常春藤 VIP 行動書櫃

結合記憶曲線學習系統

科學又有效率的 APP

讓你走路、搭車，連上廁所都可以學好英文

輕鬆 6 步驟，英文隨身讀

1 掃描 QR Code

2 下載 VIP APP

IVY English VIP

3 註冊會員

Welcome!
常春藤VIP行動書櫃

登入會員

註冊會員

常春藤結合 Mebook 學習系統，幫助你更有效地記憶單字、複習所學，第一次註冊時將引導至 Mebook 系統！

4 加入會員

歡迎您加入 Mebook 會員！
請按步驟填寫資料，以完成註冊。

請輸入手機號碼

Taiwan(+886)

上一步　下一步

5 輸入序號

用賴世雄筆記法學英文

請輸入序號

確定　取消

6 開啟書籍進入學習

常春藤 VIP 行動書櫃

用賴世雄筆記法學英文　已註冊

新概念 900 句 旅遊英文　需註冊

新概念 900 句 社交英文

新概念 900 句 職場英文

VIP 行動書櫃 序號

【安裝說明】

＊序號僅限註冊 1 個會員帳號。

＊ 1 個會員帳號可以提供 3 台載具使用。

＊本序號有效開通期限至 2027 / 12 / 31，下載後即可使用。

＊載具系統限制：❶ iOS：支援最新版本以及前兩代

❷ Android OS：支援最新版本以及前四代

客服專線 02 2331-7600 # 10 ～ 13　服務時間 週一至週五 9:00 ～ 11:50、13:00 ～ 17:30

智慧學習功能　給你最便利的學習

幫你加強記憶

採用艾賓豪斯「遺忘曲線」與萊特納「間隔式複習」兩大理論所設計的 AI 單字背誦系統，不再背過就忘！

1 提供單字講解

詳聽賴世雄老師講解，增加單字記憶點。

2 支援背景播放

在行進中一樣可以用聽的背單字、例句，學習不受限。

3 背單字練發音

在「背誦模式」中，透過語音辨識，測試自己的單字發音後再持續背單字。

幫你節省時間

把零碎時間拿來做真正的學習，其他事情我們來就好！

4 背誦／學習雙模式

「背誦模式」系統化地背單字，逐步成為長期記憶；「學習模式」可進行系統外的複習。

5 單字簿管理

可設定自己的單字簿，收藏需要隨時複習的單字。

6 睡眠學習

睡前可設定時間，在淺眠期以「耳讀學習法」聽單字。

提供 iOS / Android 手機學習模式，下載後可離線使用！

給你數位便利

不同場域不同學習載具，我們都幫你想好了！

7 單字練功房

提供「聽音辨字」、「單字選擇題」、「中譯選擇題」三種練習題型，提升學習成果。

8 我的單字量

將已完成背誦的單字具體量化。

9 學習計畫

系統制訂每天背誦字數或完成天數，高效達成學習目標。

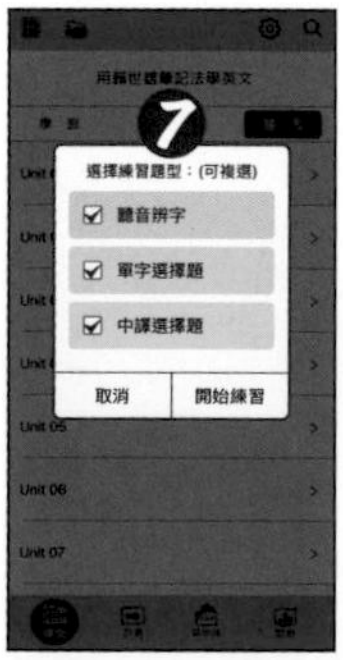

用賴世雄筆記法學英文

每天 10 分鐘，單字片語一本通

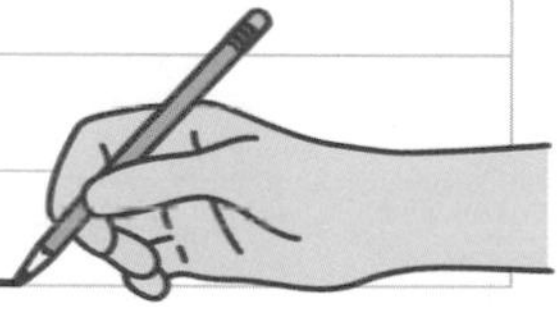

Preface
序

許多人在學習英語時，會急著要增加單字量，而一股腦兒地將大量單字片語塞進腦中，卻在實際應用時腦袋空白、不知如何開口。你是否曾經陷入或正在苦惱於這樣的「學習窘境」呢？

為了製作本書，我精心挑選了總共 **720 則英文單字片語**，給讀者們最精華、最實用的內容。使用時可搭配我親自錄製的**講解音檔**，以及由專業美籍老師錄製的**朗讀音檔**，雙管齊下使學習效果加倍！且順應時代潮流，我們特將本書內容及音檔製作成 **APP**，方便讀者們隨時隨地學習。每天只要 10 分鐘，就能讓你變身為英語達人。編排方面，全書搭配療癒插圖，以及精心設計的圖解內容，一撇一般單字片語書枯燥乏味的印象，讓你發現原來學英文也可以如此輕鬆愜意！

本書共分 24 個單元，每兩頁即附上一則包含該範圍部分單字片語的**雙人會話**，充分展現單字片語最貼切的應用方式。此外，每單元皆附有**練習題**，全書共有 5 大題型供讀者學習後牛刀小試，測試自己的學習成果。

希望各位讀者能夠藉由本書，體會到學習英文的樂趣，並在學習中獲得滿滿的成就感。祝大家學習愉快！

User's Guide
使用說明

朗讀音檔　講解音檔

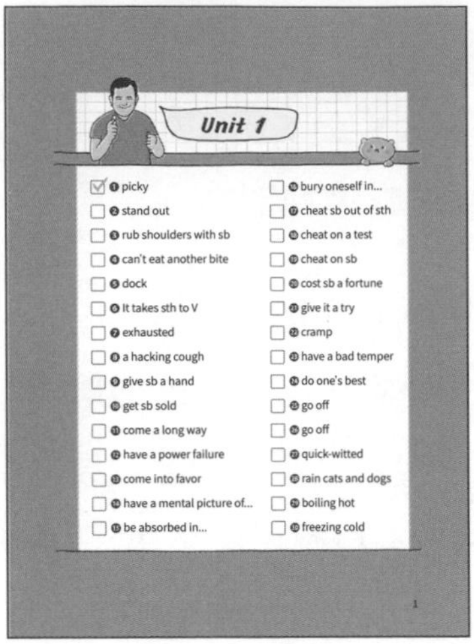
Unit 1
☑ ❶ picky
❷ stand out
❸ rub shoulders with sb
❹ can't eat another bite
❺ dock
❻ It takes sth to V
❼ exhausted
❽ a hacking cough
❾ give sb a hand
❿ get sb sold
⓫ come a long way
⓬ have a power failure
⓭ come into favor
⓮ have a mental picture of...
⓯ be absorbed in...
⓰ bury oneself in...
⓱ cheat sb out of sth
⓲ cheat on a test
⓳ cheat on sb
⓴ cost sb a fortune
㉑ give it a try
㉒ cramp
㉓ have a bad temper
㉔ do one's best
㉕ go off
㉖ go off
㉗ quick-witted
㉘ rain cats and dogs
㉙ boiling hot
㉚ freezing cold
1

聆聽音檔雙重選擇

下載 APP 或掃描 QR Code 下載全書音檔，練習發音、聽力，也強化口語能力！

精選 720 則單字片語

全書 24 個單元，每單元含 30 則單字片語，全彩內容豐富多元、實用又方便。

一覽學習完整成果

記錄每天學習進度，一步步邁向英語達人！

圖解單字加強記憶

以療癒插圖設計 單字圖解 ，讓你觸類旁通、一看就懂！

Unit 3
❶ smash (windows) 敲壞（窗戶）
• Those rioters ran through the city, smashing windows and looting shops.
那些暴民在城裡到處流竄、砸毀窗戶並搶劫商店。
❷ mess [mɛs] n. & vt. (使) 淩亂
make a mess of... 將……弄得很淩亂
mess up... 將……弄亂
• How come your room is always a mess? / in a mess? / so messy?
你的房間為何老是那麼亂？
• Don't mess up my desk.
別把我的桌子弄亂了。
❸ pull over 把車開到路旁停下來
• The policeman signaled me to pull over.
警察示意我把車停在路邊。
❹ mood [mud] n. 心情
be in a good / bad mood 心情好 / 壞
be not in the mood to V / for sth 沒有心情做某事
• Don't bother Dad now. He seems to be in a bad mood.
現在別去煩老爸。他似乎心情不好。
• I didn't do well on the test, so I'm not in the mood to go to the movies with you this evening.
我考試沒考好，所以今晚我沒心情跟你去看電影。
34

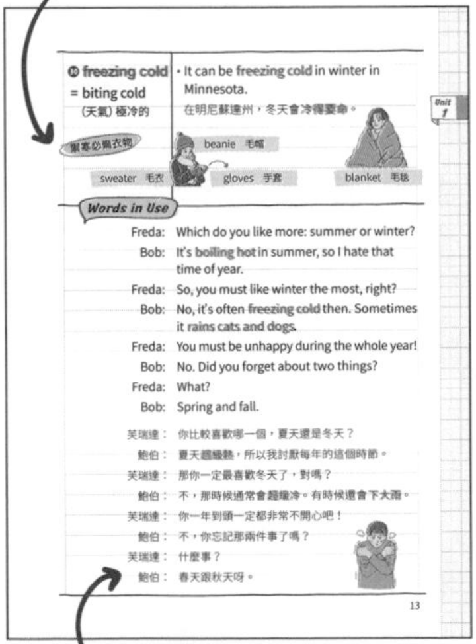
㉚ freezing cold = biting cold (天氣) 極冷的
• It can be freezing cold in winter in Minnesota.
在明尼蘇達州，冬天會冷得要命。
禦寒必備衣物
beanie 毛帽
sweater 毛衣
gloves 手套
blanket 毛毯
Words in Use
Freda: Which do you like more: summer or winter?
Bob: It's boiling hot in summer, so I hate that time of year.
Freda: So, you must like winter the most, right?
Bob: No, it's often freezing cold then. Sometimes it rains cats and dogs.
Freda: You must be unhappy during the whole year!
Bob: No. Did you forget about two things?
Freda: What?
Bob: Spring and fall.
芙瑞達： 你比較喜歡哪一個，夏天還是冬天？
鮑伯： 夏天超級熱，所以我討厭每年的這個時節。
芙瑞達： 那你一定最喜歡冬天了，對嗎？
鮑伯： 不，那時候通常會超級冷。有時候還會下大雨。
芙瑞達： 你一年到頭一定都非常不開心吧！
鮑伯： 不，你忘記那兩件事了嗎？
芙瑞達： 什麼事？
鮑伯： 春天跟秋天呀。
13

精闢解析單字片語

每則皆有精闢解析與實用例句，輕鬆提升英語力！

雙人對話實際應用

模擬生活情境，讓你輕鬆了解單字片語最貼切的應用方式。

五大題型練習題

每單元後方皆附上精心設計的練習題，驗收學習成果並強化實力，書末附有練習題解答供比對。

看圖選單字

選出正解

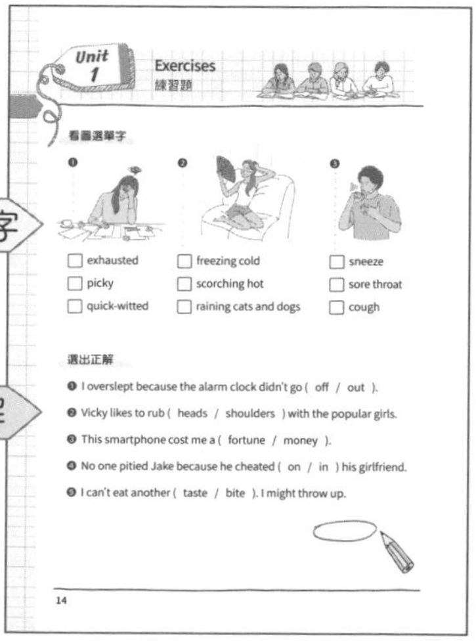
Unit 1 Exercises 練習題

看圖選單字

❶ ❷ ❸

- [ ] exhausted
- [ ] picky
- [ ] quick-witted
- [ ] freezing cold
- [ ] scorching hot
- [ ] raining cats and dogs
- [ ] sneeze
- [ ] sore throat
- [ ] cough

選出正解

❶ I overslept because the alarm clock didn't go (off / out).
❷ Vicky likes to rub (heads / shoulders) with the popular girls.
❸ This smartphone cost me a (fortune / money).
❹ No one pitied Jake because he cheated (on / in) his girlfriend.
❺ I can't eat another (taste / bite). I might throw up.

14

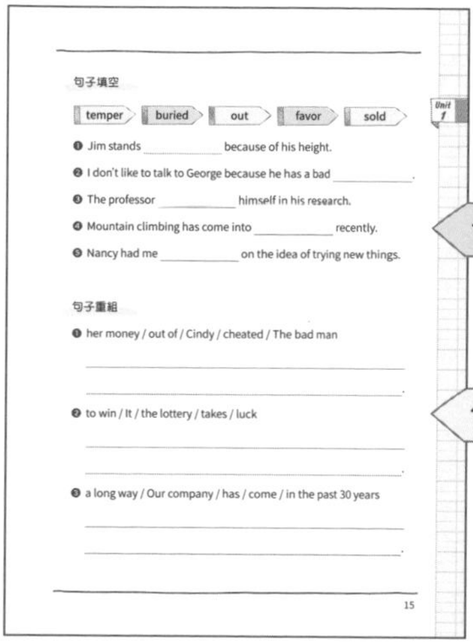
句子填空

temper | buried | out | favor | sold

❶ Jim stands ________ because of his height.
❷ I don't like to talk to George because he has a bad ________.
❸ The professor ________ himself in his research.
❹ Mountain climbing has come into ________ recently.
❺ Nancy had me ________ on the idea of trying new things.

句子重組

❶ her money / out of / Cindy / cheated / The bad man
❷ to win / It / the lottery / takes / luck
❸ a long way / Our company / has / come / in the past 30 years

15

句子填空

句子重組

看圖連連看

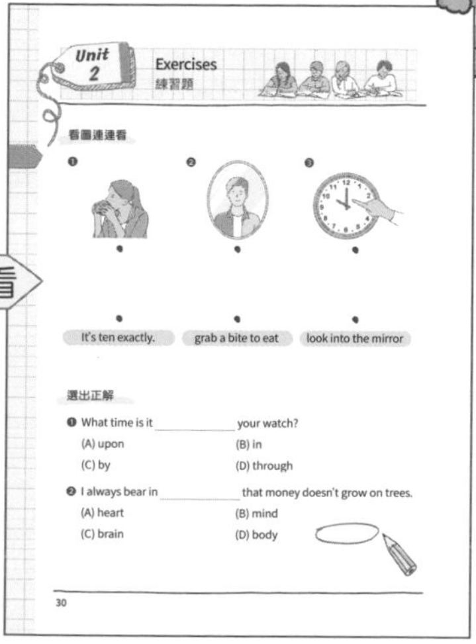
Unit 2 Exercises 練習題

看圖連連看

❶ ❷ ❸

It's ten exactly. | grab a bite to eat | look into the mirror

選出正解

❶ What time is it ________ your watch?
(A) upon (B) in
(C) by (D) through

❷ I always bear in ________ that money doesn't grow on trees.
(A) heart (B) mind
(C) brain (D) body

30

練習題解答

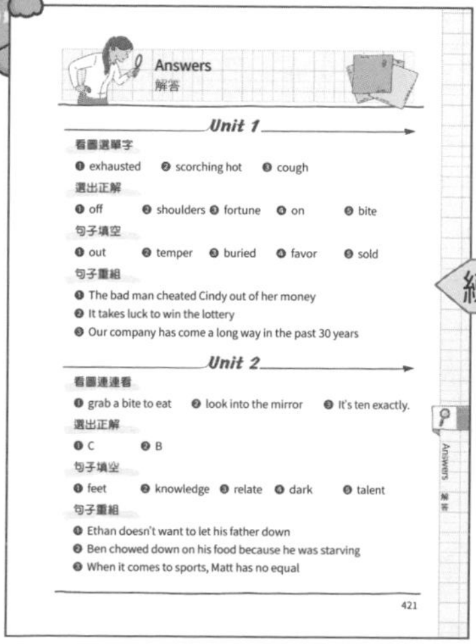
Answers 解答

Unit 1

看圖選單字
❶ exhausted ❷ scorching hot ❸ cough
選出正解
❶ off ❷ shoulders ❸ fortune ❹ on ❺ bite
句子填空
❶ out ❷ temper ❸ buried ❹ favor ❺ sold
句子重組
❶ The bad man cheated Cindy out of her money
❷ It takes luck to win the lottery
❸ Our company has come a long way in the past 30 years

Unit 2

看圖連連看
❶ grab a bite to eat ❷ look into the mirror ❸ It's ten exactly.
選出正解
❶ C ❷ B
句子填空
❶ feet ❷ knowledge ❸ relate ❹ dark ❺ talent
句子重組
❶ Ethan doesn't want to let his father down
❷ Ben chowed down on his food because he was starving
❸ When it comes to sports, Matt has no equal

421

Contents
目錄

Unit 1 → 1
Unit 2 → 17
Unit 3 → 33
Unit 4 → 49
Unit 5 → 65
Unit 6 → 81
Unit 7 → 97
Unit 8 → 113
Unit 9 → 129
Unit 10 → 149
Unit 11 → 165
Unit 12 → 183
Unit 13 → 201
Unit 14 → 217
Unit 15 → 235
Unit 16 → 255
Unit 17 → 273
Unit 18 → 291
Unit 19 → 311
Unit 20 → 329
Unit 21 → 347
Unit 22 → 365
Unit 23 → 385
Unit 24 → 403
解答 → 421

Unit 1

- [x] 1 picky
- [ ] 2 stand out
- [ ] 3 rub shoulders with sb
- [ ] 4 can't eat another bite
- [ ] 5 dock
- [ ] 6 It takes sth to V
- [ ] 7 exhausted
- [ ] 8 a hacking cough
- [ ] 9 give sb a hand
- [ ] 10 get sb sold
- [ ] 11 come a long way
- [ ] 12 have a power failure
- [ ] 13 come into favor
- [ ] 14 have a mental picture of...
- [ ] 15 be absorbed in...
- [ ] 16 bury oneself in...
- [ ] 17 cheat sb out of sth
- [ ] 18 cheat on a test
- [ ] 19 cheat on sb
- [ ] 20 cost sb a fortune
- [ ] 21 give it a try
- [ ] 22 cramp
- [ ] 23 have a bad temper
- [ ] 24 do one's best
- [ ] 25 go off
- [ ] 26 go off
- [ ] 27 quick-witted
- [ ] 28 rain cats and dogs
- [ ] 29 boiling hot
- [ ] 30 freezing cold

Unit 1

❶ picky
[ˋpɪkɪ] *a.*
挑剔的

- John is picky / particular / choosy about food.

約翰對吃的很**挑剔**。

❷ stand out
傑出，出眾

- Brian **stands out** among his peers.

布萊恩在同儕中很**傑出**。

❸ rub shoulders with sb
與某人交往

- Sam likes to rub shoulders / associate with celebrities.

山姆喜歡**與**名人**交往**。

❹ can't eat another bite
吃不下了

- I'm so full I **can't eat another bite**.

=I can't eat any more because I'm stuffed.

我已經飽了，再也**吃不下了**。

❺ dock [dak] *vt.* 扣除（薪資）	• Because of your tardiness, I'll **dock** your pay. 由於你遲到的關係，我要**扣**你的薪水。
❻ It takes sth to V 從事……需要某事物	• It takes perseverance to master any foreign language, including English. 精通任何外語，包括英文在內，均**需要**毅力。

Unit 1

Words in Use

Mark: Hey, Alice. You didn't finish your lunch.

Alice: Oh, I'm really full. **I can't eat another bite!**

Mark: Do you mind if I eat the French fries on your plate, then?

Alice: My French fries?

Mark: It's OK. I'm not **picky**.

Alice: Mark! You are on a diet, aren't you? **It takes** effort to lose weight.

馬克： 嘿，愛麗絲。妳午餐沒吃完。

愛麗絲： 喔，我真的很飽。我**吃不下了**！

馬克： 那妳介意我吃妳盤子上的薯條嗎？

愛麗絲： 我的薯條嗎？

馬克： 沒關係，我不**挑剔的**。

愛麗絲： 馬克！你在節食中，不是嗎？減肥是**需要**努力的。

❼ exhausted

[ɪgˋzɔstɪd] *a.*

疲憊的

• I was exhausted / beat / worn out / tired out after a hard day's work.

=I was exhausted after a long day of back-breaking, hard work.

經過一天的辛勞工作後，我累趴了。

❽ a hacking cough

咳個不停

• I can't stand his hacking cough.

他咳個不停，讓我受不了。

感冒症狀

cough 咳嗽

sneeze 打噴嚏

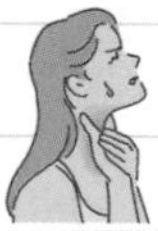

sore throat 喉嚨痛

headache 頭痛

❾ give sb a hand

幫助某人

• Please give me a hand with my baggage.

請幫我提行李。

旅遊達人

tourist 觀光客

boarding pass 登機證

passport 護照

baggage / luggage 行李

⑩ **get sb sold** 說服某人	• You've **got** me **sold**. =You've persuaded me. =I accept what you've said. 我**被**你**說服**了 / 我接受你的說法。

Words in Use

Timmy: (*coughing*) I really hate this cough.

Georgina: Yes, it sounds like **a hacking cough**.

Timmy: Plus, I feel **exhausted** after a hard day's work.

Georgina: You went to work with that cough? You should see a doctor right now!

Timmy: Yes, you're right. I'll do that now.

Georgina: And cover your mouth when you cough, Timmy!

Timmy: But I have a mask on.

Georgina: I know, but you should still cover your mouth.

提米：(咳嗽中) 我真討厭咳嗽。

喬治娜：是呀，你聽起來**咳個不停**。

提米：而且我努力工作一整天後**累癱了**。

喬治娜：你咳成這樣還去工作？你應該馬上去看醫生！

提米：妳是對的。我馬上就去。

喬治娜：還有，咳嗽時要把嘴巴遮住，提米！

提米：但我戴著口罩。

喬治娜：我知道，但你還是應該要遮住嘴巴。

⑪ come a long way

大有進步

• Medicine has come a long way in recent years.

近幾年來，醫學方面**大有進步**。

⑫ have a power failure

停電

• We had a power failure last night.

=The electricity went out last night.

昨晚**停電**了。

⑬ come into favor

= become popular

受到喜愛 / 流行起來

• Coffee-drinking has come into favor only recently in that country.

直到最近，喝咖啡才在那個國家**蔚成風氣**。

⑭ have a mental picture of...

想像……

• I have a mental picture of how happy John will be when he hears the good news.

=I can imagine how happy John will be when he hears the good news.

我可以**想像**約翰聽到這個好消息時會有多高興。

⑮ **be absorbed in...**
專注於……

• Ben was so | absorbed / immersed | in his book that he didn't notice me come in.
阿班**非常專心**看書，因此沒注意到我走進來。

⑯ **bury oneself in...**
埋首於……

• Ever since his girlfriend broke up with him, Tom has **buried himself in** his work to keep from crying all day.
湯姆自從女友與他分手後便**埋頭**工作，以免整天哭泣。

Words in Use

Teacher: It's good to see that you **are absorbed in** reading, Rupert.
Rupert: What? Um, yes. I like to **bury myself in** English books.
Teacher: That will really help your English ability **come a long way**. Wait! Is that a comic book?
Rupert: Um, well, yes, I guess it is, teacher.
Teacher: Give that to me right now, Rupert.

老師： 魯伯特，看到你這麼**專心**讀書真讓人欣慰。
魯伯特： 什麼？嗯，是的。我喜歡**埋首於**英文書籍中。
老師： 那會幫助你**大大提升**英文能力。等等！那是漫畫書嗎？
魯伯特： 嗯，是……是的，老師。
老師： 魯伯特，馬上把那本書給我。

⑰ cheat sb out of sth
騙走某人的某物

- The conman **cheated** the old woman **out of** all her money.
這名金光黨徒**騙走**了老婦人所有的錢。

⑱ cheat on a test
考試作弊

- Peter was caught **cheating on** the math **test**.
彼得數學**考試作弊**被逮個正著。

⑲ cheat on sb
對某人不忠；
欺騙某人

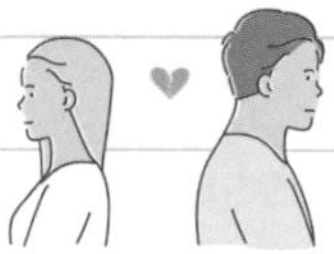

- If you ever **cheat on** me, I'll dump / ditch you right away.
= If you ever two-time me, I'll dump you right away.
你要是對我**不忠**，我會立刻把你甩了。

⑳ cost sb a fortune
花某人很多錢

- That car **cost** me **a fortune**. / an arm and a leg. / lots of money.
那輛車**花了**我**大把銀子**。

㉑ give it a try
試試看

- Many friends of mine say paragliding is a lot of fun. I hope I'll **give it a** **try** / shot / go someday.
我有許多朋友都說滑翔傘活動好玩極了。
我希望有朝一日能**試試看**。

極限戶外運動

surfing 衝浪

rock climbing 攀岩

diving 潛水

Words in Use

Allan: (*whispering*) Hey, Sarah. What's the answer to question 17?

Sarah: Allan! You can't **cheat on a test**!

Allan: Well, I'll fail if I don't. I didn't study.

Sarah: You should **give it a try** instead of trying to cheat!

Allan: Come on, Sarah. Help me out.

Sarah: No. I think I'm going to dump you.

Allan: What? Why?

Sarah: If you'll **cheat on a test**, you'll **cheat on** me, too.

亞倫：(小聲地說) 嘿，莎拉。第 17 題的答案是什麼？

莎拉：亞倫！**考試**不能**作弊**！

亞倫：喔，如果我不作弊會考不及格。我沒念書。

莎拉：你應該**試著作答**，而不是試著作弊！

亞倫：莎拉，別這樣嘛。幫幫我。

莎拉：不。我想我要把你甩了。

亞倫：什麼？為什麼？

莎拉：如果你會**考試作弊**，你也會**對**我**不忠**。

㉒ cramp [kræmp] *n.* &. *vi.* 抽筋	• If you tend to have leg **cramps** at night, stretch before bedtime. 晚上你的腿容易**抽筋**的話，睡前要拉拉筋。 • My left leg **cramped**, so I gave up the race at once. 我左腿**抽筋**，因此立刻放棄比賽。
㉓ have a bad temper = be bad-tempered 脾氣不好，很容易發脾氣	• David has few friends because he has **a bad temper.** an ill temper. a hot temper. a quick temper. =David has few friends because he's **bad-tempered.** ill-tempered. quick-tempered. hot-tempered.  大衛**脾氣不好**，因此朋友不多。
㉔ do one's best 盡力 	• Paul's in trouble. We should **do our best** / do whatever we can / do everything we can / do the best we can / do our level best / try our best / try as hard as we can — to help him. 保羅有困難，我們應**鼎力**相助。

㉕ **go off** (鬧鐘) 響	• The alarm clock **went off** at seven. 鬧鐘七點**響**了。
㉖ **go off** **= explode** (炸彈) 爆炸	• The bomb | **went off** / **exploded** |, killing five people on the spot. 炸彈**爆炸**，五個人當場喪命。

Words in Use

Ruby: Why are you so mad, Glen? You are so **bad-tempered**.

Glen: The service is so bad in this restaurant!

Ruby: That's no reason to **explode** into anger. You really need to try harder to control your **anger**.

Glen: OK, OK. I'll **do my best** to stay calm.

Ruby: I hope so. Getting so angry is not good for your health.

露比： 葛倫，你為什麼這麼生氣？你的**脾氣**真**不好**。

葛倫： 這間餐廳的服務太爛了！

露比： 沒有必要大發雷霆。你真應該要試著更努力控制脾氣。

葛倫： 好，好。我**盡量**保持冷靜。

露比： 希望如此。這麼生氣對你的健康不好。

㉗ quick-witted
有機智的，反應快的

• Peter is | quick-witted. / witty.

彼得腦袋很靈光。

㉘ rain cats and dogs
下傾盆大雨

• It's | raining cats and dogs / raining heavily / raining hard | now. Let's stay here till it | lets up. / stops.

現在正**下著大雨**。咱們就待在這裡等著雨停吧。

* It's drizzling now. Let's take shelter in that temple there.

現在正下著毛毛雨，咱們到那邊的廟躲雨吧。

大雨小雨通通記

㉙ boiling hot
= scorching hot
= baking hot
(天氣) 極熱的

• It was cloudy and cool yesterday, but it's **boiling hot** today.

昨天是陰天也很涼爽，今天則**熱死了**。

30 freezing cold

= biting cold

(天氣) 極冷的

- It can be **freezing cold** in winter in Minnesota.

  在明尼蘇達州，冬天會**冷得要命**。

禦寒必備衣物

beanie 毛帽

sweater 毛衣

gloves 手套

blanket 毛毯

Words in Use

Freda: Which do you like more: summer or winter?

Bob: It's **boiling hot** in summer, so I hate that time of year.

Freda: So, you must like winter the most, right?

Bob: No, it's often **freezing cold** then. Sometimes it **rains cats and dogs**.

Freda: You must be unhappy during the whole year!

Bob: No. Did you forget about two things?

Freda: What?

Bob: Spring and fall.

芙瑞達： 你比較喜歡哪一個，夏天還是冬天？

鮑伯： 夏天**超級熱**，所以我討厭每年的這個時節。

芙瑞達： 那你一定最喜歡冬天了，對嗎？

鮑伯： 不，那時候通常會**超級冷**。有時候還會**下大雨**。

芙瑞達： 你一年到頭一定都非常不開心吧！

鮑伯： 不，你忘記那兩件事了嗎？

芙瑞達： 什麼事？

鮑伯： 春天跟秋天呀。

Unit 1

Exercises
練習題

看圖選單字

❶

☐ exhausted
☐ picky
☐ quick-witted

❷

☐ freezing cold
☐ scorching hot
☐ raining cats and dogs

❸

☐ sneeze
☐ sore throat
☐ cough

選出正解

❶ I overslept because the alarm clock didn't go (off / out).

❷ Vicky likes to rub (heads / shoulders) with the popular girls.

❸ This smartphone cost me a (fortune / money).

❹ No one pitied Jake because he cheated (on / in) his girlfriend.

❺ I can't eat another (taste / bite). I might throw up.

句子填空

temper | buried | out | favor | sold

❶ Jim stands ______________ because of his height.

❷ I don't like to talk to George because he has a bad ______________.

❸ The professor ______________ himself in his research.

❹ Mountain climbing has come into ______________ recently.

❺ Nancy had me ______________ on the idea of trying new things.

句子重組

❶ her money / out of / Cindy / cheated / The bad man

____

____.

❷ to win / It / the lottery / takes / luck

____

____.

❸ a long way / Our company / has / come / in the past 30 years

____

____.

Notes

Unit 2

- [x] ❶ by your watch
- [ ] ❷ ten exactly
- [ ] ❸ be into sth
- [ ] ❹ hang out with sb
- [ ] ❺ hang in there
- [ ] ❻ relate to...
- [ ] ❼ a walking dictionary
- [ ] ❽ a walking encyclopedia
- [ ] ❾ when it comes to...
- [ ] ❿ after a hard day at work
- [ ] ⓫ put up with...
- [ ] ⓬ bear in mind that...
- [ ] ⓭ look into the mirror
- [ ] ⓮ To my knowledge, ...
- [ ] ⓯ favor
- [ ] ⓰ after dark
- [ ] ⓱ darkness
- [ ] ⓲ keep sb in the dark about sth
- [ ] ⓳ tower over sb
- [ ] ⓴ be jam-packed with...
- [ ] ㉑ grab a bite (to eat)
- [ ] ㉒ chow down (on) sth
- [ ] ㉓ put one's feet up
- [ ] ㉔ be down
- [ ] ㉕ let sb down
- [ ] ㉖ weaken
- [ ] ㉗ be a must
- [ ] ㉘ be a must-read
- [ ] ㉙ have an innate talent for...
- [ ] ㉚ a smash hit

Unit 2

❶ by your watch

(手錶顯示) 幾點

• What time is it by your watch now?
=What time does your watch say?
您的錶現在**幾點**了？

❷ ten exactly

十點整

• It's ten | exactly now. / sharp. / on the dot.

現在是**十點整**。

⋆ Amy showed up | on the dot of ten. / at ten on the dot.

艾咪十點整出現了。

時間的說法

It's five past...
……點五分

It's a quarter past...
……點十五分

It's half past...
……點半

It's a quarter to...
……點四十五分

❸ be into sth

喜愛某事

• Talking | of / about | hobbies, I'm really into music.
=Speaking of hobbies,
| I enjoy music.
| I'm fond of music.
| I have a passion for music.

談到嗜好，我很**喜歡**音樂。

❹ **hang out with sb** 與某人混在一起	• I enjoy hanging out with my friends on weekends. 我週末都愛**與**朋友**玩在一起**。
❺ **hang in there** 挺下去，堅持下去 = don't give up 別放棄	• I know the situation is pretty tough, but just hang in there / don't give up, and you'll make it. 我知道情勢艱困，不過你要**堅持下去**，這樣就會成功。

Words in Use

Jordan: Amy, what time is it by your watch?

Amy: Let's see. It's four exactly.

Jordan: It can't be 4 p.m. We left school at four. That was at least an hour ago.

Amy: You're right. I wonder what time it really is.

Jordan: Don't worry. I know what time it is.

Amy: Huh? What time is it then?

Jordan: Time for you to get a new watch!

Amy: I hate your jokes.

喬丹：艾咪，**妳的錶**現在**幾點**了？

艾咪：我看看。**四點整**。

喬丹：不可能是下午四點。我們是四點離開學校的，那至少是一小時前了。

艾咪：你說得對。不知道現在到底是幾點。

喬丹：別擔心，我知道現在幾點。

艾咪：什麼？那到底是幾點？

喬丹：是妳該買新手錶的時候了！

艾咪：我不喜歡你的玩笑。

❻ relate to... 認同……	• I can **relate to** your situation because I've been through it before. =I can **identify with** you because I've been through the situation before. 我曾經歷這個情況，因此我很**認同**你 / 能體會你的處境。
❼ a walking dictionary 活字典	• Go ask Tom if there's any word you don't know. He is **a walking dictionary**. 你若遇到任何不懂的字，就去問湯姆吧。他是**活字典**。
❽ a walking encyclopedia 活百科全書； 飽學之士	• Mary is **a walking encyclopedia** when it comes to music. 說到音樂，瑪麗猶如一套**活百科全書**。 
❾ when it comes to... = speaking about / of ... 說到……	• **When it comes to** singing, Jane is second to none. unrivaled. unequaled. the best. = **When it comes to** singing, Jane has no rival. equal. **說到**唱歌，沒人比得上阿珍。
❿ after a hard day at work 經過一整天的辛勞之後	• I enjoy relaxing by listening to music **after a hard day at work**. **經過一整天的辛勞之後**，我喜歡聽音樂放鬆一下。 

⓫ put up with... 容忍……	• To tell you the truth, I can't put up with / tolerate / stand your hot temper. 老實對你說，我**受不了**你的壞脾氣。 

Words in Use

Bonnie: My brother is like **a walking dictionary**.

Jacob: Yeah. He's probably the smartest guy I know. I'm smart, too.

Bonnie: Um... Well, I guess so.

Jacob: Don't you believe me? Ask me a question.

Bonnie: How far is the Sun from Earth?

Jacob: No, I don't mean that type of question. I mean one like, "Who is the greatest superhero?"

Bonnie: Yes, **when it comes to** unimportant things, you are **a walking encyclopedia**.

邦妮： 我哥就像是一本**活字典**。

雅各： 是，他應該是我認識最聰明的人。我也很聰明。

邦妮： 喔……嗯，應該吧。

雅各： 妳不相信我嗎？問我問題。

邦妮： 太陽距離地球多遠？

雅各： 不，我不是指那種問題。我是指例如「誰是最厲害的超級英雄？」

邦妮： 對，**說到**不重要的事情，你就像是本**活百科全書**。

⓬ bear in mind that... 牢記在心…… **bear sth in mind** 牢記某事	• **Bear in mind / Keep in mind / Remember** that you'll get nowhere without working hard. **記住**：不努力就不會有出息。 • Whatever happens, **bear my words in mind**: "Never give up." 不管發生什麼事，要**牢記**我的話：「千萬別放棄。」
⓭ look in / into the mirror 照鏡子 **look at the mirror** 看著鏡子外觀 (不看鏡內人物)	• I looked at the mirror... (×) →**I looked into the mirror** and suddenly found some of my hair had turned gray. (○) 我**照鏡子**，突然發現一些頭髮變灰白了。
⓮ To my knowledge, ... 就我所知，……	• **To my knowledge / As far as I know / As I understand it**, Tom has moved to Beijing. **就我所知**，湯姆已搬遷到北京。 • **To the best of my knowledge**, this is the only novel the writer has ever written. **就我所知**，這是該作家唯一的一本小說。

廁所常見物品

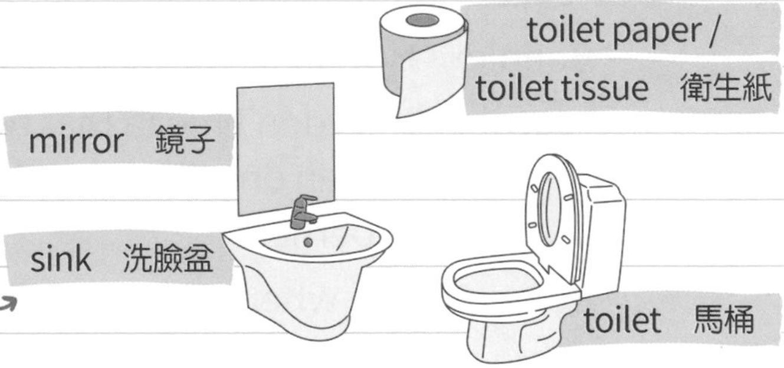

⑮ favor

[ˋfevɚ] *n.*

恩惠

do sb a favor

幫某人忙

• Could you **do me a favor** and do the laundry for me?

請**幫**我**一個忙**，幫我洗衣服好嗎？

Words in Use

Harry: What's the matter, Rita? Why are you so unhappy?

Rita: I just **looked in the mirror**. I didn't like what I saw.

Harry: Don't worry. Your haircut isn't that bad.

Rita: Yes, it is. I can't bear it.

Harry: Cheer up, honey. Just **bear in mind that** no matter how you look, I'll always love you.

哈利： 麗塔，怎麼了？妳為什麼這麼不開心？

麗塔： 我剛剛**照**了**鏡子**，不喜歡我看到的樣子。

哈利： 別擔心。妳剪的髮型沒有那麼糟糕。

麗塔： 很糟糕。我無法忍受。

哈利： 開心點，親愛的。只要**記住**不管妳看起來是什麼樣子，我都會一直愛著妳。

⑯ after dark
天黑後

- Don't go out alone **after dark**.
天黑後不要獨自外出。

⑰ darkness
[ˋdɑrknɪs] *n.*
暗處，黑暗

- I couldn't see anything in the **darkness**.
我在**暗處**什麼都看不見。

⑱ keep sb in the dark about sth
向某人隱瞞某事

- They **kept** me **in the dark about** their wedding date.
他倆**向**我**隱瞞**他們結婚的日子。

⑲ tower over sb
身材比某人高出很多

- Though he is only 15 years old, Peter | **towers over** / is far taller than | his dad.
彼得雖然只有十五歲，**個頭**卻**比**他老爸**高出許多**。

⑳ be jam-packed with...
擠滿了……

- The small town **is jam-packed with** tourists on weekends.
每逢週末，小鎮被遊客**擠得水洩不通**。

- The freeway **is** always **jam-packed with** cars during Chinese New Year.

  春節期間高速公路總是**擠滿了**車輛。

過年氣氛不可少

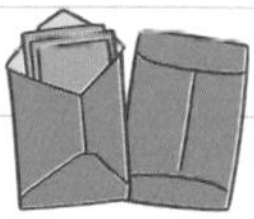

red envelope　紅包

lantern　燈籠

firecracker　鞭炮

Words in Use

George: This store **is jam-packed with** customers. Phoebe, where did Ben go?

Phoebe: I don't know. He just disappeared into thin air.

George: He shouldn't be too hard to find. He **towers over** most people.

Phoebe: I see him. Oh, now I'm mad.

George: What's wrong? Don't **keep** me **in the dark**.

Phoebe: He's talking to another girl!

喬治：店裡**擠滿了**客人。阿班去哪了，菲比？

菲比：我不知道。他消失了。

喬治：應該不難找。他**比**大多數的人還**高很多**。

菲比：我看到他了。喔，我現在生氣了。

喬治：怎麼了？**快告訴我**。

菲比：他在跟另一個女生說話！

㉑ grab a bite (to eat)
匆匆吃點東西

- I haven't had lunch yet. Let's | **grab a bite to eat.** / grab a quick bite. |
我午餐還沒吃。咱們**匆匆吃點東西**吧。

㉒ chow down (on) sth
大口吃某物

- Let's find an eatery where we can **chow down** something. I'm starving.
咱們找個小吃店好好**大吃一頓**。我餓死了。

㉓ put one's feet up
= relax (especially by sitting with one's feet supported above the ground)
(翹起雙腳) 休息

- You look tired. You need to go home and **put your feet up.**
你看起來很疲憊，應該要回家好好**休息**。

㉔ be down
消沉

- You've been so | **down** / depressed | lately. Come on! Cheer up!
你近來都很**沮喪**。別這樣嘛！振作起來！

㉕ let sb down 使某人失望	• Keep working hard. Don't **let** me **down**. 繼續努力。別**讓**我**失望**。
㉖ weaken [ˋwikən] *vi. & vt.* 減弱	• Your immune system will **weaken** if you don't get enough sleep. 你若睡眠不足，免疫系統就會**衰弱**。 • My dad's health was **weakened** by work. 我爸爸因為過勞而健康**衰弱**了。

Words in Use

Rose: I'm hungry. Let's **grab a bite to eat** somewhere.

Grant: Sure. I'd like to **chow down on** a hamburger right now.

Rose: It depresses me that you only eat junk food, Grant.

Grant: Oh, don't **be so down**, Rose. A hamburger will cheer you up.

Rose: Grant! You never fail to **let** me **down**.

蘿絲：我餓了，我們找個地方**快速地吃**點東西吧。

葛倫特：好啊。我現在想要**大口吃**漢堡。

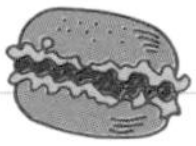

蘿絲：葛倫特，你只吃垃圾食物真讓我沮喪。

葛倫特：喔，別這麼**消沉**，蘿絲。漢堡會讓妳開心的。

蘿絲：葛倫特！你總是**讓**我**失望**。

㉗ **be a must**
是必要的東西

- A good dictionary **is a must** if you want to learn English well.
你若想把英文學好，**非得**有本好字典不可。

㉘ **be a must-read**
是必讀物

- That book **is a must-read** for those who want to improve their writing skills.
凡是想精進寫作技巧的人，那本書**非讀不可**。

be a must-see
是必看的景色

- Machu Picchu **is a must-see** for any visitor to Peru.
馬丘比丘是任何到祕魯的遊客**非看不可的景點**。

be a must-do
是必做的事

- Shopping **is a must-do** when you visit Venice.
你到威尼斯去玩時血拼**是非做不可的事**。

㉙ **have an innate / inborn talent for...**
有……與生俱來的天分

be talented in...
在……方面有天分

- Linda **has an innate / inborn talent for** music.
琳達**天生就有**音樂**天分**。

- John **is talented in / has a talent for** languages.
約翰**有**學習語言**的天賦**。

㉚ **a smash hit**
(歌曲、劇作、電影) 很成功 / 很賣座

- The album became **a smash hit** soon after it was released.
這張專輯問世之後**大受歡迎**。

- Tom Cruise's first movie was **a** box-office **smash (hit)**.
阿湯哥的第一部電影**很賣座**。

電影常見小物

3D glasses 3D 眼鏡

popcorn 爆米花

clapperboard 場記板

movie / cinema ticket 電影票

film reel 電影捲軸

Words in Use

Mother: That music is awful. How can you do your homework with it so loud?

Son: What? This song was **a smash hit** a few years ago.

Mother: If you don't turn it down, I'll smash your smartphone!

Son: OK, OK. Why don't you rest for a while?

Mother: Who is going to clean up the house if I take it easy?

Son: Not me. Sorry, Mom. My teacher said this assignment is **a must-do** for tomorrow!

媽媽： 那音樂真難聽。音樂這麼大聲你要怎麼做功課？

兒子： 什麼？這首歌幾年前可是**賣座歌曲**呢。

媽媽： 如果你不轉小聲點，我會把你的手機砸爛！

兒子： 好吧，好吧。妳何不休息一下？

媽媽： 如果我休息的話，誰要去打掃房子呢？

兒子： 抱歉，不會是我，媽媽。我的老師說這項功課明天**一定要交**！

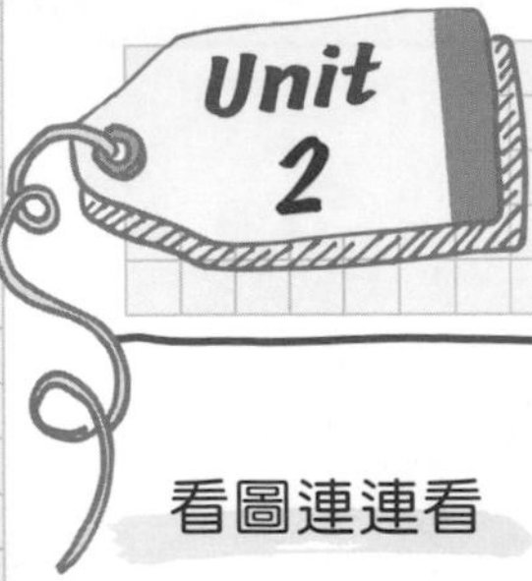

Unit 2 Exercises 練習題

看圖連連看

❶ 

❷ 

❸ 

It's ten exactly. | grab a bite to eat | look into the mirror

選出正解

❶ What time is it ______________ your watch?

(A) upon (B) in

(C) by (D) through

❷ I always bear in ______________ that money doesn't grow on trees.

(A) heart (B) mind

(C) brain (D) body

句子填空

feet | relate | knowledge | talent | dark

❶ Vicky just wants to go home and put her ______________ up.

❷ To my ______________, Sam has quit his job.

❸ I can ______________ to what you are saying.

❹ Judy kept her mother in the ______________ about her illness.

❺ We all think that James has an inborn ______________ for drawing.

句子重組

❶ down / Ethan / his father / doesn't want to / let

____

____.

❷ Ben / on his food / because he was starving / down / chowed

____

____.

❸ comes to sports / has no equal / Matt / it / When / ,

____

____.

Notes

Unit 3

- [x] 1 smash (windows)
- [ ] 2 mess
- [ ] 3 pull over
- [ ] 4 mood
- [ ] 5 have a crush on sb
- [ ] 6 plate
- [ ] 7 well-read
- [ ] 8 be well-known for...
- [ ] 9 have a runny nose
- [ ] 10 get the runs
- [ ] 11 run for one's life
- [ ] 12 (某地) boast sth
- [ ] 13 can afford sth
- [ ] 14 book
- [ ] 15 close down (...)
- [ ] 16 dye one's hair + 顏色
- [ ] 17 appreciate
- [ ] 18 be out of this world
- [ ] 19 a world of...
- [ ] 20 word
- [ ] 21 word
- [ ] 22 wording
- [ ] 23 close one's mind to sth
- [ ] 24 Great minds think alike.
- [ ] 25 Out of sight, out of mind.
- [ ] 26 sight
- [ ] 27 go sightseeing
- [ ] 28 overwhelm
- [ ] 29 make a reservation for...
- [ ] 30 without reservation

Unit 3

❶ smash (windows)

敲壞（窗戶）

• Those rioters ran through the city, smashing windows and looting shops.

那些暴民在城裡到處流竄、**砸毀窗戶**並搶劫商店。

❷ mess

[mɛs] *n.* & *vt.* (使) 凌亂

make a mess of...

將……弄得很凌亂

mess up...

將……弄亂

• How come your room is always
  | a mess?
  | in a mess?
  | so messy?

你的房間為何老是那麼**亂**？

• Don't **mess up** my desk.

別**把**我的桌子**弄亂**了。

❸ pull over

把車開到路旁停下來

• The policeman signaled me to **pull over**.

警察示意我**把車停在路邊**。

❹ mood

[mud] *n.* 心情

be in a good / bad mood

心情好 / 壞

be not in the mood to V / for sth

沒有心情做某事

• Don't bother Dad now. He seems to be **in a bad mood**.

現在別去煩老爸。他似乎**心情不好**。

• I didn't do well on the test, so I'm **not in the mood to** go to the movies with you this evening.

我考試沒考好，所以今晚我**沒心情**跟你去看電影。

5 have a crush on sb 迷戀／暗戀某人	• While I was in junior high school, I had a crush on the girl sitting next to me. 我在念國中時，**暗戀**坐在我旁邊的女孩子。
6 plate [plet] *n.* 盤子 **have too much on one's plate** 有太多事要做	• I'm sorry, but I can't help you. **I have too much on my plate** today. =I'm sorry, but I can't help you. I have too many things to do today. 抱歉，我沒辦法幫你。我今天**有很多事要忙**。

Words in Use

Mom: John, your room is in a mess! Clean it up right now.

Son: But, Mom, I really **have too much on my plate** at the moment. First, I have to play basketball with my friends. Then, we're going to a movie.

Mom: I see. Well, if you want anything on your **plate** for dinner, you'd better clean up your room right now.

Son: Aw, Mom!

媽媽：約翰，你的房間**一團亂**！馬上打掃乾淨。

兒子：但是，媽，我現在**有太多事情要忙**。首先，我得要跟朋友去打籃球。然後，我們要去看電影。

媽媽：了解。嗯，如果你想要晚餐時**盤子**上有食物吃的話，最好立刻打掃房間。

兒子：喔，媽！

❼ **well-read** 飽讀詩書 / 很有學問的	• The scholar is **well-read**; there is hardly anything he doesn't know. 這位學者**很有學問**；他幾乎無所不知。
well-received (書、電影、作品等) 受到好評的	• All Ted's books were **well-received**. 泰德的書全都**受到好評**。
well-traveled 去過許多地方的	• John is **well-traveled**. In other words, he has been to many countries around the world. 約翰**去過許多地方**。換句話說，他去過世界眾多國家。
well-bred 很有教養的	
well-built 體格很棒的	• I used to be **well-built** until I turned 50. 五十歲以前我**體格很棒**。
❽ **be** **well-known** **famous** **renowned** **noted** **for...** 以……聞名	• The restaurant **is well-known for** its delicious food. 那家餐廳的菜好吃得**出了名**。 
❾ **have a runny nose** 流鼻涕 **run a fever / temperature** 發燒	• I've got **a runny nose** and a fever. I think I must go see my doctor now. = My nose is running, and I'm **running a fever**. I've gotta see my doctor now. 我**流鼻涕**又**發燒**。我想我現在就得去看醫生。

⑩ get / have the runs 拉肚子	• I ate something bad this morning, and now I've **got the runs**. 今天早上我吃壞東西，現在在**拉肚子**。
⑪ run for one's life 拔腿逃命	• At the sight of the cops, the thief **ran for his life**. 一見到這些警察，小偷就趕緊**逃命**。 

Words in Use

Joan: (*sniffs*) Oh, I hate that I **have a runny nose**.

Max: Do you have a fever, too?

Joan: I'm not sure. I still need to take my temperature. I think I **have the runs**, though.

Max: Uh-oh. See you later.

Joan: Where are you going? You look like you want to **run for your life**.

Max: I do. Bye!

喬安：(吸鼻涕) 喔，我討厭**流鼻涕**。

麥克斯：妳也有發燒嗎？

喬安：我不確定。我還需要量一下體溫。但我想我有在**拉肚子**。

麥克斯：糟糕。再見。

喬安：你要去哪？你看起來像是要**拔腿逃命**去了。

麥克斯：沒錯，再見囉！

⑫ (某地) **boast sth** 某地以擁有某物而自豪	• Though small, the town **boasts** the best summer resorts in this country. 這個鎮雖小，卻**以擁有**該國最棒的避暑勝地**而自居**。
(人) boast of / about sth 某人吹噓某事	• Nobody likes David because he likes to **boast of / brag about** how rich he is. 大家都不喜歡大衛因為他喜歡**吹噓**他多有錢。
⑬ **can afford sth** 有能力買得起 / 負擔得起某物	• I don't think I **can afford** such an expensive car. 這麼貴的車，我想我**買**不**起**。 
can afford to V 有能力從事⋯⋯	• I **can't afford to** study abroad. 我可**負擔不起**出國留學。
⑭ **book** [bʊk] *n.* 書	• Do not judge a **book** by its cover. 勿以貌取人。(諺語)
read sb like a book 對某人瞭若指掌	• To be frank with you, I **read** Frank **like a book**. 老實對你說，我**對**法蘭克**瞭若指掌**。
in one's book 依某人之見⋯⋯	• **In my book**, Tim is not cut out for the job. **依我之見**，這份工作提姆不適任。
be a closed book to sb 對某人而言一竅不通	• English used to **be a closed book to** me. 我曾對英文**一竅不通**。
do things by the book 做事一板一眼	• If you **do things by the book**, you'll lose your creativity. 你**做事一板一眼**的話，就會失去創意。

⑮ **close down (...)** 關閉（……）	• The company has decided to **close down** its Tokyo office. / branch in Tokyo. 公司已決定**關閉**位於東京的辦事處。
⑯ **dye one's hair + 顏色** 把頭髮染成……的顏色	• To keep up with the trends, I've decided to **dye my hair** green. 為了趕潮流，我決定把**頭髮染成**綠色。

Words in Use

Diana: Hey, Craig. That's a nice car. Is it yours? How could you **afford to** buy that?

Craig: Well, I don't like to **boast about** my job, but it really pays well.

Diana: Your job at that fast-food restaurant? It's not really your car, is it, Craig?

Craig: No, it's my dad's.

Diana: I thought so. I can **read you like a book**.

黛安娜： 嘿，克雷格。這輛車真不錯，是你的嗎？你怎麼**買得起**這輛車？

克雷格： 嗯，我不喜歡**吹噓**我的工作，但薪水還蠻不錯的。

黛安娜： 你在那間速食餐廳的工作？這並不真的是你的車，對吧，克雷格？

克雷格： 不是，這是我爸的車。

黛安娜： 我就知道。我**對**你簡直**瞭如指掌**。

⑰ appreciate

[əˋpriʃɪˏet] *vt.*

感激；欣賞

• It's a pity that Nancy's talents are not **appreciated** in her company.

南西的才幹未受到她公司的**欣賞**，可惜了。

• I would **appreciate** it if you could give me a hand.

你若肯幫我一個忙，我會很**感激**。

(it 指之後 if 引導的整個子句)

⑱ be out of this world

非常好

• The food at the buffet restaurant **is out of this world**.

這家自助餐廳的食物**好吃極了**。

⑲ a world of...

= a large amount of...

大量的……

(接不可數名詞)

• Exercising will **do you** | **a world of good**. / lots of good.

運動會對你**大有好處**。

* do sb a world of good

對某人大有好處

⑳ word

[wɝd] *n.* 字，話

have a word with A about B

與 A 談論 B

• Could I **have a** | **word** / talk | **with** you **about** your son?

我可以**跟**你**談一下有關**令郎的事嗎？

without (saying) a word 一言不發地	• Patrick left **without (saying) a word**. 派翠克**一言不發地**離開了。
translate sth word for word 逐字翻譯某文章	• Don't **translate** the article **word for word**, or it'll be difficult and boring to read. 這篇文章不要**逐字翻譯**，否則讀起來既艱澀又無聊。
have words with sb 與某人爭執	• Mary **had words with** her husband over how to educate their children. 瑪麗**與**老公為如何教育孩子的事**起爭執**。
wordy [ˋwɝdɪ] *a.* 冗長的	• The politician's speech was **wordy** and not to the point. 這個政治人物的演講既**冗長**又沒切中主題。

Words in Use

Bart: Hi, Gail. You look **out of this world** in that dress.

Gail: OK, Bart. What do you want now?

Bart: What? I'm just saying you look nice today.

Gail: Bart, you want something. I know it.

Bart: Well, I would **appreciate** it if you could lend me some money. Gail? Gail? Where are you going, Gail?

巴特： 嗨，蓋兒。妳穿那件洋裝真是美得**不得了**。

蓋兒： 好了，巴特。你現在想要什麼？

巴特： 什麼？我只是在說妳今天看起來很美。

蓋兒： 巴特，你想要東西。我知道。

巴特： 嗯，如果妳能借我點錢我會**感激不盡**的。蓋兒？蓋兒？妳要去哪裡，蓋兒？

㉑ **word** [wɝd] *n.* 字，話 (作不可數名詞的重要用法) **word has it that...** = **rumor has it that...** 謠傳…… **keep one's word / promise** 守信	• Word has it / Rumor has it / It is rumored / It is said that the general manager will resign tomorrow. **據說**總經理明天將辭職。 • You can trust Roy because he always **keeps his word.** never goes back on his word. never breaks his word. 羅伊一向**守信** / 從不食言，因此你可以信任他。
㉒ **wording** [ˋwɝdɪŋ] *n.* 措辭 (不可數)	• I don't like the **wording** of this letter. It's too ambiguous. 這封信的**措辭**我不喜歡。太模稜兩可了。 
㉓ **close one's mind to sth** 別再想某事	• Paul has decided to become a monk and **close his mind to** the outside world. 保羅已下定決心出家**忘卻**紅塵。
㉔ **Great minds think alike.** 英雄所見略同。	• I had exactly the same idea. **Great minds think alike!** 我也有同樣的想法。 **英雄所見略同！** 

㉕ **Out of sight, out of mind.** 眼不見，心不煩。	• A: I've forgotten all about my ex-girlfriend. B: Well, as they say, "**Out of sight, out of mind.**" A：我已經完全忘記前女友了。 B：嗯，俗云：「**眼不見，心不煩。**」

Words in Use

Roger: I haven't seen Don in the office this week. I need him to check the **wording** on this advertisement.

Peggy: **Rumor has it that** he quit last Friday, but there's been no official announcement.

Roger: Well, if that's true, I know exactly the right person to take over his job.

Peggy Pete, right?

Roger: Yes! **Great minds think alike!**

羅傑： 這禮拜都沒有在辦公室看到唐。我需要他檢查一下這則廣告上的**用字遣詞**。

佩姬： **謠傳**他上週五辭職了，但還沒有正式公布。

羅傑： 如果謠言屬實的話，我知道可以接手他的工作的合適人選。

佩姬： 彼特，對嗎？

羅傑： 沒錯！**英雄所見略同！**

㉖ sight

[saɪt] *n.*

視力；景象

at the sight of...

一見到……

at first sight

初次看見

- I can't be a doctor because I will faint **at the sight of** blood.
  我當不了醫生，因為我**一見到**血就會昏倒。
- Amy and Henry fell in love **at first sight**.
  艾咪與亨利**一見**鍾情。
- **At first sight**, I thought he was but a poor old man. It turned out he is a billionaire.
  猛一看去，我還以為他是個窮老頭。原來他竟然是個億萬富翁。

㉗ go sightseeing

去觀光

- We didn't go to the meeting. We **went sightseeing** instead.
  我們沒去開會，反而**觀光**去了。

世界知名觀光景點

㉘ overwhelm

[ˌovɚˋwɛlm] *vt.*

使招架不住

be overwhelmed with joy / grief

高興極了 / 傷心透了

- I **was overwhelmed with joy**
  at the good news.
  when I heard the good news.
  我聽到這好消息時**樂透了**。
- The parents **were overwhelmed with grief** when they learned their baby died.
  這對父母獲知小寶寶過世時**傷心欲絕**。

㉙ **make a reservation for...** 預訂……	• I'd like to **make a reservation for** / **book** a table for five people for 8 o'clock, please. 我想要**預訂**八點的五人桌，麻煩你。
㉚ **without reservation** = completely 毫不保留地	• John accepted my advice **without reservation.** 約翰**完全**接受我的建議。

Words in Use

Rick: Anne, you look different today. Has anything good happened to you?

Anne: I **am overwhelmed with joy**, Rick. I am in love!

Rick: Really? Who's the lucky guy?

Anne: You know him—it's Dallas.

Rick: Dallas? But he's not handsome, nor is he a nice guy.

Anne: Well, Rick, it was love **at first sight**.

Rick: Well, Anne, maybe you need new glasses.

瑞克： 安妮，妳今天看起來很不一樣。發生什麼好事了嗎？

安妮： 我**開心極了**，瑞克。我談戀愛了！

瑞克： 真的嗎？是誰那麼幸運？

安妮： 你認識他的 —— 是達拉斯。

瑞克： 達拉斯？但他長得不帥，心腸也不好。

安妮： 嗯，瑞克，我們是**一見**鍾情。

瑞克： 嗯，安妮，也許妳需要配副新眼鏡了。

Unit 3

Exercises
練習題

看圖選單字

❶

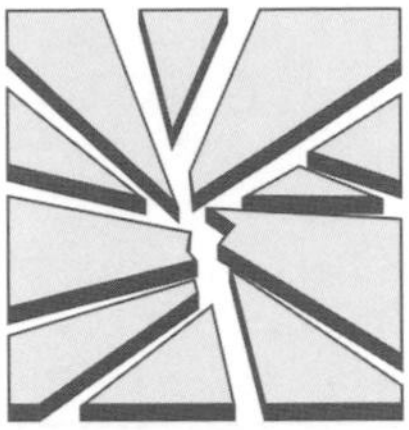

- ☐ smash into pieces
- ☐ get the runs
- ☐ close down

❷

- ☐ mess up
- ☐ pull over
- ☐ make a reservation

❸

- ☐ go sightseeing
- ☐ keep one's word
- ☐ be in a bad mood

選出正解

❶ This city is (well-traveled / well-known) for its rich history.

❷ I can't (afford / pay) to take risks.

❸ Joshua is boring because he does everything (by / to) the book.

❹ Allison wants to (die / dye) her hair red.

❺ You can count on Ethan to keep his (word / wording).

句子填空

plate | boast | wordy | appreciate | sight

❶ Allen likes to ______________ about how popular he is.

❷ Kate screamed at the ______________ of the cockroach.

❸ Your essay is too ______________. Please revise it.

❹ Don't disturb Nathan. He has too much on his ______________.

❺ I would ______________ it if you could lend me some money.

句子重組

❶ recommend / Henry / without / I / reservation

____

____.

❷ having an affair / Sam / Word has it / is / that

____

____.

❸ games / in the mood / Claire / is not / for

____

____.

Notes

Unit 4

- [x] 1 chip in (...)
- [ ] 2 baggage
- [ ] 3 give rise to...
- [ ] 4 breath
- [ ] 5 breed
- [ ] 6 sharp
- [ ] 7 sharpen
- [ ] 8 fancy
- [ ] 9 option
- [ ] 10 earn a / one's living
- [ ] 11 awareness
- [ ] 12 cautious
- [ ] 13 fit the bill
- [ ] 14 fringe benefits
- [ ] 15 litter
- [ ] 16 make ends meet
- [ ] 17 coin
- [ ] 18 break one's back
- [ ] 19 show off (...)
- [ ] 20 show up
- [ ] 21 steal the show
- [ ] 22 (battery) be dead
- [ ] 23 over my dead body
- [ ] 24 be dead hungry
- [ ] 25 be dead set against + N/V-ing
- [ ] 26 be too... for sb's liking
- [ ] 27 bumper
- [ ] 28 be fed up with...
- [ ] 29 feed
- [ ] 30 bite the hand that feeds you

Unit 4

❶ chip in (...)
分擔，湊出 (錢)

• Tomorrow is Dad's birthday. Let's each **chip in** $50 to buy a gift for him, OK?
明天是老爸的生日，我們**出錢湊**五十美元買個禮物給他，好嗎？

❷ baggage
[ˋbægɪdʒ] *n.*
= luggage
[ˋlʌgɪdʒ]
行李 (總稱)

a piece of baggage / luggage
一件行李

• How many baggages / luggages do you have with you? (×)
→ How many **pieces of baggage / luggage** do you have with you? (○)
你一共有**幾件行李**？

• You are only allowed **one piece of** carry-on / hand **baggage** on the plane.
你只准攜帶**一件**手提**行李**上飛機。

機上常見事物

❸ give rise to...
= result in...
= cause...
造成……

• Heavy rain has **given rise to** / **resulted in** / **caused** flooding in the village.
大雨**造成**整個村莊淹水。

❹ **breath**

[brεθ] *n.* 呼吸

- The beautiful landscape of the valley **took my breath away.**

山谷美得**令**我**歎為觀止**。

⋆ take sb's breath away　令某人歎為觀止

❺ **breed**

[brid] *vt.*

扶養；孕育；導致（三態為：breed, bred [brεd], bred）

- Poor living conditions **breed** violence and depression.

貧困的生活環境**是**暴力與憂鬱的**溫床**。

- Nothing **breeds** success like success.

字面翻譯：沒有一件事會像成功那樣，成功地**孕育**出成功。

實際翻譯：一事成功，萬事亨通。（只有成功才能孕育成功。）

Words in Use

Lucille: Clara is leaving the company. Do you want to **chip in** to buy a present for her?

Kent: I don't think so. I don't like what **chipping in** will **give rise to** in the future.

Lucille: What will it **give rise to**?

Kent: Being asked to **chip in** again sometime.

露西爾：克萊拉要離開公司了。你想要一起**攤錢**買個禮物送她嗎？

肯特：不了，我不喜歡未來**攤錢導致**的後果。

露西爾：會**導致**什麼後果？

肯特：又要繼續被問是否要一起**攤錢**。

❻ sharp

[ʃɑrp] *a.*

明顯的；尖銳的；時尚的

be in sharp contrast with / to...

與……形成明顯的對比

have a sharp tongue

牙尖嘴利

- I respect our current mayor because his honesty **is in sharp contrast with** many other politicians.
  我尊敬現任的市長，因為他的誠實**與**許多其他政治人物**有很大的區別**。
- I don't like Tom because he **has a sharp tongue**.
  湯姆**牙尖嘴利**，因此我不喜歡他。
- **Keep a sharp eye on** that man; he might be a thief.
  好好盯著那男子，他可能是個賊。
  ⋆ keep a sharp eye on sb　好好盯著某人
- You **look** pretty **sharp in** that suit.
  你**穿上**那套西裝**很帥氣**。
  ⋆ look sharp in + 衣服　穿某衣服很好看

❼ sharpen

[ˋʃɑrpn̩] *vt.*

削尖；磨練（技巧）

- My pencil is blunt. I'll have to **sharpen** it.
  我的鉛筆鈍了，得把它**削尖**。
- Keeping a diary is a good way to **sharpen** your writing skills.
  寫日記是**磨練**寫作技巧的好方法。

❽ fancy

[ˋfænsɪ] *vt.*

想要 & *a.* 豪華昂貴的

- Do you **fancy** a drink this evening?
  你今晚**想要**喝點酒嗎？
- We had a good time drinking and singing at that **fancy** restaurant last night.
  我們昨晚在那家**豪華的**餐廳又喝酒又唱歌，玩得很愉快。

take a fancy to sth 喜歡上某物 比較 **take a shine to sb** 立刻喜歡上某人	• The moment I saw the house, I **took a fancy / liking to it.** 我一看到那棟房子，便**喜歡上**它了。 • John really **took a shine to** the new girl in the office. 約翰非常**喜歡**辦公室新來的女孩。
9 option [ˋɑpʃən] *n.* 選擇 **have no option but to V** 除了……之外別無選擇	• You **have no option** / choice / alternative **but to** apologize to Tammy. 你**除了**向譚美道歉**外別無選擇**。

Words in Use

Melinda: You **look** very **sharp in** that suit, Austin.

Austin: Thank you. I've **taken** a bit of **a shine to** the new girl on reception. I'm going to ask her if she **fancies** going for a drink after work.

Melinda: I'm sure when she sees you looking that handsome, she'll **have no option but to** go out with you!

梅琳達：奧斯丁，你**穿**那套西裝**很帥氣**。

奧斯丁：謝謝。我有點**喜歡**接待櫃檯的那個新來的女生。我要問她下班後是否**想**跟我去喝杯酒。

梅琳達：我確定當她看到你如此帥氣的模樣的時候，**除了**跟你出去**之外也別無選擇**了！

Unit 4

⑩ **earn a / one's living / livelihood** 賺錢謀生 **livelihood** [ˋlaɪvlɪˏhʊd] *n.* 生計	• Peter earns his living / livelihood by teaching and writing. 彼得靠教書及寫作**維生**。 • People on the island depend on fishing for their **livelihood**. 島上的居民靠捕魚**維生**。
⑪ **awareness** [əˋwɛrnɪs] *n.* 意識 **raise awareness of...** 提高對……的意識	• We need to raise public **awareness** of the dangers of smoking. 我們必須**提高**大眾**對**抽菸危險的**意識**。 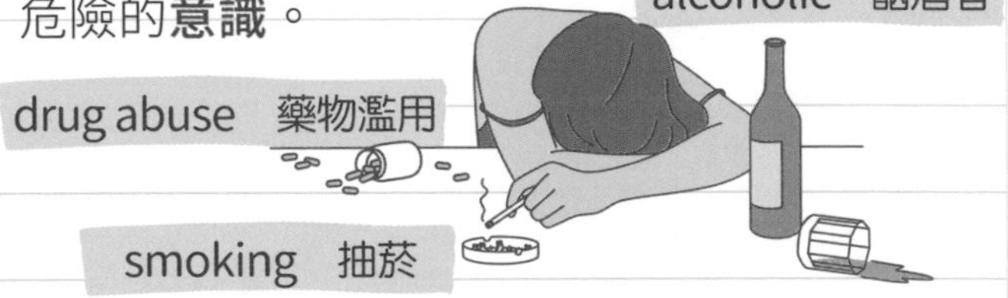
⑫ **cautious** [ˋkɔʃəs] *a.* 謹慎的 **be cautious about...** 謹慎處理…… **cautiously** [ˋkɔʃəslɪ] *adv.* = **with caution** 小心翼翼地 **caution** [ˋkɔʃən] *n.* 小心	• You should be **cautious about** everything you say or do. 你的一言一行都要**小心**為是。 • At times like this, you should spend money **cautiously**. 在這個時候，你花錢應**謹慎**。 • Paris is indeed a beautiful city, but a **word of caution**: Robberies are very common here. 巴黎的確是個美麗的城市，不過我要**提醒你**，這裡經常發生搶案。

a word of caution 提醒你，給你一句警言 **take caution** 小心	• **Take caution** / Be careful when driving in the rain. 雨天開車要**小心**。
⑬ fit the bill **= fill the bill** **= be suitable for the job** 適合（職位）	• We need an experienced editor. Do you know who **fits the bill?** / **fills the bill?** / **is suitable for the job?** 我們需要一位有經驗的編輯。你知道有哪一位是**適當人選**嗎？

Words in Use

Vivien: I'm worried about the number of cigarettes our father is smoking.

Drew: He does smoke a lot. We need to **raise** his **awareness of** the dangers of smoking.

Vivien: I'm going to have a word with him about it.

Drew: **A word of caution**: Be gentle. You know he doesn't like being told what to do.

薇薇安：我擔心我們老爸的抽菸量。

德魯：他的確抽得蠻兇的。我們需要**提高**他**對**抽菸危險**的意識**。

薇薇安：我要去跟他談一談這件事。

德魯：**提醒妳**：要溫柔。妳知道他不喜歡人家告訴他該怎麼做。

⑭ **fringe benefits** 附加福利	• John has found quite a good job. **Fringe benefits** include a company car and free health insurance. 約翰找到一份很不錯的工作。**附加福利**包括一輛公司車及免費的健保。
⑮ **litter** [ˋlɪtɚ] *n.* 垃圾（不可數）& *vi.* 亂丟垃圾	• The ground is covered with **litter**. 地上到處都是**垃圾**。 • Don't **litter**, or people will call you a **litter** bug. 別**亂丟垃圾**，否則人家會說你是**垃圾**蟲。

成為環保小尖兵

⑯ **make ends meet** 勉強維持生計	• Because of the economic recession, many families are struggling to **make ends meet**. 由於經濟不景氣，許多家庭只能**勉強糊口**。
⑰ **coin** [kɔɪn] *n.* 錢幣 & *vt.* 創造（新詞） **toss / flip a coin** 擲錢幣	• Let's open the map and **toss a coin** to decide where to go. 咱們把地圖打開**擲錢幣**來決定去哪兒吧。 • The word "hippie" was **coined** in the 1960s. 「嬉皮」一詞**創**於 1960 年代。

⑱ **break one's back** = put forth a great deal of effort 辛苦工作	• All parents are willing to **break their backs** to give their kids a better life. 所有父母都心甘情願**努力打拼**讓孩子生活得更好。

Words in Use

Sally: Have you found a job yet, Terry?

Terry: No. I've really made an effort, but I haven't found one yet.

Sally: I hope you can find one with good **fringe benefits**.

Terry: I don't care about those so much. I just want one that can help me **make ends meet**. But the only ones I've been offered pay so poorly.

Sally: Good luck!

莎莉：泰瑞，你找到工作了嗎？

泰瑞：還沒，我真的盡力了，但還沒找到工作。

莎莉：希望你能找到**附加福利**好的工作。

泰瑞：我不太在乎那些東西。我只想要一份能夠讓我**勉強維持生計**的工作。但目前為止願意聘請我去的工作薪水都少得可憐。

莎莉：祝你好運！

⓳ show off (...)
炫耀 (……)

- Tom has just bought a brand new sports car. Whenever he can, he likes to **show** it **off** to his friends.
  湯姆剛買了一輛全新的跑車。只要有機會，他就喜歡**炫耀**給朋友看。
- People who **show off** have few friends.
  愛**炫耀**的人朋友不多。

⓴ show up
= turn up
出現

- David waited for almost two hours, but his girlfriend didn't **show** / **turn** **up**.
  大衛等了幾近兩個小時，但是他女友就是沒**出現**。

㉑ steal the show
= become the main focus of attention
大出風頭

- The singer **stole the show** throughout the concert.
  演唱會從頭到尾，這位歌手**出盡了風頭**。

㉒ (battery) be dead
(電池) 沒電

- The batteries **are dead**. They have to be recharged.
  電池**沒電**，需要充電了。

㉓ **over my dead body**
門兒都沒有

- A: Can I borrow your new car?
  B: **Over my dead body!**
  A：你的新車可以借給我嗎？
  B：**門兒都沒有！**

㉔ **be dead / very hungry**
餓死了
be dead right
對極了
be dead tired
累壞了

- I'm **dead hungry**. Let's find a place to eat.
  =I'm starving to death. Let's find a place to eat.
  我**餓死了**。咱們找個地方吃東西吧。

Words in Use

Graeme: Chris is so annoying! He **showed up** late to my birthday dinner last night and still managed to **steal the show**! He was **showing off** about his latest promotion at work.

Sheila: Don't get so worked up about him. I think I'll invite him to our house this weekend so you guys can make up.

Graeme: **Over my dead body!**

葛雷姆：克里斯好煩啊！昨晚我的生日晚餐他很晚才**到**，而且還**搶盡風頭**！他當時在**炫耀**他最近升職。

席拉：別為了他這麼激動。這個週末我想邀請他到我們家，這樣你們兩個可以和好。

葛雷姆：**門都沒有！**

Unit 4

㉕ **be dead set against + N/V-ing** 堅決反對……	• The villagers are dead set against / completely opposed to having a nuclear power plant built near their village. 村民們**堅決反對**把核電廠蓋在村莊附近。
㉖ **be too... for sb's liking** 太……因此某人並不喜歡	• The cake is too sweet for my liking. 這蛋糕**太**甜了，**因此**我**不喜歡**。 
㉗ **bumper** [ˋbʌmpɚ] *n.* (汽車) 保險桿 bumper to bumper 車子一輛接著一輛	• On holidays, the traffic on the freeway is **bumper to bumper**. 每逢假日，高速公路上的車流量都是**車子一輛接一輛地**開（車流量很大）。
㉘ **be fed up with...** = be sick and tired of... 受夠 / 厭倦……	• I'm fed up with this boring job. I think I need to find a new one. 這個無聊的工作讓我**受夠了**。我想我得找份新工作。 
㉙ **feed** [fid] *vt.* 餵養 (三態為：feed, fed [fɛd], fed) feed on... (動物) 以……為食	• I do two jobs every day because I have a large family to feed. 我每天做兩份工作因為我有一大家子要**養**。

比較 **live on...** (人或動物) 以……為食 **live by...** 憑藉……為人處事	• Small birds feed on / live on insects. 小鳥**靠**吃昆蟲**維生**。 • Most Asians live on rice. 大多數亞洲人**吃**米飯**維生**。 • "Honesty" is the word I live by. 「誠實」一詞是我**為人處事的根本**。
30 bite the hand that feeds you 忘恩負義	• Stay away from Paul. He's the kind of man that will bite the hand that feeds him. 遠離保羅。他是會**恩將仇報**的那種人。

Words in Use

Tracy: Where is Brandon? And why hasn't he called me? He's 20 minutes late.

Keith: Maybe the battery is dead on his phone.

Tracy: Maybe. Anyway, he'd better show up soon.

Keith: It sounds like you're tired of him being late all the time.

Tracy: Yes. I'm starting to think our relationship has come to a dead end.

崔西：布蘭登在哪裡？還有，他為什麼還沒打電話給我？他已經遲到 20 分鐘了。

凱斯：也許他電話**沒電了**。

崔西：也許吧。總之他最好趕快出現。

凱斯：妳聽來**對**他總是遲到**覺得厭煩了**。

崔西：沒錯，我開始認為我們的關係已經走到盡頭了。

Unit 4

Unit 4

Exercises
練習題

看圖連連看

❶

❷

❸

toss a coin | litter | bumper to bumper

選出正解

❶ Unfortunately, none of the candidates fit the ____________.

(A) bill (B) place

(C) spot (D) point

❷ Gina's comments ____________ rise to a heated discussion.

(A) made (B) caused

(C) had (D) gave

句子填空

cautious | ends | show | liking | chipped

❶ This restaurant is too fancy for my ______________.

❷ My siblings and I all ______________ in for the present.

❸ Rick is working three jobs to make ______________ meet.

❹ You should be ______________ about what you say on the internet.

❺ James is considered arrogant because he likes to ______________ off.

句子重組

❶ looks / in / Frank / sharp / that outfit

____

____.

❷ start over / but to / have / no option / We

____

____.

❸ is dead set / a new house / The old man / against / moving to

____

____.

Unit 4

Notes

Unit 5

- [x] 1 put sb off
- [ ] 2 put sth off
- [ ] 3 strive for...
- [ ] 4 call sb... for short
- [ ] 5 In short, ...
- [ ] 6 be tied up
- [ ] 7 in turn
- [ ] 8 be in a tough spot
- [ ] 9 come into existence
- [ ] 10 know the ins and outs of sth
- [ ] 11 be anything but + N/adj.
- [ ] 12 be nothing but + N
- [ ] 13 of all time
- [ ] 14 with care
- [ ] 15 for days on end
- [ ] 16 for + 數字 + consecutive days
- [ ] 17 be a carbon copy of sb/sth
- [ ] 18 learn sth by heart
- [ ] 19 miss out on...
- [ ] 20 slip one's mind
- [ ] 21 a slip of the pen
- [ ] 22 a slip of the tongue
- [ ] 23 slip
- [ ] 24 It's just as well that...
- [ ] 25 be of like mind
- [ ] 26 be well-liked
- [ ] 27 You said it!
- [ ] 28 You don't say!
- [ ] 29 weigh
- [ ] 30 weight

Unit 5

❶ put sb off
拒絕某人

• Tom keeps asking Mary out, and she keeps **putting him off**.
湯姆不斷約瑪麗出去，她則不斷**拒絕**他。

❷ put sth off
將某事延期

• The meeting was **put off** / **postponed** until next Monday because of bad weather.
因為天氣不好，會議**延**到下星期一再舉行。

❸ strive for...
努力爭取……

strive to V
努力要……

• The coach encouraged his team to **strive for** the championship.
教練鼓勵他的球隊要**力爭**冠軍。

• The government is **striving to** narrow the gap between rich and poor.
政府正**努力**縮減貧富差距。

❹ call sb... for short
把某人簡稱為……

• My co-worker's name is Alexandra, but I often **call** her Alex **for short**.
我的同事名叫亞麗珊卓，不過我常**簡稱**她**為**亞麗絲。

❺ In short, ... = In a word, ... = To sum up, ... = In brief, ... 簡言之/總之，……	• Peter never does things right and always makes many mistakes. **In short,** he is not suitable for the job. 彼得從未把事情做好過，也總會犯錯。**簡言之**，他並不適任這份工作。
❻ be tied up 被纏住	• I am **tied up** in a meeting at the moment, so call me later. 目前我正在開會人**走不開**，因此稍後再打電話給我。

Words in Use

Hank: So, Chloe, how do you like being married?

Chloe: Married? I haven't tied the knot with anyone.

Hank: Oh, I heard you and Paul were getting married. Did you **put off** the wedding?

Chloe: Ha! We did more than just **put it off**.

Hank: I don't understand.

Chloe: Well, **in short**, he's no longer even my boyfriend!

漢克：克羅伊，妳對結婚的感覺是如何？

克羅伊：結婚？我還沒跟任何人結婚呢。

漢克：喔，我之前聽說妳跟保羅要結婚了。你們把婚禮**延期**了嗎？

克羅伊：哈！我們做的可不止是**延期**而已。

漢克：我不懂妳的意思。

克羅伊：嗯，**總之**，他連我的男友都不是了！

❼ in turn = because of this / that 因此	• Paul stopped eating out, and, in turn because of this , he was in better shape and was able to save more money. 保羅不再到外頭餐館用餐，也**因為如此**，他身材變好了，也省下更多錢。
❽ be in a tough spot = be in a difficult situation 陷入困境	• Ever since he lost his job, Tom has been in a tough spot. difficult situation. =Losing his job has put Tom in a tough spot. 自從失業後，湯姆就**陷入困境**。
❾ come into existence = come into being 開始存在，問世	• To my understanding, the Earth came into existence being around 4.5 billion years ago. 就我所知，地球大約在四十五億年前就**存在**了。 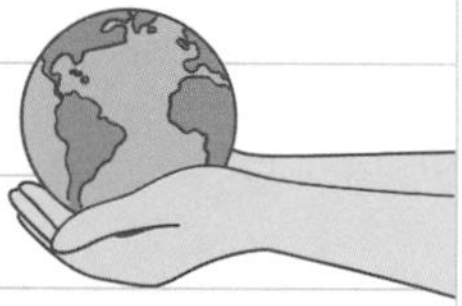
❿ know the ins and outs of sth = know the detailed facts about sth 了解某事物的全部細節	• I know how to use computers, but I don't really know / understand the ins and outs of how they work. 我知道如何使用電腦，不過至於電腦是如何運作的，這方面的**細節**我就不**清楚**了。 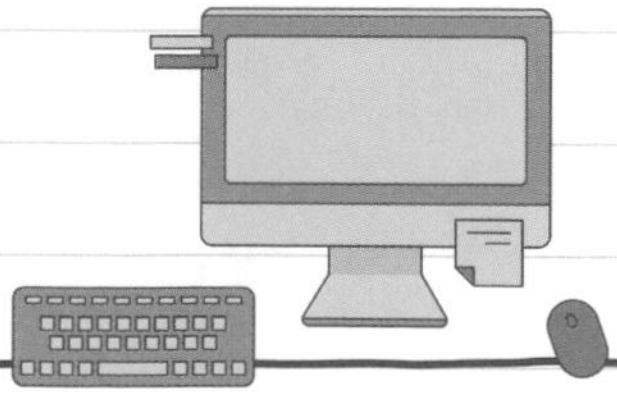

⑪ **be anything but + N/adj.** = be not + N/adj. + at all = be far from + N/adj. 絕不是……	• Tom is anything but a fool. =Tom is not a fool at all. 湯姆**絕不是**個傻子。 • Frankly, your boyfriend is anything but good-looking / not good-looking at all / far from good-looking, but he has a good heart. 坦白說，妳的男友**一點都不**帥，但他心腸很好。
	• You can trust Peter. He is anything but a liar. / not a liar at all. / far from a liar. 你可以信任彼得。他**絕不是**個騙子。

Unit 5

Words in Use

Joan: Keith's life is anything but good these days. I feel bad for him.

Ronnie: That's too bad. What's the problem?

Joan: He got fired from his job, and, in turn, he doesn't have enough money these days.

Ronnie: It sounds like he's in a tough spot.

Joan: He sure is.

喬安： 凱斯最近過得**一點也不**好。我替他感到難過。

朗尼： 太糟糕了。發生什麼事了？

喬安： 他被開除了，**因此**，他最近沒有足夠的錢過日子。

朗尼： 聽起來他是**陷入困境**了。

喬安： 一定是的。

⓬ **be nothing but + N** = be nothing more than + N = be only / just + N 只不過是……	• Billy is | nothing but nothing more than only / just | a little child. Don't expect too much of him. 比利**只不過是**個小孩子。別對他期望過高。 
⓭ **of all time** 有史以來 (與最高級形容詞並用) 	• It is not too much to say that William Shakespeare is the greatest writer **of all time**. 威廉·莎士比亞堪稱是**有史以來**最偉大的作家，這樣說並不為過。 • This is my favorite song **of all time**. 這是**有史以來**我最喜歡的歌。
⓮ **with care** = carefully 小心地	• The road is | icy slippery |, so drive **with care**. 馬路結冰了 / 很滑，因此要**小心**駕駛。
⓯ **for | days hours | on end** 連續好幾天 / 好幾個小時	• It has been raining here for three | days hours | on end. (×，不可與數字並用) →It has been raining here **for | days hours | on end**. (○) 這裡**連續**下了**好幾天** / **好幾個小時**的雨。

⑯ for + 數字 + consecutive days / hours
= for + 數字 + days / hours in a row
連續……天 / ……個小時

- It has been raining here for three consecutive days. / days in a row.

這裡**連續**下了三**天**雨。

下雨必備雨具

Words in Use

Frank: Oh! The Calves lost again. They have lost nine consecutive games! I think they are the worst basketball team **of all time.**

Ally: Maybe you care about sports too much.

Frank: Every player on that team **is nothing but** a loser. I could talk about how bad they are **for hours on end.**

Ally: Yes, I'm sure you could. See you later.

法蘭克： 喔！小牛隊又輸了。他們已經連續輸九場比賽了！我覺得他們是**有史以來**最爛的籃球隊。

艾麗： 也許你關心運動過了頭。

法蘭克： 那個球隊裡的每個隊員都**只不過是**個魯蛇。我可以講他們有多爛，**連續**講**好幾個小時**。

艾麗： 是，我確定你行。再見。

Unit 5

⑰ **be a carbon copy of sb/sth** 與某人 / 某物長得很像	• Mary is a **carbon copy of** her mother. =Mary looks very much like her mother. 瑪麗跟她媽媽**長得很像**。
⑱ **learn sth by heart** 憑記憶背下某物	• I **learned** a lot of poems **by heart** when I was in elementary school. Even today, I can still recite most of them. 小學時我**背**過許多詩。甚至到今天大部分的詩我仍會背誦。
⑲ **miss out on...** = miss... 錯過 (機會)	• Don't **miss out on** / **miss** any opportunities to learn English. 不要**錯過**任何一個學習英文的機會。
⑳ **slip one's mind** 忘記 (某事)	• I forgot it's your birthday today. It totally **slipped my mind**. 我忘了今天是你的生日。我**忘得一乾二淨**。
㉑ **a slip of the pen** 筆誤	• Sorry, it was **a slip of the pen**. I meant to write "dig," not "dog." 抱歉，那是**筆誤**。我原本要寫的是 dig，而不是 dog。

㉒ a slip of the tongue

口誤

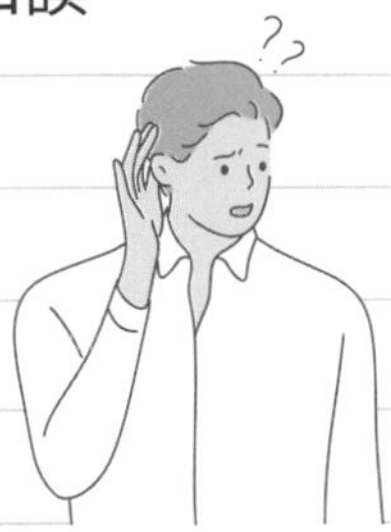

• Sorry, I meant to say “Tainan,” not “Taichung.” It was obviously **a slip of the tongue**.

抱歉，我原本要說「臺南」，而非「臺中」。這顯然是**口誤**。

Words in Use

Eric: It’s so hard to remember all the words for the play.

Chloe: Oh, I’ve **learned** all my words **by heart** already.

Eric: You must have a great memory.

Chloe: Thanks. I do.

Eric: By the way, why didn’t you come to my party on Saturday? Did you forget?

Chloe: Um... I guess it just **slipped my mind**. Sorry.

Eric: Hmm.

艾瑞克：要記住這齣戲的所有臺詞好難啊。

克羅伊：喔。我已經把我的臺詞都**背好**了。

艾瑞克：妳的記憶力一定很好。

克羅伊：謝謝，沒錯。

艾瑞克：對了，妳星期六怎麼沒來參加我的派對？妳忘了嗎？

克羅伊：喔……我想我是**忘記**了，抱歉。

艾瑞克：嗯。

㉓ slip

[slɪp] *vi.*

滑跤（三態為：slip, slipped, slipped）

- Peter slipped on the ice and landed right on his bottom.

  彼得在冰上**滑了一跤**，一屁股坐在地上。

- The old man slipped in the bathtub and broke his leg.

  老先生在浴缸**滑了一跤**，把一隻腿跌斷了。

受傷治療

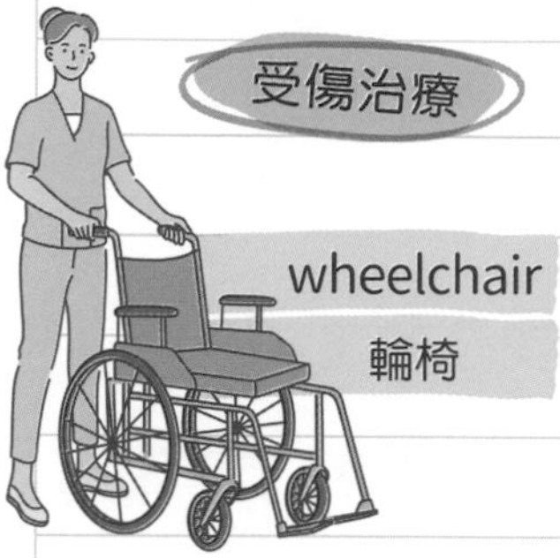

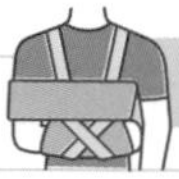

㉔ It's just as well that...

= It's a good thing that...

還好……

- It's beginning to rain. It's just as well that we've brought our umbrellas.

  開始下雨了。**還好**我們帶了傘。

㉕ be of like mind

意見相同

- I enjoy working with people of like mind.

  我喜歡和**意見相同的**人共事。

- I can see that you and I are of like mind on this issue.

  我看得出來，這個議題你我**看法一致**。

㉖ be well-liked

= be popular

很受歡迎

- The new co-worker is well-liked because of her pleasant and humorous personality.

  這位新同事個性開朗又幽默，因此**很受歡迎**。

Words in Use

Jasmine: It seems like Jessy has become really **popular** in our school.

Chuck: Yes, she is one of the most **well-liked** students.

Jasmine: I don't understand it. She's neither smart nor pretty. And she's boring.

Chuck: Maybe it's because she doesn't criticize other people.

Jasmine: What do you mean?

Chuck: **It's just as well that** we're not **of like mind** on this issue.

潔思敏： 潔西在學校似乎變得**很受歡迎**。

查克： 沒錯，她是最**受歡迎**的學生之一。

潔思敏： 我不懂。她既不聰明也不漂亮。而且她這個人很無聊。

查克： 也許是因為她不亂批評別人。

潔思敏： 你是什麼意思？

查克： **幸好**我們在這個議題上**看法不一致**。

㉗ You said it!
你說得沒錯 / 我同意你的話！

• A: I shouldn't have lent Ricky the money. He is nowhere to be found now.
B: **You said it!**
A：我不該把錢借給瑞奇的。他現在連一個人影都沒有。
B：**你說得沒錯！**

㉘ You don't say!
= Really?
真的嗎？

• A: Eric and I are getting married next week.
B: **You don't say!**
A：艾瑞克與我下星期就要結婚了。
B：**真的嗎？**

感情的階段

date 約會

propose 求婚

divorce 離婚

break up 分手

㉙ weigh
[we] *vt.* & *vi.*
量（某人 / 物的）重量
weigh sb down
讓某人承受不起

• To lose weight, I watch what I eat and **weigh** myself twice a day.
為了減重，我很注意吃，而且每天量兩次**體重**。
• I **weigh** 85 kilos.
我的**體重**是八十五公斤。
• How much do you **weigh**?（常用）
= What's your weight?（少用）
你多重？
• John was **weighed down** by the heavy burden of raising his big family.
約翰要養一大家子的人，這負擔把他**壓垮**了。

weigh one's words 字字斟酌	• You must **weigh your words** when you answer the judge's questions. 你回答法官的問題時要**字字斟酌**。
30 weight [wet] *n.* 重量 **carry weight** (講話) 有影響力	• The CEO's words **carry** a lot of **weight** with the president. 執行長的話對董事長很**有影響力**。

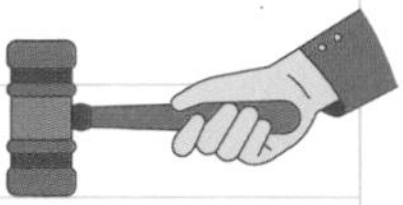

Words in Use

Paul: We always get so much homework. All this homework **weighs** us **down**.

Wanda: **You said it!**

Paul: Maybe we should talk to the teacher about it.

Wanda: I don't think what the students say will **carry** much **weight** with the teacher.

Paul: Maybe not, but if we **weigh our words** carefully, maybe we can persuade the teacher to give us less homework.

保羅： 我們的回家作業總是好多。這些作業要把我們**壓垮**了。

汪達： **你說得沒錯！**

保羅： 也許我們應該要跟老師談談。

汪達： 我不認為學生說的話會對老師**有**太大的**影響力**。

保羅： 也許不會，但是如果我們**字字斟酌**小心地說，也許我們能說服老師給我們少一點回家作業。

Unit 5

Exercises
練習題

看圖選單字

❶

☐ slip

☐ weigh

☐ be tied up

❷

☐ weight

☐ a carbon copy

☐ a slip of a pen

❸

☐ put sb off

☐ carry weight

☐ with care

選出正解

❶ Gina has been in a tough (point / spot) ever since her mother died.

❷ To be honest, Greg is (anything / something) but smart.

❸ Jane and I are of like (heart / mind). That's why we work well together.

❹ I can't meet you this week. I'm tied (in / up) all week.

❺ Joanne keeps putting (off / out) doing her homework.

句子填空

well | miss | short | end | mind

❶ I forgot to set up the meeting. It completely slipped my ______________.

❷ Dan is thirsty after talking for hours on ______________.

❸ His name is Jonathan. I call him Jon for ______________.

❹ It's just as ______________ that I took the train. The traffic was bad.

❺ Don't ______________ out on the flash sale.

Unit 5

句子重組

❶ is striving / Sally / a healthy lifestyle / maintain / to

____

____.

❷ knows / of / the project / Mason / the ins and outs

____

____.

❸ by / Ben / the responsibilities / down / is weighed

____

____.

Notes

Unit 6

- [x] ❶ drive
- [ ] ❷ drive
- [ ] ❸ take sb on a ride
- [ ] ❹ heartbreaking
- [ ] ❺ favor
- [ ] ❻ feast
- [ ] ❼ have a heated debate over sth
- [ ] ❽ though
- [ ] ❾ have dual nationality
- [ ] ❿ jump at the opportunity to...
- [ ] ⓫ by any chance
- [ ] ⓬ by chance
- [ ] ⓭ take chances
- [ ] ⓮ a slim chance
- [ ] ⓯ Chances are that...
- [ ] ⓰ come as no surprise
- [ ] ⓱ want nothing more than to V
- [ ] ⓲ stubborn
- [ ] ⓳ there is no point in + V-ing
- [ ] ⓴ be on the point of + V-ing
- [ ] ㉑ What's the point of...?
- [ ] ㉒ be to the point
- [ ] ㉓ push sb to the point of...
- [ ] ㉔ by far the + 最高級形容詞 + N
- [ ] ㉕ stardom
- [ ] ㉖ feel at home
- [ ] ㉗ be home to...
- [ ] ㉘ make yourself at home
- [ ] ㉙ at times
- [ ] ㉚ foundation

Unit 6

❶ drive
[draɪv] *n.*
駕車行駛
go for a drive
開車兜風
a five-hour drive to + 某地
到某地的車程是五個小時

- Now that we're finished with all the work, let's go for a drive.
  既然我們把工作都做完了，我們去**開車兜風**吧。
- It's | a five-hour drive / five hours' drive | from my house to the amusement park.
  從我家**到**遊樂園**的車程是五個小時**。

❷ drive
[draɪv] *n.* 精力，衝勁（不可數）
be full of
| drive
| great energy
充滿幹勁

- We all believe Sam will get somewhere someday—he's full of | drive. / great energy.
  我們都相信山姆有朝一日會成大器 —— 他**充滿幹勁**。

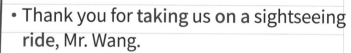

❸ take sb on a ride
開車載某人兜風

- Thank you for taking us on a sightseeing ride, Mr. Wang.
  王先生，謝謝您**開車載**我們觀光。

❹ heartbreaking
[ˋhɑrt͵brekɪŋ]
a. 令人心碎

- My son does nothing but play video games day and night. It's heartbreaking to see him wasting his life away like this.
  我兒子整天什麼事都不做只會打電玩。看到他這樣虛度光陰真**令人難過**。

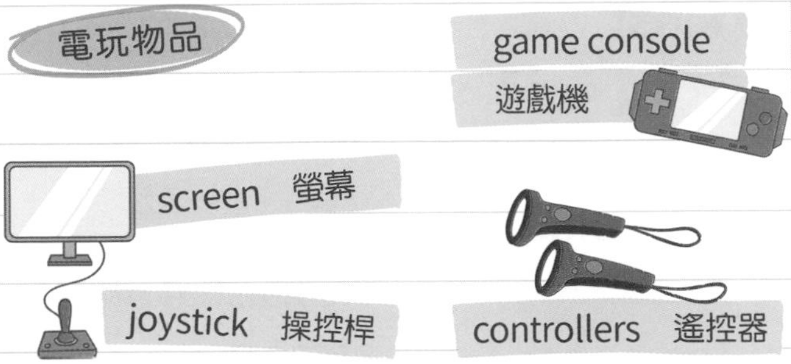

❺ **favor** [ˋfevɚ]

n. 寵愛（不可數）

fall out of favor

失寵

curry favor with sb

巴結某人

- Peter **fell out of favor** with his boss soon after he was found lying to him.

  彼得被老闆發現他撒謊之後，立刻就**失寵**了。

- I look down upon Carl because he likes to **curry favor** with his boss.

  我瞧不起卡爾，因為他喜歡**巴結**老闆。

Words in Use

Jake: Hey, Andrea. Would you like to go for a drive?

Andrea: Thanks, Jake, but I'm meeting Tony for lunch.

Jake: Tony? I thought he **fell out of favor** with you.

Andrea: He did. But he's been trying to **curry favor** with me lately.

Jake: So, is he taking you to an expensive restaurant?

Andrea: Of course!

傑克： 嘿，安德莉亞。妳想**開車兜兜風**嗎？

安德莉亞： 謝了，傑克，但是我要跟湯尼見面吃午餐。

傑克： 湯尼？我以為妳已經**不喜歡**他了。

安德莉亞： 沒錯。但他最近一直試著要**巴結**我。

傑克： 所以他要帶妳去很昂貴的餐廳吃飯嗎？

安德莉亞： 當然！

❻ feast [fist] *n.* 盛宴 & *vi.* 享用 & *vt.* 款待 **feast on...** 盡情享用…… **feast one's eyes on...** 飽覽……，將……一飽眼福	• We held a **feast** in celebration of our victory in the basketball game. 我們舉辦了一場**盛宴**以慶祝我們在籃球比賽的勝利。 • We **feasted on** all the delicious dishes at the party. 派對上我們**大啖**所有的美食。 • I took a seat by the window, sipping coffee and **feasting my eyes on** the beauty of the valley. 我坐在窗邊的座位，邊啜飲著咖啡，邊**飽覽**山谷的美景。

不同種類的咖啡

❼ have a heated debate over sth 因某事產生激烈的爭執	• Mr. & Mrs. White **had a heated debate / argument over** how to educate their children. 懷特夫婦**對**如何教育子女**產生了激烈的爭執**。
❽ though [ðo] *conj.* 雖然（置主詞之前）& *adv.* 然而（置句尾）	• **Though / Although** he is old, Mr. Smith keeps learning. = Old **though** he is, Mr. Smith keeps learning. **雖然**史密斯先生年歲已高，他仍不斷在學習。

- Mr. Smith is old. He keeps learning, **though**.

= Mr. Smith is old; **however**, he keeps learning.

史密斯先生年歲已高，**不過**他仍不斷在學習。

9 have dual nationality / citizenship

擁有雙重國籍

- According to the law, you can't **have / hold dual nationality** if you want to work for the government.

根據法律的規定，你若想擔任公職就不得**擁有雙重國籍**。

Words in Use

Juliet: Hi, David. **Feast your eyes on** these. I have two tickets to the Tigers game for you!

David: Oh, thanks.

Juliet: You don't seem excited. I thought you liked the Tigers.

David: Sorry. I just had **a heated debate** with my parents.

Juliet: **Though** you are unhappy, I hope you can still go to the game.

David: Sure—thanks!

茱麗葉： 嗨，大衛。**享用**吧。我有兩張老虎隊的票要給你！

大衛： 喔，謝謝妳。

茱麗葉： 你好像不怎麼興奮。我以為你喜歡老虎隊。

大衛： 抱歉，我剛跟我爸媽**大吵一架**。

茱麗葉： 雖然你心情不好，我還是希望你能去看比賽。

大衛： 我一定會去 —— 謝謝！

⑩ jump at the opportunity to...
= seize the chance to...
抓住機會從事……

• You should jump at every opportunity / seize every chance you have to learn English.
你應**把握所有**學英文**的機會**。

⑪ by any chance
可能

• Do you **by any chance** know that guy?
那個傢伙你**可能**認識嗎？

• Are you Mr. Stark, **by any chance**?
您**會是**史塔克先生嗎？

⑫ by chance
碰巧

• I met an old friend **by chance** a couple of days ago.
= I chanced on / ran into / bumped into / came across an old friend a couple of days ago.
幾天前我**偶然**遇見一位老朋友。

⑬ take chances
= do risky things
冒險，做有風險的事

• A: Don't **take chances** while driving.
B: What do you mean by that?
A: Don't do things like speeding or tailgating while driving.
A：開車時不要**冒險**。
B：你這話是什麼意思？
A：不要做超速或近距離跟車這類的事。

⑭ **a slim chance** 機會渺茫	• There is only **a slim chance** that Sam will pass the test because he hardly ever studies. 山姆通過考試的**機會很渺茫**因為他幾乎從不念書。
⑮ **Chances are that...** = It is very likely that... 很可能……	• The sky is overcast. Chances are / It's very likely that it's going to rain soon. 天空烏雲密布。**很可能**隨即會下雨。

Words in Use

Jerry: Hey, Tina. Watch me do the tricks on my bike.

Tina: You'll hurt yourself.

Jerry: Ha! There's only **a slim chance** of that!

Tina: But it's raining. **Chances are that** you'll fall.

Jerry: You worry too much. Watch this! Oops!

Tina: I knew you would fall. Are you hurt?

Jerry: A bit. You don't have a Band-Aid, by any chance, do you?

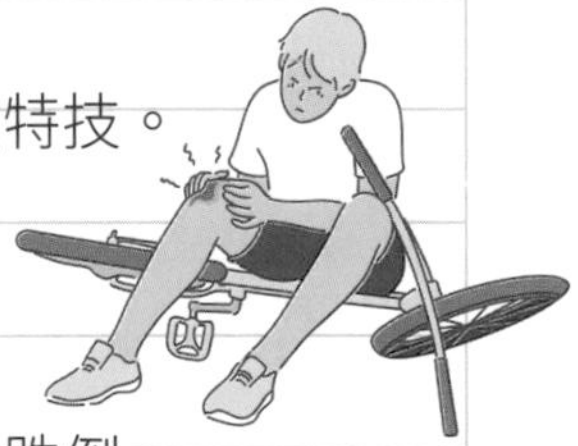

傑瑞： 嘿，蒂娜。看我在腳踏車上表演特技。

蒂娜： 你會受傷的。

傑瑞： 哈！**不太可能**啦！

蒂娜： 但現在正在下雨。你**很有可能會**跌倒。

傑瑞： 妳擔心太多了。妳看！糟糕！

蒂娜： 我就知道你會跌倒。受傷了嗎？

傑瑞： 一點點。妳身上**應該**沒有 OK 繃吧，有嗎？

⑯ come as no surprise 不令人驚訝 **come as a big surprise** 令人吃驚 	• The singer has such an amazing voice that her phenomenal success **comes as no surprise**. 這位歌手的嗓音十分動聽，因此她卓越的成就一點也**不令人驚訝**。 • Adam studies very hard. It **came as no surprise** that he passed the test with flying colors. 亞當很用功。他高分通過考試也就**不足為奇**了。 • Mary broke up with her boyfriend last week. The news really **came as a big surprise** to everyone. 瑪麗上星期與她男友分手了。消息傳來著實令大家**大吃一驚**。
⑰ want nothing more than to V = just want to V 只想要……	• I'm so tired that I **want nothing more than to** take a good rest now. 我好累，現在我什麼都不想，**只想**好好休息一下。
⑱ stubborn [ˋstʌbɚn] *a.* 固執的 **be (as) stubborn as a mule** 非常固執	• Mark is (as) stubborn as a mule / bullheaded / obstinate. I can't reason with him. 馬克**很固執**。我無法跟他講理。

⑲ **there is no point in + V-ing** = it is no use + V-ing = there is no use (in) + V-ing ……是無意義 / 沒用的	• There is no point in / It is no use / There is no use (in) arguing with Nathan—he is very stubborn. 跟奈森爭論**是沒用的**——他很固執。
⑳ **be on the point of + V-ing** 正要……之時	• I was on the point of giving up hope / about to give up hope when my friend Tom came to help. 當我**正要**放棄希望**時**，我的朋友湯姆就前來伸出援手了。

Words in Use

Gareth: Dad is so **stubborn**!

Hanna: Well, Gareth, that should **come as no surprise**. He's always been that way.

Gareth: Yeah! He won't give me any money to buy new video games because my grades are low. But I have the right to buy games when I want!

Hanna: Listen to yourself. Maybe you are the one being **stubborn** this time.

蓋瑞斯：老爸好**固執**！

漢娜：喔，蓋瑞斯，那應該**不算太讓人驚訝**吧。他一直都是那樣的。

蓋瑞斯：是啊！他因為我成績太糟糕而不肯給我錢買新的電玩遊戲，但我有權利買遊戲！

漢娜：聽聽你自己說的話。也許這次你才是**固執**的人。

Unit 6

㉑ What's the point / purpose of...? ……的目的何在？	• What's the **point / purpose** of holding this meeting? 開這個會議**的目的何在？**
㉒ be to the point 切中要點	• Mr. Lee's speech was brief and **to the point.** 李先生的演講簡短又**中肯**。
㉓ push sb to the point of... 把某人逼到……的地步	• David's selfishness **pushed** his wife **to the point of** hysterics. 大衛的自私作風**把**他太太**逼到**歇斯底里**的地步**。
㉔ by far the + 最高級形容詞 + N 最最……的…… 比較 **so far = up to the present** 到目前為止	• William is **by far the** best student I've ever taught. 威廉是我教過**最最**棒**的**學生。 • Teresa is **by far the** most beautiful girl in our school. 泰瑞莎是我們學校**最最**美**的**女孩子。 • We have only finished half of the project **so far.** 這個計畫**到目前為止**我們只完成了一半。
㉕ stardom [ˋstardəm] *n.* 明星地位	• Taylor Swift's rise to **stardom** is due to all her hard work and self-confidence. 泰勒絲躍升為**巨星**全歸因於她的努力與自信。

Words in Use

Kathy: I hate math. **What's the point of** learning it? I'm going to be a famous singer.

Martin: You're **by far the** best singer that I know, Kathy. But you still need to know math.

Kathy: I don't think so. **What's the purpose of** being good at math?

Martin: Well, once you rise to **stardom**, you'll need math to count all your money!

Kathy: I guess you're right about that.

凱西： 我討厭數學。學數學**的目的是什麼？**我未來要當知名歌手。

馬丁： 凱西，妳是我目前所知**最最**棒**的**歌手。但是妳仍然得了解數學。

凱西： 我不這麼認為。學好數學**的目的何在？**

馬丁： 嗯，妳一旦成為**巨星**之後，就會需要數學來數妳所有的錢！

凱西： 我想這點你說得對。

㉖ **feel at home** 感到很自在輕鬆	• In less than two weeks, Walter was beginning to **feel at home** in his new job. 還不到兩個禮拜的時間，華特就對他的新工作**得心應手**了。
㉗ **be home to...** 是……的大本營 / 棲息地	• This small town **is home to** many artists. 這座小鎮**是**許多畫家**的大本營** / 住了許多畫家。 • The forest **is home to** several rare species of insects. 這片森林**是**數種稀有昆蟲**的棲息地**。
㉘ **make yourself at home** 請隨便 / 別拘束	• Come on in and **make yourself at home**. 請進，**別拘束**。 
㉙ **at times** = sometimes = on occasion 有時候	• Tom is amiable, but he may lose his temper **at times / sometimes / on occasion**. 湯姆為人親切，不過**有時候**他會發脾氣。
㉚ **foundation** [faʊnˋdeʃən] *n.* 基礎 **provide / lay a solid foundation for...** 為……提供堅固基礎	• Mutual trust **provides a solid foundation for** marriage. 互信**為**婚姻**提供了牢固的基礎**。 • A good knowledge of grammar helps you **lay a solid foundation for** your English. 充分了解文法能**為**你的英文**打下堅固的基礎**。

be without foundation 沒有事實根據	• It's a rumor which is totally **without foundation.** 那是謠言，完全**沒有事實根據**。
rock the foundations of... 動搖……的基礎	• Racism is **rocking the foundations of** that country. 種族主義正**動搖**該國的**國本**。

Words in Use

Jackie: Hi. Come on in and **make yourself at home.**

Ken: Thanks, Jackie. Hey—chocolates!

Jackie: Yes, they are really expensive Godiva chocolates. Would you like...

Ken: Godiva! Move out of the way. Oh, boy, these are yummy!

Jackie: Ken! You just ate all of the chocolates!

Ken: Sorry, but you told me I should **feel at home**.

Jackie: Ken, **at times** you really annoy me.

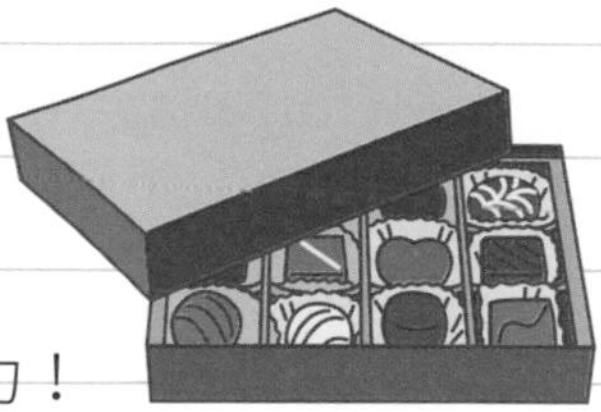

潔姬： 嗨。請進，**別拘束**。

阿肯： 謝了，潔姬。嘿，是巧克力！

潔姬： 是的。這些是很貴的 Godiva 巧克力。你想要……。

阿肯： Godiva！讓一讓。喔，天啊，好好吃啊！

潔姬： 阿肯！你把所有的巧克力都吃掉了！

阿肯： 抱歉，但是妳要我**別拘束的**。

潔姬： 阿肯，**有時候**你真的讓我覺得很煩。

Unit 6 Exercises
練習題

看圖連連看

❶

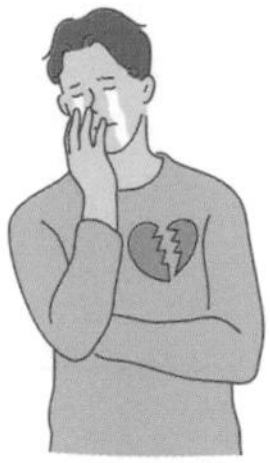

❷

❸

stubborn　　heartbreaking　　take sb on a ride

選出正解

❶ I felt fortunate to feast my ______________ on such beautiful scenery.

(A) mind　　(B) ears

(C) eyes　　(D) heart

❷ Karen is ______________ far the nicest person I've ever worked with.

(A) of　　(B) by

(C) through　　(D) with

句子填空

home | nothing | slim | Though | point

❶ Katie wants ______________ more than to get a doll for her birthday.

❷ There is a ______________ chance that our team will win.

❸ Los Angeles is ______________ to many movie stars.

❹ You should make your article short and to the ______________.

❺ ______________ Kim is odd, I enjoy being with her.

句子重組

❶ a one-hour drive / to the beach / It's / my house / from

____

____.

❷ her idol / Irene / to meet / at the chance / jumped

____

____.

❸ as no surprise / It / came / Gary proposed to Helen / that

____

____.

Notes

Unit 7

- [x] 1 (It is) no wonder (that)...
- [ ] 2 a wonder drug
- [ ] 3 work / do wonders
- [ ] 4 bolt
- [ ] 5 a bolt from the blue
- [ ] 6 out of the blue
- [ ] 7 dance to + 音樂 / 節奏
- [ ] 8 dance the waltz
- [ ] 9 cheek to cheek
- [ ] 10 cheeky
- [ ] 11 to the fullest
- [ ] 12 thrill
- [ ] 13 date back to + 過去某時間
- [ ] 14 date
- [ ] 15 the expiration date
- [ ] 16 date
- [ ] 17 ask sb out on a date
- [ ] 18 be on a date with sb
- [ ] 19 a blind date
- [ ] 20 date
- [ ] 21 in one's eye(s)
- [ ] 22 keep an eye on...
- [ ] 23 eye-catching
- [ ] 24 catch sb's eye
- [ ] 25 beholder
- [ ] 26 be low in...
- [ ] 27 reference
- [ ] 28 with reference to...
- [ ] 29 come in handy
- [ ] 30 pastime

Unit 7

❶ (It is) no wonder (that)...
難怪……

• Bill was late for work again this morning. **No wonder** the boss wants to
| let him go.
| fire him.

比爾今天早上上班又遲到了。
難怪老闆想開除他。

❷ a wonder drug
靈丹妙藥

• Research has shown that this new medicine is **a wonder drug** for patients with liver cancer.
研究顯示這種新藥對肝癌病患**有奇效**。

❸ work / do | wonders / miracles |
產生奇蹟，有奇效

• A good night's sleep can **work / do | wonders / miracles |** for your body and mind.
晚上一覺好眠會對你的身心**有奇效**。

❹ bolt
[bolt] *n.*
一道（閃電）
a bolt of lightning
一道閃電

• The farmer died when **a bolt of lightning** struck him.
一道閃電打在那位農夫身上，
他當場死亡。

❺ a bolt from the blue 突如其來，晴天霹靂	• The news of Max and Kate's divorce came as **a bolt from / out of the blue**. 麥克斯與凱特離婚的消息**突如其來，猶如晴天霹靂**。
❻ out of the blue 出奇不意地，突然地	• The general manager's resignation came **out of the blue**. 總經理的辭呈來得**極為突然**。

Words in Use

Walter: You look really tired, Anita.

Anita: I couldn't sleep at all last night.

Walter: **It's no wonder that** you look exhausted.

Anita: Yes, I can hardly keep my eyes open. It will be a miracle if I finish this assignment today.

Walter: Why don't you take a nap? A half-hour nap can **do wonders** for you. Anita? Anita?

Anita: (*snoring*)

Walter: It looks like she's already taking my advice.

華特：安妮塔，妳看起來很累。

安妮塔：我昨晚完全睡不著。

華特：**難怪**妳看起來非常疲倦。

安妮塔：是，我眼睛都快睜不開了。如果我今天能完成這項工作，那簡直就是奇蹟。

華特：不如妳小睡一會吧？小睡半小時**會有很好的效果**。安妮塔？安妮塔？

安妮塔：（打呼中）

華特：看來她已經接受我的建議了。

❼ dance to + 音樂 / 節奏
隨著（音樂）起舞
dance with sb
與某人跳舞

- Let's dance to the music / song.
咱們**隨著**這首音樂 / 歌曲**起舞**吧。
- Can I dance with you?
我可以**跟**你**跳舞**嗎？

❽ dance the waltz
跳華爾滋

- Can you dance the waltz? / the cha-cha? / the jitterbug? / the rumba?
你會**跳華爾滋** / 恰恰 / 吉魯巴 / 倫巴（舞）嗎？

舞蹈的種類

❾ cheek to cheek
臉頰貼著臉頰

- Look! Peter and Mary are dancing cheek to cheek.
瞧！彼得和瑪麗正在**臉貼著臉**跳舞。

❿ cheeky [ˋtʃikɪ] *a.*
= **sassy** [ˋsæsɪ]
粗魯無禮的，放肆的

- Behave yourself! You're getting far too cheeky.
守規矩！你太過**放肆**了。

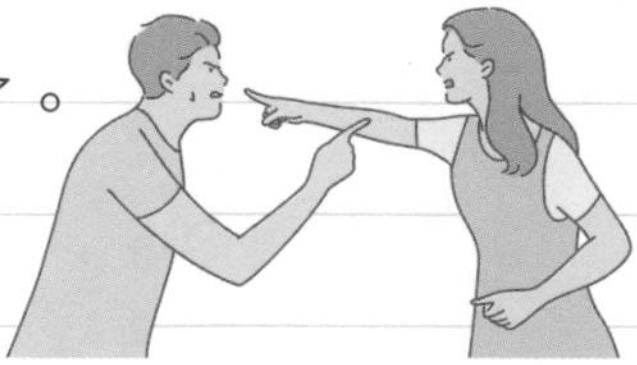

⑪ to the fullest

= as much as possible

盡情地

• Life is too short, so we should enjoy it **to the fullest**.

人生苦短，因此我們應**盡情**享受人生。

Words in Use

Fritz: Did that guy just ask you to **dance the waltz** with him?

Yuki: Yes, but I told him it was not a good song to **dance to**.

Fritz: What did he say then?

Yuki: He said he would ask me to **dance to** the next song with him. But I told him that song wouldn't be good to **dance to**, either.

Fritz: Ha! That's a pretty **cheeky** comment.

Yuki: I think he got my point, though.

費茲：那傢伙剛剛邀請妳**共跳華爾滋**嗎？

由紀：對，但我跟他說那首歌不好**跳**。

費茲：那他說什麼呢？

由紀：他說下首歌他會再邀請我**共舞**。但我跟他說那首歌也不好**跳**。

費茲：哈！那真是很**大膽的**說法。

由紀：但我想他知道我的意思。

⑫ **thrill**
[θrɪl] *n.*
興奮感 & *vt.* 使興奮

- It gave me a big **thrill** to meet the famous writer in person.

= It **thrilled** me to meet the famous writer in person.

能親自見到這位知名作家讓我**興奮**不已。

⑬ **date back to + 過去某時間**
追溯至……；自……起就存在了

- The vase | **dates back to** / dates from / goes back to | the Ming dynasty.

這個花瓶**自**明朝**就有了**。

date back + 一段時間
追溯至……前

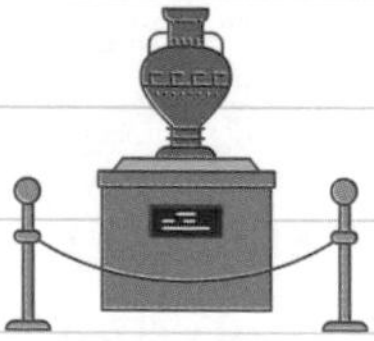

- It is said that the head-hunting practice in that tribe **dates back to** the 1700s.

= It is said that the head-hunting practice in that tribe **dates back** around 300 years.

據說那個部落的獵頭習俗可**追溯到**十八世紀 / 三百年前左右。

⑭ **date**
[det] *n.*
日期

- What date is today? (×)

→ What's the **date** today? (○)

= What's today's **date**? (○)

今天是**幾月幾日**？

- A: What's the **date** today? / What's today's **date**?

  B: It's May 6. (讀作 May sixth / May the sixth，不可讀作 May six)

  A：今天是**幾月幾日**？

  B：今天是五月六日。

比較

A: What day is it today?　A：今天是星期幾？

B: It's Friday (today).　B：（今天是）星期五。

⑮ **the expiration date** (美)

= **the expiry date** (英)

到期日，有效期限

• Read **the expiration date** before you buy the milk.

買牛奶之前先看它的**有效期限**。

Words in Use

Jared: Hey, Kerry. Look at **the expiration date** of these eggs.

Kerry: What do you mean? It says August 10.

Jared: And what **date** is it today?

Kerry: It's the 9th.

Jared: That means you should eat them as soon as possible.

Kerry: It's July 9 today, not the 9th of August.

Jared: Oops. Never mind.

傑瑞德：嘿，凱莉。妳看這些蛋的**有效期限**。

凱莉：什麼意思？上面寫八月十號。

傑瑞德：今天是**幾月幾號**？

凱莉：今天是九號。

傑瑞德：意思是妳應該盡快吃掉這些蛋。

凱莉：今天是七月九號，不是八月九號。

傑瑞德：喔，那沒事了。

⑯ **date** [det] *n.* (戀愛中的) 約會 **have / go on a date with sb** 與某人約會	• It thrills me to think that I'm having / going on a date with Jill this evening. 想到今晚要和吉兒約會，真讓我感到很高興。 
⑰ **ask sb out on a date** 約某人去約會	• James plucked up the courage to ask Amy out on a date. 詹姆士鼓起勇氣約了艾咪去約會。
⑱ **be on a date with sb** 與某人約會中	• A: Where's David now? B: Well, he's on a date with Cindy. A：大衛現在人在哪兒？ B：噢，他正在跟辛蒂約會。
⑲ **a blind date** 相親	• Scott and Shelley met on a blind date, and in less than two months, he proposed to her. 史考特與雪莉在相親上認識，兩個月不到，他就向她求婚了。 
⑳ **date** [det] *vt.* 約會 **date sb** 與某人約會	• Paul has been dating Mary for years, but they have not decided to get married yet. 保羅與瑪麗約會多年，不過他們尚未有結婚的打算。

㉑ **in one's eye(s)** 在某人眼中	• Honey, in my eyes, you're the most beautiful girl on the planet. / in the world. / on earth. 親愛的，在我眼中，妳是世上最漂亮的女孩子。

Unit 7

Words in Use

Wayne: I'm going on a date tomorrow night.

Petra: Wow! So, you finally plucked up the courage to ask somebody out on a date?

Wayne: No, it's a blind date. My friend organized it.

Petra: Well, good luck!

Wayne: Do you want to come, too?

Petra: What? No! I don't want to go on a date with you and a girl. That's not a good idea.

Wayne: But I'm so nervous!

韋恩：我明天晚上要去約會。

佩德拉：哇塞！所以你終於鼓起勇氣約某人去約會了？

韋恩：不是，我是去相親。我朋友安排的。

佩德拉：嗯，祝你好運！

韋恩：妳也想來嗎？

佩德拉：什麼？不！我不想要跟你和某個女生去約會。這不是個好主意。

韋恩：但我好緊張啊！

㉒ keep an eye on...

好好盯著……

• Keep an eye on your kids wherever they go.

不論你的孩子走到哪裡，都要**好好看著**他們。

㉓ eye-catching

[ˋaɪˏkætʃɪŋ] *a.*

= attractive

[əˋtræktɪv]

引人注目的

• The dress you're wearing is really eye-catching.

妳穿的這件洋裝真**吸睛**。

㉔ catch sb's eye

= attract sb

吸引某人

• The girl sitting in the corner really
  | caught my eye.
  | attracted me.

坐在角落的那個女孩子很**吸引我**。

㉕ beholder

[bɪˋholdɚ] *n.*

觀看者（少用）

• Beauty is in the eye of the beholder.

情人眼裡出西施。（諺語）

㉖ be low in...

……的含量低

be | high / rich | in...

富含……

• I'm choosy about what I eat. Basically, I like things that are high in nutrition and low in calories.

我對吃的很講究。基本上，我喜歡吃**高營養**、**低熱量**的東西。

均衡飲食

whole grains
全穀物

fish, poultry, and eggs
魚、（雞鴨）肉、蛋

milk and dairy products
牛奶與乳製品

fruits and vegetables
蔬菜水果

Words in Use

Selena: It looks like someone has really **caught** your **eye**.

Neil: What do you mean?

Selena: You keep looking at that girl over there. You must like her.

Neil: Well, she is wearing an **eye-catching** dress.

Selena: Why don't you go over and talk to her?

Neil: Oh, an **attractive** girl like that wouldn't be interested in me. I'm not handsome.

Selena: She might like you. Beauty is in the eye of the **beholder**, you know.

瑟琳娜：看來有個人非常**吸引**你。

尼爾：什麼意思？

瑟琳娜：你一直在看那邊那個女孩。你一定是喜歡她吧。

尼爾：嗯，她穿的衣服很**引人注目**。

瑟琳娜：你何不走過去跟她說說話？

尼爾：喔，像那樣**有魅力的**女生不會對我有興趣的。我又不帥。

瑟琳娜：她可能會喜歡你啊。**情人**眼裡出西施，你知道的。

㉗ reference

[ˋrɛfərəns] *n.*

提及

make (a) reference to...

提及……

make no reference to...

沒提及……

- In his speech, Mr. Johnson
  | **made reference to** / mentioned | his poor childhood |
  several times.

  強森先生在他的演講中數度**提及**他貧困的童年。

- For fear that his aged mother couldn't stand it, Paul **made no reference to** his father's serious illness in their chat.

  在閒聊中，保羅**未提到**父親的重病，以免年邁的母親受不了。

㉘ with reference to...

= in reference to...

= with regard to...

= in regard to...

有關……

- | **With reference** / **In reference** / **With regard** / **In regard** | to your application for |
  the job, we regret to tell you that the vacancy has been filled.

  有關你應徵本職務一事，我們很抱歉通知你，職缺已被遞補了。

㉙ come in handy

派上用場

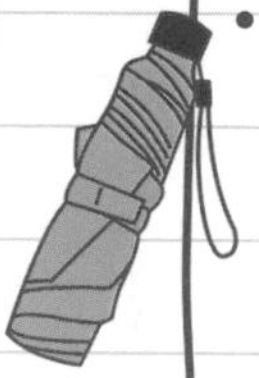

- You'd better carry an umbrella with you—it may | **come in handy.** / be useful. |

  你最好隨身帶把傘 —— 它可能會**派上用場**。

㉚ pastime

[ˋpæs,taɪm] *n.*

消遣，娛樂

- Listening to music is my favorite
  | **pastime.** / recreation. |

  聽音樂是我最喜歡的**消遣活動**。

消遣活動

exercising 運動 | drawing 繪畫 | reading 閱讀 | cooking 烹飪

Words in Use

Liz: Hey, Anders. Why are you reading the dictionary so carefully?

Anders: Well, Elizabeth, improving my knowledge is my favorite **pastime**.

Liz: Elizabeth? You always call me Liz. **Pastime**? You mean hobby? I've never seen you look at the dictionary before.

Anders: **With reference to** your comment, Elizabeth, I think you are mistaken.

Liz: What? Why are you talking that way?

Anders: OK, OK. I have a job interview tomorrow. I'm practicing being smart.

Liz: I think you'd better keep practicing, then.

麗茲： 嘿，安德斯。你為什麼這麼仔細地在讀字典？

安德斯： 嗯，伊莉莎白，增進知識是我最喜歡的**消遣活動**。

麗茲： 伊莉莎白？你總是叫我麗茲啊。**消遣活動**？你是指嗜好嗎？我以前從未見你看過字典。

安德斯： **關於**妳的評論，伊莉莎白，我想妳是誤會了。

麗茲： 什麼？你為什麼那樣講話？

安德斯： 好，好，我明天有個工作面試。我在練習裝聰明。

麗茲： 我想你最好還是繼續練習好了。

Unit 7

Exercises
練習題

看圖選單字

❶

❷

❸

❶	❷	❸
☐ come in handy	☐ a bolt of lightning	☐ eye-catching
☐ catch sb's eye	☐ a wonder drug	☐ cheeky
☐ dance to the music	☐ a blind date	☐ blind

選出正解

❶ Grandfather's death is such a bolt from the (blue / black).

❷ Let's enjoy our vacation to the (richest / fullest).

❸ Lily set me up on a blind (date / day) with her friend.

❹ (By / With) reference to your letter, this is our response.

❺ If you don't keep an (ear / eye) on the puppy, it'll run away.

Unit 7

句子填空

handy | dates | reference | pastime | wonders

❶ Try this medicine. It'll work ____________ for your headache.

❷ Simon made a ____________ to his team in his acceptance speech.

❸ Joan's favorite ____________ is scrolling through her phone while lying in bed.

❹ This portrait ____________ back to the 18th century.

❺ Don't throw the bags away. They may come in ____________.

句子重組

❶ on a date / Henry / I can't / asked me out / believe

____

____.

❷ the prettiest girl / Tess / is / In Sam's eyes / in school / ,

____

____.

❸ calories / low / This meal / in / is

____

____.

Notes

Unit 8

- [x] ❶ get into the habit of...
- [ ] ❷ be in the habit of...
- [ ] ❸ kick the habit of...
- [ ] ❹ out of habit
- [ ] ❺ be associated with...
- [ ] ❻ spoil
- [ ] ❼ spare
- [ ] ❽ be fast approaching
- [ ] ❾ slow down
- [ ] ❿ speed up
- [ ] ⓫ be the last person to V
- [ ] ⓬ to the last
- [ ] ⓭ last but not least
- [ ] ⓮ The last thing sb would ever do is...
- [ ] ⓯ call off...
- [ ] ⓰ call for...
- [ ] ⓱ call on sb
- [ ] ⓲ call sb down
- [ ] ⓳ call sb names
- [ ] ⓴ call sth one's own
- [ ] ㉑ be on call
- [ ] ㉒ be on duty
- [ ] ㉓ call in sick
- [ ] ㉔ ask for sick leave
- [ ] ㉕ flood
- [ ] ㉖ be flooded with...
- [ ] ㉗ get going
- [ ] ㉘ be on the go
- [ ] ㉙ go bad
- [ ] ㉚ 名詞 + 介詞 to

Unit 8

❶ **get into the habit of...** **= cultivate / develop the habit of...** 養成……的習慣	• You should **get into the habit of** going to bed early. It will do a lot of good for your health. 你應**養成**早睡**的習慣**。那會對你的健康大有好處。
❷ **be in the habit of...** 有……的習慣	• I'm **in the habit of** taking a walk after a meal. 我吃完飯後都**有**散步**的習慣**。
❸ **kick / break the habit of...** 戒掉……的習慣	• There is probably no hope that Dad can **kick / break the** bad **habit of** smoking. He's been a chain smoker for years. 老爸要**戒掉**抽菸**的惡習**恐怕是沒希望了。他多年來一直都是個老菸槍。
❹ **out of habit** 出自習慣	• I say hi to people whether I know them or not. I guess I do it **out of habit**. 我見到人，不論認不認識，都會向他們打招呼。我想這是**習慣成性**了。
❺ **be associated with...** 與……有關聯	• A majority of lung cancers **are associated with / linked to** tobacco smoking. 大多數的肺癌都**與**抽菸**有關**。

❻ **spoil** [spɔɪl] *vt.* 寵壞；破壞，使掃興（三態為：spoil, spoiled / spoilt [spɔɪlt], spoiled / spoilt）	• Billy is an only child, but his parents never **spoil** him. 比利是獨生子，不過他爸媽從不**寵**他。 • Spare the rod and **spoil** the child. 孩子不打不成器。（諺語） • John's phone call **spoiled** my mood. 約翰的一通電話**打壞了**我的心情。

Words in Use

Father: Your room is so messy. Why do you throw your clothes on the floor?

Daughter: I guess I just do it **out of habit**.

Father: You need to **kick the habit of** being so lazy.

Daughter: It's hard. Sometimes I feel too tired.

Father: That's because you stay up late watching TV. You should **get into the habit of** going to bed earlier.

Daughter: But I'm **in the habit of** going to bed late.

Father: Haven't you been listening to anything I've said?

爸爸： 妳的房間真亂。妳為什麼把衣服都丟到地板上？

女兒： 我想我就是**習慣**這樣。

爸爸： 妳得要**戒掉**懶惰**的習慣**。

女兒： 很難，有時候我覺得好累。

爸爸： 那是因為妳熬夜看電視。妳要**養成**早點睡**的習慣**。

女兒： 但我**習慣**晚睡了。

爸爸： 我說的話妳都沒在聽嗎？

❼ spare

[spɛr] *a.*

備用的，多出的

& *vt.* 騰出⋯⋯

a spare key
備用鑰匙

a spare room
備用房間

a spare tire
備胎

sb's spare time
某人的休閒時間

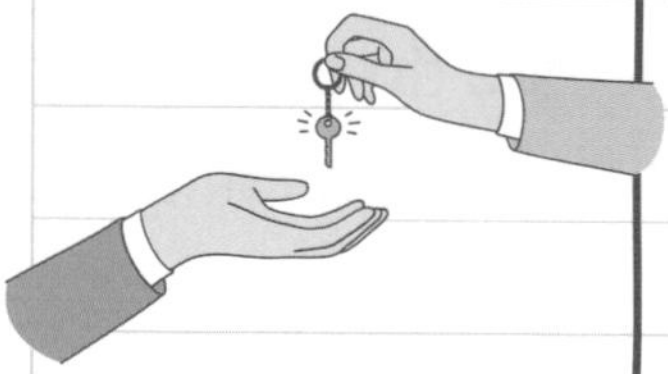

- I lost my **spare key**, so I had no choice but to have the lockset replaced.

  我把我的**備用鑰匙**弄丟了，因此只好把整套鎖換掉了。

- We have **a spare room**, so you can stay overnight with us.

  我們有**一間空房**，你可以留下來跟我們過夜。

- What do you often do in your
  | **spare time**?
  | leisure time?

  你**休息時間**通常在做什麼？

- I'd like to help you, but I can't **spare** the time.

  我很想幫助你，可是我**騰不出**時間。

- Can you **spare** me | a minute / a few minutes | ? I'd like to have a word with you about your son.

  你可否**撥**點時間給我？我想跟你談一下令郎的事。

❽ be fast approaching

快到了

- A typhoon is | **fast approaching** / around the corner / coming soon |, and we should do something before it's too late.

  颱風**快要到了**，我們應有所作為以免為時已晚。

❾ slow down

（車速）慢下來

- **Slow down**! You're driving too fast.

  慢下來！你車開得太快了。

⑩ speed up (車速) 加快	• Speed up! You're driving at a snail's pace. like a snail. **加速**！你車開得太慢了， 簡直像個蝸牛一樣。

Unit 8

Words in Use

Lance: Are you **speeding up**? Don't drive so fast!

Charlotte: I'm not going too fast. Calm down.

Lance: No, you need to **slow down**.

Charlotte: I'm driving safely. Don't worry.

Lance: Look out! That bus **is fast approaching**, and it might hit us!

Charlotte: No, it won't. I think something else **is fast approaching**, too.

Lance: Oh, no! What?

Charlotte: A headache! So, please don't talk so much while I'm driving.

蘭斯：妳在**加速**嗎？不要開這麼快！

夏綠蒂：我沒有開很快，冷靜點。

蘭斯：不，妳需要**慢下來**。

夏綠蒂：我開車很安全，別擔心。

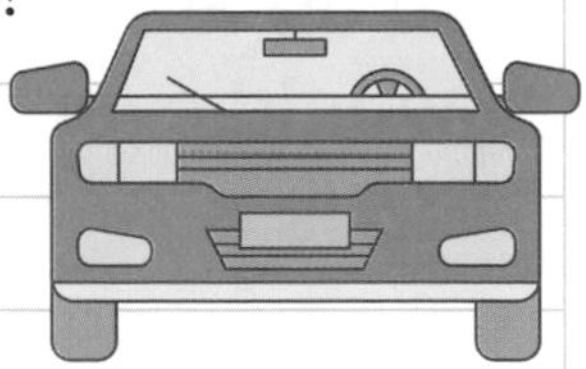

蘭斯：小心！那臺公車正在**快速接近**我們，它有可能會撞到我們！

夏綠蒂：不，不會的。我想還有其他東西也在**快速接近**。

蘭斯：喔，不！是什麼？

夏綠蒂：頭痛！所以我開車時請不要一直說話。

⑪ be the last person to V 是最不可能做……的人	• John always means what he says. In other words, he **is the last person to lie.** 約翰向來心口如一。換言之，他**是個絕不會**說謊**的人**。
⑫ to the last 直到最後一刻；直到死亡	• The soldiers vowed to fight for freedom **to the last.** 士兵們誓言要捍衛自由**直到生命最後一刻**。
⑬ last but not least 最後但也蠻重要的 (插入語，常用於演講) 	• I would like to thank you all for cooperating with me over the past 10 years. And, **last but not least,** I would like to thank Mr. Smith. Without his support and encouragement, I wouldn't be who I am today. 我要謝謝大家在過去十年內與我合作。**最後但也挺重要的是**，我要謝謝史密斯先生。若無他的支持及鼓勵，就不會有今天的我。
⑭ The last thing sb would ever do is... 某人最不願做的一件事是……	• Honey, trust me. **The last thing I would ever do is** lie to you. 親愛的，相信我。我**最不願做的一件事就是**欺騙妳。 
⑮ call off... **= call... off** 取消 (會議、活動等)	• The meeting was **called off** | **cancelled** because of the coming typhoon. 因颱風即將來襲，所以會議**取消**了。

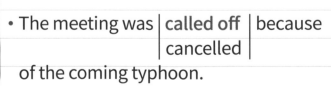

公司會議

video conference / online meeting
視訊 / 線上會議

presentation 簡報

⑯ call for...

= require...

需要……

• There is no denying that success

| calls for | hard work.
| requires |

不可否認，成功**需要**努力。

Words in Use

Alvin: Everyone, I would like to introduce Iris.

Iris: Oh, I thought you forgot about me.

Alvin: Iris, **the last thing I would ever do is** forget about you.

Iris: Really? I don't believe you.

Alvin: OK. This **calls for** a different introduction. Ladies and gentleman, **last but not least**, I would like to introduce Iris.

Iris: OK. That's better.

艾爾文：請注意到我這邊，我想介紹艾瑞絲給大家認識。

艾瑞絲：喔，我以為你忘記我的存在了。

艾爾文：艾瑞絲，我**最不願做的事情就是**忘記妳。

艾瑞絲：真的嗎？我不相信你。

艾爾文：好。這樣就**需要**不同的引薦了。各位先生女士，**最後但也很重要的**，我想介紹艾瑞絲給大家認識。

艾瑞絲：好吧，這樣好多了。

⑰ **call on sb** = pay sb a visit = visit sb 探訪某人	• I'm planning to **call on** my grandparents in the country this weekend. 這個週末我打算到鄉下**看**我爺爺奶奶。 
⑱ **call sb down** = scold sb = rebuke sb 斥責某人	• The teacher **called** me **down** in front of the class after he caught me cheating on the test. 老師發現我考試作弊時，就當著全班的面前**痛斥**我。
⑲ **call sb names** 辱罵某人 (此處 names 指不雅的綽號)	• When he gets angry, Johnny tends to **call** people **names**. 強尼生氣時，往往會用不雅的字眼**罵人**。 
⑳ **call sth one's own** 有屬於某人自己的東西	• Except for an old dog, the poor old man has nothing to **call his own**. 這位可憐的老先生除了一隻老狗外，沒有一樣東西是**屬於自己的**。
㉑ **be on call** (醫生等) 隨時待命 / 隨傳隨到	• Two doctors and five interns **are on call** this weekend. 這個週末有兩名醫生及五名實習醫生**待命**。 

22 be on duty
值班 / 上班
be off duty
不值班 / 不上班

- Dad **is on duty** tonight and won't be back until 7 tomorrow morning.
  老爸今晚**值班**，要到明天早上七點才回家。
- I'**m off duty** today, but I'll **be** | **on duty** / at work | all day tomorrow.
  我今天**不上班**，不過明天要**上班**一整天。

Words in Use

Melvin: Are you **on duty** at the hospital this weekend?
Agatha: No, but I will **be on call**. I have to go there if there are too many emergencies.
Melvin: Oh, I guess you can't go to the beach, then.
Agatha: No, I shouldn't leave the city this weekend. But you can **call on** me if you like. Maybe we can watch a movie on TV together at my place.
Melvin: Hey, that's a great idea!

梅爾文：妳這個週末會在醫院**值班**嗎？
愛葛莎：不會，但我會在**待命**。如果有太多急救案件的話，我就得去。
梅爾文：喔，那我想妳就沒辦法去海灘了。
愛葛莎：不行，我這個週末不能出城。但是你願意的話可以來**找**我喔。也許我們可以在我家用電視一起看部電影。
梅爾文：嘿，這點子棒呆了！

㉓ call in sick 打電話請病假	• Peter **called in sick** this morning, but he actually went to the movies with his girlfriend. 彼得今早**來電請病假**，但是他其實跟女友看電影去了。
㉔ ask for **sick / personal / marriage / bereavement / maternity** **leave** 請病假 / 事假 / 婚假 / 喪假 / 產假 be on... leave 正在放……假	• Mark had the runs all night last night, so he **asked for** a day's **sick leave**. 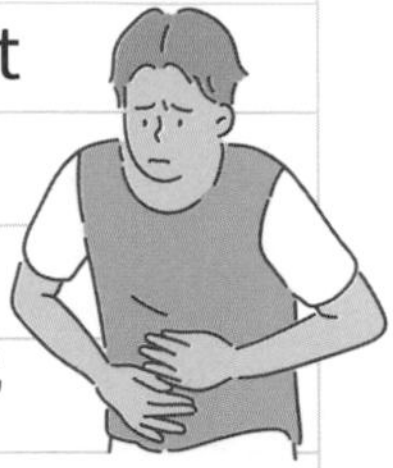 馬克昨晚拉了一整晚的肚子，因此他**請**了一天的**病假**。 • David is **on sick leave / on personal leave** today. 大衛今天**請了病假 / 事假**。 • Katie **is on marriage leave** all this week. Sam is covering for her. 凱蒂**請**了一整個星期的**婚假**。山姆在幫她代班。
㉕ flood [flʌd] *vi.* & *vt.* 淹沒；充斥	• The whole village **flooded** when the river burst its banks. = The river burst its banks and **flooded** the whole village. 河流潰堤時，整個村莊都**淹沒**了。 • It comes as no surprise that Japanese cars are **flooding** the market. 市場到處**充斥**著日製汽車，這已是不足為奇的事。

㉖ be flooded with...

擠滿 / 充滿……

- The department store **is** always **flooded** / packed / filled **with** people on weekends.
  每逢週末，百貨公司總是人**滿**為患。
- Jim **was flooded with** joy when his baby boy was born.
  吉姆的兒子出生時，他**滿心**歡喜。

百貨公司購物

credit card　信用卡

Words in Use

Tracy: Joyce just **called in sick**.

Nigel: Really? Rick is already **on sick leave**. We'll never finish all this work today.

Tracy: I was thinking of **asking for personal leave** for today. It's a good thing I didn't.

Nigel: Yes. We **are** completely **flooded with** work.

Tracy: Yes. It's starting to make me feel sick.

Nigel: Uh-oh!

崔西：喬伊絲剛剛**打電話進來請病假**。

奈吉爾：真的嗎？瑞克已經**請病假**了。我們沒辦法今天完成這些工作了。

崔西：我還在想著今天要**請事假**。還好我後來沒請。

奈吉爾：是啊，我們工作**滿檔**呢。

崔西：沒錯。而這開始讓我覺得想吐了。

奈吉爾：糟糕！

㉗ **get going / moving** 出發 / 動身	• It's getting dark. Let's **get going / moving** now. 天色漸漸暗了，咱們**動身**吧 / **該走**了。
㉘ **be on the go** 忙個不停	• I've **been on the go / quite busy** all day. I really need a good rest. 我**忙了一整天**，真的需要好好休息一下。
㉙ **go bad** = spoil [spɔɪl] *vi.* = go sour = go stale (食物) 變壞，餿掉	• You should put the food in the fridge or it will **go bad / spoil** quickly. 你應把食物放在冰箱裡，否則它很快就會**餿掉**。 • The milk **has gone bad / sour / stale**. It's undrinkable. 牛奶**變酸**了，不能再喝了。
㉚ **以下名詞均接介詞 to (to 表「針對」的意思)：** answer (答案，回答) solution (解決之道) key (鑰匙)	• Who knows the **answer to** the question? 誰知道這個問題**的答案**？ • Teaming up is the only **solution to** this problem. 團結合作是**解決**這個問題的唯一**之途**。 • I lost the **key to** the door / room. 這門 / 房間**的鑰匙**我弄丟了。

response (回應) ambassador (大使) reaction (反應) approach (途徑，方法) access (接觸)	• I wrote Jim a letter last week, but there hasn't been any **response to** my request. 我上星期寫了封信給吉姆，但迄今尚未有任何**針對**我的請求**的回應**。 • Having a good command of Japanese, Mr. Johnson was appointed British **ambassador to** Japan yesterday. 強森先生日文造詣不錯，昨天被派任英國駐日**大使**。 • The billionaire owns a fancy villa with easy **access to** the beach. 這位億萬富翁擁有**離**海灘**很近**的豪華別墅。

Words in Use

Raul: Well, it's getting late. I should **get going**. Thanks very much for dinner.

Sophia: You're very welcome, Raul. Would you like to take some food home with you?

Raul: Um... Are you sure? Don't you want it?

Sophia: There's too much for me to eat by myself. It will **go bad** before I eat it all.

Raul: OK, thanks a lot, Sophia!

拉爾：嗯，時間不早了。我該**走了**。謝謝款待我這頓晚餐。

蘇菲亞：拉爾，不必這麼客氣。你想要帶點食物回家嗎？

拉爾：嗯……妳確定嗎？妳不要嗎？

蘇菲亞：我自己一個人吃太多了。我還來不及吃完就會**壞掉**了。

拉爾：好，太謝謝妳了，蘇菲亞！

Unit 8

Exercises
練習題

看圖連連看

❶

❷

❸

flood

a spare tire

go bad

選出正解

❶ We're helping Sam ________ the habit of sleeping late.

(A) pull (B) push

(C) knock (D) kick

❷ The game was called ________ due to recent events.

(A) off (B) on

(C) down (D) up

句子填空

duty | leave | go | to | associated

❶ Crime is often ____________ with money.

❷ Jim has never taken a vacation. He is always on the ____________.

❸ Sally will be on two weeks' maternity ____________ next month.

❹ The doctor helped save the man even though he was off ____________.

❺ Kevin came up with the solution ____________ this problem.

句子重組

❶ my boyfriend / would ever do / betray me / The last thing / is

____

____.

❷ my own / call / I'm happy / this house / to

____

____.

❸ the last person / Karen / from me / is / who would steal things

____

____.

Notes

Unit 9

- [x] 1 shape
- [ ] 2 courage
- [ ] 3 lend
- [ ] 4 borrow
- [ ] 5 land sb in trouble
- [ ] 6 plus
- [ ] 7 get on with your life
- [ ] 8 Not on your life!
- [ ] 9 impulse
- [ ] 10 for a long time to come
- [ ] 11 有關 time 的英文諺語
- [ ] 12 有關 money 的英文諺語
- [ ] 13 immune
- [ ] 14 "Did / Do you know...?" 的區別
- [ ] 15 time-consuming
- [ ] 16 consult the dictionary
- [ ] 17 look it up
- [ ] 18 get to the root of the problem
- [ ] 19 Upon / On + N/V-ing
- [ ] 20 go / come + (and) + V
- [ ] 21 smile from ear to ear
- [ ] 22 paint the town red
- [ ] 23 see red
- [ ] 24 be green with envy
- [ ] 25 be in the pink (of health)
- [ ] 26 a white lie
- [ ] 27 a black sheep
- [ ] 28 yellow
- [ ] 29 brown-nose
- [ ] 30 blue

Unit 9

❶ shape
[ʃep] *n.* 狀態

be in good / bad shape
狀態佳 / 糟；身體很好 / 不好

keep / stay in shape
保持健康

- Even though the car is quite old, it's still **in good shape.**
即使這輛車相當老舊，**車況仍很好**。
- I work out at a gym every day to **keep / stay in shape.**
我每天都在健身房鍛鍊以**維持健康**。

❷ courage
[ˋkɝɪdʒ] *n.* 勇氣

pluck up (the) courage to V
鼓起勇氣……

- Paul **plucked up the courage to** propose to Jenny. Much to his delight, she nodded and said yes immediately.
保羅**鼓起勇氣**向珍妮求婚。令他頗高興的是，她立刻點頭答應了。

❸ lend [lɛnd] *vt.*
借給 (三態為：lend, lent [lɛnt], lent)

lend sth to sb
= lend sb sth
把某物借給某人

- I need money to buy a second-hand bike. Could you **lend some to me** / **lend me some**?
我需要錢買一輛二手腳踏車，你可否**借**些錢**給**我？

❹ **borrow**

[ˋbaro] *vt.*

(向某人) 借

borrow sth from sb

向某人借某物

• Can I **borrow** some money (**from** you)? I want to buy a second-hand bike.

我可否 (**向**你) **借**點錢？我想要買輛二手腳踏車。

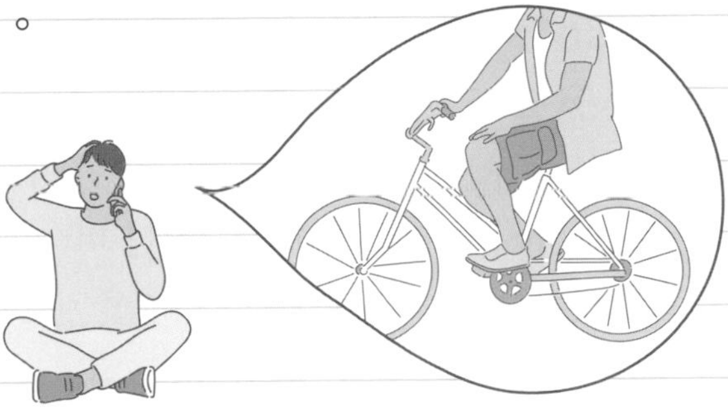

Words in Use

Travis: Hey, Yolanda. How do you **keep in shape**?

Yolanda: I exercise a lot, especially by cycling.

Travis: Cool! I really should lose some weight. Say, could you **lend** me your bike for a while?

Yolanda: How will I exercise then? You need to buy a bicycle for yourself.

Travis: Yeah, you're right. Can you **lend** me some money to buy one?

崔維斯： 嘿，友蘭達，妳如何**維持身體健康**？

友蘭達： 我大量運動，尤其是騎腳踏車。

崔維斯： 太酷了！我真該減肥一下。那麼妳能把腳踏車**借**我一陣子嗎？

友蘭達： 那我要怎麼運動？你得自己買臺腳踏車才行。

崔維斯： 妳說得對。那妳能**借**我點錢買腳踏車嗎？

❺ land sb in trouble
使某人陷入麻煩

land sb in jail
使某人入獄

land sb / a company in bankruptcy
使某人／某公司破產

- Our boss is narrow-minded. If you argue with him, it will certainly land you in big trouble.
  我們老闆心胸狹窄。你若跟他起爭執，肯定會有大麻煩。
- Don't do anything illegal or you'll be landed in jail.
  別做非法的事，否則你會吃牢飯。
- Financial problems eventually landed the company in bankruptcy.
  財務問題最終導致該公司破產。

❻ plus
[plʌs] *prep.*
加上，外加

比較
inclusive of...
包括……

- The house rent is $1,000 per month, plus gas and electricity.
  房子每個月租金是一千美元，瓦斯及電費另計。
- The house rent is $1,000 per month, inclusive of gas and electricity.
  房子每個月租金是一千美元，包括瓦斯及電費在內。

❼ get on with your life
(別想過去令你後悔的事) 好好過日子

- Look on the bright side and get on with your life.
  看開點，往後的日子好好過。

❽ **Not on your life!** 休想！	• A: Will you marry me, Jane? B: **Not on your life!** = Dream on! A：阿珍，妳願意嫁給我嗎？ B：**休想！門兒都沒有！**
❾ **impulse** [ˋɪmpʌls] *n.* 衝動 **on impulse** 衝動地	• I resisted the **impulse** to laugh when I saw Peter's funny-looking face. 我看到彼得那一副滑稽模樣的臉龐時強忍著要笑的**衝動**。 • I don't make much money, so I never shop **on impulse.** 我錢賺得不多，因此我從不會在**衝動之下**購物。

Words in Use

Kiki: That's a nice car! It must have cost a lot of money.

Bruno: It really did. I kind of bought it **on impulse.**

Kiki: You are always buying expensive things. That might **land** you **in trouble** some day.

Bruno: Yeah, it already has. I owe a lot of money.

Kiki: Well, if you need money, maybe you can sell me that car at a cheap price.

Bruno: **Not on your life!**

琪琪：這臺車太棒了！它一定很貴吧。

布魯諾：沒錯。我有點是在**衝動之下**買的。

琪琪：你總是買貴的東西。總有一天**會有大麻煩**的。

布魯諾：已經造成麻煩了。我欠了一大筆錢。

琪琪：嗯，如果你需要錢，也許你可以用便宜的價格把那臺車賣給我。

布魯諾：**休想！**

⑩ **for a long time to come** 未來好長一段時間	• There is no doubt that the pandemic will be with us **for a long time to come.** 毫無疑問的是，這個大規模流行病將會持續到**未來好一陣子**。
⑪ **有關 time 的英文諺語**	• **Time** flies. **光陰**似箭。 • **Time and tide** wait for no man. **歲月**不饒人。 • A stitch **in time** saves nine. **及時**一針省了九針 / 小洞**及時**補，免遭大洞補。 * stitch [stɪtʃ] *n.* (縫紉的) 一針 • **Time** is money. **時間**就是金錢。 • **Time** lost never returns. **時光**一去不復返。 • Procrastination is the thief of **time.** 拖延是**時間**的賊 / 拖延就是浪費**時間**。
⑫ **有關 money 的英文諺語**	• **Money** talks. 有**錢**能使鬼推磨。 • **Money** makes the world go round. **金錢**萬能 / **金錢**極為重要。 • **Money** is something, but not everything. **金錢**固然重要，但並非萬能。 • (The love of) **Money** is the root of all evil. (愛) **錢**是萬惡的根源。

不可不知的金錢用語

save money 存錢

cash 現金

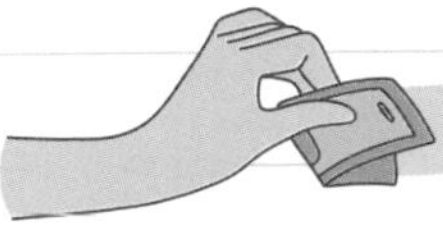

bill 鈔票

coin 硬幣

⑬ immune

[ɪˋmjun] *a.*

免疫的

be immune to...

對……免疫；免於……

- No one **is immune to** the virus yet.
  針對該病毒目前尚未有人能**免疫**。
- No one **is immune to** failure, but failing early in your career can make you more successful in the future.
  每個人都會失敗，這是在所難**免**，不過在你的職涯中早年失敗會讓你的未來更加成功。

Words in Use

Yoshi: Come on. Hurry up! **Time is money.**

Donatella: Oh, it's 5 p.m. already. Wow, **time flies!**

Yoshi: Yes, and the customer needs his shirt ironed today.

Donatella: OK, I'll work faster on it.

Yoshi: Please do. If this customer is happy, I think he will give us business **for a long time to come.**

耀西：拜託，快一點！**時間就是金錢**。

唐娜特拉：喔，都已經傍晚五點了。哇，**時間過得真快！**

耀西：沒錯，客人今天就要拿到燙好的襯衫。

唐娜特拉：好，我會加快速度。

耀西：請加快。如果這個客人滿意的話，我想**未來好長一段時間**他都會給我們生意做。

⓮ **"Did you know...?" 與 "Do you know...?" 的區別：**	• **Did you know** that the blue whale is the largest mammal on earth? 藍鯨是世上最大的哺乳類動物，這件事**你以前知道嗎？** • **Did you know** that around the world, over 2.25 billion cups of coffee are consumed each day? 全球各地每天飲用咖啡的總量超過二十二億五千萬杯，這點**你知道嗎？** • **Do you know** when David and Betty are getting married? **你知道**大衛和貝蒂何時結婚**嗎？** • **Do you know** where Sam and Joan's wedding will take place? **你知道**山姆與喬恩的婚禮將在何處舉辦**嗎？**

TIPS

ⓐ 使用 "Did you know...?" 時，問者已知道某件事，卻不確定被問者原先知不知道該件事，故用 Did you know 起首，之後接表示事實的 that 子句。

ⓑ 使用 "Do you know...?" 時，問者並不知道某件事，期望被問者告訴問者答案，故用 Do you know 起首，之後多接以疑問詞（如 what、when、why、whether 等）起首的名詞子句。

⓯ **time-consuming** [ˋtaɪmkənˏsjumɪŋ] *a.* 耗時的	• Compiling a dictionary is a **time-consuming** job. 編字典是很**耗時的**工作。

⑯ consult / refer to the dictionary 查字典	• Consult / Refer to the dictionary if you don't know the word. (正式) =Check the dictionary if you don't know the word. (口語) 你若不懂這個字就查字典吧。
⑰ look it up 查 (資訊、單字等)	• If you don't know the spelling of this word, look it up in the dictionary. 你若不知道這個字的拼法，就去查字典吧。

Words in Use

Sonia: Do you know what the capital of Switzerland is?

Ray: Actually, I'm not sure. Why don't you look it up on the internet?

Sonia: That's too time-consuming. Can you find out for me? Please!

Ray: OK, it's Canada.

Sonia: Canada? Did you know Canada is a country, not a city in Switzerland?

Ray: Did you know you don't understand my jokes?

桑妮雅： 你知道瑞士的首都是什麼嗎？

雷： 我其實不太確定。妳何不上網查一查？

桑妮雅： 那太花時間了。你能幫我找嗎？拜託！

雷： 好吧，是加拿大。

桑妮雅： 加拿大？你知道加拿大是國家，不是瑞士的某個城市嗎？

雷： 那妳知道妳沒聽懂我的笑話嗎？

⑱ get to the root of the problem
找到問題的根源

- To solve this, we must **get to the root of** the problem.
要解決這個問題，我們就得**找到**它的**根源**。

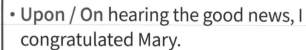

⑲ Upon / On + N/V-ing
= As soon as / Once...
一……就……

- **Upon / On** hearing the good news, I congratulated Mary.
= **As soon as / Once** I heard the good news, I congratulated Mary.
我**一**聽到這個好消息**就**立刻向瑪麗致賀。
- **Upon / On** your arrival at the train station, call us and we'll go pick you up.
= **As soon as / Once** you arrive at the train station, call us and we'll go pick you up.
你**一**到火車站就打電話給我們，我們**就**會去接你。

⑳ go / come + (and) + V
去 / 來……

- **Go (and)** buy me a newspaper now, son.
兒子，現在就**去**給我買份報紙。
- **Come (and)** see me when you have time.
有空時**來**看我。

TIPS

go 或 come 以原形動詞出現在句中時，之後可接連接詞 and，再接另一原形動詞，而 and 可省略。

㉑ smile / beam / grin from ear to ear
笑得合不攏嘴 / 笑得開心極了

• Paul smiled from ear to ear upon hearing that he was promoted to manager.
保羅獲知他升遷為經理一職後就**笑得合不攏嘴**。

各式各樣的表情

Words in Use

Sasha: Why are you **smiling from ear to ear**?
Igor: I've finally **gotten to the root of the problem**.
Sasha: What do you mean? The root of what problem?
Igor: Oh, I can't tell you that. It's private.
Sasha: You are a strange person, Igor. Did you know that?
Igor: No, I didn't know that.
Sasha: I think that is your real problem.

莎夏：你為什麼**笑得這麼開心**？
伊果：我終於**找到問題的根源**了。
莎夏：你指的是什麼？什麼問題的根源？
伊果：喔，我不能告訴妳。那是隱私。
莎夏：伊果，你是個奇怪的人。你知道嗎？
伊果：不，我不知道。
莎夏：我想那才是你真正的問題所在。

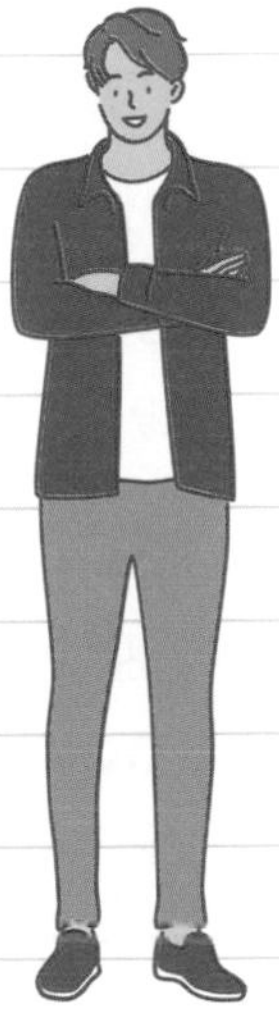

㉒ **paint the town red** 到市區痛快吃喝一番	• Now that the finals are all over, let’s **paint the town red** tonight. 既然期末考全都考完了，咱們今晚就**到市區痛快吃喝玩樂**吧。
㉓ **see red** = become very angry 變得極為生氣	• The mere thought of her boyfriend smooching her best friend Kate made Mary **see red**. 瑪麗光是想到她男友吻了她的手帕交凱特就**氣壞了**。
be in the red (公司)財務虧損中 	• Because of the rampage of the infectious disease, most businesses across the world **are in the red**. 由於傳染病的猖獗，全球大多數的公司企業都陷入**財務虧損中**。
㉔ **be green with envy** = be very jealous 非常嫉妒的	• When I heard James was promoted to a new position, I **was green with envy**. 我聽說詹姆士升遷到新職位時，心中**滿是嫉妒**。
a green thumb 善於種花草、盆栽、蔬果的人	• John’s garden is filled with beautiful flowers. He sure has **a green thumb**. 約翰的花園長滿了美麗的花朵。他確實**很會種花草**。
greenhorn [ˋgrin͵hɔrn] *n.* = rookie [ˋrʊkɪ] 新手	• Don’t be so harsh. The new staff member is just a **greenhorn** who doesn’t have as much experience. 不要那麼苛刻。這位新職員是個**新手**，經驗沒有那麼豐富。

be green
= be inexperienced
缺乏經驗

- Twenty years ago, the world-famous doctor was just an intern at a small hospital, (who was) **green** and immature.
  二十年前，這位世界知名的醫師還只是一家小醫院的實習醫師，既**缺乏經驗**又不夠成熟。

各式各樣的醫生

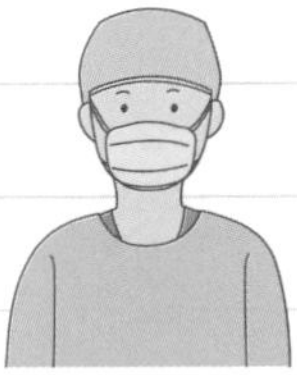

surgeon （外科）醫生

physician （內科）醫生

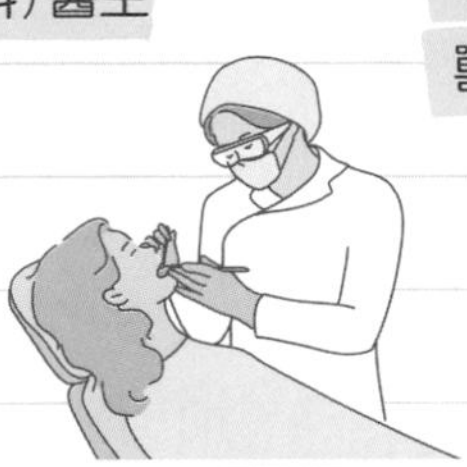

dentist 牙醫

veterinarian / vet
獸醫

Words in Use

Antonio: Every time I think of what Harry did, I **see red**!

Tara: It happened a long time ago. Why don't you just forget about it?

Antonio: I can't. And it bothers me that such a bad guy is so rich. He's got an expensive car and a big house with a swimming pool.

Tara: Oh, now it sounds like you're just **green with envy**.

安東尼歐： 我每次想到哈利做的好事就**超級生氣**！

塔拉： 那是好久以前發生的事了。你何不就忘了呢？

安東尼歐： 沒辦法。而且讓我討厭的是，這麼糟糕的人居然這麼有錢。他有一輛價值不斐的車還有附帶游泳池的大房子。

塔拉： 喔，現在聽起來像是你在**嫉妒**而已。

㉕ **be in the pink (of health)** = be in very good health 容光煥發的，身體狀況極佳的	• Mr. Wang recovered from the surgery in less than a week and **is in the pink** now. 王先生手術不到一個星期就復原了，現在**身體狀況好得很**。 • I have recovered from the flu, and **I'm in the pink** again. 我流感已復原了，現在再次覺得自己很**健康**。
㉖ **a white lie** 善意的謊言 go / turn (as) white as a sheet 臉色發白（如一張白紙似的） 	• I knew my boyfriend was telling **a white lie** when he said I was the prettiest girl in the world. 我男友說我是世上最美的女孩子時，我知道他只是**說說算了**。 • | Mary **went (as) white as a sheet** | | Mary's **face turned pale** | upon hearing that her son was seriously injured. 瑪麗聽到兒子受到重傷時，**臉色**立刻**蒼白起來**。
㉗ **a black sheep** 害群之馬 have a blackout = have a power failure 停電	• Sam idles around all day. It is safe to say that he is **the black sheep** of his family. 山姆啥事不做整天鬼混。可以肯定地說，他是家中的**害群之馬**。 • A huge typhoon | hit / battered / struck | our city, and we **had a blackout** for 10 hours. 強颱侵襲本市，造成十小時的**停電**。

black out = **pass out** = **faint** 昏倒	• The old man was too weak to walk. For a few seconds, he felt like he was going to **black out.** 老先生虛弱得走不動了。有片刻的時間他覺得自己快**昏倒**了。
put sth down in black and white 將某事用白紙黑字寫下來	• My boss promised to give me a huge bonus after the project was finished, but I asked him to **put it down in black and white** first. 老闆承諾計畫完成時要給我一大筆的獎金，但我要求他先**將**他的話**訴諸文字**。

Words in Use

Darla: Hi, Gregory. You look much better than before.

Gregory: Yes, thanks, Darla. Today, I feel like I'**m in the pink of health.**

Darla: That's wonderful! Did the doctor explain to you why you **blacked out** a few days ago?

Gregory: He said it's probably nothing to worry about. I hope he's not just telling me **a white lie** to make me feel better.

Darla: No, I'm sure everything will be fine.

達拉：嗨，葛瑞格里。你看起來比先前好多了。

葛瑞格里：是的，謝謝妳，達拉。今天我感覺**身體好極了**。

達拉：太棒了！醫生跟你解釋你前幾天**昏倒**的原因了嗎？

葛瑞格里：他說應該沒有什麼好擔心的。我希望他不是說**善意的謊言**讓我感覺好過一點。

達拉：不，我確定會沒事的。

㉘ yellow

[ˋjɛlo] *a.*

膽怯的

• To tell you the truth, I'm too **yellow** / cowardly / chicken to go bungee jumping.

老實跟你說，我**膽子太小**不敢玩高空彈跳。

㉙ brown-nose

[ˋbraʊn͵noz]

vt. & *vi.*

拍 (某人) 馬屁

brown-noser

[ˋbraʊn͵nozɚ]

n. 馬屁精

• Nobody in the company likes Peter because he likes to | **brown-nose** / flatter / curry favor with | the boss whenever possible.

彼得隨時都愛**拍**老闆的**馬屁**，因此全公司的人都不喜歡他。

• I'm sick of that **brown-noser**.

那個**馬屁精**令我討厭。

㉚ blue

[blu] *a.*

憂鬱的，難過的

have the blues

= feel sad

心情難過

• Ever since his girlfriend ditched / dumped / deserted him, Steven has been feeling quite **blue**.

自從被女友拋棄後，史蒂芬心情都**鬱鬱悶悶的**。

• My pet dog passed away last week, and I have **had the blues** ever since.

自從我的寵物狗上個星期離世，我一直都很**低落**。

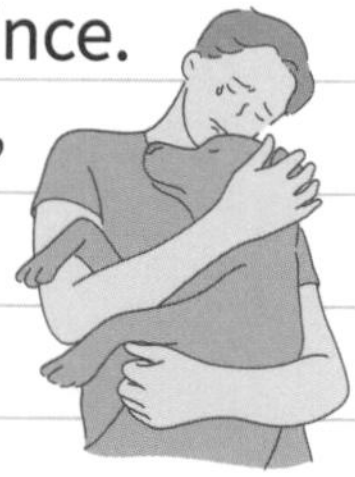

養狗必備

Words in Use

Hadji: Did you hear that Marlon got promoted? That really came as a surprise!

Jackie: Maybe you were surprised by it, but I wasn't.

Hadji: Really? Why not? He's only been with the company a short time.

Jackie: He's such **a brown-noser**. He's always saying nice things about the boss, but he doesn't mean them at all.

Hadji: Oh, I thought Marlon was a nice guy.

Jackie: That's because he **brown-noses** you, too, Hadji!

哈吉： 妳聽說馬龍升職了嗎？那真是令人意外啊！

潔姬： 也許會嚇到你，但不會嚇到我。

哈吉： 真的嗎？為什麼？他來公司才很短的時間而已。

潔姬： 他是個超級**馬屁精**。他總是會說老闆好話，但他根本不是真心的。

哈吉： 喔，我以為馬龍是個好人。

潔姬： 哈吉，那是因為他也會**拍**你**馬屁**！

Unit 9

Exercises
練習題

看圖選單字

❶

- ☐ see red
- ☐ black out
- ☐ brown-nose

❷

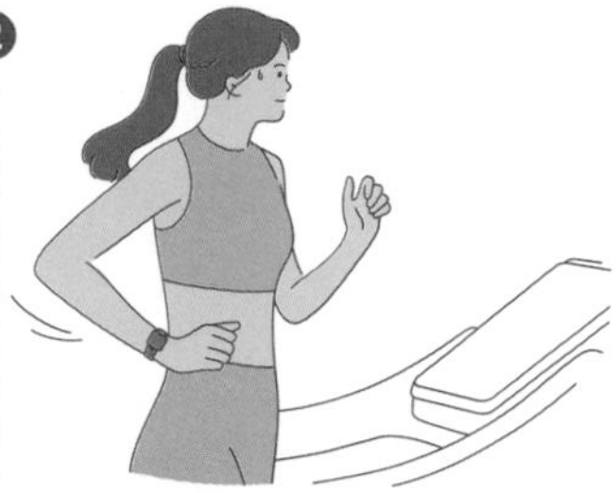

- ☐ lend a hand
- ☐ keep in shape
- ☐ look the word up

❸

- ☐ immune
- ☐ time-consuming
- ☐ yellow

選出正解

❶ Harry (borrowed / lent) some money from me.

❷ Stop thinking about it and get (on / by) with your life.

❸ (Once / Upon) talking to John, I knew that he was the perfect candidate.

❹ Helen is a great gardener; she's got such a green (hand / thumb).

❺ It's fine to tell a (white / black) lie from time to time.

句子填空

black | smiled | root | immune | impulse

❶ Sally ______________ from ear to ear when Frank proposed to her.

❷ I already had chickenpox, so I'm ______________ to it.

❸ Zack needs to think rationally and stop acting on ______________.

❹ Everyone thinks that Ben is the ______________ sheep of the family.

❺ It's critical that we get to the ______________ of the problem.

句子重組

❶ will / for a long time / Oil prices / remain high / to come

____

____.

❷ paint the town / Let's / to celebrate / red / your birthday

____

____.

❸ after / in the pink / Roger / a good rest / is

____

____.

Unit 9

Notes

Unit 10

- [x] 1 stress
- [ ] 2 fart
- [ ] 3 leaf
- [ ] 4 leaf
- [ ] 5 leafy
- [ ] 6 on top of...
- [ ] 7 On top of that, ...
- [ ] 8 feel on top of the world
- [ ] 9 ups and downs
- [ ] 10 beat the traffic
- [ ] 11 budget
- [ ] 12 be short of...
- [ ] 13 be short for...
- [ ] 14 be in short supply
- [ ] 15 be in high demand
- [ ] 16 genuine
- [ ] 17 fake
- [ ] 18 signature
- [ ] 19 物品 + come in + 尺寸 / 顏色
- [ ] 20 A is above B
- [ ] 21 be not above + V-ing
- [ ] 22 above all, ...
- [ ] 23 merits and demerits
- [ ] 24 drawback
- [ ] 25 有關 bird 的英文諺語
- [ ] 26 eat like a bird
- [ ] 27 eat like a horse
- [ ] 28 hold your horses
- [ ] 29 idle
- [ ] 30 needy

Unit 10

❶ stress
[strɛs] *n.*
壓力；強調

be under stress
處在壓力之下

lay / put | stress / emphasis | on... 強調……

• John has **been under** a lot of **stress** ever since he took over the new position.
約翰自從接任新職後就一直**處在**很大的**壓力下**。

• Time and again, our manager **lays | stress / emphasis | on** punctuality.
我們經理不時**強調**守時的重要性。

⋆ time and (time) again
屢次；常常

❷ fart [fɑrt] *vi.*
= cut the cheese
= pass gas
放屁

• I know Peter **farted** just now, but he won't admit it.
我知道彼得剛才**放了個屁**，但他卻不承認。

❸ leaf [lif] *n.*
樹葉；(書的) 一頁

turn over a new leaf
翻開新的一頁 / 改過自新，重新做人

take a leaf out of sb's book
效法某人

• It has been two months since Jimmy quit smoking. Obviously, he has **turned over a new leaf.**
吉米戒菸已有兩個月了。顯然他現在已**改過自新**了。

• Maybe I should **take a leaf out of** Peter's **book** and start exercising every morning.
也許我該**效法**彼得，開始每天早上運動。

❹ leaf

[lif] *vi.* 翻閱

leaf / browse through...

隨便翻閱 / 瀏覽 (書籍、雜誌)

• On weekends, I like to **leaf through** books and magazines at the bookstore near my house.

週末的時候，我喜歡在我家附近的一家書店**瀏覽**書籍或雜誌。

❺ leafy

[ˋlifɪ] *a.*

綠樹成蔭的

• The **leafy** view of the valley is breathtaking!

山谷**綠意盎然的**景色真是令人歎為觀止啊！

Words in Use

Mother: Tom, your grades at school aren't very good. I think you need to **put** more **stress on** studying.

Son: OK, Mom, but I'm already **under** a lot of **stress** in my life.

Mother: Well, being an adult is a lot more stressful. Hey, did you just **fart** while I was talking to you, young man?

Son: (*laughing*) Sorry, Mom. I had to **cut the cheese**.

Mother: Instead of **passing gas**, you need to concentrate on passing your tests!

媽媽： 湯姆，你的成績不好，我想你得在課業上**多用點心**。

兒子： 好吧，媽媽。但我的生活中已經**有許多壓力**了。

媽媽： 嗯，長大成人之後會有更多壓力。嘿，你是在我跟你講話時**放屁**嗎，年輕人？

兒子： (大笑) 抱歉，媽咪。我得**排氣**一下。

媽媽： 與其**放屁**，不如專注於通過測試！

❻ on top of... 在……的頂端	• My house lies / is situated / is located on top of the hill, overlooking the whole valley. 我家就坐落在山頂，可以俯瞰整個山谷。
❼ On top of that, ... 此外，……(尤指不愉快的事)	• I lost my wallet. On top of that, the last train bound for Kaohsiung had just left. 我把錢包弄丟了。更糟的是，開往高雄的最後一班火車也剛駛離。
❽ feel on top of the world = feel extremely happy 感到高興極了	• When Nick got down on one knee and showed her the diamond ring, Sandy felt on top of the world. 尼克單腳下跪把鑽戒拿給她看時，珊蒂感到高興極了。 
❾ ups and downs = successes and failures 起起落落；成敗的經驗	• Life is full of ups and downs. 人生充滿了起起落落。 • Every marriage has its ups and downs. 每段婚姻都有波折。 
❿ beat the traffic (提早上路) 避免交通阻塞	• In order to beat the traffic, many people hit the road early. 許多人提早上路以避免交通阻塞。 ⋆ hit the road 上路，出發 = begin a journey

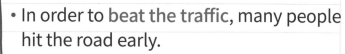

⑪ **budget** [ˋbʌdʒɪt] *n.* 預算 & *vt.* 規劃 (時間或金錢) **on a tight budget** 預算吃緊，精打細算	• Because of the economic recession, more and more people are living **on a tight budget.** 由於經濟不景氣，**勒緊褲帶**過生活的人愈來愈多。 • **Budgeting** your money enables you to save money and get out of debt. 把你的錢**精打細算**可以幫你省錢也免陷債務。

Words in Use

Samantha: We should leave now if we want to **beat the traffic** to the airport.

Malcolm: Why? It's only 2 p.m. Our flight doesn't leave until 6 p.m.

Samantha: The traffic will get really bad soon. **On top of that,** we should be at the airport about three hours before the departure time.

Malcolm: OK. I'm really looking forward to finally starting our holiday. I **feel on top of the world** right now.

莎曼珊： 如果我們想要**避開塞車**到機場，現在就應該要出門了。

馬康： 為什麼？現在才兩點。我們的飛機要六點才起飛。

莎曼珊： 交通很快就會癱瘓了。**除此之外**，我們要在起飛時間三個小時前到機場。

馬康： 好吧。我真的很期待終於要去度假了。我現在**覺得高興極了**。

⑫ be short of...

缺乏……

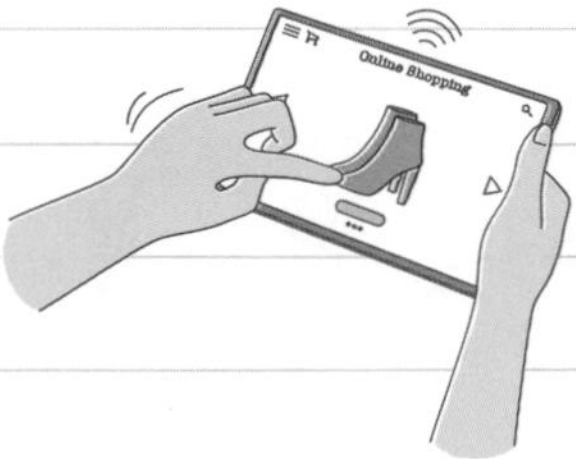

- Cindy has a passion for online shopping, which is why she **is** often **short of** money.

  辛蒂很喜愛線上購物，這也是她經常錢**不夠用**的原因。

- Can you lend me some money? I'**m** a little **short** (**of** money).

  你可否借我一點錢？我手頭有點**緊**。

⑬ be short for...

是……的簡稱

- The name Bob **is short for** Robert.

  Bob 這個名字**是** Robert **的簡稱**。

⑭ be in short supply

供應短缺

- Basic foodstuffs **were in short supply** across the country soon after the epidemic broke out.

  該流行病爆發不久後，全國基本糧食的**供應**就**短缺**了。

⑮ be in high demand

需求量大

- To our surprise, the new product has **been in high demand** since it was released last month.

  令我們吃驚的是，自從該新產品上個月上市，**需求量一直都很大**。

⑯ genuine

[ˋdʒɛnjʊɪn] *a.*

真實的；真跡的

- This is | **a genuine** / an authentic | painting / watch, not a fake one.

  這是**真**畫 / 錶，不是假貨。

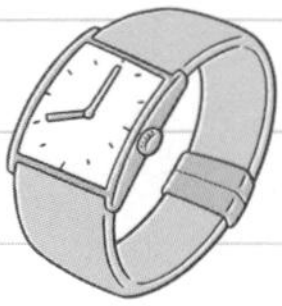

⑰ fake
[fek] *a.*
仿冒的 & *n.* 假貨
& *vt.* 偽造

• The connoisseur said that all the paintings on display at this gallery were **fake**.
這位鑑定家稱該藝廊所展出的所有畫作全是**贗品**。

• While in high school, I once **faked** / forged my father's signature on my report card.
念高中時，有一次我曾在成績單上**偽造**我爸爸的簽名。

Words in Use

Kim: Will said he wants to join us for lunch.
Stan: Uh-oh. He's always **short of** money. I'll have to buy him lunch again.
Kim: He's not that bad.
Stan: You don't know him as well as I do. You know what his name **is short for**, don't you?
Kim: Will? It's **short for** William, isn't it?
Stan: In this case, it's **short for** "Will he ask me for money again?"

金： 威爾說他想跟我們一起吃午餐。
史坦： 糟糕，他總是**缺**錢。我又得請他吃午餐了。
金： 他人沒那麼壞吧。
史坦： 妳不像我這麼了解他。妳知道他名字**是**什麼**的簡稱**，不是嗎？
金： 威爾嗎？**是**威廉**的簡稱**，不是嗎？
史坦： 在這種情況下，**是**「威爾會不會又跟我要錢」**的簡稱**。

⑱ signature
[ˋsɪgnətʃɚ] *n.*
(文件上的) 簽名

比較

autograph
[ˋɔtə͵græf] *n.*
(向名人索取供作紀念的) 簽名

• Put your **signature** here, please.
= Sign your name here, please.
請在此處**簽名**。

• Could I have your **autograph**, Shakira?
夏奇拉小姐，我可以獲得您的**簽名**嗎？

⑲ 物品 + come in + 尺寸 / 顏色
某物有……的尺寸 / 顏色

• This shirt **comes in** three sizes: small, medium, and large.
這件襯衫**有**大、中、小三種尺寸。

• This car **comes in** five colors: black, white, silver, dark green, and red.
這輛車**有**五種顏色：黑色、白色、銀色、深綠色及紅色。

交通工具

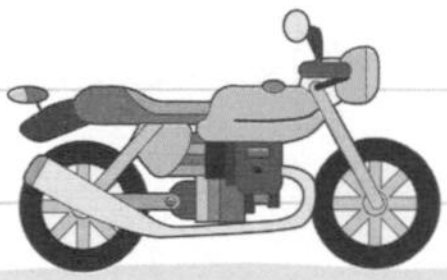

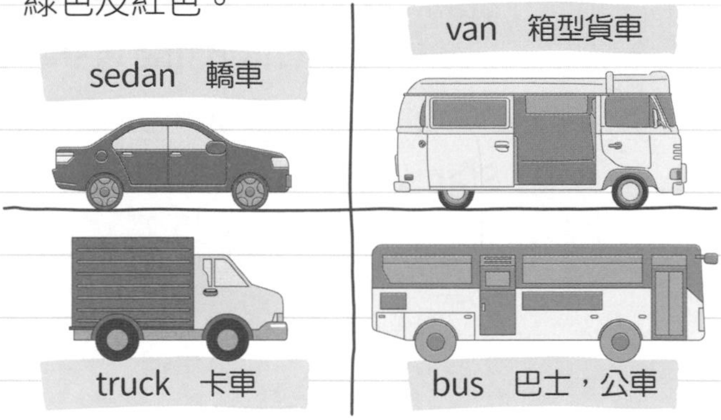

⑳ A is above B
= A is more important than B
A 比 B 重要

• (Good) Health **is above** wealth.
健康**勝於**財富。(諺語)

㉑ **be not above + V-ing** = be willing to V 願意做⋯⋯(尤指令人感到委屈的事情)	• John **is not above** working as a security guard. After all, work is work. 約翰**甘心**做個警衛。畢竟，工作無貴賤之分。 • Though a famous scholar, Dr. Smith **is never above** asking questions. 史密斯博士雖然是位知名學者，卻**從不恥**下問。
㉒ **above all, ...** = most importantly, ... 尤其是，⋯⋯； 最重要的是，⋯⋯	• To stay fit, you should watch what you eat. **Above all,** you should exercise regularly. 你若想保持健康，就應注意飲食。**最重要的是**，你要規律運動。

Unit 10

Words in Use

Rosa: So, what do you think of the running shoes?

Evan: I like the style, but they are a bit tight. Do they **come in** a larger size?

Rosa: I'm sorry, these ones don't. Would you like to look at a different pair?

Evan: I guess so. Comfort **is above** style, after all.

Rosa: You are right. **Above all,** sports shoes should fit well.

羅莎： 那麼你覺得這雙慢跑鞋如何？

艾文： 我喜歡這款式但是有點太緊，**有大一點的尺寸**嗎？

羅莎： 抱歉，這款沒有。你想看看不一樣的款式嗎？

艾文： 好吧。舒適度終究是**比**款式**重要**的。

羅莎： 你說得對。**最重要的是**，運動鞋得要很合腳才行。

㉓ **merits and demerits** 利與弊	• What are the | merits and demerits / advantages and disadvantages | of living in the country? 鄉村生活的**利與弊**是什麼？ 
㉔ **drawback** [ˋdrɔˏbæk] *n.* (機器、計畫、地方等事物的) 缺點 比較 **shortcoming** [ˋʃɔrtˏkʌmɪŋ] *n.* (人的) 缺點	• Shanghai is no doubt a fun city. The only **drawback** is the weather. It can be biting cold there in winter. 毫無疑問，上海是個好玩的城市。唯一的**缺點**就是天氣。冬天時那兒會冷得要命。 • Tell me the **drawbacks** / disadvantages of this car. 告訴我這輛車的**缺點**。 • One of Peter's **shortcomings** is that he has a tendency to lie. 彼得的**缺點**之一就是他愛說謊。
㉕ **有關 bird 的英文諺語** 	• A **bird** in the hand is worth two in the bush. 一鳥在手勝於兩鳥在林 / 珍惜現有東西以免貪心失去了它。(諺語) • **Birds** of a feather flock together. 物以類聚。(諺語) • The early **bird** catches the worm. 早起的**鳥兒**有蟲吃 / 捷足者先登。(諺語)

㉖ **eat like a bird** 吃得很少，食量很小	• Jane **eats like a bird**. No wonder she looks so thin. 阿珍**食量很小**。難怪她看起來那麼瘦。
㉗ **eat like a horse** 吃得很多，食量很大	• Dean **eats like a horse**, but strangely, he never gains weight. 迪恩**食量奇大**，不過怪的是，他從不發胖。

Words in Use

Pauline: How do you like working from home, Chuck?

Chuck: There are some good things about it, but there are also some **drawbacks**.

Pauline: There are **merits and demerits** to it, for sure.

Chuck: For example, I still **eat like a horse**, even though I don't get as much exercise as I used to.

Pauline: Yes, that could be a problem. I **eat like a bird** most of the time, but even I have gained some weight.

寶琳： 查克，你覺得居家工作如何？

查克： 有好有**壞**。

寶琳： 當然會有**利弊**。

查克： 舉例來說，雖然我沒有像從前那麼常運動，但**食量還是很大**。

寶琳： 是，那可能會是個問題。我大多時候**食量都很小**，但連我也變胖了。

㉘ **hold your horses** = hold it 且慢，別急	• **Hold your horses!** I don't think it's the right time to take any action now. **且慢！**我認為現在不是採取任何行動的時機。
straight from the horse's mouth (消息) 直接從可靠的來源獲得	• I heard the news **straight from the horse's mouth**, so it's absolutely not a rumor. 這消息我是**直接從可靠的管道聽來的**，因此絕不是謠言。
put the cart before the horse 本末倒置	• If you buy a fancy car before finding a stable job, you are **putting the cart before the horse**. 你若還沒有獲得穩定的工作就想買一輛豪華的車，就是在**本末倒置**。
horse around 胡鬧；鬼混	• If you **horse** / goof / idle **around** every day, you'll certainly get nowhere. 你若每天**鬼混無所事事**，肯定不會有出息。
㉙ **idle** [ˋaɪdḷ] *a.* 閒蕩的，無所事事的 & *vi.* 閒蕩	• An **idle** youth, a needy age. = If you **idle** around when young, you'll become poor and helpless when old. 少小不努力，老大徒傷悲。(諺語)
㉚ **needy** [ˋnidɪ] *a.* 窮困的 the needy / poor (泛指所有的) 窮人	• All the money we have raised will go to **the needy / poor**. 我們所募得的錢將會全數用來救濟**窮困的人**。

慈善不分你我

blood donation
捐血

food donation
捐贈食物

volunteer 義工

charity 慈善(機構)

Words in Use

Fran: Wait a minute. I'm going to give that guy some money.

Ricardo: **Hold your horses!** I don't know if that's a good idea.

Fran: What do you mean? He's obviously poor and needs help. I think it's important to give to **the needy**.

Ricardo: What about me? I need money, too.

Fran: You? You're not **needy**. You're just a lazy guy who likes to **idle** all day!

法蘭： 等等。我要給那個人一點錢。

雷卡多： **別急**！我不確定這個主意好不好。

法蘭： 什麼意思？他顯然很窮苦而且需要幫助。我覺得施予**窮苦的人**是很重要的。

雷卡多： 那我呢？我也需要錢。

法蘭： 你？你不**窮**，你只是個整天**遊手好閒**的懶鬼！

Unit 10

Exercises
練習題

看圖連連看

❶

❷

❸

eat like a horse

needy

signature

選出正解

❶ Dean left the house early to ______________ the traffic.

(A) punch (B) beat

(C) throw (D) hit

❷ Dan is a good role model. I should take a ______________ out of his book.

(A) leave (B) cover

(C) leaf (D) word

句子填空

top | budget | genuine | drawbacks | short

❶ The project was canceled because we're on a tight ______________.

❷ Most people call me Lizzie. It's ______________ for Elizabeth.

❸ The painting is worth a lot of money because it's ______________.

❹ Mike felt on ______________ of the world when he got his dream job.

❺ There are many ______________ to working in a large company.

句子重組

❶ everything else / well-being / above / is / Your

____

____.

❷ This jacket / various / in / comes / sizes

____

____.

❸ the environment / laid stress / The chairman / on / protecting

____

____.

Notes

Unit 11

- [x] ❶ do one's best
- [ ] ❷ a man of his word
- [ ] ❸ eat one's words
- [ ] ❹ go through...
- [ ] ❺ relate to...
- [ ] ❻ chord
- [ ] ❼ string
- [ ] ❽ stand sb up
- [ ] ❾ disappear without a trace
- [ ] ❿ burn (oneself) out
- [ ] ⓫ have money to burn
- [ ] ⓬ set aside...
- [ ] ⓭ put aside...
- [ ] ⓮ fulfilled
- [ ] ⓯ awaken (sb) to sth
- [ ] ⓰ dare
- [ ] ⓱ dare
- [ ] ⓲ dare 的其他重要用法
- [ ] ⓳ I dare say...
- [ ] ⓴ daring
- [ ] ㉑ for fear that...
- [ ] ㉒ company
- [ ] ㉓ hornet
- [ ] ㉔ a garbage dump
- [ ] ㉕ marry
- [ ] ㉖ married
- [ ] ㉗ shut-eye
- [ ] ㉘ ditch sb
- [ ] ㉙ follow suit
- [ ] ㉚ news

Unit 11

❶ do one's best
盡己之力

• **Do your best** and then let God do the rest.
凡事**盡力而為**，其他的就交給上天了 / 盡人事聽天命。（諺語）

❷ a man of his word
守信用的人

• Tim is **a man of his word**. In other words, he never | goes back on / breaks | his word.
提姆是個**言而有信的人**。
換言之，他從不食言。

❸ eat one's words
收回所說過的話；承認所說過的話是不對的

• My teacher said I will never achieve anything. I'll make him **eat his words**. Just wait and see!
我的老師說我將來絕對一事無成。我會要他**收回這句話**。等著瞧吧！

❹ go through...
= experience...
歷經……

• Edward | **went through** / **experienced** | a lot of hardships before becoming what he is today.
愛德華**吃了**許多苦頭才有今日的成就。
* hardship [ˋhardʃɪp] *n.* 艱困，困難

❺ relate to...

對……感同身受；認同……

be related to sb 與某人有親戚關係

• The movie attracted many people because it told a story that everyone could | **relate to**. / identify with.

這部電影因為述說所有人都能**感同身受**的故事而吸引了很多人觀看。

• Little did I know that Peter **is related to** our English teacher.

我想都沒想到／一點也沒料到彼得**與**我們的英文老師**有親戚關係**。

Words in Use

Sydney: Good luck in the game today, Alicia. I'm sure you'll win.

Alicia: Well, I will **do my best** during the game.

Sydney: Of course you will. You are the best! You should be more confident.

Alicia: I don't want to have to **eat my words** if I lose, though.

Sydney: Yeah, I can **relate to** what you're saying. That's happened to me before.

席妮： 祝妳今天的比賽順利，愛麗莎，我確定妳會贏的。

愛麗莎： 比賽時我會**盡力**。

席妮： 我確定妳會。妳是最棒的！妳應該要更有信心。

愛麗莎： 但是我不希望我得**收回這些話**。

席妮： 是，**對**妳說的話我能**感同身受**。這種事以前曾經發生在我身上過。

❻ chord [kɔrd] *n.*
(吉他的) 和弦

strike / touch a chord with sb
引起某人的共鳴 / 同情

- The singer's song **struck a chord with** the audience, and many were moved to tears after listening to it.

  這位歌手的歌**引起**觀眾的**共鳴**，許多人聽完歌之後都感動得落淚了。

❼ string [strɪŋ] *n.*
(樂器的) 弦

heartstrings [ˋhɑrt͵strɪŋz] *n.*
心弦 (恆用複數)

tug / pull at sb's heartstrings
觸動某人的心弦

- The sight of the starving children **pulled at my heartstrings.**

  看到那些飢餓的孩子，我**心痛不已**。

❽ stand sb up
對某人爽約

- I had been waiting for my date for almost an hour, but she didn't show / turn up. Obviously, she had **stood me up.**

  我等約會的對象等了將近一個小時，不過她並未出現。顯然她**放**我**鴿子**了。

❾ disappear without a trace
= disappear into thin air
消失得無影無蹤

- The man disappeared without a trace / into thin air / from the face of the earth after committing several murders.

  該男子犯下數起謀殺案後**消失得無影無蹤** / 便從人間蒸發了。

⑩ **burn (oneself) out** 心力交瘁	• You need to take a vacation from time to time, or you'll **burn out** soon. 你時不時就該放個假，否則很快就會**身心俱疲**。
⑪ **have money to burn** 錢多得花不完	• The snobbish girl likes to associate with boys who **have money to burn**. 那個勢利的女孩子喜歡和**有錢的**男孩子交往。 * snobbish [ˋsnɑbɪʃ] *a.* 勢利的

Words in Use

Gillian: Hi, Burt. How are you? Are you going to eat at this restaurant, too?

Burt: Yes, if my date ever arrives. She's 45 minutes late already. I thought I saw her on the street over there, but then she **disappeared without a trace**.

Gillian: Oh, 45 minutes is a long time to wait. I hope she didn't **stand you up**.

Burt: Me, too. I'm getting tired of waiting.

吉莉安：嗨，伯特。你好嗎？你也要在這間餐廳用餐嗎？

伯特：是，如果我約會的對象會到的話。她已經遲到 45 分鐘了。我以為我有看到她在對街，但她卻**消失得無影無蹤**。

吉莉安：喔，等了 45 分鐘的確很久。希望她不是**放你鴿子**。

伯特：我也是。我等得有點煩了。

⑫ **set aside...** = put aside... 撥出 / 騰出 (時間)	• However busy I am, I manage to **set aside** some time every evening to play with my children. 不管我多忙，我每晚都會設法**撥出**一點時間跟孩子們玩耍。
⑬ **put aside...** = save... 存 (錢) 以 從事…… 	• My wife and I are planning to | **put aside** / **save** | some money every month, hoping one day we can travel. 我與我太太打算每個月**存**一些錢，期望有朝一日可以去旅遊。
⑭ **fulfilled** [fʊlˋfɪld] *a.* 感到滿足的	• I feel **fulfilled** / satisfied every time I help the needy. 每次幫助窮困的人之後我都很**滿足** / 很有成就感。
⑮ **awaken (sb) to sth** (使) 某人意識到 某事	• Everyone should | **awaken to** / be awakened to | the fact that all men are created equal. 每個人都應**意識到**人人生而平等這件事。
⑯ **dare** [dɛr] *vt.* 挑戰；敢於 dare / challenge sb to V 挑戰某人 / 賭某人不敢……	• I **dare** you **to** swim across the river. 我向你**挑戰**，賭你**不敢**游過這條河。 

dare (to) V
膽敢……

- If you **dare to** stand me up again, you'll be in big trouble.（常用）

=If you dare stand me up again, you'll be in big trouble.（少用）

你若**敢**再放我鴿子，你就要倒大霉了。

游泳要物

bikini　比基尼

flip-flops / thongs
人字拖

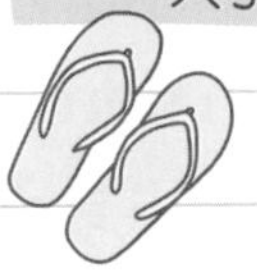

trunks　游泳褲

swimming cap
泳帽

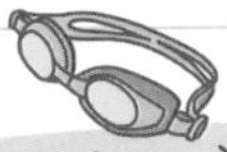

goggles　泳鏡

Words in Use

Kevin: Wow! This city is so expensive to live in. I can't seem to **put aside** any money to save.

Stacy: I don't think living in this city is expensive. You spend a lot of money on things like entertainment and expensive meals.

Kevin: I **dare** you **to** name one thing that I bought that I didn't need.

Stacy: What about the video games that you have never played?

Kevin: Come on, I need to feel **fulfilled** in life!

凱文：哇！住這城市好花錢。我似乎**撥**不**出**錢來存了。

史黛西：我不認為住城市裡很花錢，而是你把很多錢花在像是娛樂與大餐這樣的事情上。

凱文：我**諒**妳說不出一件我買的東西卻是我不需要的。

史黛西：那些你買了卻沒玩過的電動遊戲要怎麼解釋？

凱文：別這樣，我需要在人生中**感到滿足**！

⑰ **dare** [dɛr] *aux.* 膽敢	• **Dare** John lie to you again? 約翰**膽敢**再對你說謊？ (dare 是助動詞，可置主詞前，形成問句)
dare not + V 不敢……	• I believe John dares not lie to me again. (×) dare 與 not 並用時，dare 已成助動詞，主詞即使是第三人稱單數 (如 he, she, John, Mr. Li 等)，均無 dares not 的說法，故上句應改成：
won't dare (to) + V 不敢……	→ I believe John **dare not** lie to me again. (○) 我相信約翰**不敢**再對我說謊了。 • John **dare not** lie to me again. = John **won't dare to** lie to me again. 約翰**不敢**再對我說謊了。

一秒搞糟人際關係

⑱ **dare 的其他重要用法：** ⓐ **dare not 的過去式為 dared not。**	• Afterwards, Roy **dared not** jaywalk again. = Afterwards, Roy didn't dare (to) jaywalk again. 之後，羅伊再也**不敢**闖越馬路。
ⓑ **no one dares (to) + V** 沒人敢……	• **No one dares (to)** tell Mary the truth. **沒人敢**把真相告訴瑪麗。 • **No one dared (to)** tell Mary the truth then. 當時**沒人敢**把真相告訴瑪麗。

ⓒ **Who dares (to) + V?** 誰敢……？	• Who dares to challenge me? (常用) = Who dares challenge me? (少用) 誰敢挑戰我？
ⓓ **How dare you / they / he / she + V?** (你 / 你們 / 他們 / 他 / 她等) 怎麼敢……！	• How dare you call me a liar! 你好大的膽子，竟敢稱我為騙子！ • How dare Anna imply that I'm a liar! 安娜好大的膽子，竟敢暗示我是個騙子！

Words in Use

Charlotte: How dare you do that? You dare not tell me the truth, right?

Marlon: Huh? Are you really talking to me?

Charlotte: Oh, sorry. I'm practicing the new vocabulary I learned in English class today.

Marlon: Let me guess—your teacher taught you how to use "dare," right?

Charlotte: Yes! How did you know that?

Marlon: "Dare" to guess?

夏綠蒂： 你怎麼敢這麼做？你不敢告訴我真相，對不對？

馬龍： 什麼？妳真的是在跟我說話嗎？

夏綠蒂： 喔，抱歉。我是在練習今天英文課學到的新單字。

馬龍： 我來猜猜看 —— 妳的老師今天教妳使用 dare 這個字，對嗎？

夏綠蒂： 沒錯！你怎麼會知道？

馬龍： 妳「敢」猜猜看嗎？

⑲ **I dare say...** (美) = **I daresay...** (英) 我敢說……	• I dare say (that) Adam doesn't have the guts to do it. = I daresay Adam doesn't have the guts to do it. **我敢說**亞當沒膽做這件事。
⑳ **daring** [ˋdɛrɪŋ] *a.* 勇敢的，敢於冒險的	• Jerry is a daring man who is willing to try anything risky. 傑瑞是個**敢於冒險的**人，任何危險的事他都願意嘗試。
㉑ **for fear that...** = **lest...** 唯恐……；以免……	• Kyle dared not make any sound for fear that he might wake up the baby. = Kyle didn't dare to make any sound lest he (should) wake up the baby. 凱爾不敢發出任何聲響**以免**吵醒小寶寶。

TIPS

lest 引導的副詞子句只可使用 should，且往往均予省略。

㉒ **company** [ˋkʌmpənɪ] *n.* 公司，行號(可數)；陪伴(不可數) **keep sb company** 陪伴某人 **enjoy sb's company** 喜歡某人的陪伴	• Though young, Mr. Smith runs / owns two big companies. 史密斯先生雖然年輕，卻擁有兩家大**公司**。 • My girlfriend kept me company while I was waiting for the train. 我等火車時，女友**陪著**我。 • I enjoy Paul's company because of his pleasant personality. 保羅個性爽朗，因此我**喜歡與他為伍**。

the company sb keeps 某人所交往的朋友們	• One is known by **the company** one **keeps**. 從一個人**所交往的朋友**就可看出他是什麼樣的人／觀其友而知其人。（諺語）
㉓ **hornet** [ˋhɔrnɪt] *n.* 大黃蜂 be (as) mad as a hornet 氣炸了	• When he found out his son had stolen his money, Mr. Wang **was mad as a hornet.** 王先生發現他兒子偷了他的錢時，他**氣炸了**。

Words in Use

Norman: **I'm mad as a hornet** right now!

Valerie: What's the matter, Norman?

Norman: I found out that Sandra doesn't love me at all.

Valerie: Your girlfriend? But I thought you said she **enjoys** your **company**.

Norman: She does. But the **company** she really enjoys is the store that I own! She only likes my money!

Valerie: Oh, I'm so sorry to hear that, Norman.

諾曼：我現在**氣炸了**！

薇拉蕊：諾曼，怎麼了？

諾曼：我發現珊卓根本不愛我。

薇拉蕊：你的女友？但我以為你說過她**喜歡**你**的陪伴**。

諾曼：沒錯。但她真正喜歡的是我的那間店！她只喜歡我的錢！

薇拉蕊：喔，諾曼，聽到你這麼說真讓我遺憾。

Unit 11

㉔ a garbage dump
垃圾場（無規劃）

landfill
[ˋlændfɪl] *n.*
垃圾掩埋場（有規劃）

• I chose to live near a **garbage dump** because it's so smelly there that few people would come and bother me.
我選擇住在**垃圾場**附近，因為那兒很臭，沒幾個人會來煩我。

㉕ marry
[ˋmærɪ] *vi.* 結婚 & *vt.* 將某人出嫁；與某人結婚

marry sb
娶／嫁給某人

• Kate **married** young. She is less than 30 years old, and yet she has three children now. 凱特很早就**結婚**。她還不到三十歲，卻已有三個孩子。

• Cindy's father refused to **marry** his daughter to that poor young boy.
辛蒂的父親拒絕**將**女兒**嫁**給那個窮小子。

• I won't **marry** you until you've found a good job and have a steady income.
你找到好工作且收入穩定後我才會**跟**你**結婚**。

• Jane married with Dan 10 years ago. (×)
→ Jane **married** Dan 10 years ago. (○)
阿珍十年前**嫁給**阿丹。

㉖ married
[ˋmærɪd] *a.* 結婚的，已婚的

be married to sb
與某人結婚

• Jane was / got **married to** Dan 10 years ago.
= Jane and Dan got **married** 10 years ago.
= Jane and Dan tied the knot 10 years ago.
阿珍與阿丹是十年前**結婚**的。

be getting married 即將結婚	• It came as a big surprise that Ivan and Jenny **are getting married** next month. 艾凡與珍妮下個月**就要結婚**了，消息傳來令人頗感意外。
㉗ **shut-eye** [ˋʃʌtˏaɪ] *n.* = sleep 睡眠 get some shut-eye 小睡一下	• You look very tired. You'd better **get some shut-eye.** 你看起來很累，最好**睡個覺**。

Words in Use

Alex: You must be so excited. Your wedding day is tomorrow!

Lana: I'm so nervous about it that it's hard for me to sleep. I haven't been **getting** much **shut-eye** lately.

Alex: You should get some soon. You'll be really busy after you **get married**. You'll have to take care of everything.

Lana: You never **married**, did you, Alex?

艾力克斯： 妳一定很興奮。明天就是妳的大喜之日了！

拉娜： 我好緊張，緊張到難以入眠。我最近都**睡**不好。

艾力克斯： 妳應該補眠。**結婚**後妳會變得很忙。妳得要處理每件事情。

拉娜： 你沒**結**過**婚**對吧，艾力克斯？

Unit 11

㉘ ditch sb

= dump sb
= desert sb
把某人 (指情人、夫、妻) 甩了

• David has isolated himself from the world ever since his wife | ditched / dumped / deserted | him for another. 大衛的老婆**把**他**甩了**又跟人跑了，從此他就隔絕於世。

㉙ follow suit

= follow in sb's footsteps
仿效某人，追隨某人

• Kevin is a barber by trade, and he expects his son to follow | suit / in his footsteps | when he grows up.
凱文是個理髮師，他也期盼兒子長大後能**步**他的**後塵**。

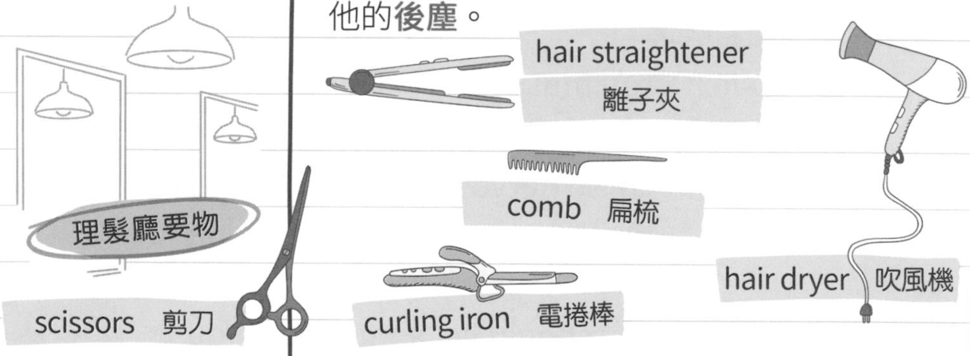

㉚ news

[njuz] *n.*
新聞；消息
(不可數)

• I have a good news to tell you. (×)
→ I have | a good piece of news / a piece of good news / good news / some good news | to tell you. (○)
我有 (一則) 好**消息**要告訴你。

• No news is good news.
沒**消息**就是好**消息** / 不出事就是好事。(諺語)

be in the news 被媒體報導	• The sudden death of that celebrity has **been in the news** recently. 最近媒體**大肆報導**那位名人猝死的事。
be on the news 被影音媒體（指電視、電臺）報導	• The local election results **are** | **on the news** / TV | now. | **being broadcast** | 電視 / 電臺正在**報導**當地選舉結果。
break the news to sb 將（壞）消息告訴某人	• I dare not **break the news** about her husband's death **to** Mrs. Lee. 我不敢**把**李太太的丈夫逝世**的消息告訴**她。

Words in Use

Ben: I heard some good **news** today! Amanda has **ditched** her boyfriend.

Carol: And you think you can date her now? I hate to **break the news to** you, but...

Ben: No, please don't tell me!

Carol: Why not?

Ben: I think in this case, no **news** is good **news**.

班： 我今天聽到了一些好**消息**！亞曼達**甩掉**她男友了。

卡蘿： 你認為你現在可以找她約會嗎？我不想**把**這**消息告訴你**，但是……。

班： 不，拜託別跟我說！

卡蘿： 為什麼不要？

班： 我想就這件事而言，沒**消息**就是好**消息**。

Unit 11 Exercises 練習題

看圖選單字

❶

☐ shut-eye
☐ company
☐ string

❷

☐ daring
☐ married
☐ fulfilled

❸

☐ marry sb
☐ ditch sb
☐ stand sb up

選出正解

❶ You can trust Ronald. He's a man of his (word / speech).

❷ The poem struck a (string / chord) with Annie.

❸ Lily was devastated when the police (broke / threw) the news to her.

❹ Tim stood still for (fright / fear) that the dog might bite him.

❺ I'm so busy that I can't set (aside / away) some time for my family.

句子填空

burn | trace | best | suit | dares

❶ No one ______________ to say no to the boss.

❷ After Walt joined in, he convinced the others to follow ______________.

❸ The thief disappeared without a ______________.

❹ If James continues working overtime, he'll ______________ out soon.

❺ Don't be so tough on Carol. She did her ______________ on the test.

句子重組

❶ the dangers of / was awakened / smoking / to / Samuel

____

____.

❷ company / enjoy / each / Charlie and I / other's

____

____.

❸ married / her childhood friend / is / to / Betty

____

____.

Notes

Unit 12

- [x] ❶ uneasy
- [ ] ❷ ease
- [ ] ❸ ease
- [ ] ❹ take it easy
- [ ] ❺ focus (...) on...
- [ ] ❻ stay focused
- [ ] ❼ treat
- [ ] ❽ treat
- [ ] ❾ map
- [ ] ❿ map out...
- [ ] ⓫ read sb's mind
- [ ] ⓬ a (wide) variety of...
- [ ] ⓭ potential
- [ ] ⓮ make the most of...
- [ ] ⓯ As the saying goes, "..."
- [ ] ⓰ threat
- [ ] ⓱ threaten
- [ ] ⓲ Are you putting me on?
- [ ] ⓳ pencil
- [ ] ⓴ lips
- [ ] ㉑ cut down on...
- [ ] ㉒ be cut out for...
- [ ] ㉓ bony
- [ ] ㉔ make no bones about...
- [ ] ㉕ amount to + 數字
- [ ] ㉖ spice
- [ ] ㉗ haste
- [ ] ㉘ hurry up
- [ ] ㉙ halt
- [ ] ㉚ grind to a halt

Unit 12

❶ uneasy
[ʌnˋizɪ] *a.*
= **worried**
[ˋwɝɪd] 不安的

比較
not easy
= **difficult**
[ˋdɪfəˏkʌlt]
不容易的

• You look **uneasy**. Is there anything
the matter / wrong with you?
你看起來很**憂心的**樣子。出了什麼事？

• The math test I took this morning was really **not easy**.
今天早上我考的數學考試實在**很難**。

❷ ease
[iz] *vi.* & *vt.*
(使疼痛、壓力等) 減輕，緩解

• Right after I took the medicine, the pain started to **ease**.
我吃了這個藥不久，疼痛就開始**減輕**了。

• My family doctor said this medicine would **ease** / relieve my stomachache.
我的家庭醫生稱這種藥可以**緩解**我的胃痛。

• Listening to music can help **ease** / relieve your stress.
聽音樂可以幫助你**減輕**壓力。

❸ ease
[iz] *n.* 容易；輕鬆自在 (不可數)
with ease
輕鬆地

• Because he was well-prepared for the test, Peter passed it **with ease**. / easily.
因為彼得有充分準備考試，所以**輕鬆**及格了。

feel at ease / relaxed 感到很自在	• I **feel** more **at ease** with my friends than I do with my parents. 跟我朋友在一起比跟我爸媽在一起**自在**多了。
feel ill at ease 感到不自在	• I **felt ill at ease** when I found my teacher standing behind me. 我發現老師站在我身後時**感到渾身不自在**。
❹ **take it easy** = relax and don't worry 放寬心，別緊張	• You've been working too hard recently, buddy. **Take it easy** and have fun during the weekend. 老兄，你最近工作得太辛苦了。週末的時候**放輕鬆**、好好玩玩。
easy does it (做事) 小心，慢慢來	• Move the bookcase to the corner there. It's very heavy. **Easy does it!** 把書櫃移到角落那裡。它很重。**小心，慢慢來！**

Words in Use

Scott: I'm feeling **uneasy** about that test on Friday.

Marsha: If we study for it, we can pass it **with ease**.

Scott: I think I need to **ease** my stress by eating some chocolate.

Marsha: OK, but you'd still better study after you **take it easy** and eat some chocolate.

史考特：禮拜五的那場考試讓我**坐立難安**。

瑪莎：如果我們努力讀書，我們就可以**輕鬆**過關。

史考特：我想我需要吃點巧克力來**減輕**壓力。

瑪莎：好，但在你吃點巧克力**放輕鬆**後，你最好還是要念書。

❺ focus (...) on... 把注意力、精力等集中在⋯⋯；專心於⋯⋯	• You should **focus** / concentrate **on** your studies, or there is no chance you will pass the entrance exams for college. 你應**專心於**學業，否則你不可能通過大學的入學考試。
❻ stay focused 保持專注	• Jonas always **stays focused** on whatever he does. 喬納斯做什麼事都很**專心**。
❼ treat [trit] *n.* 令某人開心的事；款待；請客 	• When I was a kid, chewing gum was a **treat**. 我小時，能吃到口香糖是**一大享受**。 • Let me foot / pay the bill. It's my **treat** today. 我來結帳。今天由我**請客**。
❽ treat [trit] *vt.* 對待(某人)；處理(某問題)；治療，醫治；請(某人) **treat sb well / badly** 善待 / 不善待某人 **treat sb like a dog / dirt** 不把某人當人看 **treat a problem** 處理某問題	• If you **treat** people **well**, they will **treat** you the same way. 你若**善待**大家，大家也會**善待**你。 • Jim's wife **treated** him **like a dog**. Eventually, he divorced her and has remained unmarried ever since. 吉姆的老婆**把**他**當狗看待**。他最後跟她離婚，從此一直保持未婚狀態。 • Tell me how you are going to **treat** this thorny **problem**. 告訴我你要怎麼**處理**這個棘手的**問題**。 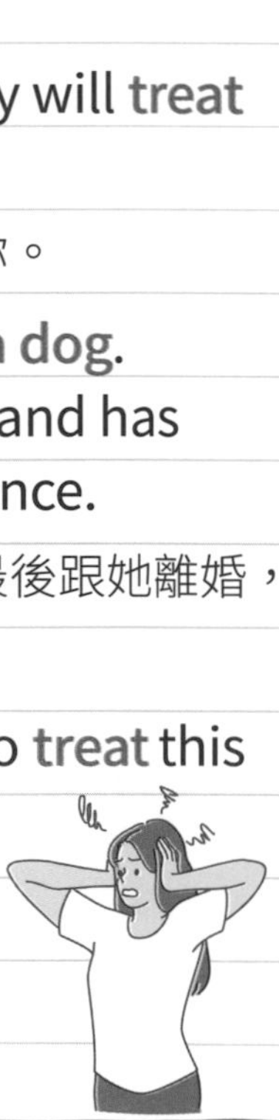

treat sb / an illness 醫治某人 / 治療某疾病 **treat sb to sth** 請某人吃 / 享受某物	• The doctor **treated** the patient with a new medicine. 醫生用新的藥物**治療**這位病人。 • It is indeed hard to **treat** this **illness**. 這種病確實很難**醫治**。 • I **treated** my girlfriend **to** a hearty dinner last night. 我昨晚**請**我女友**吃**了一頓豐盛的晚餐。 • Can you **treat** me **to** a movie? 你可以**請**我看場電影嗎？

Words in Use

Son: My homework is so difficult, Mom. I'll never finish it.

Mom: Just **stay focused**.

Son: I'll try, but it's hard.

Mom: If you **focus on** your homework, you can do it. And, if you do it well, I'll give you a **treat**—a big piece of chocolate cake.

Son: OK, Mom. Now, I think I can do it.

兒子：媽媽，回家功課好難寫。我永遠都寫不完了。

媽媽：只要**專心**就可以。

兒子：我會試試看，但這個功課好難。

媽媽：如果你**專心**寫功課，你就可以完成。而且，如果你寫得好，我會拿點心**請**你吃 —— 一大塊巧克力蛋糕。

兒子：好的，媽媽。現在我覺得我做得到了。

❾ map [mæp] *n.* 地圖 & *vt.* 在地圖上標示（三態為：map, mapped, mapped）

put a place / sb on the map
= make a place / sb famous
使某地方 / 某人出名

- Read the **map** and find where the small town is.
  查看**地圖**，找出該小鎮的位置。

- Ever since the smartphone came into being, very few people have used road **maps**.
  自從智慧型手機問世後，使用交通**地圖**的人少了許多。
- The delicious food the chef cooks has **put** his restaurant **on the map**.
  這位主廚燒得一手好菜，**使**他的餐廳**名聲大噪**。

- The news report has **put** our small town **on the map**.
  這則新聞報導**使**我們的小鎮**一舉成名**。

❿ map out...
詳細規劃……

- Nick had **mapped out** his career path long before he graduated from college.
  尼克早在他大學畢業前就已把他的職涯發展**規劃**好了。

⓫ read sb's mind
看透 / 了解某人的想法 / 心思

read sb's palm / face
算某人的手相 / 面相

- I can **read** your **mind**. You've got a crush on my sister.
  我**看透**你在想什麼。你暗戀我妹妹。
- The fortune-teller was a fake. He couldn't **read** my **palm** at all.
  這個算命師是冒牌的。他根本不會**算**我的**手相**。

⑫ a (wide) variety of... 各式各樣的……	• The newly opened store around the corner sells **a wide variety of** goods. 轉角處那家新開幕的店販賣**各式各樣的**商品。
⑬ potential [pəˋtɛnʃəl] *n.* 潛力（不可數）& *a.* 潛在的；可能的 **reach one's full potential** 完全發揮潛力	• As a teacher, I will do | all I can / my best | to help my students **reach their full potential**. 身為老師，我會盡力幫助我的學生**發揮他們最大的潛力**。 • Treat the young men well because they are our **potential** customers. 善待這群年輕人，因為他們是我們的**潛在**客戶。

Words in Use

Austin: Before I start this assignment, can you please **map out** exactly what you want me to do and when I should finish it?

Paula: Don't worry. You'll do a good job on it.

Austin: But I can't **read your mind**. I would really like more details about it first. I want to avoid **potential** problems.

Paula: Austin, you'll never **reach your full potential** if I tell you everything.

奧斯丁：在我開始這項工作之前，能麻煩妳**仔細規劃**好妳要我做的事情及期限嗎？

寶拉：別擔心。你能表現地很好。

奧斯丁：但我不是**妳肚子裡的蛔蟲**。我真的很想先知道更多細節。我想避開**可能發生的**問題。

寶拉：奧斯丁，如果我告訴你所有事情，你永遠也無法**完全發揮你的潛力**。

⓮ make the most of...
充分利用……

比較

make the best of...
盡力扭轉(不利的情勢，以創造好的契機)

- I'll be on business in New York. I'll | make the most / take full advantage | of this opportunity to polish up my spoken English.

  我會到紐約出差。我會**充分利用**這個機會精進我的英文會話能力。

- Though life is pretty tough, I'll **make the best of** it and carve (out) a bright future for myself.

  雖然生活很不好過，不過我會**盡力扭轉**這個不好的情況，並為自己開創光明的前途。

⓯ As the saying goes, "..."
= "...," so goes the saying.
俗云：「……。」

- **As the saying goes**, "One is never too old to learn."
  ="One is never too old to learn," **so goes the saying.**

  俗云：「學不厭老。」

學習的階段

⓰ threat
[θrɛt] *n.* 威脅

pose a threat / menace to...
對……構成威脅

- Drug abuse **poses a major** | threat / menace | to social stability.

  濫用藥物**對**社會安穩**構成重大威脅**。

⑰ threaten

[ˋθrɛtn̩] *vt.* & *vi.*

威脅

threaten to V

威脅要……

threaten sb

威脅某人

be threatening

(暴風雨) 即將來臨

• The hijackers **threatened to** blow up the plane if their demands were not met.

= The hijackers **threatened** that they would explode the plane if their demands were not met.

劫機者**威脅**若要求未獲滿足的話就要炸掉飛機。

• The robber **threatened** the bank clerk with a gun.　搶匪用槍**威脅**銀行行員。

• The wind is getting stronger and the clouds are gathering. It seems like a storm is | **threatening.** / fast approaching. / coming soon.

風逐漸增強，雲愈來愈多。看來暴風雨**要來了**。

Words in Use

Nick: You really should start doing your homework now. **As the saying goes,** "There is no time like the present."

Joy: I know. But I'm so occupied with the cleaning today. Can you help me with it?

Nick: Sorry. I want to **make the most of** such a beautiful day and take a walk along the river.

尼克：妳真的應該要現在開始寫作業了，**俗話說**：「把握當下。」

喬依：我知道。但我今天忙打掃忙翻了。你能幫忙嗎？

尼克：抱歉。我想要**充分利用**今天這美好的天氣去河邊散散步。

⑱ **Are you putting me on?** = Are you kidding (me)? = Are you pulling my leg? 你在開玩笑嗎？	• A: Cindy and I are getting married next week. B: **Are you putting me on?** You've known each other for only two months! A：我和辛蒂下星期就要結婚了。 B：**你是在開玩笑嗎？**你們彼此認識才兩個月而已！
⑲ **pencil** [ˋpɛnsḷ] *n.* 鉛筆 & *vt.* 用鉛筆寫 **with a pencil** 用（一支）鉛筆 **in pencil** 用鉛筆寫／塗 **pencil sb/sth in** 把某人／某事暫時安排進來	• Sam scribbled a note **with a pencil** / **in pencil** before rushing out of the door. 山姆**用鉛筆**草草寫了一張便條就匆匆出門了。 • The doctor is on holiday this week. Would you like me to **pencil** you **in** for next Wednesday at 10? 醫生這個星期度假去了，要不要我**把您暫定**在下星期三早上十點約診？ • The meeting is **penciled in** for August 10. 該會議**暫定**在八月十日召開。
⑳ **lips** [lɪps] *n.* 嘴唇（因有兩片，常用複數）	• Loose **lips** sink ships. **嘴巴**守不緊必會釀成大禍／口風不緊船艦沉。（諺語）

read my lips 好好聽著我要說的話 **lip service** 空話	• Don't tell Peter any secrets. He has loose **lips** / a big mouth. 別告訴彼得任何祕密。他守不住祕密。 • My **lips** are sealed. 我**口風**很緊，絕不洩密。 • **Read my lips**: John is by no means a man you can trust. **聽好**：約翰絕不是你可信賴的人。 • David keeps saying he'll help me whenever I'm in trouble, but he has never put his words into practice. I'm sick and tired of his **lip service**. 大衛不斷說只要我有困難他都會幫助我，但從未付諸行動。他的**空話**讓我厭惡透了。
㉑ **cut down on...** 減少……	• To lose weight, you should first **cut down on** the amount of sugar you consume. 你若想減肥，首先要**減少**你攝取的含糖量。

Words in Use

Brown: **Are you putting me on?** I can't lend you my **pencil**. I need it to take notes.

Leah: Come on, I need a **pencil** to take notes, too.

Brown: **Read my lips**: No! Go ask somebody else.

Leah: Fine!

布朗：**妳是在跟我開玩笑嗎？**我不能借妳**鉛筆**，我要用來做筆記。

莉雅：拜託，我也需要一支**鉛筆**做筆記。

布朗：**聽好**：不行！去跟別人借吧。

莉雅：好啦！

㉒ **be cut out for...** 能勝任……	• Why do you think you **are cut out** / competent **for** the job? 你為何認為你**能勝任**這份工作？
be cut out to be... 適合擔任……	• Tom is too shy, so I don't think he **is cut out to be** a teacher. 湯姆太害羞，因此我認為他並不**適合當**老師。
㉓ **bony** [ˈbonɪ] *a.* (魚體內) 多刺的	• Many Westerners don't like to eat fish because it's **bony**. 許多西方人不喜歡吃魚肉因為魚肉**多刺**。
比較 **thorny** [ˈθɔrnɪ] *a.* (體外) 多刺的； 棘手的 (問題)	• Those bushes are **thorny**. = Those bushes have thorns. 那些小樹叢**有刺**。 • Nobody dares to deal with that **thorny** problem. 沒人敢處理那個**棘手的**問題。
㉔ **make no bones about...** 直言不諱地指出……	• John's boss **made no bones about** his incompetence. 約翰的上司**開門見山就道出**他的無能 / 不適任。
㉕ **amount to +** 數字 總共是……	• All this **amounts to** $3,000. 這些東西**總共是**三千美元。
amount to nothing 一文不值	• If we don't attain / fulfill / reach / achieve the goal, all our efforts will **amount to nothing**. 我們如果沒達到目標，所有的努力全都會**白費**了。

❷❻ **spice** [spaɪs] *n.* 香料；刺激，趣味 & *vt.* 給……增加趣味

add spice to one's life
= spice up one's life
增添生活情趣

• Variety is the **spice** of life.
體驗不同的事物能增添生活**趣味**。（諺語）

• We need to take a trip abroad every now and then to **add spice to our lives.** / **spice up our lives.**
我們偶爾需要到國外走走以**增添生活情趣**。

常見的香料

mint 薄荷

ginger 薑

garlic 大蒜

chili 辣椒

cinnamon 肉桂

basil 羅勒葉

Words in Use

Arlene: I became rich because of my former boss.
Jacob: How so?
Arlene: Well, he **made no bones about** the fact that he thought I was stupid. He even said I would **amount to nothing.**
Jacob: How did that help you get rich?
Arlene: After that, I never wanted to have another boss again. So, I started my own business.

艾琳：我會變得富裕是因為我的前任老闆。
雅各：怎麼說？
艾琳：嗯，他**直接點出**他認為我很笨。他甚至說我簡直**一文不值**。
雅各：那件事如何幫助妳變有錢？
艾琳：那件事之後，我再也不想幫另一個老闆做事。所以我開了自己的公司。

㉗ haste [hest] *n.* 匆忙（不可數）	• When he heard the news, Paul left in **haste** / a rush / a hurry, without saying goodbye to us. 保羅聽到這消息時就**匆匆**離去，連再見也沒對我們說一聲。 • Marry in **haste**, repent at leisure. **匆匆**結婚，慢慢後悔 / 草率結婚後悔多。（諺語） • More **haste**, less speed. = Haste makes waste. 欲**速**則不達。（諺語）
㉘ hurry up 動作快 **hurry sb up** 使某人加快速度	• **Hurry up** or we'll miss the train. = Make it snappy or we'll miss the train. **動作快一點**，否則我們就要趕不上火車了。 • **Hurry** Philip **up**, or we'll be late for the meeting. 叫菲利浦**動作快一點**，否則我們開會要遲到了。
㉙ halt [hɔlt] *n.* 停止 **bring... to a halt** 使……停頓	• The power failure yesterday afternoon **brought** our work **to a halt**. 昨天下午停電**使**我們的工作**停擺**了。
㉚ grind to a halt = **grind to a standstill** 慢慢停頓下來	• If the government doesn't take immediate action to deal with the economic recession, every industry will **grind to a halt**. 如果政府不立即採取行動處理經濟不景氣，各行各業將會**陷入停頓**。

(grind 的三態為：grind, ground [graund], ground)

道路交通常見物品

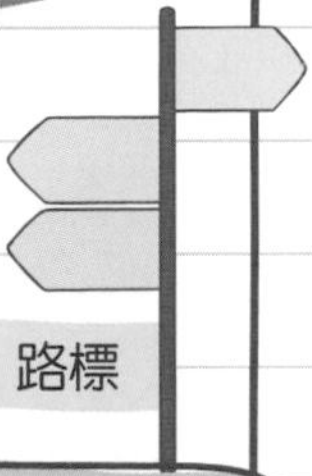

signpost 路標

• Because of a car accident ahead, the traffic **ground to a halt.**

由於前面發生車禍，交通**陷入了癱瘓**。

roadblock 路障

traffic light 紅綠燈

traffic cone 交通錐

traffic sign 交通標誌

Words in Use

Joshua: Hey, why are we going so slowly? **Hurry up!**

Mona: Don't be in such **haste**. Traffic has **ground to a halt**. I think there is an accident up ahead.

Joshua: Oh, no. I'll be late for an important meeting.

Mona: Hopefully, we will start moving again soon. But there's no way I can **hurry up** the traffic myself.

Joshua: Yes, I know.

喬書亞： 嘿，我們為什麼這麼慢？**動作快一點**！

夢娜： 別這麼**匆忙**。車流**停下來**了。我想前方應該是有車禍。

喬書亞： 喔，不。我有個重要的會議要遲到了。

夢娜： 希望我們能趕快開始動。但光靠我一個人可沒辦法**使車流加快速度**。

喬書亞： 是，我知道。

Unit 12

Exercises
練習題

看圖連連看

❶

❷

❸

map | bony | feel at ease

選出正解

❶ It's hard to stay ______________ when the TV is on.

(A) uneasy (B) thorny

(C) focused (D) difficult

❷ Greg devoted himself to helping students reach their full ______________.

(A) potential (B) threat

(C) spice (D) haste

句子填空

halt | amount | penciled | threatened | treats

❶ The assistant ______________ me in for an appointment with Dr. Dylan.

❷ I'm glad that Sarah's boyfriend ______________ her well.

❸ The earthquake has brought all trains to a(n) ______________.

❹ Our purchases ______________ to $1,000 in total.

❺ Karen ______________ to divorce Charles if he doesn't quit smoking.

句子重組

❶ and went hiking / the beautiful day / made / Sam / the most of

____

____.

❷ cut out / because / Ben was replaced / he wasn't / for the job

____

____.

❸ no bones / The customer / his dissatisfaction / made / about

____

____.

Notes

Unit 13

- [x] ❶ a nervous breakdown
- [ ] ❷ break down
- [ ] ❸ break a promise
- [ ] ❹ break the law
- [ ] ❺ break in...
- [ ] ❻ break a record
- [ ] ❼ (sth) break
- [ ] ❽ break out
- [ ] ❾ break into...
- [ ] ❿ day is breaking
- [ ] ⓫ break up with sb
- [ ] ⓬ seclusion
- [ ] ⓭ be reduced to + V-ing
- [ ] ⓮ be hospitalized
- [ ] ⓯ horizon
- [ ] ⓰ broaden one's horizons
- [ ] ⓱ efficient
- [ ] ⓲ effective
- [ ] ⓳ take effect
- [ ] ⓴ realize one's dreams
- [ ] ㉑ a dream come true
- [ ] ㉒ hit the sack
- [ ] ㉓ heyday
- [ ] ㉔ set
- [ ] ㉕ set
- [ ] ㉖ set a good example
- [ ] ㉗ set out for + 地方
- [ ] ㉘ set off a bomb
- [ ] ㉙ set up...
- [ ] ㉚ set sb up

Unit 13

❶ a nervous breakdown
精神崩潰

breakdown
[ˋbrek͵daʊn] *n.*
(機器) 故障

- Sarah was on the verge of **a nervous breakdown** after she heard the terrible news.
  莎拉聽到噩耗後**精神**幾近**崩潰**。
- The **breakdown** of your car was due to a mechanical failure.
  你的車**拋錨**是機械故障造成的。

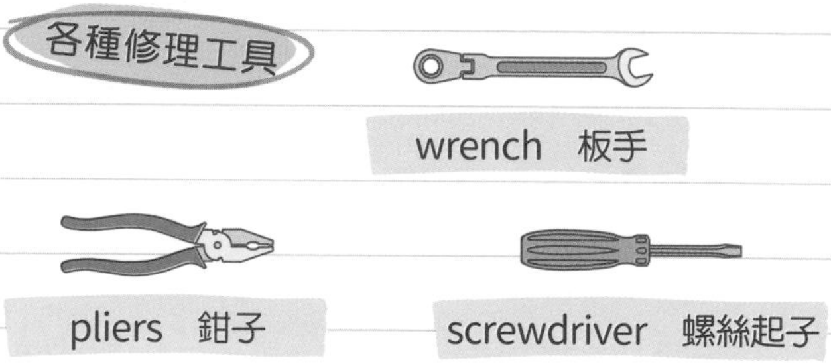

❷ break down
(尤指汽車) 拋錨，故障 (break 的三態為：break, broke [brok], broken [ˋbrokn̩])

- Our car **broke down** halfway home, so we had to walk the rest of the way back.
  我們的車子在回家的半途**拋錨**，因此我們得一路走回去。

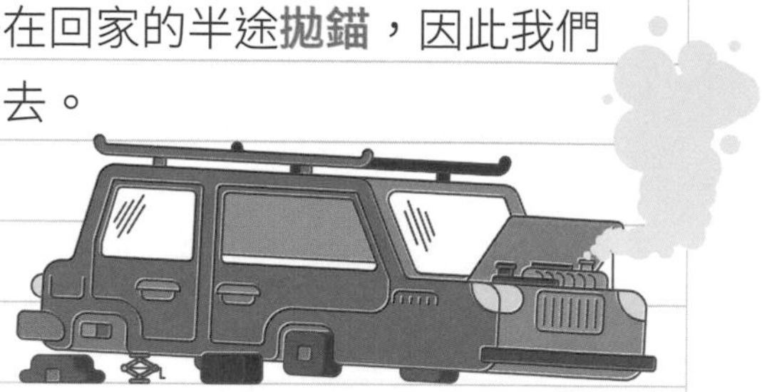

❸ break a promise
食言，失信

- If you **break a promise**, people will think you are unreliable.
  你若**食言**，大家會認為你這個人不可靠。

Unit 13

④ break the law
= violate the law
犯法

- You'll be put in jail / prison if you **break the law**.
你若**犯法**就會坐牢。
- Charles was fined NT$6,000 for **breaking** the speed limit.
=Charles was fined NT$6,000 for speeding.
查爾斯因為**超**速被罰新臺幣六千元。

⑤ break in...
將 (新鞋) 穿合腳

- It took me almost a month to **break in** my new shoes.
我花了幾近一個月才**把**新鞋**穿合腳**。

Words in Use

Tammy: I had a **breakdown** this morning.
Alvin: Oh, no! Are you OK? Is the workload getting too much for you?
Tammy: Not **a *nervous* breakdown**, Alvin; my car **broke down**. Could you give me a ride home tonight?
Alvin: Of course. I promise I won't leave without you. And I never **break** my **promise**!

譚美：我今天早上很**崩潰**。
艾爾文：喔，不！妳還好嗎？工作量對妳來說是不是太多？
譚美：艾爾文，不是我**精神崩潰**，是我的車子**拋錨**了。你今晚可以載我回家嗎？
艾爾文：當然。我保證我不會拋下妳離開。我從不**失信**！

❻ break a record
打破紀錄

set a record
寫下／創下紀錄

keep a record
保持紀錄

- The 100-meter runner **set a new record** three years ago and **kept** it for two years. Unfortunately, **the record was broken** by another runner this year.
  這位百米賽跑選手三年前**創下**了新**紀錄**，這項紀錄他**保持**了兩年。很不幸，今年另一位選手**打破**了這項**紀錄**。

❼ (sth) break
(尤指電器、手錶、儀器等) 損壞／不能運作

break sth
= damage sth
把某物弄壞

- My watch has **broken** / doesn't work now. I guess I need to buy a new one.
  我的錶**壞**了。我想我得買一只新的。
- I have **broken** my brand-new computer, so I'll have to get by with my old one.
  我**把**我全新的電腦**弄壞**了，因此我只好將就使用我那臺舊電腦了。

❽ break out
(尤指戰爭、疾病) 爆發

- Kevin joined the army soon after war **broke out.**
  戰爭**爆發**沒多久凱文便從軍了。

❾ break into...
闖入……

• A thief **broke into** my house and took all the jewelry he could find.
有個小偷**闖入**我的房子，把他能找到的珠寶全都拿走了。

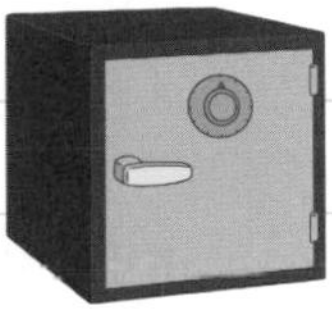

❿ day is breaking
= dawn is breaking
破曉

• We set out for Alishan just as **day / dawn was breaking**.
我們於**破曉時分**前往阿里山。

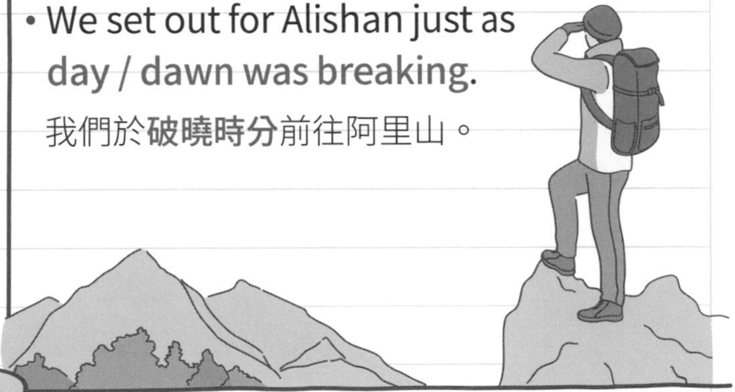

Words in Use

Michael: My alarm clock has **broken**. What time is it?
Jessica: Well, **day is breaking**, so it must be around 5 a.m. Let's get up and watch the sunrise.
Michael: Wow—5 a.m. I must've **broken** my **record**. I don't think I've ever woken up before 6:30. I'm going back to sleep, then.

麥可： 我的鬧鐘**壞掉了**。現在幾點？
潔西卡： 嗯，剛**破曉**，所以一定是早上五點左右。我們起床去看日出吧。
麥可： 哇 —— 早上五點。我肯定**破了**自己的**紀錄**。我想我未曾在六點半之前起床過。那麼，我要回去睡覺了。

⑪ **break up with sb** 與某人分手	• Ever since Paul **broke up with** Gina, he has led / lived a secluded life. 保羅自從**與**吉娜**分手**後便過著離群索居的生活。 ⋆ secluded [sɪˋkludɪd] *a.* 與世隔絕的
⑫ **seclusion** [sɪˋkluʒən] *n.* 幽僻，清淨	• I like the **seclusion** and peace of country life. 我喜歡鄉間生活的**幽僻寧靜**。
⑬ **be reduced to + V-ing** 淪落到……的地步	• Much to my surprise, the billionaire was eventually **reduced to** begging for a living. 令我大感驚訝的是，這位億萬富豪最後竟**淪落到**靠乞討維生**的地步**。
⑭ **be hospitalized** 住院 **hospitalize** [ˋhɑspɪtḷˏaɪz] *vt.* 使住院治療(常用被動)	• Frank **was hospitalized** two months ago because he had a sudden stroke. 法蘭克兩個月前突然中風**住院**了。 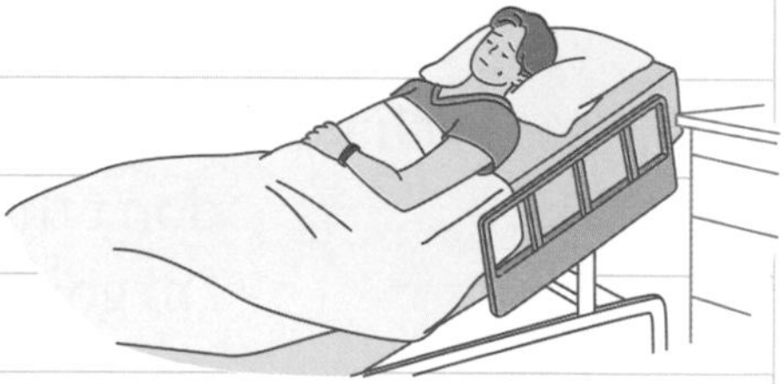
⑮ **horizon** [həˋraɪzṇ] *n.* 地平線；海平線 **be on the horizon**	• The sun is rising above the **horizon**. 太陽從**地平線**冉冉升起。 • Look! There's a ship on the **horizon**. 瞧！**海平線**上有艘船。

= be likely to happen / exist 即將發生 / 問世	• A new drug **is on the horizon** for the treatment of this strange disease. 一種專治這種怪病的新藥**即將問世**。
⑯ **broaden one's horizons** 增廣見聞	• There is no doubt that traveling **broadens our horizons.** 毫無疑問，旅遊可讓我們**增廣見聞**。

TIPS

此處 horizons 恆用複數，表示「範圍」、「眼界」。

Words in Use

Thomas: What are you doing here, Rachel? I thought you were going traveling to **broaden your horizons.**

Rachel: That was the plan. Unfortunately, my mom **was hospitalized** with a heart problem.

Thomas: Oh, I'm really sorry to hear that. I hope she gets better soon.

Rachel: Thanks, Thomas. Hopefully a new treatment **is on the horizon.**

湯瑪士：瑞秋，妳在這裡做什麼？我以為妳要為了**增廣見聞**去旅遊。

瑞秋：原本計畫是那樣。但不幸地，我媽媽心臟出問題**住院了**。

湯瑪士：喔，聽到這消息我真的很難過。希望她早日康復。

瑞秋：謝謝你，湯瑪士。希望**很快會有**新的治療方式。

⑰ **efficient**

[ɪˋfɪʃənt] *a.*

有效率的

• All bosses like **efficient** employees.

所有的老闆都喜歡做事**有效率的**員工。

⑱ **effective**

[ɪˋfɛktɪv] *a.*

產生作用的

• This medicine is highly **effective** in treating the flu.

這種藥在治療流感方面很**有效**。

⑲ **take effect**

(法律、規定、政策等) 生效；(藥物) 發生作用，見效

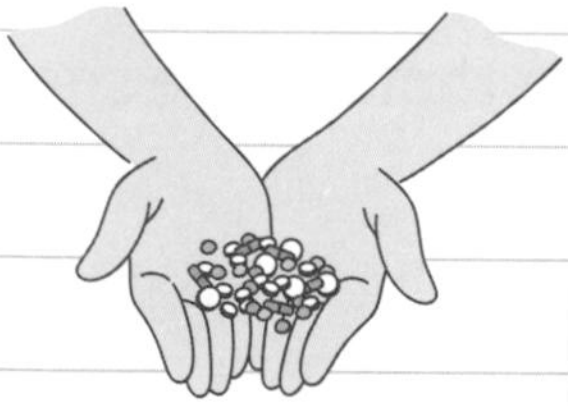

• The new regulations will **take effect** as of January 1.

=The new regulations will

| go into effect
come into effect
be effective | from January 1. |

這些新規定將自元月一日起**生效**。

• This medicine will **take effect** in an hour.

這種藥一個小時後就會**見效**。

⑳ **realize one's dreams**

實現夢想

• Only by working hard can you **realize your dreams**.

=Only by working hard can you make your dreams come true.

你唯有努力才能**實現夢想**。

㉑ a dream come true
美夢成真

- When Sandy promised to marry me, I felt it was really a beautiful dream come true.
  珊蒂答應嫁給我時，我有一種美夢成真的感覺。
- Every moment (which is) spent with you is like a beautiful dream come true.
  跟妳在一起的每個時刻就如美夢成真一般。

TIPS

本片語原為 a dream which has come true，但實際使用時 which has 已省略。

Words in Use

Katie: I am so happy here, Daniel. It's a dream come true to live by the ocean.

Daniel: I'm glad I could help you realize your dreams, Katie.

Katie: I just wish the house didn't cost us so much money.

Daniel: That doesn't matter. Happiness is above wealth in my eyes.

凱蒂： 丹尼爾，我在這裡很高興。住在海邊真是美夢成真。

丹尼爾： 凱蒂，我很慶幸可以幫妳實現夢想。

凱蒂： 我只希望這房子沒有讓我們花費那麼多錢。

丹尼爾： 這不重要。對我而言，幸福比財富重要。

㉒ **hit the sack** = hit the hay = go to bed 去睡覺 * sack [sæk] *n.* 大布袋 hay [he] *n.* 乾草	• Turn off the TV. It's time to **hit the sack**. 把電視關掉。是該睡的時候了。 
㉓ **heyday** [ˋhede] *n.* 全盛時期	• In her **heyday**, the world-famous singer made tens of millions of dollars a year. 這位全球知名的歌手在她的**鼎盛時期**，每年都可賺進數千萬美元。
㉔ **set** [sɛt] *vt.* 放置；備妥； 決定；設定 (三態同形) set the table 擺碗筷 set to work + V-ing = start + V-ing 開始做某事 set the alarm clock 設定鬧鐘	• The guests are coming. Help me **set the table** now. 客人就要到了。現在就幫我**上餐具擺好桌子**吧。 • Peter has **set to work** writing a memoir about his teaching career. 彼得已經**著手開始**撰寫他教書生涯的回憶錄。 * memoir [ˋmɛmwɑr] *n.* 回憶錄 • Be sure to **set the alarm clock** for 6 tomorrow morning. 務必要把**鬧鐘設定**在明天早上六點。 

Unit 13

㉕ **set** [sɛt] *a.* 準備好的，預定好的 **be set / scheduled to V** 準備好 / 預定要…… **be all set for...** **= be ready for...** **= be prepared for...** 為……已準備妥當	• Ready, (get) **set**, go! 各就各位，**預備**，跑（鳴槍）！ • The meeting **is set to** take place at 10 this morning. =The meeting **is scheduled to** take place at 10 this morning. 會議**預定**在今天早上十點舉行。 • I'm **all set for** the exam tomorrow. 明天的考試我**準備好了**。 • Is everything **all set for** the party? 派對的籌備一切都**就緒**了嗎？

Words in Use

Richard: Well, it's time for me to **hit the sack**.

Kelly: It's only 9 o'clock! In your **heyday**, you used to stay up till midnight!

Richard: That was before I was a manager. I've got a very important meeting that's **scheduled to** start first thing in the morning. Good night!

理查：嗯，該是我去**睡覺**的時候了。

凱莉：現在才九點鐘！在你的**年少時代**，你都會熬夜到半夜！

理查：那是我成為經理之前。我明天一大早**排定**了一場非常重要的會議。晚安！

㉖ set a good example

樹立一個好榜樣

- You should **set a good example** to / for your younger brother.

  你應為弟弟**樹立一個好榜樣**。

㉗ set out for + 地方

= set off for + 地方

出發前往某地

- Mr. Lee | **set out** / **set off** / **departed** / **left** | for Tokyo early this morning.

  李先生今天一大早就**出發前往**東京了。

㉘ set off a bomb

使炸彈爆炸

set off firecrackers / fireworks

施放鞭炮 / 煙火

- Terrorists **set off a bomb** near the city center, killing 20 people on the spot and injuring many others.

  恐怖分子在市中心附近**引爆一枚炸彈**，當場讓二十人喪命，另有多人受傷。

- The Chinese **set off firecrackers** to ring in the Lunar New Year.

  華人**放鞭炮**以迎接農曆新年的到來。

危險爆裂物

missile 飛彈

grenade 手榴彈

bomb 炸彈

dynamite 炸藥

㉙ set up... = establish... 設立 (機構、組織、系統、制度等)	• We've decided to set up / establish a new management system to help improve the efficiency of our company. 我們已決定**設立**一個新的管理制度以協助改善公司的效率。 
㉚ set sb up = frame sb 誣陷 / 陷害某人	• I got very mad when I learned my best friend Jerry had set me up. 我獲知我最要好的朋友傑瑞**陷害**我時，我氣極了。

Words in Use

Son: I'm sad. I wish Dad were here to set off the fireworks.

Mom: You know he would be if he could, but he set off for Tainan right after breakfast. He's setting up a new branch of his company. Now, be strong and set a good example for your little brother.

Son: OK, Mom.

兒子： 我好難過。我希望爸爸可以在這**放煙火**。

媽媽： 你知道如果他可以的話他會來的，可是他吃完早餐就**出發去**臺南了。他要**設立**公司的新分部。來，堅強點，為你的弟弟**立個好榜樣**。

兒子： 好的，媽媽。

Unit 13

Exercises
練習題

看圖選單字

❶

☐ break a promise
☐ break a record
☐ break down

❷

☐ hit the sack
☐ set a good example
☐ a dream come true

❸

☐ set off a bomb
☐ set the table
☐ break the law

選出正解

❶ Annie will set (out / up) for the airport this afternoon.

❷ Victor (realized / made) his dreams when he started his own company.

❸ Taking this trip will broaden your (horizon / horizons).

❹ I called the police because a man broke (out / into) my house.

❺ The new law will take (effect / affect) starting from tomorrow.

句子填空

seclusion | nervous | record | example | heyday

❶ Everyone cheered when the athlete broke the world

____________.

❷ Carl set a good ____________ to his siblings by working hard.

❸ In their ____________, the band sold millions of records worldwide.

❹ Andy had a(n) ____________ breakdown due to his heavy workload.

❺ The hiker is enjoying the ____________ of the mountains.

句子重組

❶ was / her colleague / Fiona / set up / by

____

____.

❷ the trip to / Phil / is all set / Paris / for

____

____.

❸ Dylan / living / was / on the streets / reduced to

____

____.

Notes

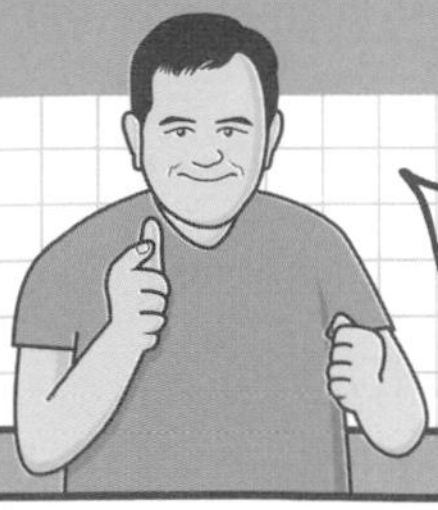

Unit 14

- [x] ❶ (as) clear as day
- [ ] ❷ be dressed in...
- [ ] ❸ beyond description
- [ ] ❹ It's beyond me...
- [ ] ❺ 有關 want 的重要用法
- [ ] ❻ shortcut
- [ ] ❼ master
- [ ] ❽ trade-off
- [ ] ❾ be full of...
- [ ] ❿ in the face of...
- [ ] ⓫ quit
- [ ] ⓬ all in all, ...
- [ ] ⓭ insist on + N/V-ing
- [ ] ⓮ hype
- [ ] ⓯ for good
- [ ] ⓰ cut to the chase
- [ ] ⓱ bush
- [ ] ⓲ bushy
- [ ] ⓳ on condition that...
- [ ] ⓴ reach a record high / low
- [ ] ㉑ caregiver
- [ ] ㉒ cheap
- [ ] ㉓ slimy
- [ ] ㉔ discount
- [ ] ㉕ discreet
- [ ] ㉖ distinct
- [ ] ㉗ classic
- [ ] ㉘ historic
- [ ] ㉙ be around the corner
- [ ] ㉚ give A an advantage over B

Unit 14

❶ (as) clear as day

(像晴天那樣清晰) 顯而易見的

- It's **(as) clear as day** that the host team will beat the visiting team.

= It's certain that the host team will defeat the visiting team.

顯而易見的是，地主隊肯定會打敗客隊。

❷ be dressed in...

穿著……

比較

put on...

穿上……(指動作)

be dressed to kill

穿得很帥氣 / 火辣 (耀人眼目)

- The man (who is) **dressed in** a dark suit is our general manager.

= The man (who is) wearing a dark suit is our general manager.

那位**穿著**深色西裝的男士是我們總經理。

- Dad **put on** a grey suit before driving to work.

老爸**穿上**一套灰色西裝後便開車上班去了。

- Wow! Look at Mary! She's really **dressed to kill**!

哇！瞧瞧瑪麗！她**穿得可真吸睛**！

- Peter **was dressed to kill** at the party, knowing that the girl he had a crush on would show up.

彼得在派對上**穿得很帥氣**，因為他知道他暗戀的那個女孩子會到場。

❸ **beyond description** 非筆墨所能形容	• The girl's beauty is indeed **beyond description.** = The girl is indeed beautiful **beyond description.** 這女孩確實美得**難以形容**。
❹ **It's beyond me...** 我無法理解……	• | **It's beyond me** / I can't understand | why Mary divorced Walter. **我無法理解**瑪麗為何跟華特離婚了。

Words in Use

Jack: Wow! That girl is beautiful **beyond description**!

Laura: You're right! That's Mandy. She's really **dressed to kill** tonight.

Jack: Do you know if she has a boyfriend?

Laura: Actually, her boyfriend just broke up with her, so she's single.

Jack: **It's beyond me** why anyone would break up with her!

傑克： 哇！那女孩美得**難以形容**！

蘿拉： 你說得對！那是曼蒂。她今晚真是**穿得很吸睛**。

傑克： 你知道她有沒有男友嗎？

蘿拉： 其實，她男友才剛與她分手，所以她單身中。

傑克： **我無法理解**為何有人會想跟她分手！

❺ 有關 want 的重要用法

- Excuse me. You're **wanted** on the phone.
  不好意思，有你的電話。
- Waste not, **want** not.
  =If you don't waste anything, you'll lack nothing.
  不浪費，就不虞**匱乏** / 勤儉節約，吃穿不缺。（諺語）

❻ shortcut
[ˋʃɔrtˏkʌt] *n.*
捷徑

a shortcut to + N/V-ing
……的捷徑

- There is no shortcut to learn English. (×)
  → There is no **shortcut to** learning English. (○)
  學習英文無**捷徑**。

❼ master
[ˋmæstɚ] *n.*
大師；主人 & *vt.* 精通

a master of...
……的大師

- Mr. Bobson is a skilled artist. Many people consider him **a master of** pastel painting.
  鮑勃遜先生是個技藝高超的畫家。許多人都認為他是粉彩畫作**大師**。
  * pastel [pæsˋtɛl] *n.* 粉彩，蠟筆
- It is impossible to **master** a language overnight.
  一夕之間就想把某種語言**學通**是不可能的事。

❽ **trade-off** [ˋtredɔf] *n.* (為了得到好處而必須付出的) 妥協，代價	• One **trade-off** of online shopping is that you give up some privacy when browsing these websites. 網路購物的**代價**就是你在瀏覽那些網站時得放棄一些隱私。 
❾ **be full of...** = be filled with... 充滿……	• The road to success **is** always **full of** / **filled with** potholes. 通往成功的道路總是**充滿**坑洞。 * pothole [ˋpɑt͵hol] *n.* 坑洞

Words in Use

Gavin: You're **a master of** dance, Marie! You'll be a professional dancer in no time.

Marie: I've still got a lot to learn. After all, there's no **shortcut to** becoming a professional dancer.

Gavin: I have faith in you. They say the road to success **is full of** potholes, but I'm sure you'll dance right round them!

蓋文：瑪莉，妳是舞蹈**大師**！妳很快就會成為專業舞者。

瑪莉：我還有很多需要學習。畢竟，成為專業舞者並沒有**捷徑**。

蓋文：我對妳有信心。大家都說，通往成功的道路總是**充滿**坑洞，但我相信妳會跳呀跳地越過這些坑洞！

⑩ **in the face of...** 面對……	• Success comes to those who never give up **in the face of** any challenge. 成功屬於那些**面對**任何挑戰從不放棄的人。
⑪ **quit** [kwɪt] *vi.* & *vt.* 放棄，投降；離職（三態同形）	• Winners never **quit**; quitters never win. 勝利者絕不會**放棄**；放棄者絕不會獲勝。 （諺語）
⑫ **all in all, ...** = **to sum up, ...** 總之，……	• **All in all,** if you persist in learning English, you'll master this language someday. **總之**，如果你堅持下去持續學習英文，總有一天你會精通英文。

學習的形式

⑬ **insist on + N/V-ing** (執著地) 堅持要求…… 比較 **persist in + N/V-ing** (從不放棄地) 堅持……	• I told James that the meal was on me, but he **insisted on** paying for it. 我跟詹姆士說這頓飯我請客，不過他**堅持**要付錢。 • Whatever David does, he **persists in** doing it well. 大衛不論做什麼事，他都會**堅持**要把它做好。

Words in Use

Amelia: What's wrong, Darren?

Darren: Nothing.

Amelia: Come on—tell me. I **insist on** knowing!

Darren: OK. Ever since our school switched to **distance learning**, I'm finding teaching too difficult. To sum up, I want to **quit**.

Amelia: That's not like you. You usually thrive **in the face of** a challenge.

艾蜜莉亞：戴倫，你怎麼了？

戴倫：沒事。

艾蜜莉亞：來啦 —— 告訴我。我**堅持**一定要知道！

戴倫：好吧。自從我們學校換成**遠距學習**，我覺得教書太困難了。總而言之，我想**辭職**。

艾蜜莉亞：這不像你。你通常**遇到**挑戰都會有出色的表現。

⑭ hype

[haɪp] *n.*

炒作；誇大的宣傳 (不可數)

media hype

媒體炒作 / 大肆宣傳

• Despite the **media hype**, I found the new film starring Tom Cruise very disappointing.

儘管**媒體的大肆宣傳**，我卻覺得這部由阿湯哥主演的新電影令人非常失望。

電影的種類

⑮ for good

= **forever**

[fɚˋɛvɚ]

= **eternally**

[ɪˋtɝnəlɪ] 永遠

• Trust me, Jane. I'll love you | **for good.** / **forever.** / **eternally.**

相信我，阿珍。我會**永遠**愛妳。

⑯ cut to the chase

切入正題 / 重點

• We don't have enough time, so I'm going to | **cut to the chase.** / get to the point.

我們時間不多了，因此我就**切入重點**了。

⑰ bush

[bʊʃ] *n.* 矮樹叢

beat around the bush

(講話) 拐彎抹角，兜圈子

• Don't **beat around the bush**. Get to the point!

別**拐彎抹角**。打開天窗說亮話吧！

⑱ **bushy** [ˋbʊʃɪ] *a.* (毛髮) 濃密的	• That young man has big eyes and **bushy** eyebrows. 那位年輕人有一雙**濃**眉大眼。
be / look bright-eyed and bushy-tailed 愉快並精神抖擻的	• You **look bright-eyed and bushy-tailed** today, John. Do you have some good news? 約翰，你今天一臉**容光煥發**的樣子。有什麼好消息嗎？

Unit 14

Words in Use

Jenny: What did you think of the movie?

Mark: Well, it was OK, I guess. I mean, it wasn't bad. Hmm... It was decent, I suppose.

Jenny: Don't **beat around the bush**. **Cut to the chase** and give me a straight answer!

Mark: It didn't live up to the **hype**. It was disappointing.

珍妮： 你認為那部電影如何？

馬克： 嗯，我想還可以。我的意思是，它並不糟。嗯……。我想它是部像樣的電影。

珍妮： 不要**拐彎抹角**。**切入重點**告訴我直接的回答！

馬克： 它沒有跟**宣傳**上說的一樣好。讓人頗為失望。

⑲ on condition that... 條件是……	• I will tell you the story on condition that my name is not revealed. =I will tell you the story on condition of anonymity. =I will tell you the story provided (that) / if / as long as I'm not identified. 我會把事情經過告訴你，**條件是**不得透露我的名字。/ 如果我的身分不被發現，我就會把事情經過告訴你。 * reveal [rɪˋvil] *vt.* 透露 anonymity [ˌænəˋnɪmətɪ] *n.* 匿名 identify [aɪˋdɛntəˌfaɪ] *vt.* 認出

TIPS

本片語可替換為 if（如果）、provided that（設若，如果）、as long as（只要），均視作連接詞。

⑳ reach a record high / low 創下歷史新高 / 低	• Because of the bad economy, the unemployment rate in that country reached a record high last year. 由於經濟不景氣，該國的失業率去年**創下歷史新高**。

TIPS

此處 record [ˋrɛkɚd] 是形容詞，表示「破紀錄的」。

㉑ caregiver [ˋkɛrˌgɪvɚ] *n.* 看護者	• Many families in Taiwan hire foreign in-home caregivers. 臺灣有許多家庭雇用外籍居家**看護**。

㉒ cheap

[tʃip] *a.*

便宜的（修飾事物）；吝嗇的（修飾人）

• Everything they sell in that store is quite **cheap**.

那家店賣的每樣東西都挺**便宜**的。

• Biking is a **cheap** way to get around.

騎腳踏車是到處逛逛的**省錢**方式。

• Paul is **cheap** / **stingy**. He never treats people to a meal.

保羅很**小氣**。他從不會請人吃飯。

Words in Use

Journalist: What will the unemployment figures say when they're released tomorrow?

Politician: I'm sorry—I can't tell you that.

Journalist: Come on. I need it for my story.

Politician: OK. I'll tell you **on condition that** you keep my name out of the story. Unemployment has **reached a record high**. The country is in big trouble.

記者：明天失業率的數據公布會顯示什麼呢？

政治人物：很抱歉 —— 我無法告知。

記者：拜託。我的報導需要這項資訊。

政治人物：好吧。我會告訴你，**條件是**你的報導不能包含我的名字。失業率已**創下史上最高**。全國已陷入重大危機之中。

㉓ slimy

[ˋslaɪmɪ] *a.*

黏答答的；(為人) 假惺惺的

- Eels are slimy and difficult to hold.

  鰻魚黏答答的，很難抓住。

- Don't you think most politicians are slimy and cunning?

  你不覺得大多數政客對人假裝熱心，心地卻很狡猾嗎？

  * cunning [ˋkʌnɪŋ] *a.* 狡猾的

㉔ discount

[ˋdɪskaʊnt] *n.*

折扣 &

[dɪsˋkaʊnt] *vt.*

打折

offer a discount on...

針對……打折優惠

- That supermarket is offering a 20% discount on all skincare products this weekend.

= That supermarket is selling all skincare products at a 20% discount this weekend.

  那家超市會在這週末針對所有的護膚產品打八折優惠。

㉕ discreet

[dɪˋskrit] *a.*

(言行) 謹慎的

比較

discrete

[dɪˋskrit] *a.*

= **separate**

[ˋsɛpərɪt]

分離的，個別的

- A career diplomat is always discreet about what he says and does.

  職業外交官一向言行謹慎。

- This company is composed of three discrete departments.

  這家公司由三個個別部門組成。

㉖ distinct
[dɪˋstɪŋkt] *a.*
明顯的；清晰的

比較
distinctive
[dɪˋstɪŋktɪv] *a.*
獨特的，很特別的

- Mr. Smith speaks English with a very **distinct** southern accent.
  史密斯先生說英語時帶著**明顯的**南方口音。
- The man's voice was low, but every word he said was **distinct**.
  該男子講話的聲音很低沉，不過他說的每個字都很**清晰**。
- I'm attracted to the singer's **distinctive** voice.
  這位歌手的**獨特**嗓音很吸引我。

Words in Use

Waitress: Can I interest you in the fried eel? We're **offering a** 50% **discount on** all orders.
Customer: I don't really like eel. It's too **slimy** for me.
Waitress: Then how about some oysters? They have a very **distinctive** taste.
Customer: They're not my cup of tea, either. Let me look at the menu.

服務生：您有興趣試試看炒鰻魚嗎？本店所有訂單都有**提供半價折扣**。
顧客：我不太喜歡鰻魚。對我來說太**黏糊**了。
服務生：那麼一些生蠔如何？它們有相當**獨特的**味道。
顧客：它們也不合我胃口。讓我看看菜單。

㉗ classic

[ˋklæsɪk] *a.*

經典的，歷久不衰的 & *n.* 經典作品

比較

classical

[ˋklæsɪkḷ] *a.*

古典的

- *Gone with the Wind* is a **classic** novel.
  《亂世佳人》是一本**經典**小說。
- Henry Mancini wrote many **classic** songs, one of which is "Moon River."
  亨利．曼西尼寫過許多**經典的**歌曲，其中一首就是《月河》。
- Even today, "Moon River" is widely admired as a **classic**.
  即使在今日，《月河》仍廣受讚譽為**經典之作**。
- I'm not very much into **classical** music.
  我不是很喜歡**古典**樂。

古典樂器

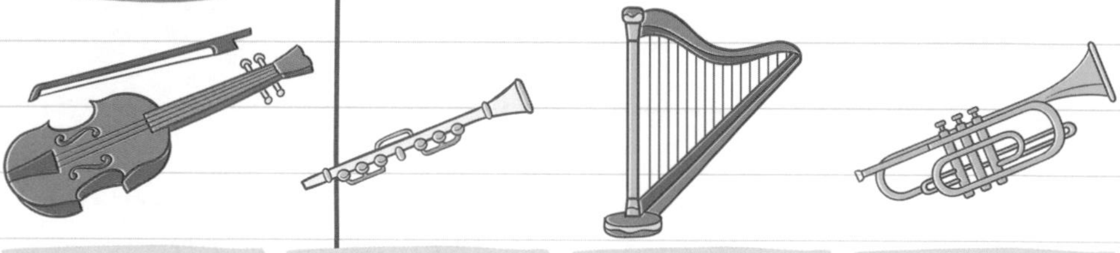

violin 小提琴　oboe 雙簧管　harp 豎琴　trumpet 小號

㉘ historic

[hɪsˋtɔrɪk] *a.*

在歷史上占有重要地位的，可留名青史的

比較

historical

[hɪsˋtɔrɪkḷ] *a.*

(有關) 歷史的

- The Confucian Temple in Tainan is no doubt a **historic** building.
  位於臺南的孔廟毫無疑問是**具有歷史價值的**建築物。
- Have you read the **historical** novel entitled *Journey to the West*?
  那本名為《西遊記》的**歷史**小說你看過了嗎？

㉙ **be around the corner** = be coming soon = be fast approaching 即將到來	• Frogs begin to croak when summer is **around the corner.** 夏天**快到**時，青蛙就開始呱呱叫了。 
㉚ **give A an advantage over B** 使 A 比 B 占優勢	• David's ability to speak French **gave** him **an advantage over** his opponents. 大衛能說法語，這**使得**他**比**對手**占到優勢**。 ⋆ opponent [əˋponənt] *n.* 對手，敵手

Words in Use

Ray: That song is beautiful. What is it?

Mina: It's a **classic** song called "Let It Be" by The Beatles. I'm learning to play it on the violin for a competition.

Ray: Cool. When's the competition?

Mina: Actually, it's just **around the corner**—it's next week.

Ray: I'm sure you will win!

阿瑞： 那首歌真美。歌名是什麼？

米娜： 這是一首披頭四樂團的**經典**曲，歌名叫《讓它去》。我正為了一場比賽學習如何拉小提琴演奏這首歌。

阿瑞： 太酷了。比賽是什麼時候？

米娜： 其實，就**快到了**——在下週。

阿瑞： 我相信妳會贏的！

Unit 14

Exercises
練習題

看圖連連看

❶

❷

❸

caregiver　　slimy　　bush

選出正解

❶ It's as clear as ______________ that we will win the competition.

(A) night　　(B) day

(C) sky　　(D) glass

❷ It's best to ______________ to the chase in business meetings.

(A) point　　(B) get

(C) cut　　(D) run

句子填空

cheap | discreet | discount | hype | quitting

❶ The store is offering a ______________ on last season's items.

❷ Jamie plans on ______________ his job at the end of the year.

❸ This product is of good quality and is actually quite ______________.

❹ Karen is very ______________ when it comes to secrets.

❺ There has been a lot of ______________ around the movie.

句子重組

❶ around / are / New job opportunities / just / the corner

____

____.

❷ has reached / The number / a record low / new students / of

____

____.

❸ would hate chocolate / It's / why / anyone / beyond me

____

____.

Notes

Unit 15

- [x] 1 come close to + N/V-ing
- [ ] 2 odd
- [ ] 3 do odd jobs
- [ ] 4 odds
- [ ] 5 conceive
- [ ] 6 perceive
- [ ] 7 deceive
- [ ] 8 receive
- [ ] 9 be independent of...
- [ ] 10 answer the phone
- [ ] 11 be jailed
- [ ] 12 launch
- [ ] 13 unfazed
- [ ] 14 leave + 人數 + dead / injured
- [ ] 15 habitat
- [ ] 16 habitable
- [ ] 17 inhabit
- [ ] 18 live
- [ ] 19 heaven
- [ ] 20 alert
- [ ] 21 alert
- [ ] 22 chaos
- [ ] 23 put into practice...
- [ ] 24 work one's way through college
- [ ] 25 fight one's way through the crowd
- [ ] 26 instruction
- [ ] 27 abandon
- [ ] 28 pace
- [ ] 29 pace
- [ ] 30 elbow grease

Unit 15

❶ come close to + N/V-ing
差一點就要……

• I was so mad that I came close to hitting the naughty boy.
我氣得**差一點要**揍這個頑皮的男童。

❷ odd
[ɑd] *a.*
奇怪的
(= strange [strendʒ]);
不成對的，不相配的
odd number
奇數
數字-odd
約……多

• It was odd that when I said hello to my friend Kevin this morning, he didn't recognize me.
奇怪的是，今天早上我向我朋友凱文打招呼時，他卻認不出我。

• One and three are odd numbers, whereas two and four are even numbers.
一和三是**奇數**，而二和四是偶數。

• John has been working for our company for thirty-odd / thirty-some years.
約翰在本公司服務已有三十多年了。

❸ do odd jobs
打零工

• The old man does odd jobs for a living.
這位老伯伯靠**打零工**維生。

❹ **odds**

[ads] *n.*

可能性，機率

(恆用複數)

The odds are that...

很可能……

- The odds are in our favor. Keep going, men.

  我方勝算很大。兄弟們，繼續拚吧。

- Even though the odds were against the host team, they kept fighting till the end.

  即使地主隊勝算不大，他們仍然賣力奮鬥直到最後一刻。

- | The odds are / Chances are / It's very likely | that it's going to rain soon.

  可能很快就要下雨了。

Words in Use

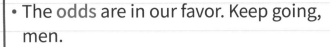

Christine: Do you think Ken was acting odd at work today?

Liam: Yes, I do. He was just sitting there, not saying a word. In fact, I came close to asking him about it.

Christine: Why didn't you?

Liam: I figured he was just tired. The odds are that he didn't get much sleep last night.

克莉絲汀：你不覺得阿肯今天工作時表現很奇怪嗎？

連恩：沒錯，我有這樣覺得。他就只是坐在那裡，不發一語。老實說，我差點要去問問他。

克莉絲汀：你怎麼沒去問呢？

連恩：我想他只是累了。很有可能是他昨晚睡眠不足。

❺ conceive [kən`siv] *vt.* & *vi.* 想出 (點子)；懷孕 conceive of + N/V-ing 想像……（多與 cannot 並用） conceive of sb as... 把某人當作……	• Paul eventually conceived / came up with a good idea to solve this problem. 保羅最後**想出**了一個解決這個問題的好點子。 • Jane was conceived when her mother was 45. 阿珍的媽媽四十五歲時**懷**了她。 • Many Asians cannot conceive of a meal without rice. = Many Asians cannot conceive that they'll have a meal without rice. 許多亞洲人無法**想像**少了米飯的一餐。 • Though I'm close to forty, Dad still conceives of me as a young kid. 雖然我已年近四十，老爸仍**把**我**當作**年輕小伙子看待。

❻ perceive [pə`siv] *vt.* = become aware of... 察覺到，意識到 perceive oneself as... = regard oneself as... 把自己看待成……	• Tom's mouth fell open when he perceived the truth. 湯姆**了解**真相時，嘴巴張得大大的。 • Roy has been in a wheelchair for years, but he never perceives himself as disabled. 羅伊坐輪椅多年，卻從不**視**自己**為**殘障。 

7 deceive

[dɪˋsiv] *vt.*

欺騙；對某人感情不忠

- The con artist **deceived** the old man into giving all his money to her.
  這個金光黨把那位老先生的錢全都**騙**走了。
- Mary broke up with her boyfriend shortly after she found out he had been **deceiving** her for years.
  瑪麗發現她男朋友多年來**對**她**不忠**後就馬上跟他分手了。

Words in Use

Malcolm: Olivia... Will you marry me?

Olivia: Oh, my God! Yes, of course I'll marry you, Malcolm! I've been waiting for this day all my life! Just promise me one thing.

Malcolm: Name it.

Olivia: Promise you'll never **deceive** me.

Malcolm: I promise. I can **conceive of** no situation where I would ever **deceive** you.

麥爾肯：奧莉薇亞……。妳願意嫁給我嗎？

奧莉薇亞：喔，我的天啊！願意，我當然願意嫁給你，麥爾肯！我這輩子都等著這一天。你只要向我保證一件事。

麥爾肯：妳儘管說。

奧莉薇亞：保證你絕對不會**欺騙**我。

麥爾肯：我保證。我**想不到**任何情況我會**欺騙**妳。

❽ receive

[rɪˋsiv] *vt.*

收到（東西、禮物、信等），接到（電話、訊息等）；受到（熱情款待）；（藝術作品、影片、新書等）大獲好評

- I **received** a letter from a friend from afar.
  我**收到**一位住在遠地的朋友寄來的一封信。
- Before I go to bed, I turn off my phone so I don't **receive** any messages.
  我睡前都會關掉我的手機，以免**接收**任何訊息。
- We **received** a warm welcome from the host and his wife at the party last night.
  昨晚的派對上，我們**受到**主人及其夫人熱情的招待。
- The new film was well **received** by the critics.
  這部新片頗**受**影評家的**好評**。

❾ be independent of...

脫離……獨立

be dependent on...

依賴 / 依靠……

- In the process of growing up, children should learn to **be** more and more **independent of** their parents.
  孩子在成長的過程中應學習要愈來愈**獨立**，不要一直依靠父母。
- You can't **be dependent on** your parents all your life.
  你不可能一輩子都**靠**父母生活。

⑩ **answer the phone** 接電話 answer the door 應門	• The phone is ringing. Go **answer** it. 電話在響。快去**接電話**。 • Somebody is knocking on the door. Go **answer** it. 有人在敲門。快去**應門**。
⑪ **be jailed** = be put in jail = be put in prison = be imprisoned 入獄	• The man **was** | **jailed** / **put in jail** | for drug trafficking. 這位男子因販毒**入獄**。

Words in Use

Isabel: We've just **received** an invitation to Olivia and Malcolm's wedding.

Fred: They're getting married? That's great news! Now he can finally move out of his parents' house. I was worried he was going to **be dependent on** them for the rest of his life.

Isabel: I think this calls for a bottle of champagne!

Fred: I agree!

伊莎貝爾： 我們剛**收到**奧莉薇亞與麥爾肯的婚禮請帖。

佛萊德： 他們要結婚了？那真是好消息！現在他終於可以搬出他父母家了。我原本很擔心他會一輩子**依賴**著他們。

伊莎貝爾： 我想這值得開一瓶香檳慶祝！

佛萊德： 我同意！

⑫ launch

[lɔntʃ] *vt.*

發射（武器、人造衛星等）；（船隻）下水；發表（新作品、新產品等）；發動（攻擊）；發起（運動、活動等）

launch
- **a missile**
- **a rocket**
- **a satellite**
- **a spaceship**
- **a torpedo**

發射飛彈 / 火箭 / 人造衛星 / 太空船 / 魚雷

launch an attack on...
對……發動攻擊

launch a campaign
發起活動

- More than 300 missiles were **launched** on the first day of the war.
  戰爭爆發的第一天就**發射**了三百多枚飛彈。
- The new cargo ship was **launched** at 10 o'clock sharp this morning.
  這艘新貨輪於今天上午十點整**下水**。
- The writer's new novel will be **launched** this weekend.
  該作家新寫的小說將於本週末**發表上市**。
- Ten jet fighters **launched an attack on** the enemy troops at sunrise.
  十架戰機於破曉時分**向**敵軍**發動攻擊**。
- Ever since the president of that country **launched an** anti-corruption **campaign**, quite a few corrupt officials have been put under arrest.
  自從該國總統**發起**反貪腐**運動**後，不少貪官汙吏遭到拘捕。

⑬ **unfazed**
[ʌnˋfezd] *a.*
泰然自若的
faze [fez] *vt.*
使驚慌失措

• The pandemic is ravaging the world, but Jeremy seems to be **unfazed** by it.
流行病在世界各地肆虐，不過傑瑞米似乎**絲毫不擔憂**。

⑭ **leave + 人數 + dead / injured**
造成若干人死亡 / 受傷

• A devastating explosion destroyed a large section of the city, **leaving** more than 150 **dead** and over 5,000 **injured**.
發生了一起毀滅性的爆炸事件，炸毀城市大片區域，**造成**一百五十多人**死亡**，另有五千多人**受傷**。

Words in Use

Jerry: What's that on TV?
Maggie: It's a news story about Kevin Maxwell. He's **launching** his **campaign** to be the next president.
Jerry: Wow—he's surrounded by thousands of supporters holding banners. And he's completely **unfazed** by it all.
Maggie: Yeah, he's very cool. I'm certainly going to vote for him.

傑瑞： 電視在播什麼？
瑪姬： 是一則關於凱文・麥斯威爾的新聞報導。他要**發起活動**競選下一任總統。
傑瑞： 哇 —— 有上千名拿著布條的支持者圍繞著他。他完全不受這影響，十分**泰然自若**。
瑪姬： 對啊，他很從容。毫無疑問，我會投給他。

⑮ habitat

[ˋhæbəˏtæt] *n.*

(動植物) 棲息地

- Jane Goodall spent a lot of time studying chimpanzees in their natural **habitat**.

  珍．古德花了很長的一段時間在黑猩猩的自然**棲息環境**研究牠們。

- **Habitat** loss is the primary threat to the survival of wildlife.

  喪失**棲息地**是對野生動植物生存的主要威脅。

⑯ habitable

[ˋhæbɪtəbl̩] *a.*

= **inhabitable**

[ɪnˋhæbɪtəbl̩]

可居住的，適合居住的

uninhabitable

[ˏʌnɪnˋhæbɪtəbl̩]

a. 不適合居住的

- The house being built will be **habitable** / **inhabitable** by the end of this year.

  這棟正在蓋的房子年底就**可住進去**了。

- Without a roof, the house is **uninhabitable**.

  這房子若沒屋頂是**不能住人的**。

⑰ inhabit

[ɪnˋhæbɪt] *vt.*

(動物、部落、種族) 居住於，棲息於

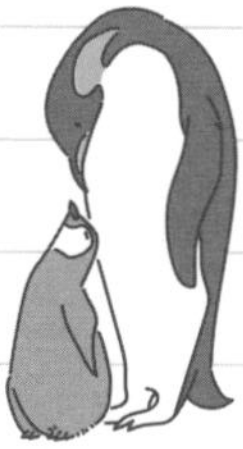

- Dinosaurs **inhabited** Earth hundreds of millions of years ago.

  恐龍幾億年前曾**棲息於**地球。

- The tribe still **inhabits** that area.

  該部落仍**居住在**那個地區。

- That island is **inhabited** by penguins only.

  只有企鵝**棲息在**那座島上。

⑱ **live**
[lɪv] *vi.*
= **dwell** [dwɛl]
= **reside** [rɪˋzaɪd]
居住

• I **live** in Taipei. Where do you **live**?
我**住**在臺北。你**住**在哪兒？

• I prefer to | live / dwell / reside | in the countryside because of its tranquility.
我比較喜歡**住**在鄉下，因為那裡很寧靜。
* tranquility [træŋˋkwɪlətɪ] *n.* 寧靜

TIPS

這三個動詞之後必須接介詞，再置地方名詞。live 的主詞可為人或動物；dwell 及 reside 的主詞則為人。

Words in Use

Paige: Mr. Williamson, this is Paige calling from your apartment on South Road. There is damp on the walls and there are rats in the kitchen. In short, it's **uninhabitable**.

Mr. Williamson: That's nonsense. I resided there for years myself. It's completely **habitable**.

Paige: I disagree, and I want you to sort out the problems now!

佩琪：威廉森先生，這是珮琪打來，我在你位於南方路的公寓。牆上有水漬，廚房也有老鼠。簡言之，這裡**不適合居住**。

威廉森先生：那是一派胡言。我自己在那裡住了多年。那裡完全**適合居住**。

佩琪：我不同意，我想要你現在就來解決這些問題！

⑲ heaven

[ˋhɛvən] *n.*

天堂

TIPS

heaven 之前不置冠詞 the 或 a。

- **Heaven** helps those who help themselves.
  自助者**天**助。(諺語)
- Sitting by the window with a cup of coffee in hand is like **heaven** for me.
  對我而言端著一杯咖啡坐在窗邊就像是**天堂**一般。

- Sam and Joy are a match made in **heaven**.
  山姆與喬依可謂是**天**作之合。

⑳ alert

[əˋlɝt] *vt.* 使警覺

alert sb to sth

使某人警覺某事物

be alerted to sth

被警告某事物

- The authorities concerned **alerted** the public **to** the dangers of the pandemic.
  有關當局針對此全球流行病**向**大眾**提出警告**。
- Passengers **were alerted to** the possibility of a terrorist attack at the airport.
  乘客**接獲**在機場可能會發生恐攻的**警告**。

㉑ alert

[əˋlɝt] *a.* 警覺的

be / stay alert to sth

對某事物保持警覺

be / stay on the alert for sth

注意 / 提防某事物

- We must **stay alert to** any dangers ahead of us.

= We must **stay on the alert for** any dangers ahead of us.
  我們必須**保持警覺**以避開眼前的任何危險。

㉒ **chaos** [ˋkeas] *n.* 混亂（不可數） **send... into a state of chaos / confusion** 將……處於混亂的狀態	• The whole country was in **chaos** after war broke out. 戰爭爆發，全國陷入**一片混亂**。 • In recent months, the pandemic has **sent** the world **into a state of chaos**. 近幾個月，全球流行病**讓**整個世界**陷入混亂的狀況**。
㉓ **put into practice...** = **put... into practice** 將……付諸行動	• The government hopes to **put into practice** a ban on the use of disposable chopsticks. = The government hopes to impose a ban on the use of disposable chopsticks. 政府希望對免洗筷子的使用**實施**禁令。

Words in Use

Tamara: Oh, lying here on the beach with a cocktail in hand is just **heaven**! I hope this lasts forever. Wait... What's that noise?

Callum: It's my phone **alerting** me **to** the fact that a typhoon is coming.

Tamara: A typhoon? Why can't I relax for five minutes before the world descends **into a state of chaos**?

塔瑪拉：喔，手中拿著雞尾酒躺在沙灘上真是**天堂**！我希望這可以永遠持續下去。等等……那是什麼聲音？

卡倫：是我的手機在**警告**我有颱風來襲。

塔瑪拉：颱風？為什麼不能在世界**陷入混亂的狀態**前讓我放鬆五分鐘呢？

㉔ **work one's way through college** 半工半讀念完大學 **work one's way to the top** 一路努力爬到高層職位	• I respect Sean because he **worked his way through college**. 尚恩**半工半讀念完大學**，令我敬佩。 • Peter started as a janitor and **worked his way to the top** of the company. 彼得一開始擔任工友，接著在公司**一路力爭上游最後達到高層職位**。
㉕ **fight one's way through the crowd** 費力穿越群眾	• When the train was approaching, I **fought** / struggled / squeezed / elbowed **my way through the crowd**, trying to get on board. 火車駛近時我**費力穿越群眾**，想要登上火車。 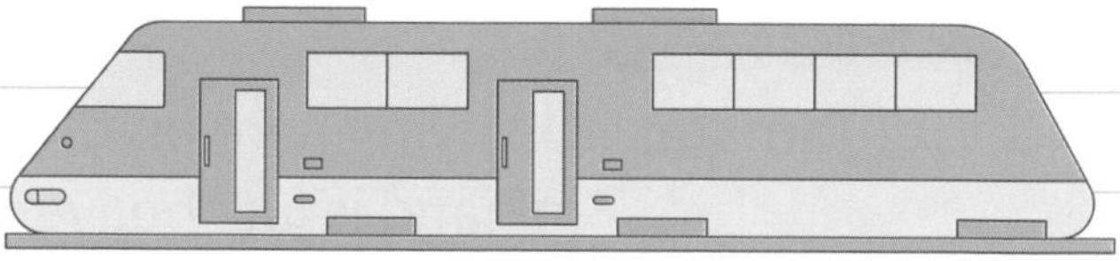
㉖ **instruction** [ɪnˋstrʌkʃən] *n.* 教導（不可數）；指示（常用複數）；使用說明（常用複數） **under sb's instruction** 在某人的指導下	• **Under** Professor Lee's **instruction**, I have made a lot of progress in English. **在李教授的教導下**，我的英文大有進步。 • Read the **instructions** carefully before you operate the machine. 操作該機器之前先仔細看完**操作說明**。 

27 **abandon**
[əˋbændən] *vt.*
= **desert**
[dɪˋzɝt]
拋棄

abandon oneself to...
沉溺於 / 縱情於……

• The baby girl was **abandoned** by her mother.
這個女嬰被生母**拋棄**。

• After her husband passed away, Lily **abandoned herself to** grief / depression.
丈夫過世之後，莉莉就**陷入**悲傷 / 憂鬱之中。

• On a chilly fall day, I like to **abandon myself to** the comforts of hot coffee and a warm blanket.
在微涼的秋天，我喜歡躺在溫暖的毯子喝杯熱咖啡**放縱**一下。

Words in Use

Grace: How was Peter's speech?

Warren: Well, I had to **fight my way through the crowd** so I could hear it. But once I did, it was very inspirational.

Grace: What did he talk about?

Warren: He described how he **worked his way through college**, and he told us to **abandon ourselves to** our studies.

葛瑞絲：彼得的演講如何？

華倫：嗯，我得**費力穿越人群**才聽得到。不過我一聽到演講，就非常受其鼓舞。

葛瑞絲：他講到了什麼？

華倫：他描述了他**半工半讀念完大學**的事，也告訴我們要**沉浸在**學業之中。

28 pace [pes] *n.*
速度；步調

work at one's own pace
按照自己的步調做事

quicken one's pace 加快腳步

keep pace with the times
= **keep up with the times**
跟上時代潮流

- Mr. Brown allows us to **work at our own pace**, so we can leave the office anytime we want to.
  布朗先生允許我們**按自己的步調工作**，因此我們可以隨時離開辦公室。
- As the finish line was in sight, the runners **quickened their pace**.
  終點線在望時，賽跑者**加快腳步**了。
- I don't really like using the internet, but you have to **keep pace with the times**.
  我實在不喜歡使用網際網路，不過你必須**與時俱進**啊。

29 pace
[pes] *vt. & vi.*
踱步，來回走動

pace oneself
調整自己的步速

- Evan was waiting outside the operating room, **pacing** the floor.
  艾凡在手術室外頭**來回走動**守候著。
- **Pace yourself** and don't run so fast, or you'll run out of energy well before the finish line.
  你要**調整步調**別跑得那麼快，否則還沒到終點線你就筋疲力盡了。

跑步好處多

30 elbow grease 費勁，用體力幹活 **elbow** [ˋɛlbo] *n.* 手肘 **grease** [gris] *n.* 油脂（不可數）	• It took me a lot of **elbow grease** to paint the house. 粉刷這間屋子**費**了我很大的**體力**。 • I know we're running out of time, but if we all use a bit of **elbow grease**, I think we'll be able to finish the job on time. 我知道我們快沒時間了，不過如果我們大夥**使點勁**的話，我認為我們可以準時完工。

Unit 15

Words in Use

Tom: Come on, Gina. **Quicken your pace**! You'll never be a good runner if you move at a snail's **pace**.

Gina: I'm sorry, Tom. I had to use a lot of **elbow grease** to clean the kitchen this morning, so I'm a bit tired. I think it's best if I jog **at my own pace** today.

Tom: Suit yourself!

湯姆：來吧，吉娜。**加快腳步**！如果妳**步調**那麼慢，永遠都不會成為傑出的跑者。

吉娜：抱歉，湯姆。我今早**費了很大的體力**打掃廚房，所以我有點疲倦。我想我今天最好**以自己的步調**慢跑。

湯姆：隨妳的便！

Unit 15

Exercises
練習題

看圖選單字

❶

- ☐ do odd jobs
- ☐ launch a rocket
- ☐ put into practice

❷

- ☐ keep pace with the times
- ☐ be put in prison
- ☐ answer the phone

❸

- ☐ habitat
- ☐ heaven
- ☐ chaos

選出正解

❶ We'll need to use some (elbow / knee) grease to get the floor clean.

❷ Due to the flood, our house is no longer (habitable / uninhabitable).

❸ After working for a few years, Jim is already (independent / dependent) of his parents.

❹ Karen (receives / perceives) herself as an important asset to the company.

❺ It's crucial to (abandon / alert) the public to the importance of wearing masks.

句子填空

odds | fought | pace | unfazed | conceive

❶ Sally likes to work at her own ____________.

❷ Ben ____________ his way through the crowd to see his idol.

❸ It amazes me how Jim could ____________ such a good idea.

❹ The ____________ are that we will win the tournament.

❺ The politician seems ____________ by the scandal.

句子重組

❶ came close / Gary / the match / to / winning

____

____.

❷ five / injured / The car accident / people / left

____

____.

❸ put / your ideas / Let's / practice / into

____

____.

Notes

Unit 16

- [x] 1 fill the air
- [ ] 2 put on airs
- [ ] 3 be on (the) air
- [ ] 4 weigh sb/sth up
- [ ] 5 lose weight
- [ ] 6 credit
- [ ] 7 credit
- [ ] 8 assist sb in + V-ing
- [ ] 9 assistance
- [ ] 10 terms
- [ ] 11 in terms of...
- [ ] 12 drop out of school
- [ ] 13 achieve a goal
- [ ] 14 be in luck
- [ ] 15 as luck would have it, ...
- [ ] 16 try one's luck
- [ ] 17 It is bad luck on sb that...
- [ ] 18 tend to sb
- [ ] 19 tend to + V
- [ ] 20 sniff
- [ ] 21 maze
- [ ] 22 recover
- [ ] 23 handle sth
- [ ] 24 dispose of...
- [ ] 25 have a huge following
- [ ] 26 take... by storm
- [ ] 27 be not as good as sb/sth is cracked up to be
- [ ] 28 be in for sth
- [ ] 29 takeaway
- [ ] 30 author

Unit 16

❶ fill the air
瀰漫在空氣中

• Romantic love songs **filled the air** in that fancy Italian restaurant.
那家高檔義大利餐廳**瀰漫著**浪漫情歌。

❷ put on airs
擺架子；裝腔作勢

• Stop **putting on airs**, Jane. You're not some world-class singer. You're just an amateur like the rest of us.
阿珍，別再**擺架子**了。妳不是什麼世界級的歌手。妳跟我們其他人一樣只不過是個業餘歌手。

❸ be on (the) air
= being broadcast on radio / TV
在廣播 / 電視節目播出
be off (the) air
廣播或電視節目結束 / 停播

• The new program is scheduled to **be on the air** at eight tonight.
這個新節目預定於今晚八點**播出**。

• Please wait until I **am off the air** before you call me.
請等到我**下了節目**後再打給我。

廣播節目元素

❹ **weigh sb/sth up** 評估某人 / 某事物	• You must **weigh up** the advantages and disadvantages of the two proposals. 你必須**權衡**這兩項提案的利弊。
❺ **lose weight** 減肥，瘦下來 put on weight = gain weight 胖了，增重	• To **lose weight**, you must stop eating between meals from now on. 想**瘦身**的話，從現在開始兩餐之間別再吃東西了。 • Jim has **put on** a lot of **weight** since he quit smoking. 吉姆自從戒菸後**胖了**許多。

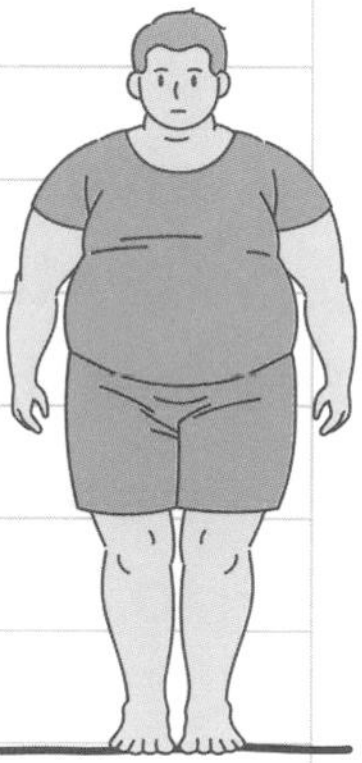

Words in Use

Albert: I love hearing the sound of your beautiful voice **fill the air**.

Audrey: You'll be hearing a lot more of it—my musical TV show **is on the air** soon, so I need to practice. I also need to **lose** some **weight**.

Albert: But you're already so slim!

Audrey: Don't you know the camera adds five kilos?

艾伯特： 我好喜歡聽到妳的美妙歌聲**瀰漫在空氣中**。

奧黛莉： 你會有更多機會聽到 —— 我的音樂電視節目快要**播出**了，所以我需要練習。我也需要**減肥**。

艾伯特： 可是妳已經很苗條了！

奧黛莉： 你難道不知道攝影機會讓我看起來胖五公斤嗎？

❻ credit [ˋkrɛdɪt] *n.* 功勞（不可數）； 獎勵，讚揚； 賒帳，貸款	• Give **credit** where **credit** is due. 該**表揚**的就該**表揚**。（諺語）
take / get credit for sth 因某事獲得功勞	• I can't **take** all the **credit for** the success of the project—it was a team effort. 這項企畫的成功不能都算是我個人**的功勞**——這是團隊努力的結果。
give sb credit for sth 把某事歸功於某人	• We **gave** Daisy **credit for** completing the tough mission. 我們**將**完成這項艱鉅任務的成就**歸功於**黛西。
be a credit to... 是……的光榮	• Josh won three gold medals in the E-sports World Championship. He **is** really **a credit to** our school. 喬許在世界電競大賽贏了三面金牌。他實在是本校**的光榮**。
	• We bought the TV set on **credit**. 我們用**貸款**的方式買了這臺電視。

❼ credit [ˋkrɛdɪt] *vt.* 使有功勞（常用被動）	• The company is **credited** with inventing the industrial robot. = The invention of the industrial robot is **credited** to the company. 工業機器人的發明要**歸功於**這間公司。

❽ assist sb in + V-ing **= help sb (to) + V** 幫助某人做⋯⋯	• Don't worry. We'll **assist you in finding** somewhere to stay for the night. 別擔心。我們會**幫助**你找到過夜的地方。
❾ assistance [əˋsɪstəns] *n.* 幫助 **come to sb's assistance / help / aid** 前來幫助某人	• Upon learning David was in trouble, we all **came / rushed to his assistance**. 一知道大衛有難，我們全都**趕來幫助**他。

Words in Use

Mr. Brown: Congratulations on winning the spelling competition again, Jenna. You really **are a credit to our school**. Here is your trophy.

Jenna: Thank you, sir.

Mr. Brown: Now, I need to ask for your **assistance**. I'd like you to **come to the aid of** some of the other students who aren't as good at spelling.

Jenna: Of course, sir.

布朗老師：珍娜，再次恭喜妳在拼字比賽中獲勝。妳真**是本校的光榮**。這是妳的獎盃。

珍娜：老師，謝謝您。

布朗老師：現在我需要尋求妳的**幫忙**。我想要妳**來幫助**一些並不那麼擅長拼字的學生。

珍娜：好的，老師。

⑩ **terms** [tɝmz] *n.* 條款；措詞；關係（恆用複數） **under the terms of...** 根據……的條款 **be on good terms with sb** 與某人關係良好 **be on nodding terms with sb** 與某人是點頭之交 **be not on speaking terms with sb** 與某人不講話了	• **Under the terms of** the agreement, you'll have to pay for the damage caused to the goods during shipment. **根據**協議**條款**，貴方必須賠償貨品運送時所蒙受的損害。 • I'll try to explain the case in simple **terms**. 我會嘗試用簡單的**措詞**來解釋該事例。 • Even though Dylan and Vicky are divorced, they**'re** still **on good terms with** each other. 即使迪倫與薇琪已離異，他們仍**保持良好的關係**。 • Sam is not a friend of mine. I**'m** just **on nodding terms with** him. 山姆並非我的朋友。我跟他只**是點頭之交**。 • After the quarrel, John **was** no longer **on speaking terms with** me. 吵過架後，約翰再也**不跟**我**講話了**。
⑪ **in terms of...** = with regard to... = regarding... 就……而言	• **In terms of** salary, this job is great, but it has its demerits. **就**薪資**而言**，這份工作挺不錯的，不過它也有其缺點。 * demerit [diˋmɛrɪt] *n.* 缺點
⑫ **drop out of school / college** 輟學	• George **dropped out of school** because he couldn't afford the college tuition fees. 喬治因付不出學費念大學而**輟學**了。 * tuition [tjuˋɪʃən] *n.* 學費

drop out of a race / competition
退出比賽

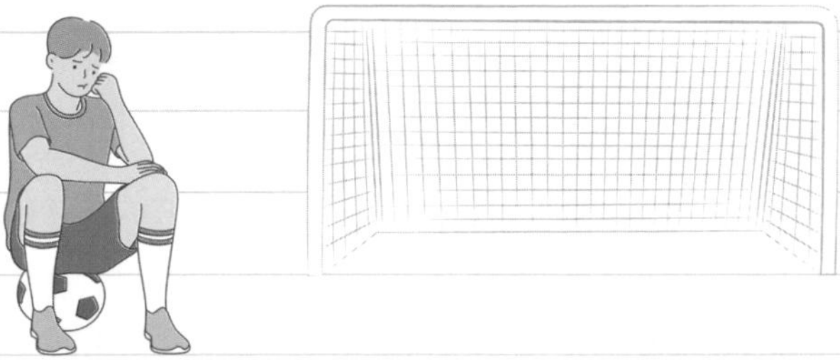

⑬ **achieve a / one's goal**
達成目標

• You can achieve / attain / fulfill / reach your goals if you work hard and stay focused.
只要努力並保持專心，你就能**達成目標**。

Words in Use

Carrie: Have you heard that Dominic has **dropped out of college**?

Boris: Who's Dominic?

Carrie: Your classmate and friend, Dominic!

Boris: Oh, Dominic's not my friend; I'm only **on nodding terms with** him.

Carrie: Well, anyway, apparently he wants to set up his own business. His goal is to be a millionaire by the time he's thirty.

凱莉： 你有聽說多米尼克**從大學輟學**了嗎？

鮑里斯： 誰是多米尼克？

凱莉： 你的同學跟朋友多米尼克啊！

鮑里斯： 喔，多米尼克不是我的朋友；我**跟**他只**是點頭之交**。

凱莉： 嗯，反正，看來他想要自己創業。他的目標是三十歲前成為百萬富翁。

⑭ **be in luck** = be lucky 走運，運氣好	• You **are in luck**. We still have a twin room available. 你真**走運**。我們還有一間雙床雙人房。
⑮ **as luck would have it, ...** = luckily, ... 所幸的是，……	• We ran out of gas on the way home, but **as luck would have it,** we were near a gas station. 我們在回家途中汽油用完了，不過**所幸的是，**附近有間加油站。
比較 as luck would have it, ... = unluckily, ... 不幸的是，……	• I arrived a little late, and, **as luck would have it,** the last ticket had just been sold. 我到得有點晚，**不幸的是，**最後一張票才剛被賣掉。
⑯ **try one's luck** 碰碰運氣	• Mr. Chan has decided to **try his luck** at opening a Chinese restaurant in Italy. 陳先生決定要**試試運氣**在義大利開一家中華料理餐館。
⑰ **It is bad luck on sb that...** 某人……真不幸	• **It was bad luck on** Bill **that** he was ill on his birthday. 比爾生日當天生病**真倒霉**。

⑱ tend to sb
= attend to sb
= care for sb
= take care of sb
照顧某人

- I have to ask for leave to **tend / attend** to my sick daughter.
我必須請假以**照顧**生病的女兒。

⑲ tend to + V
容易會……

- When I'm tired, I **tend to** make mistakes.
=When I'm tired, I'm **inclined / liable / apt / prone** to make mistakes.
我累時**很容易**出錯。

Words in Use

Gordon: Hi, is this Maya's Restaurant? I know this is a bit of a long shot, but do you have any tables for two left for tonight?

Maya: Yes! **As luck would have it,** we've just had a cancelation.

Gordon: That's great news. I **tend to** leave things to the last minute, but I'**m in luck** today!

高登：喂，是麥雅餐廳嗎？我知道這不太可能，但是妳今晚還有任何兩人桌嗎？

麥雅：有的！**所幸的是**，我們才剛有客人取消。

高登：真是大好消息。我**總會**將事情留到最後一刻，但今天我**走運**了！

⑳ **sniff** [snɪf] *vi.* 抽鼻子（哭泣或感冒時，鼻子用力吸氣所發出的聲音）& *vt.* 聞 / 吸（空氣） **sniff out sth** 嗅出某物 **sniff at sth** 嗅 / 聞某物；對某事物嗤之以鼻 / 不以為然 	• We all catch colds at times and can't help **sniffing** and sneezing. 我們有時都會感冒，忍不住**抽鼻子**及打噴嚏。 • I enjoy living in the mountains, **sniffing** the fresh air all around me. 我喜歡住在山中，**呼吸**周遭新鮮的空氣。 • These dogs are trained to **sniff out** drugs in passengers' luggage. 這些狗受過訓練會**嗅出**乘客行李箱中的毒品。 • The dog **sniffed at** my shoes and barked at me. 這隻狗**嗅一嗅**我的鞋子後對我吠了幾聲。 • It's not a big profit, but it's not to be **sniffed at**. 這個利潤雖不多，但也不容**小覷**。
㉑ **maze** [mez] *n.* = labyrinth [ˋlæbərɪnθ] 迷宮	• We lost our way in the | **maze** / **labyrinth** | of streets. 我們在**迷宮**般的街道中迷路了。
㉒ **recover** [rɪˋkʌvɚ] *vt.* & *vi.* 尋回，找回；恢復	• The police have **recovered** all the stolen oil paintings. 警方把失竊的油畫全都**尋獲**了。

recover from... 從……康復，從(不愉快的經驗)復原 / 恢復常態	• Dad is still recovering from his operation. 老爸開了刀，仍在康復中。 • It took Phil many years to recover from the death of his wife. 菲爾經過多年才從愛妻的過世中釋懷。
recover oneself = recover / regain one's composure 恢復鎮靜，回神	• Kate was astonished when she saw me, but she soon recovered herself. 凱特見到我時很驚訝，不過很快她就回神了。

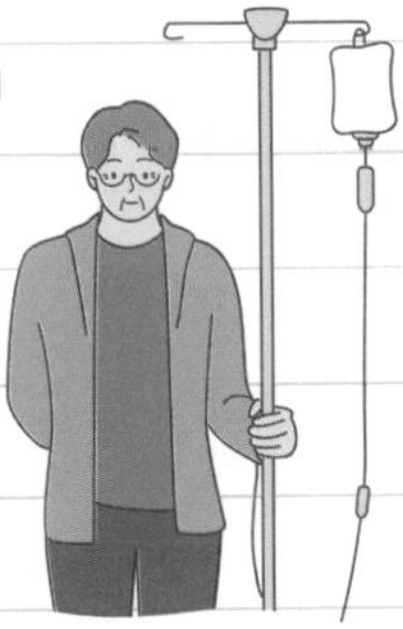

Words in Use

Lorraine: Don't sniff at your food like that, Lewis. You're not a dog.

Lewis: I'm still recovering from my upset stomach, so I just want to make sure the meal is not too spicy.

Lorraine: It's macaroni and cheese, not an Indian curry. Stop worrying and eat up, or you'll never get better.

洛琳：路易斯，不要那樣聞你的食物。你又不是狗。

路易斯：我剛才肚子不舒服，還在復原中，所以我只想確認這餐點不會太辣。

洛琳：這是起司通心麵，不是印度咖哩。別憂心了，趕快吃不然你永遠都不會康復。

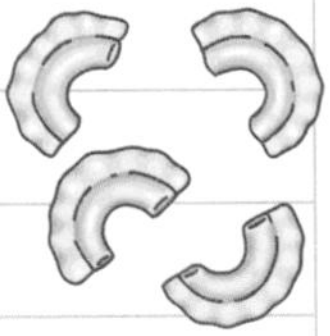

Unit 16

㉓ handle sth

= cope with sth

= deal with sth

處理/對付某事物

• When Paul didn't know how to **handle** the situation, he turned to Barbara for help.

保羅不知道如何**處理**這個情況時，便向芭芭拉求助。

• The psychiatrist advised Peter on how to **cope with** the stresses and strains of his job.

精神科醫師向彼得建議如何**處理**他的工作所帶給他的緊張及壓力。

* psychiatrist [saɪˋkaɪətrɪst] *n.* 精神科醫師

㉔ dispose of...

= get rid of...

將……處理掉

• Tell me how to | **dispose** / **get rid** | of the garbage.

告訴我這些垃圾要如何**處理**。

㉕ have a huge following

= have many fans

有許多支持者 / 粉絲

• The band **has** | **a huge following** / **many fans** | in Japan.

該樂團在日本**有許多粉絲**。

㉖ **take... by storm** 風靡／征服……	• When Audrey Hepburn starred in her first major movie, *Roman Holiday*, she **took the world by storm.** 奧黛莉．赫本主演她第一部重大的電影《羅馬假期》時，**風靡**了全世界。
㉗ **be not as good as sb/sth is cracked up to be** 某人／某事物並不像別人說的那麼好	• Mr. Wayne **is not as good** a writer **as** he **is cracked up to be.** = Mr. Wayne is not such a good writer as he is said to be. 韋恩先生**並不是外傳如此優秀**的作家。

Words in Use

Diana: That actor **has a huge following.** He's really **taken the world by storm** since he released his first film.

Charles: Yeah, I'm impressed by how well he's **handled** the fame. If it were me, I wouldn't be able to **cope with** all the media attention.

Diana: Luckily for you, you can't act to save your life!

黛安娜： 那位演員**有很多粉絲**。自從他的首部電影上映之後，他確實**風靡**了全世界。

查爾斯： 對啊，我很佩服他如此擅於**應付**名氣。如果是我，我應該無法**應對**那些媒體的關注。

黛安娜： 算你走運，你完全不會演戲！

㉘ be in for sth

= be going to experience sth
即將經歷（不好的事物）

- The wind is getting stronger and the rain heavier. I think we **are in for** a storm.
  風愈來愈強，雨愈來愈大。我想我們**即將遭遇**暴風雨。

- If you're expecting everyone to support you, you**'re in for** a shock.
  你若預期大家都會支持你，你**將大感**震驚。

㉙ takeaway

[ˋtekə͵we] *n.*
外賣的食物
(= takeout [ˋtek͵aʊt])；
重點
(= a key fact / a key point)

- I'm too tired to cook, so let's order a
  | **takeaway.**
  | takeout.
  | carryout.

  我累得不想煮飯，咱們就叫**外賣**的食物吧。
- Excuse me, what's the **takeaway** from the meeting? I spaced out during it.
  不好意思，剛剛會議的**重點**是什麼？開會時我發呆了。
  * space out　分心，失神，發呆
- The main **takeaway** from the book is that we should all learn to accept change.
  這本書的**重點**就是我們都應學習接受改變。

㉚ author

[ˋɔθɚ] *n.*
（某本書 / 某篇文章的）作者
& *vt.* 撰寫

- The **author** of this book / article happens to be a good friend of mine.
  這本書 / 這篇文章的**作者**正巧是我的一位好友。

比較 **writer** [ˋraɪtɚ] *n.* (以寫作維生的)作家	• The researcher **authored** / wrote three articles on endangered species. 這位研究員**撰寫**了三篇有關瀕危物種的文章。 • Ernest Hemingway was one of the greatest American **writers** of the 20th century. 厄尼斯特．海明威是二十世紀美國最偉大的**作家**之一。

Unit 16

Words in Use

Alice: I don't want to cook tonight. I want to finish this book by Murakami. He's one of my favorite **authors**. Can you cook instead?

Jeremy: Haha! If you think I'm cooking, you**'re in for** a shock!

Alice: I thought so! Let's order **takeout**, then.

Jeremy: Sounds good. I'm in the mood for Mexican food.

愛麗絲： 我今晚不想煮飯，我想看完這本村上春樹的小說。他是我最喜歡的**作者**之一。可以換你煮飯嗎？

傑瑞米： 哈哈！如果妳覺得我要煮飯的話，那**將會**讓妳跌破眼鏡！

愛麗絲： 我想也是！那麼我們來訂**外食**吧。

傑瑞米： 好主意。我想來點墨西哥料理。

Unit 16

Exercises
練習題

看圖連連看

❶

❷

❸

maze   sniff   takeaway

選出正解

❶ The caregiver was hired to ________ to the patient.

(A) assist   (B) care

(C) recover   (D) tend

❷ Walt is still on good ________ with Zack, despite their argument.

(A) terms   (B) term

(C) luck   (D) credit

句子填空

handle | credited | air | dispose | cracked

❶ Martin is not as good a salesman as he is ____________ up to be.

❷ Sam gave me some pointers on how to ____________ this problem.

❸ Mr. Rogers is ____________ with the success of the new product.

❹ The episode featuring Gina will be on the ____________ next week.

❺ Is there a better way to ____________ of nuclear waste?

Unit 16

句子重組

❶ a huge following / The pop star / around / has / the world

____

____.

❷ tends to / quickly / Keith / up / weigh people

____

____.

❸ her performance / took the world / with / The actress / by storm

____

____.

Notes

Unit 17

- [x] 1 lose one's temper
- [ ] 2 There is no point (in) + V-ing
- [ ] 3 strike it rich (overnight)
- [ ] 4 an honest mistake
- [ ] 5 You made my day.
- [ ] 6 What day is it today?
- [ ] 7 the day before yesterday
- [ ] 8 all day (long)
- [ ] 9 by day
- [ ] 10 sb's days are numbered
- [ ] 11 day after day
- [ ] 12 Rome wasn't built in a day.
- [ ] 13 forever and a day
- [ ] 14 in those days
- [ ] 15 the other day
- [ ] 16 as far as sth goes
- [ ] 17 whetstone
- [ ] 18 drudgery
- [ ] 19 grin
- [ ] 20 pride
- [ ] 21 wrist
- [ ] 22 sprain
- [ ] 23 wet
- [ ] 24 before you know it
- [ ] 25 broke
- [ ] 26 affect
- [ ] 27 affect
- [ ] 28 effect
- [ ] 29 hold sb in high esteem
- [ ] 30 I beg to differ.

Unit 17

❶ lose one's temper
發脾氣
fly into a temper
= hit the ceiling
勃然大怒

- Tim **loses his temper** easily. He should curb / keep / control his temper.
  提姆很容易**動怒**。他應該控制脾氣。
- I know you're upset, but there's no point **flying into a** temper / fury / rage like that.
  我知道你很不滿，但**勃然大怒**成那個樣子毫無意義。

❷ There / It is no point (in) + V-ing
= There / It is no use (in) + V-ing
……無濟於事 / 沒有用

- **There's no** point / use getting upset—let's try to find a solution.
  = **It is no use** getting upset—let's try to find a solution.
  生氣是**沒用的** —— 咱們設法找出解決之道吧。
- **It's no use** crying over spilt milk.
  牛奶潑了，哭也**無益**。/ 木已成舟，後悔也沒用。（諺語）

❸ strike it rich (overnight) 一夕致富	• Most people don't **strike it rich overnight** unless they win the lottery or get an inheritance. 大多數人除非是中了樂透或獲得遺產，否則是不能**一夕致富**的。 ⋆ inheritance [ɪnˋhɛrɪtəns] *n.* 遺產

❹ an honest mistake 無心之過	• You shouldn't have gotten so mad at your son. It was just **an honest mistake**. 你不該對兒子如此生氣。那只是**無心之過**。

Words in Use

Josh: Our neighbor, Mr. Thompson, has won the lottery. That makes me so mad! He's never worked a day in his life, yet he's still managed to **strike it rich**!

Marie: **There's no point losing your temper** like that. That's the whole point of the lottery.

Josh: I guess so. It's just not fair.

喬許： 我們的鄰居湯普森先生中樂透了。這讓我好生氣！他一生中未曾工作過，但他還是有辦法**一夕致富**！

瑪莉： 那樣**發脾氣是沒有用的**。這就是樂透的重點啊。

喬許： 我想也是。只是覺得好不公平。

❺ You made my day. = You've made my day. 你讓我開心極了。	• When you told me I had aced all the tests, you made my day. 你告訴我我所有的考試全都過了，真讓我高興極了。
❻ What day is it today? 今天是星期幾？ 比較 What's today's date? 今天是幾月幾日？(非 What date is it today?)	• A: What day is it today? B: (It's) Sunday. A：今天是星期幾？ B：星期日。  • A: What's today's date? B: (It's) February 2nd. A：今天是幾月幾日？ B：二月二日。
❼ the day before yesterday 前天 the day after tomorrow 後天	• We set out the day before yesterday and will be back the day after tomorrow. 我們前天出發，後天回來。 
❽ all day (long) 一整天	• I've been very busy all day long. I think I should call it a day now. 我忙了一整天。我想我應到此收工了。

❾ **by day** 白天這段期間 **by night** 晚上這段期間	• Nocturnal animals sleep **by day** and hunt **by night**. = Nocturnal animals sleep during the day and hunt during the night. 夜行動物**白天**睡覺**晚上**獵食。 * nocturnal [nɑkˋtɝnḷ] *a.* 夜行的
❿ **sb's days are numbered** 某人的日子被編號了（喻某人來日不多）	• The patient's condition is worsening. His **days are numbered**. 病人的病況惡化中。他**來日不多**了。

Words in Use

Rahul: **What day is it today?**

Priya: Monday.

Rahul: That's not the answer I was looking for.

Priya: It's your birthday! Happy birthday! Are you doing anything to celebrate?

Rahul: Of course. I'm going to eat birthday cake and drink champagne **all day long**.

Priya: If you carry on like that, your **days are numbered**!

拉胡爾：　**今天是什麼日子？**

佩利雅：　星期一。

拉胡爾：　這不是我想聽的答案。

佩利雅：　今天是你的生日！生日快樂！你有慶祝活動嗎？

拉胡爾：　當然。我要吃生日蛋糕然後喝香檳喝**一整天**。

佩利雅：　如果你持續這樣，你會**來日不多**！

Unit 17

⑪ **day after day**

= **day in day out**

日復一日（從事無聊枯燥的工作）

day by day

一天天，逐日

- I am sick of having to do the same boring jobs | **day after day.** / **day in day out.**

我**每天**得做相同又枯燥的工作，令我厭惡透了。

- Under Ms. Mason's guidance, Henry's English is getting better **day by day.**

在梅森老師的指導下，亨利的英文**逐日**進步中。

⑫ **Rome wasn't built in a day.**

羅馬不是一天建成的。（諺語）

- Learning English takes time and perseverance. Keep in mind that **Rome wasn't built in a day.**

學英文需要時間和毅力。記住：**羅馬不是一天建成的**。

⑬ **forever and a day**

比永遠還多一天（喻直到天長地久）

- Honey, I'll love you | **forever and a day.** / **till the seas run dry.**

親愛的，我會愛妳到**海枯石爛**。

⑭ **in those days** 在那個時候 / 年代 in this day and age = nowadays [ˋnaʊəˏdez] 當今這個時代	• People **in those days** lived a simple, frugal life. **那個時代**的人日子過得很簡樸。 * frugal [ˋfrugl̩] *a.* 節儉的 • It's unbelievable that **in this day and age**, people are still dying from hunger. **這年頭**仍有人死於飢餓，真難以想像。

Words in Use

Aidan: I'm thinking of quitting my job at the law firm.

Caroline: Really? Why?

Aidan: I'm sick of researching boring cases **day after day** while the other lawyers get to take on the interesting cases.

Caroline: You've only been there for a year. I suggest you stick with it. **Rome wasn't built in a day.**

艾登：我在考慮要辭去律師事務所的工作。

卡羅琳：真的嗎？為什麼？

艾登：我對於**每天**研究枯燥無味的案件感到厭倦了，而其他律師卻可以負責有趣的案件。

卡羅琳：你才在那邊待一年而已。我建議你堅持下去。**羅馬不是一天建成的。**

Unit 17

⑮ the other day
前些時日（與過去式並用）

比較

someday
[ˋsʌm͵de] *adv.*
有朝一日（與未來式並用）

some other day
= another day
改天（與未來式並用）

• I ran into a friend of mine **the other day**.
前些時日我遇到一位朋友。

• If you keep working hard like this, you'll get somewhere | **someday**. / one day.
你若這樣努力下去，**有朝一日**一定會成大器。

• The boss is busy now. You can see him | **some other day**. / **another day**.
老闆現在很忙。你可以**改天**來見他。

⑯ as far as sth goes
= as far as sth is concerned
= with regard to sth
有關……一事，就……而言

• I'm struggling with my math this semester, but **as far as** chemistry **goes**, I'm doing quite well.
我這學期數學學得很苦，不過**至於**化學，我表現挺好的。

⑰ whetstone
[ˋwɛt͵ston] *n.*
磨刀石

• A mind needs books like a sword needs a **whetstone**.
要保持頭腦靈光就得看書，就像要保持劍的鋒利就得時時**磨**劍。（諺語）

⑱ **drudgery** [ˋdrʌdʒərɪ] *n.* 單調乏味的工作（不可數） **drudge** [drʌdʒ] *n.* 苦工（指人）	• Mom never seems to get tired of the **drudgery** of housework. 老媽似乎從不厭倦於做家事的**枯燥**。 • Dad works as a street cleaner, but he never thinks of himself as a **drudge**. 老爸擔任街道清潔工，不過他從不認為自己是個**苦工**。
⑲ **grin** [grɪn] *vi.* 咧著嘴笑（三態為：grin, grinned, grinned）& *n.* 咧嘴笑 **grin and bear it** 默默忍受	• I was **grinning** from ear to ear when I heard the good news. 我聽到這則好消息時，**笑得**合不攏嘴。 • I don't agree with their decision, but all I can do is **grin and bear it**. 我並不同意他們的決定，不過我能做的只有**默默接受**了。

Words in Use

Ellen: You look much better than you did **the other day**. You're **grinning** from ear to ear.

Lance: That's right, Ellen. I got into my first-choice university!

Ellen: Great news! I wish I'd heard back from the universities I applied to.

Lance: I'm sure you'll hear **someday** soon.

艾倫：你跟**前幾天**比看起來好多了。你**笑得**合不攏嘴呢。

蘭斯：沒錯，艾倫。我錄取了我第一志願的大學！

艾倫：真是好消息！我希望我申請的大學可以給我回覆。

蘭斯：我相信妳最近**這幾天**就會收到消息。

⑳ pride

[praɪd] *n.* 驕傲，自豪；令驕傲的人 / 事物；自尊 & *vt.* 以……為榮

fill sb with pride 使某人自豪

take pride in...
= pride oneself on... 以……為榮

- The sight of their son graduating from college **filled** Mr. & Mrs. Cooper **with pride**.
  看到兒子自大學畢業令庫伯夫婦**非常自豪**。
- Mr. Johnson **takes pride in** his children's achievements.
  = Mr. Johnson **prides himself on** his children's achievements.
  = Mr. Johnson is proud of his children's achievements.
  強森先生**以**孩子們的成就**為榮**。
- My son is doing very well at school. He is really my **pride** and joy.
  我兒子在校表現優異。他實在是我的**驕傲**和快樂。
- Paul just couldn't swallow his **pride** and apologize to Annie.
  保羅拉不下**臉**向安妮道歉。

畢業典禮要件

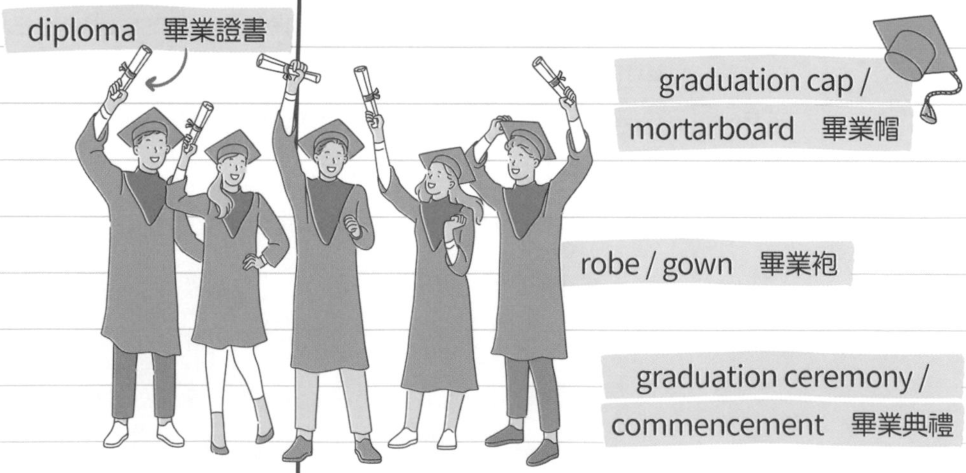

㉑ wrist
[rɪst] *n.*
手腕

- The girl is wearing a jade bracelet on her left **wrist**.
  那個女孩子左**手 (腕)** 戴了一只玉手鐲。
  ⋆ bracelet [ˋbreslɪt] *n.* 手鐲，手環

㉒ sprain
[spren] *n.* & *vt.*
扭傷

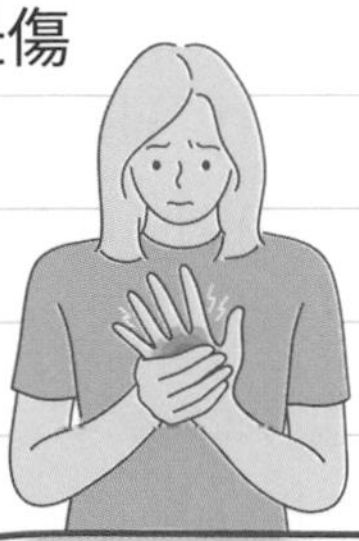

- You've got a severe ankle **sprain**. You need to go see a doctor immediately.
  你腳踝嚴重**扭傷**，需要立即看醫生。
- I stumbled and **sprained** my left wrist / ankle.
  我跌倒把左手腕 / 左腳腳踝**扭傷**了。

Words in Use

Enid: How was your catch-up with Bob?
Aaron: A bit boring, to be honest. He spent the whole time showing me photos of his daughter's graduation ceremony.
Enid: It's natural that he **takes pride in** his daughter's achievements. She's his only child, after all.
Aaron: That's true. It's clear she's his **pride** and joy.

伊妮德：你跟鮑伯聊得如何？
亞倫：老實說，有點無聊。他都在給我看他女兒畢業典禮的照片。
伊妮德：他**為**自己女兒的成就**感到驕傲**是很自然的事。畢竟她是他的獨生女。
亞倫：沒錯。顯然她是他的**驕傲**和快樂。

㉓ wet [wɛt] *a.* 溼的 & *vt.* 使潮溼（三態為：wet, wet / wetted, wet / wetted）

get / be soaking wet 溼透了

be wet behind the ears 乳臭未乾

a wet blanket 溼毯子（喻掃興的人）

wet the / one's bed 尿床

- I **got soaking wet** in the heavy rain.
  我在磅礡大雨中全身都**溼透了**。
- From the way the soldier handled the gun, everyone could tell that he **was wet behind the ears.**
  從這位士兵操槍的樣子，大家都看得出來他**乳臭未乾**。
- Don't invite Mike to the party. He is **a wet blanket** who does nothing but complain all the time.
  別邀請麥克來派對。他**很掃興**，只會一直抱怨。
- I used to **wet the bed** when I was very young.
  我小時候常**尿床**。

㉔ before you know it = very soon 沒多久，很快地

- I'll be there **before you know it.** / **very soon.**
  我**很快**就會到了。
- If you keep spending money like that, you'll be broke **before you know it.**
  你若繼續那樣花錢，**很快**就會沒錢了。

㉕ broke [brok] *a.* 沒錢的；破產的 **go broke** **= go bankrupt** [ˋbæŋkrʌpt] 破產 **be flat broke** **= be completely broke** 完全沒錢	• During the pandemic, countless small companies in that country **went broke**. 疫情大流行期間，該國無數的小型公司紛紛**破產**。 • David turned up / showed up / appeared at my house yesterday, **flat broke** and hungry. 大衛昨日出現在我家門口，**又窮**又餓。

Words in Use

Charlotte: Let's go for a walk.

Patrick: It's pretty cold outside, and the weatherman said it might rain. I don't want to **get soaking wet**.

Charlotte: Oh, don't be such **a wet blanket**!

Patrick: I'd rather stay here and keep warm under this duvet.

Charlotte: Well, I'm going. I'll be back **before you know it**.

夏綠蒂：　我們去散步吧。

派翠克：　外面蠻冷的，而且氣象主播說可能會下雨。我不想**全身溼透**。

夏綠蒂：　喔，不要那麼**掃興**！

派翠克：　我寧願待在這裡然後蓋上被子保持暖和。

夏綠蒂：　嗯，我要去散步。我**很快**就會回來。

㉖ affect
[əˋfɛkt] *vt.*
= **influence** [ˋɪnfluəns]
= **impact** [ɪmˋpækt]
影響

- Try not to let your bad mood **affect** your work.
設法別讓你的壞心情**影響**了你的工作。
- Your opinion will by no means **affect** my decision.
你的意見絕不會**影響**我的決定。

㉗ affect
[əˋfɛkt] *vt.*
= **fake** [fek]
= **pretend** [prɪˋtɛnd]
裝作，假裝

- John likes to **affect** / **fake** an English accent when he talks on the phone.
約翰講電話時愛**裝成**英國腔。

㉘ effect
[ɪˋfɛkt] *n.*
= **influence** [ˋɪnfluəns]
= **impact** [ˋɪmpækt]
影響

- Smoking will have a bad **effect** / **influence** / **impact** on your health.
= Smoking will **affect** / **influence** / **impact** your health.
抽菸對你的健康會有不良的**影響**。/ 抽菸會影響你的健康。

㉙ **hold sb in high esteem** = hold sb in high regard 極尊重/器重某人	• Nate is hardworking and helpful, so he is held in high esteem / held in high regard / highly respected / highly regarded / highly esteemed by his colleagues. 奈特工作努力又熱心助人，因此**備受**同事**尊敬**。
㉚ **I beg to differ / disagree.** 恕我難以苟同。	• You insist your idea is better, but I beg to differ. / disagree. 你堅信你的點子更好，不過**恕我難以苟同**。

Words in Use

Cassie: I've decided to promote John to assistant manager.

Gus: John? I don't know why you **hold him in** such **high regard**. He only **affects** interest in the company.

Cassie: **I beg to differ.** I think he is very genuine. Anyway, that is what I have decided. Your opinion will in no way **impact** my decision.

凱西： 我已經決定要將約翰晉升為副理。

蓋斯： 約翰？我不懂妳為何如此**器重**他。他只不過是**假裝**關心公司。

凱西： **恕我難以苟同**。我認為他很真誠。總而言之，這是我已經做的決定。你的意見絕不會**左右**我的決定。

Unit 17

Exercises
練習題

看圖選單字

❶

- ☐ fly into a temper
- ☐ be soaking wet
- ☐ strike it rich

❷
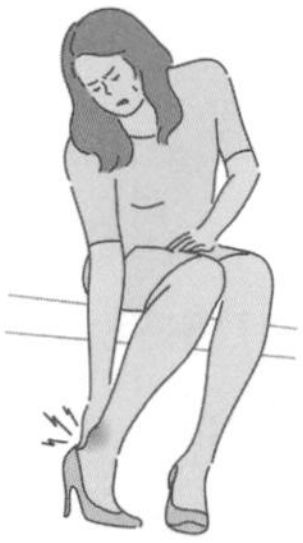

- ☐ an honest mistake
- ☐ a wet blanket
- ☐ sprain

❸

- ☐ grin
- ☐ go broke
- ☐ affect

選出正解

❶ You made my (date / day) when you told me the good news.

❷ This university takes (pride / proud) in its diversity.

❸ Bill spent all his money on medical treatments and went (broke / broken).

❹ Thank you for your comment, but I beg to (agree / disagree).

❺ We will arrive at the airport (before / after) you know it.

句子填空

drudgery | mistake | far | numbered | effect

❶ According to the doctor, the old man's days are ______________.

❷ As ______________ as singing goes, there is no one better than Joan.

❸ You should forgive Gina for that honest ______________.

❹ The ______________ of the drug will wear off soon.

❺ The job turned out to be nothing more than ______________.

Unit 17

句子重組

❶ in / her mentor / Sally / high esteem / holds

____

____.

❷ no point / about the issue / There is / arguing / in

____

____.

❸ long / Calvin / English / all day / studied

____

____.

Notes

Unit 18

- [x] ❶ lose one's sight
- [ ] ❷ have good sight
- [ ] ❸ Get out of my sight!
- [ ] ❹ lose sight of...
- [ ] ❺ catch sight of...
- [ ] ❻ there is no end in sight
- [ ] ❼ Nature calls.
- [ ] ❽ double
- [ ] ❾ sponge
- [ ] ❿ aspire
- [ ] ⓫ inspire
- [ ] ⓬ perspiration
- [ ] ⓭ sweat
- [ ] ⓮ alone
- [ ] ⓯ lonely
- [ ] ⓰ lone
- [ ] ⓱ resign
- [ ] ⓲ resignation
- [ ] ⓳ decent
- [ ] ⓴ cash
- [ ] ㉑ cash in on...
- [ ] ㉒ scramble
- [ ] ㉓ bargain
- [ ] ㉔ exacerbate
- [ ] ㉕ exasperate
- [ ] ㉖ exorbitant
- [ ] ㉗ put sb in harm's way
- [ ] ㉘ desperate
- [ ] ㉙ be derived from...
- [ ] ㉚ be quick to + V

Unit 18

❶ lose one's sight
失明

- Helen Keller **lost her sight** and hearing when she was 19 months old.

=Helen Keller went blind and deaf when she was 19 months old.

海倫・凱勒十九個月大時就**失明**又失聽了。

❷ have good sight / eyesight
視力很好

- Though he is almost 90, the old man still **has good sight / eyesight**.

雖然快九十歲了，老先生的**視力**仍然**很好**。

常見的各種眼鏡

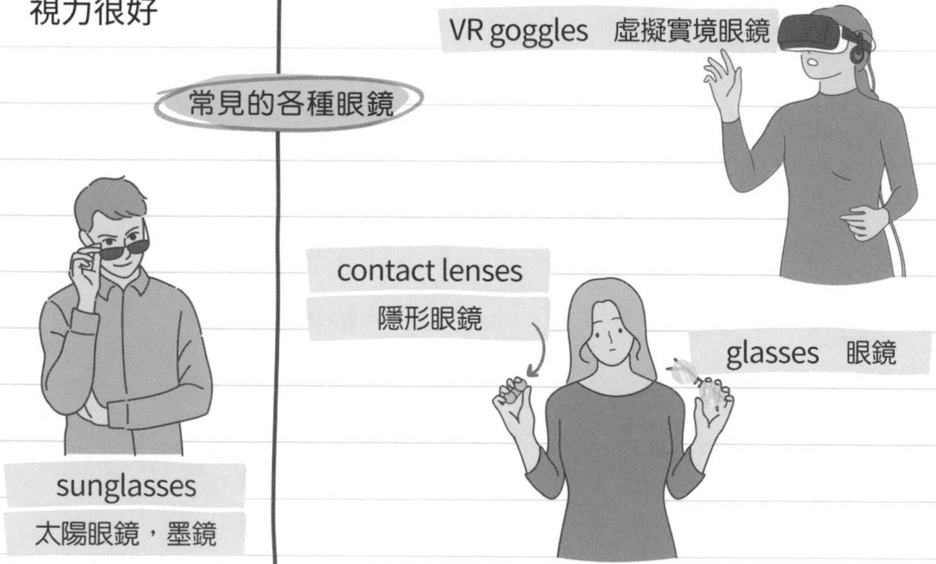

❸ Get out of my sight!
滾開！

- I'm so mad at you! **Get out of my sight!**

我對你感到很生氣！**滾開**！

❹ lose sight of... 看不見……	• The children kept waving at the train until they **lost sight of** it. 小朋友們不斷對火車揮手直到**看不見**火車。
❺ catch sight of... 看見……	• As I turned around, I **caught sight of** George kissing my sister. 我轉過身來便**看到**喬治在吻我妹妹。

Words in Use

Richie: I've **lost sight of** my dad in the huge crowd. Can you see him anywhere?

Helena: Yeah, of course. He's right over there, standing next to the person in the blue and white T-shirt.

Richie: Wow—you've **got good eyesight**!

Helena: It's these new glasses. They're great.

Richie: I think I need to go see your eye doctor!

李奇：我在人群之中**找不到**我老爸。妳有在任何地方看到他嗎？

海倫娜：當然有啊。他就在那邊，身旁站著一位身穿藍白上衣的人。

李奇：哇 —— 妳**視力真好**！

海倫娜：是這副新的眼鏡。它很厲害。

李奇：我想我需要去找妳的眼科醫生看看！

❻ **there is no end in sight**
看不到結束的跡象

• Three months have passed since the start of the strike, but **there is** still **no end in sight**.
罷工開始至今已三個月了，不過仍**看不到結束的跡象**。

❼ **Nature calls.**
我要上廁所。
(口語)

• A: Hey, what's up?
B: One moment—**nature calls**.
= One moment—I have to answer nature's call.
A：嘿，怎麼了？
B：等等 —— **我要上廁所**。

❽ **double**
[ˋdʌbḷ] *n.*
= doppelgänger
[ˋdɑpḷˏgæŋɚ]
極相像的人；分身
a body double
替身演員

• Mary | is the **double** of / looks very much like | her mother.
瑪麗的長相是她媽媽的**翻版**。

• Believe it or not, I used to be Bruce Lee's **(body) double**.
信不信由你，我曾當過李小龍的**替身演員**。

❾ sponge

[spʌndʒ] *n.*
海綿 & *vi.* 白吃白喝

sponge off sb
依賴某人生活

• Children are like **sponges**. They learn from their surroundings and people around them.

孩子就像**海綿**一樣，他們會從周圍環境及周遭的人學習。

• Get a decent job and stop **sponging off** your parents, David!

大衛，找份像樣的工作，不要再當**啃**老族了。

Words in Use

Larry: Excuse me—**nature calls.**

Joy: Again? You've just been!

Larry: I was drinking beer with my friends last night, so there's plenty of liquid to get rid of.

Joy: Shouldn't you be saving money for your own place instead of spending it on beer? You're 30 and you're still **sponging off** your parents!

Larry: They don't mind.

賴瑞：不好意思 —— **我得去廁所**。

喬依：又一次？你才剛去過！

賴瑞：我昨晚去跟朋友喝啤酒，所以有很多水分要排掉。

喬依：你不是應該存錢買自己的房子而非把錢花在啤酒上嗎？你已經三十歲了還在**依賴**你父母！

賴瑞：他們不介意。

Unit 18

⑩ aspire

[əˋspaɪr] *vi.*

渴望

aspire to sth

渴望得到某事物

aspire to + V

渴望要……

- Many college graduates **aspire to** careers in finance.

  許多大學畢業生**渴望**以金融業為終身志職。

- John **aspires** / **longs** / **yearns** to study abroad upon graduating from college.

  約翰**渴望**在大學畢業後馬上出國留學。

⑪ inspire

[ɪnˋspaɪr] *vt.*

激勵；啟發

inspire sb to + V

激勵某人從事……

- The design of the car has **inspired** many imitations.

  這輛車的設計風格**激發**了許多仿製品。

- After his trip to Spain, Peter **was inspired to** learn Spanish.

  在西班牙之行後，彼得**受到激勵要**學西班牙文。

⑫ perspiration

[ˏpɝspəˋreʃən]

n. 出汗

- Genius is one percent inspiration and ninety-nine percent **perspiration**.

  天才是百分之一的靈感，加上百分之九十九的**汗水**。（愛迪生名言）

⓭ sweat

[swɛt] *vt.* & *vi.*

= perspire

[pɚˋspaɪr] *vi.*

流汗

sweat buckets

= sweat like a pig

= sweat a lot

= sweat profusely

出大汗

• I started to sweat buckets within seconds of running on the treadmill.

= I started to sweat like a pig within seconds of running on the treadmill.

我在跑步機跑沒多久就開始出大汗。

Words in Use

Dina: How was Egypt?

Callum: It was so hot! I was sweating like a pig the whole time I was there.

Dina: So, I guess you won't be going back?

Callum: Probably not. But it did inspire me to learn Arabic.

Dina: I bet that's a tough language to learn!

Callum: Apparently, it's nearly as hard as Chinese.

迪娜： 你的埃及之旅如何？

卡倫： 那裡好熱！我在那裡都汗如雨下。

迪娜： 所以，我猜你不會再去一趟？

卡倫： 可能不會。但是這趟旅程有激勵我要學阿拉伯文。

迪娜： 我敢肯定那一定是個很難學的語言！

卡倫： 據說阿拉伯文幾乎跟中文一樣難。

⑭ alone [əˋlon] *a.* 單獨的 & *adv.* 獨自 	• I'm all **alone** by myself. Would you like to come play video games with me? 我現在**獨自**一個人。你想來跟我打電動嗎？ • Since her husband passed away ten years ago, Sherry has lived **alone**. 自從丈夫十年前過世後，雪莉就**一個人獨**居。
⑮ lonely [ˋlonlɪ] *a.* = **lonesome** [ˋlonsəm] 寂寞的 	• The old man lives alone and often feels **lonely**. 這位老人一個人住，常感到**寂寞**。 • I felt | **lonely** / **lonesome** | after my girlfriend left me for another. 我女友離開我琵琶別抱後，我感到很**寂寞**。
⑯ lone [lon] *a.* 單獨的 (之後恆置名詞) **a lone wolf** 獨行俠，獨來獨往的人	• Sharon should have known Brad would break her heart—he's **a lone wolf** who doesn't like getting close to anybody. 雪倫應該要知道布萊德會傷她的心 —— 他向來**獨來獨往**又不喜歡接近任何人。

⑰ **resign** [rɪˋzaɪn] *vt.* & *vi.* 放棄；辭職 **resign oneself to + N/V-ing** 只好……，不得不…… **resign as + 職務** 辭去某職務	• After his wife passed away, Jim **resigned himself to** living alone. 自從愛妻過世後，吉姆**只好**獨居了。 • We were shocked when Mr. Wilson **resigned as** general manager this morning. 威爾遜先生今天早上**辭去**總經理一職時，我們大感震驚。

Words in Use

Sadie: You're always on your own, Gil. Do you never wish you had a girlfriend?

Gil: I'm a bit of **a lone wolf**, to be honest with you. But I don't mind being **alone**. I've **resigned myself to** being **alone** for the rest of my life.

Sadie: Well, if you change your mind... here's my number.

莎蒂：吉爾，你向來都獨來獨往。你都不曾希望你有女朋友嗎？

吉爾：老實說，我是個有點**孤僻的人**。不過我不介意**獨自一人**。我已經**接受要孤獨**一生了。

莎蒂：嗯，如果你改變主意……這是我的電話號碼。

⑱ **resignation**

[ˌrɛzɪgˋneʃən] *n.*

辭職

hand in one's resignation

= offer one's resignation

= tender one's resignation

遞出辭職信

• After a fierce argument with the boss, Tom immediately **handed in his resignation**.

與老闆發生激烈的爭論之後，湯姆立刻**遞交辭職信**。

⑲ **decent**

[ˋdisn̩t] *a.*

像樣的，相當不錯的

a decent salary

優渥的薪水

a decent night's sleep

= a good night's sleep

一夜好眠

a decent person

很正派的人

be decent

穿好衣服

• I have a **decent** job and a **decent** house to live in. What else could I ask for?

我有份**像樣**的工作以及**相當不錯的**房子可以住。我還有什麼好求的？

• As a commercial pilot, Phil has **a decent salary** to support a family of five.

菲爾是民航機師，擁有一份**優渥的薪水**可養五口之家。

• I had **a decent night's sleep**, so I'm full of energy this morning.

我睡了**一夜好眠**，因此我今天早上精神抖擻。

• Robert is **a decent man** who never takes advantage of people.

羅伯特是個**正人君子**，從不占人便宜。

• Don't open the door. I'm not **decent** yet.

別開門。我衣服還沒**穿好**。

⑳ **cash** [kæʃ] *n.* 現金	• You can pay by card or in cash. =You can pay by card or with cash. 你可以刷卡或付現。 • How much do you have in cash? =How much cash do you have? 你有多少現金？
㉑ **cash in on...** 從……中牟利	• The TV channel is being accused of cashing in on the death of the celebrity. 該電視頻道被指控利用該名人的過世來牟利。

Words in Use

Edwin: I haven't had a good night's sleep for a long time. I've decided to hand in my resignation at work today.

Nina: What? Why?

Edwin: I need a job that pays a decent salary. I can't go on struggling to make ends meet. So, I'm going to put all my efforts into finding a well-paying job.

愛德溫：我已經很久沒有睡得一夜好眠了。我已經決定今天上班要遞交辭呈。

妮娜：什麼？為什麼？

愛德溫：我需要一份有優渥薪水的工作。我不能繼續勉強餬口。所以我會盡全力尋找一份高薪的工作。

㉒ scramble
[ˋskræmbl̩] *vi.*
(艱難地) 攀登，爬，移動；倉促做 & *vt.* 炒 (蛋)

scramble into + 衣服
匆匆穿上衣服

scramble for the exit / entrance
奮力衝向出口 / 入口

scramble to + V
倉促地做……

scramble an egg
炒蛋

- We succeeded in **scrambling up** the rocky hilltop.
  我們成功地**爬上**了滿是岩石的山頂。
- After hanging up the phone, David **scrambled into** his clothes and rushed to the hospital.
  掛上電話後，大衛**匆匆穿上**衣服火速趕往醫院。
- As the burning plane landed, the terrified passengers **scrambled for the exits.**
  起火的飛機一降落，驚恐的乘客**奮力衝往逃生門**。
- Those shoppers **scrambled to** get the best bargains.
  那些顧客**爭先恐後地**搶購最划算的特價商品。
- I prefer to have my eggs **scrambled** rather than boiled.
  我比較喜歡吃**炒**蛋而不喜歡水煮蛋。

23 bargain

[ˋbɑrgɪn] *n.*

划算品，撿到便宜的商品；協議

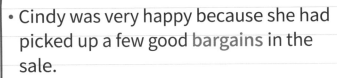

- Cindy was very happy because she had picked up a few good **bargains** in the sale.

  辛蒂在這次的特賣會買到一些很不錯的**便宜貨**，她高興極了。

- The car is really a **bargain** at that price.

  以那個價格來說，這輛車實在是很**划算**。

- After hours of negotiating, both sides finally reached / struck a **bargain**.

  經過數小時的協商後，雙方終於達成了**協議**。

Words in Use

Theresa: How would you like your eggs?

Phillip: Eggs for breakfast again?

Theresa: It was three boxes for the price of one. I couldn't say no to such a good **bargain**.

Phillip: OK. I'll have mine **scrambled**, please.

Theresa: I think you should have yours boiled. It's much healthier.

Phillip: Why bother asking me, then!

泰瑞莎：你想要吃哪種蛋？

菲利浦：早餐又要吃蛋？

泰瑞莎：當時買一送二。我無法拒絕那麼**優惠的價格**。

菲利浦：好吧。我要吃**炒蛋**，麻煩妳。

泰瑞莎：我覺得你應該要吃水煮蛋。這樣比較健康。

菲利浦：那妳為什麼問我呢？

㉔ exacerbate [ɪɡˋzæsɚ͵bet] *vt.*
= **worsen** [ˋwɝsn̩]
使惡化

比較
deteriorate [dɪˋtɪrɪə͵ret] *vi.*
= **worsen**
惡化

• This attack will exacerbate / worsen the already tense relations between the two nations.
= The already tense relations between the two nations will deteriorate / worsen because of the attack.
這起攻擊將使兩國已經緊張的關係**更加劇**。

㉕ exasperate [ɪɡˋzæspə͵ret] *vt.*
= **annoy** [əˋnɔɪ]
= **irritate** [ˋɪrə͵tet]
= **infuriate** [ɪnˋfjʊrɪ͵et]
= **anger** [ˋæŋɡɚ]
使煩惱，激怒

• I was exasperated / infuriated by the noisy neighbors, so I called the police.
我被吵鬧的鄰居**激怒**了，因此就報了警。

警察配備

bulletproof vest 防彈背心

handcuffs 手銬

sidearm 隨身武器

megaphone 擴音器

walkie-talkie 對講機

baton 警棍

26 exorbitant
[ɪgˋzɔrbɪtənt] *a.*
= **extortionate**
[ɪkˋstɔrʃənɪt]
(價格) 過高的

• A million dollars for that guitar is
| exorbitant.
| extortionate.
| way too expensive.

那把吉他要價一百萬，實在**貴得離譜**。

27 put sb in harm's way
使某人處於險境

• Parents will never **put** their children **in**
| **harm's way.**
| danger.

父母絕不會讓孩子**處於險境**。

Words in Use

Ned: Jack is such a bad driver! I can't believe he **put us in harm's way** like that.

Maude: Why didn't you mention it while we were in the car?

Ned: I should have done. I'm going to call him now to complain!

Maude: Don't do that! It will just **exacerbate** the issue. We're home safely. That's all that matters.

奈德： 傑克是個糟透的駕駛！我不敢置信他會如此這般**使我們處於險境**。

莫德： 你為何不趁我們在車上的時候提這件事？

奈德： 我本來應該要的。我現在要打電話給他抱怨！

莫德： 別這樣！這只會使狀況**更糟**。我們已安全到家。這才是重要的事。

㉘ desperate
[ˋdɛspərɪt] *a.*
非常嚴重的；奮不顧身的；走投無路的

- The situation at the refugee camps is **desperate**—they have no food, very little water, and no medical supplies.

難民營的情況**很嚴峻**——他們沒吃的，又缺水，也無醫療用品。

難民營的困境

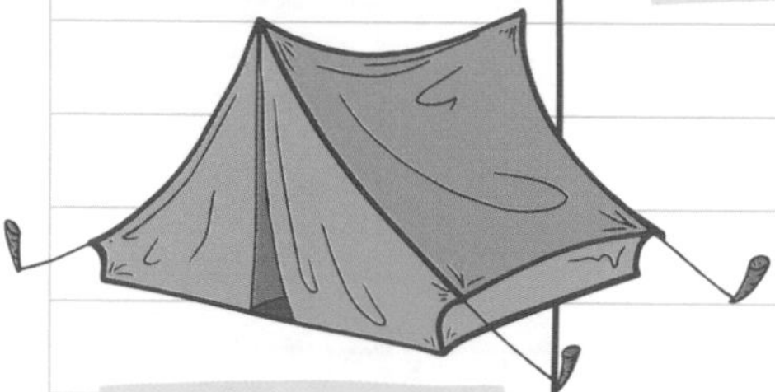

㉙ be derived from...
= derive from...
源自於……

- A lot of English words **are derived** / **derive** / are borrowed / come **from** French.

=A lot of English words are of French origin.

很多英文字**源自**法文。

㉚ be quick to + V

很快就……

- I don't like Walt because he **is quick to** anger.

=I don't like Walt because he loses his temper easily.

=I don't like Walt because he is
  quick-tempered.
  hot-tempered.
  ill-tempered.

我不喜歡華特，因為他**很容易**生氣。

- In general, kids **are quick to** learn.

一般而言，小朋友學東西**很快**。

Words in Use

Freddie: What's that you're reading?

Ingrid: It's a report about the terrible earthquake in Indonesia. The survivors are in such a **desperate** situation. It's heartbreaking.

Freddie: Is there a disaster fund we can contribute some money to?

Ingrid: Yes. A group of charities has set one up. They**'re** always **quick to** react in these situations.

佛萊迪：妳在讀什麼？

英格麗：這是一則關於印尼大地震的報導。生還者正處於**很嚴峻**的狀態。真令人心碎。

佛萊迪：有沒有災難援助基金可以讓我們捐錢？

英格麗：有的。有一群慈善機構成立了一項基金。他們在這些情況下總會**很快**有所做為。

Unit 18

Exercises
練習題

看圖連連看

❶ 

❷ 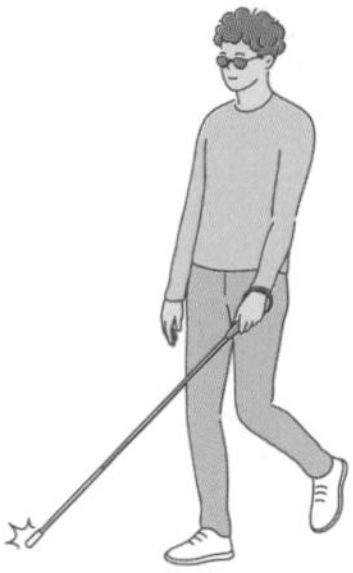

❸ 

perspiration | double | lose one's sight

選出正解

❶ The men trapped underwater are in ______________ need of help.

(A) exorbitant (B) decent

(C) desperate (D) lonely

❷ Stephen's father ______________ him to become a writer.

(A) resigned (B) aspired

(C) perspired (D) inspired

句子填空

scrambled | sight | lone | bargain | exasperated

❶ I bought this coat at half price. It's a real ______________!

❷ Victor felt ______________ when his brother was mocking him.

❸ Karen panicked when she lost ______________ of her children.

❹ Thomas is a(n) ______________ wolf. He hates social events.

❺ Upon hearing the alarm, everyone ______________ for the exit.

句子重組

❶ the CEO / Harry / of the company / as / resigned

____

____.

❷ cashed / the singer's fame / on / The manager / in

____

____.

❸ point out / is quick to / Joe / mistakes / other people's

____

____.

Notes

Unit 19

- [x] ❶ join forces with...
- [ ] ❷ mindset
- [ ] ❸ have... in stock
- [ ] ❹ online shopping cart
- [ ] ❺ faulty
- [ ] ❻ ship
- [ ] ❼ rather than...
- [ ] ❽ other than...
- [ ] ❾ to one's + 表情緒的名詞
- [ ] ❿ addict
- [ ] ⓫ addicted
- [ ] ⓬ addiction
- [ ] ⓭ in the blink of an eye
- [ ] ⓮ all eyes were on sb
- [ ] ⓯ with an eye to + V-ing
- [ ] ⓰ be up to one's eyes in work
- [ ] ⓱ have a keen eye for...
- [ ] ⓲ have trouble + (in) + V-ing
- [ ] ⓳ be of note
- [ ] ⓴ make a note of...
- [ ] ㉑ take notes of...
- [ ] ㉒ take note of...
- [ ] ㉓ lead to...
- [ ] ㉔ bottle sth up
- [ ] ㉕ meet sb's needs
- [ ] ㉖ prey
- [ ] ㉗ come to terms with...
- [ ] ㉘ course
- [ ] ㉙ tumble
- [ ] ㉚ kick off (...)

Unit 19

❶ join forces with...

= **cooperate** [koˋɑpəˏret] **with...**

與……合作

• Our CEO is considering **joining forces with** that international company.

本公司執行長正在考慮要跟那家國際公司**合作**。

❷ mindset [ˋmaɪndˏsɛt] *n.*

= **mentality** [mɛnˋtælətɪ]

心態

• I just cannot understand the | **mindset** / **mentality** | of people who abuse animals.

我實在無法了解那些虐待動物的人的**心態**。

❸ have... in stock

有……的庫存

• I'm afraid we don't **have** any of those left **in stock**. Would you like us to order one for you?

我們現在恐怕無**庫存**了。要幫您訂一個嗎？

購物常見物品

checkout counter
收銀臺

a shopping basket
購物籃

a shopping bag
購物袋

a shopping cart
購物車

❹ online shopping cart 線上購物車	• Beth loaded up her **online shopping cart** with all the gifts she had bought for her family. 貝絲的**線上購物車**裝滿了她為家人所添購的所有禮物。
❺ faulty [ˋfɔltɪ] *a.* 有瑕疵的	• Michelle realized the machine was **faulty**, so she contacted the store owner to exchange it. 蜜雪兒發覺這臺機器**有瑕疵**，因此她聯繫店家要求換貨。

Words in Use

Beth: Oh, no! The website doesn't **have** the dress I want **in stock**.

Cole: Sorry, honey.

Beth: That's OK. I'll just buy these five pairs of shoes.

Cole: Maybe we should spend money replacing the **faulty** TV instead.

Beth: Well... The shoes are already in my **online shopping cart**. And... I've just clicked "buy now!" Sorry... too late!

貝絲：喔，不！我想要的洋裝在這購物網站上沒有**庫存**了。

柯爾：很抱歉，親愛的。

貝絲：沒關係。我只好這款鞋子買五雙了。

柯爾：或許我們應該將錢花在替換這臺**壞掉的**電視。

貝絲：嗯……。這些鞋子已經在我的**線上購物車**了。而且……就在剛剛我按下「馬上購買」的按鈕了！抱歉……太遲了！

❻ **ship** [ʃɪp] *vt.* 運送 (三態為：ship, shipped [ʃɪpt], shipped)	• Once a customer completes the payment process, his or her package will be **shipped** within 24 hours. 顧客完成付款程序後，包裹將在二十四小時內**出貨**。
❼ **rather than...** 而非⋯⋯ (為對等連接詞，連接對等的動詞、形容詞等)	• Doug chose to quit **rather than** admit his mistake. = Doug chose to quit instead of admitting his mistake. 道格選擇辭職**而非**認錯。 • The problem is psychological **rather than** physiological. = The problem is psychological instead of being physiological. 這是心理層面的問題**而不是**生理層面。 • **Rather than** work hard, John fools around all day. = **Rather than** / Instead of working hard, John fools around all day. 約翰**非但**不用功，反而整天鬼混。

TIPS

ⓐ rather than 亦可用 instead of（而非），但 instead of 是介詞，故之後應置動名詞、名詞或代名詞受格作受詞。

ⓑ rather than 置句首時，可接原形動詞，但亦可將 rather than 視作介詞 instead of，之後接動名詞。

❽ other than... = **except...** 除了……之外 (與否定句並用)	• The old man has nothing other than / except an old dog. 這位老先生**除了**一條老狗**以外**一無所有。 • This form cannot be signed by anyone other than / except you. **除了**你**以外**，任何人都不可在表格上簽名。

Words in Use

Lloyd: Are you going to Sarah's party on Saturday night?

Kim: No. I've decided to go to the cinema **rather than** go to the party. What about you?

Lloyd: I guess I'll go. I've got nothing to do **other than** go to the party.

Kim: You could come to the movies with me.

Lloyd: Thanks, Kim. That sounds good!

洛伊德： 妳星期六晚上要去莎拉的派對嗎？

金： 不要。我已經決定要去電影院，**而不**去派對。你呢？

洛伊德： 我想我會去。**除了**去派對**之外**我沒有其他事要做。

金： 你可以跟我一起去看電影。

洛伊德： 謝謝，金。聽起來很棒！

❾ to one’s + 表情緒的名詞
令某人……的是，……

to one’s disappointment, …
令某人失望的是，……

to one’s delight / joy, …
令某人高興的是，……

to one’s horror, …
令某人恐懼的是，……

to one’s regret, …
令某人後悔的是，……

- **To Martha’s disappointment,** she did not make it to the spelling bee final.
  令瑪莎失望的是，她並沒有晉級至拼字比賽的決賽。
- **To Linda’s delight,** her boyfriend bought her a large bouquet of flowers.
  令琳達高興的是，她的男友買了一大束鮮花送給她。
- Much **to Mary’s horror,** she saw a huge snake on the roadside.
  頗**令瑪麗害怕的是，**她看到路邊有一條好大的蛇。

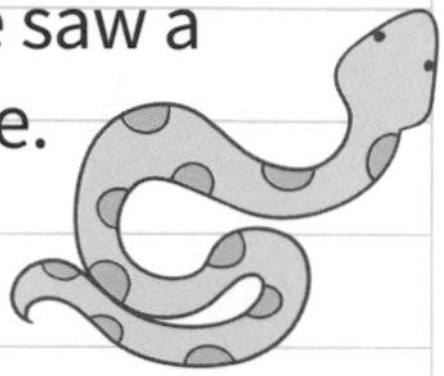

- **To my regret,** I didn’t take your advice and ended up losing everything.
  令我後悔的是，我當時沒聽你的建議，到頭來一切落空。

❿ addict
[ˋædɪkt] *n.*
對……**成癮** / 入迷的人

- The drug **addict** ended up in jail.
  這吸毒**成癮的人**最後入獄了。
- It’s a pity that most young kids today are video game **addicts**.
  很遺憾當今大多數小朋友都是電動**迷**。

⑪ **addicted** [ə`dɪktɪd] *a.* 入迷的；成癮的 be addicted to + N/V-ing 對……上癮	• Bob **was addicted to** online gambling while he was in college. 鮑勃念大學時就**沉迷於**線上賭博。

⑫ **addiction** [ə`dɪkʃən] *n.* 上癮	• Katy admits that she has been suffering from drug **addiction** for years. 凱蒂承認她飽受毒**癮**之苦已有多年了。

Words in Use

Alec: Are you still going out with your boyfriend? I've not seen him around lately.

Eden: No. We broke up. **To my horror**, he **became addicted to** gambling.

Alec: Oh, I'm sorry to hear that.

Eden: Yeah. I hope he gets the help he needs, but I just couldn't go out with an **addict**.

艾力克：妳還在跟妳男友交往嗎？我最近都沒有看到他。

伊登：沒有。我們分手了。**令我害怕的是**，他後來**沉迷於**賭博。

艾力克：喔，真是不幸。

伊登：對啊。我希望他可以得到應得的幫助，但我就是無法與一個**癮君子**交往。

⑬ in the blink of an eye

一眨眼功夫，很快地

- Children grow up in the blink of an eye. / very quickly.

=Children grow like weeds.

孩子們**很快**就長大了。

⋆ weed [wid] *n.* 雜草

養育嬰兒必備

diaper 尿布

nursing bottle / feeding bottle 奶瓶

pacifier 奶嘴

bib 圍兜

rompers （嬰兒）連身衣

⑭ all eyes were on sb

所有的眼光都集中在某人身上

- All eyes were on the celebrity as she walked onto the stage.

這位名人走上舞臺時**大家的目光都盯在**她**身上**。

⑮ with an eye to + V-ing

= with a view to + V-ing

= for the purpose of + V-ing

= in order to + V

= so as to + V

為了要 / 以便……

- We moved in with my parents with an eye to saving up for a house of our own.

我們搬進來與我父母同住**以便能**存錢買一棟屬於自己的房子。

- These measures have been taken with a view to increasing the company's profits.

採取這些措施**目的就是要**增加公司的盈收。

⑯ be up to one's eyes in work
= have a lot of work to deal with
工作很忙碌

• My colleagues and I are up to our eyes in work almost every day.
我與我的同事們幾乎每天都**忙得不可開交**。

⑰ have a keen eye for...
對……有敏銳的鑑賞力

• The judges of the drawing contest have a | keen / sharp | eye for beauty.
素描比賽的裁判都**有銳利的**審美**眼光**。

Words in Use

Roy: Are you looking at baby pictures? I thought you were **up to your eyes in work**.

Cindy: I am, but it's difficult to resist. Look at my nephew—isn't he cute!

Roy: He certainly is adorable.

Cindy: I try to spend as much time with him as possible. Children grow up **in the blink of an eye**, you know.

羅伊：妳在看小嬰兒的照片嗎？我以為妳**工作忙翻了**。

辛蒂：我是忙翻了，但是我情不自禁。你瞧我的姪子——是不是很可愛！

羅伊：他確實可愛極了。

辛蒂：我試圖要盡量與他多相處。你知道，小孩**一眨眼**就會長大。

⓲ **have** **trouble / difficulty / problems / a hard time / a tough time / a rough time** **+ (in) + V-ing** 從事……有困難	• We **had trouble** repairing the machine. 我們修理這臺機器時**遇到困難**。 • I **have problems** communicating with that stubborn guy. 我**很難**與那固執的傢伙溝通。 • Paige **had a tough time** reciting that essay. 佩琪**很難**把那篇短文背出來。
⓳ **be of note** = **noteworthy** [ˋnot͵wɝðɪ] 值得注意的；卓越的，著名的	• Many of the speaker's comments **are of note**. 演講者的評論有許多是**值得注意的**。 • The painting **is of note** because it was done during the artist's time in Paris. 這幅畫**很著名**，因為這是該畫家待在巴黎期間所畫的。
⓴ **make a note of...** 記下 / 寫下…… 	• Please **make a note of / write down / jot down** my phone number and the date we'll meet. 請**寫下**我的電話號碼及我們相見的日期。 ⋆ jot [dʒɑt] *vt.* 快速記下

㉑ **take notes of...** 將……記成筆記	• Be sure to **take notes of** everything the teacher says in class. 務必**把**老師在課堂所說的每句話**作筆記**。

TIPS

名詞 note 作為學生的課本筆記時應用複數。

㉒ **take note of...** = take notice of... = pay attention to... 注意……	• Visitors are reminded to **take** note / notice **of** local laws and customs. 遊客接獲提醒要**注意**當地的法律及風俗習慣。

Words in Use

Jamal: Hey! Did you **take notes of** Mr. Leonard's lecture for me?

Aisha: I'm sorry, Jamal. I tried to **take notes**, but I **had trouble** hearing what he said. I was sitting at the back, and he was talking so quietly.

Jamal: Don't worry about it. Thanks for trying. Hopefully, he didn't say anything **of note**!

賈邁爾：嘿！妳有幫我**將**雷納德老師的上課內容**記成筆記**嗎？

艾莎：很抱歉，賈邁爾。我有試圖要**記筆記**，但是我當時**很難**聽到他講的話。我坐在最後面，他講話又很小聲。

賈邁爾：別在意。謝謝妳的幫忙。希望他沒有講到什麼**重要的**事！

㉓ lead to...
= bring about...
= result in...
= give rise to...
= contribute to...
= cause...
導致 / 引起 / 造成……

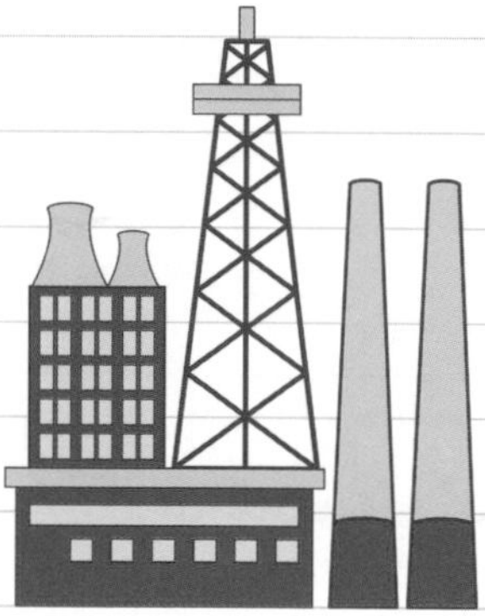

- Going to bed without brushing your teeth may **lead to** a mouthful of cavities.
  不刷牙就上床睡覺可能會**造成**滿嘴蛀牙。
- The deforestation in the Amazon will **bring about** dramatic changes in the global climate.
  亞馬遜河流域的森林砍伐會**造成**全球氣候的巨大變化。
- The CEO's poor decisions **resulted in** the failure of the company.
  執行長糟糕的決定**導致**公司的失敗。
- Those fumes emitted from the factory **contributed to** global warming.
  那些從工廠排放出來的廢氣**造成**全球暖化。
  ★ fume [fjum] *n.* 廢氣（常用複數）
  emit [ɪˋmɪt] *vt.* 排放

㉔ bottle sth up
= bottle up sth
= bottle sth in
= bottle in sth
壓抑（情緒）

- Instead of talking it out with his parents, Jack chose to **bottle** his anger **up**. / **bottle up** his anger.
  傑克沒有和他父母把話說開，而是選擇**壓抑**他的怒氣。

㉕ meet sb's needs / demands / requirements / expectations

符合／滿足某人的要求／期望

TIPS

本片語的名詞恆用複數。

• Since your company failed to **meet** our **demands**, we are going to terminate the contract.

由於貴公司未能**符合**我們**的要求**，我們將終止契約。

• Owen **met** his parents' **expectations** and became a doctor.

= Owen lived up to his parents' expectations and became a doctor.

歐文**達到**他父母**的期望**，當上了醫生。

Words in Use

Rhea: What's wrong, Jimmy?

Jimmy: Nothing.

Rhea: I can tell you're upset. You shouldn't **bottle** things **up**. Doing so can **lead to** high blood pressure and other health issues.

Jimmy: I hate my job. It hasn't **met** my **expectations** at all. But I don't know what to do about it.

Rhea: I understand. Let's talk through your options together.

蕾雅： 吉米，怎麼了？

吉米： 沒事。

蕾雅： 我看得出來你心情不好。你不應該**壓抑**。這樣會**造成**高血壓與其他身心問題。

吉米： 我討厭我的工作。它完全不**符合**我**的期望**。但是我不知道該怎麼辦。

蕾雅： 我了解。我們來一一討論你的選項。

㉖ prey [pre] *n.*
獵物（不可數）

fall prey to...
成為……的受害者

be easy prey to...
易成為……的目標，易受……的傷害

- Lions often stalk their **prey** for hours.
  獅子總會悄悄跟蹤牠們的**獵物**長達好幾個小時。
  ⋆ stalk [stɔk] *vt.* 偷偷跟蹤
- Teenagers tend to **fall** | **prey** / **victim** | **to** drugs.
  青少年很容易**成為**毒品**的受害者**。
- Elderly people **are easy prey to** conmen.
  老年人**很容易成為**詐騙集團**的目標**。

㉗ come to terms with...
逐漸接受（不好的事實）

- The young kid still has problems **coming to terms with** the fact that he was adopted.

= The young kid still has trouble accepting the fact that he was adopted.
  這個小朋友仍然很難**接受**他是領養的這個事實。

㉘ course
[kɔrs] *n.* 過程

in the course of...
在……的過程中

- With this line graph, you can see how our sales figures changed **in the course of** a year.
  根據這張折線圖，各位可看到我們的銷售數據**在**這一年**中**的變化。

㉙ tumble
[ˋtʌmbḷ] *n.* & *vi.*
摔倒，跌下

take a tumble
重摔

- The model wearing super high heels **took a tumble** on the runway.
  那名穿著超高高跟鞋的模特兒在伸展臺上**重重摔了一跤**。

tumble down 滾下來	• Tim **tumbled down** the stairs and got a few bruises. 提姆從樓梯**跌下**，身上有幾處瘀青。
㉚ **kick off (...)** = start (...) 開始（會議、比賽、活動等）	• The meeting will **kick off** on time. 會議將會準時**召開**。 • I'm going to **kick off** this meeting with a few remarks about the budget. 會議**一開始**我想就預算一事說幾句話。

Words in Use

Pedro: OK. Let's **kick off** the meeting. Hang on... Where's Manuel?

Maria: He **took a tumble** down the stairs and broke his leg, so he won't be in for a while.

Pedro: Oh, no. I hope he's OK.

Maria: He's a bit down, actually. He's not yet **come to terms with** the fact that he'll miss the company skiing trip.

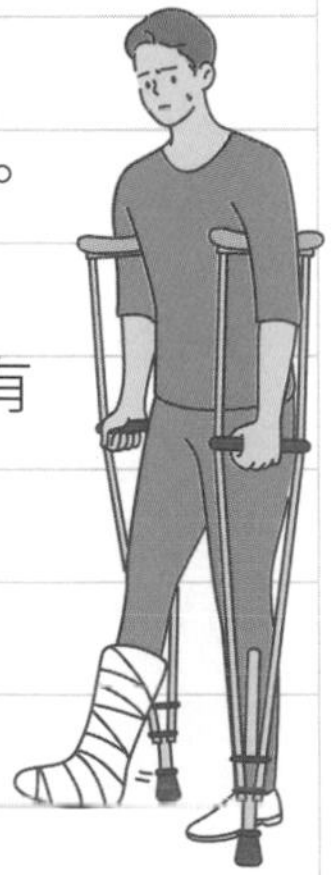

佩卓：好。咱們**開始**進行會議吧。等等……。曼奴爾在哪裡？

瑪麗亞：他從樓梯上**跌倒**並摔斷腿了，所以他有一陣子不會進辦公室。

佩卓：喔，不。希望他沒事。

瑪麗亞：其實，他心情有點低落。他還無法**接受**他會錯過公司的滑雪之旅這件事。

Unit 19

Exercises
練習題

看圖選單字

❶

☐ ship
☐ tumble
☐ kick off

❷

☐ come to terms with...
☐ have a keen eye for...
☐ take notes of...

❸

☐ course
☐ prey
☐ addict

選出正解

❶ Psychological stress can (lead / cause) to illness.

❷ There was nothing of (notice / note) in the presenter's speech.

❸ To my (disappoint / disappointment), Ben forgot about our date.

❹ You should judge people by their deeds (rather / other) than their appearance.

❺ We joined (cooperation / forces) with the other team to improve our sales.

句子填空

mindset | addicted | faulty | terms | eye

❶ Dean is still coming to ______________ with the death of his wife.

❷ You may receive a refund if the product is ______________.

❸ It is difficult to change the ______________ of the public.

❹ Jasmine traveled abroad with a(n) ______________ to broadening her horizons.

❺ Ronald has been ______________ to alcohol ever since his divorce.

句子重組

❶ your emotions / It's / to / bottle up / unhealthy

____

____.

❷ had / the customer / handling / trouble / The clerk

____

____.

❸ disappeared / an eye / in the blink / The rabbit / of

____

____.

Notes

Unit 20

- [x] ❶ end in...
- [ ] ❷ end with...
- [ ] ❸ end up + V-ing
- [ ] ❹ end up + (being) + N/Adj. / 介詞片語
- [ ] ❺ sweep
- [ ] ❻ be swept away by...
- [ ] ❼ sweep sb off his / her feet
- [ ] ❽ come what may, ...
- [ ] ❾ triumph
- [ ] ❿ precarious
- [ ] ⓫ add insult to (sb's) injury
- [ ] ⓬ bleak
- [ ] ⓭ outlook
- [ ] ⓮ glue
- [ ] ⓯ It never rains but it pours.
- [ ] ⓰ trait
- [ ] ⓱ somber
- [ ] ⓲ play possum
- [ ] ⓳ be like no other
- [ ] ⓴ get out of control
- [ ] ㉑ be out of date
- [ ] ㉒ be out of luck
- [ ] ㉓ be out of work
- [ ] ㉔ be / feel out of place
- [ ] ㉕ be out of danger
- [ ] ㉖ sing out of tune
- [ ] ㉗ stay tuned
- [ ] ㉘ try one's best to + V
- [ ] ㉙ make every effort to + V
- [ ] ㉚ go all out to + V

Unit 20

❶ end in...
以……告終

• The team's attempt to climb Mt. Everest **ended in** failure.
該登山隊企圖攻下聖母峰之舉**以**失敗**收場**。

登山配備

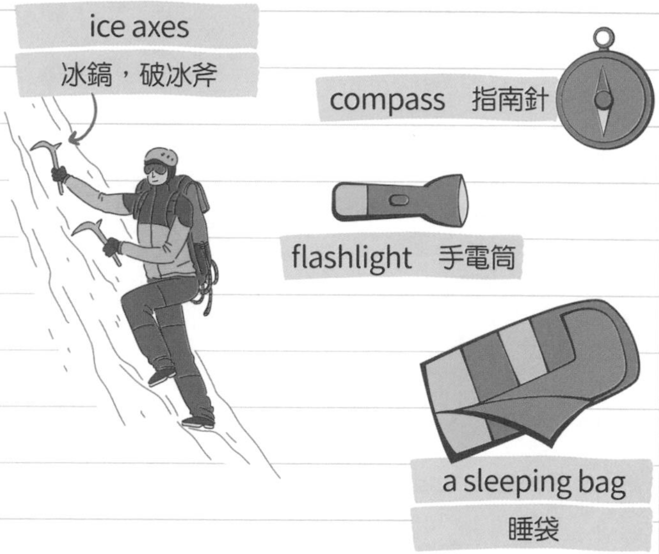

❷ end with...
以……結尾

• The word "turkey" starts with "t" and **ends with** "y."
英文單字 turkey 是**以**字母 t 開頭、字母 y **結尾**。

❸ end up + V-ing
= wind [waɪnd] up...
到頭來……

• James was so addicted to gambling that he **ended up** losing everything.
詹姆士沉迷於賭博，**到頭來**失去一切。

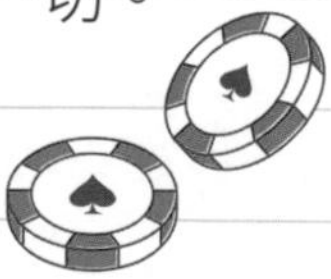

❹ end up + (being) + N/Adj. / 介詞片語

到頭來 / 最後成為……

TIPS

實際使用時現在分詞 being 一律省略。

- David spent money like water, and before he knew it, he **ended up** a beggar.
  大衛花錢如流水，很快地，他**就淪為**乞丐了。
- You'll **end up** penniless if you continue to spend like that.
  你若持續像那樣花錢，很快**就會**身無分文。
  ⋆ penniless [ˋpɛnɪlɪs] *a.* 身無分文的
- The thief **ended up** in jail.
  這小偷**到頭來**入獄了。

Words in Use

Patty: So, how was the big romantic dinner?

Bruce: Not good. It **ended in** failure.

Patty: She turned down your proposal?

Bruce: I didn't even get a chance to ask her to marry me. She had an allergic reaction to some fish, so we **ended up** going home early.

Patty: I hope she's OK!

Bruce: She's fine. I'm disappointed, though!

派蒂：所以，盛大的浪漫晚餐如何？

布魯斯：不好。**以**失敗**收場**。

派蒂：她拒絕你的求婚嗎？

布魯斯：我甚至沒有機會向她求婚。她對某些魚產生過敏反應，所以我們**最後**提早回家了。

派蒂：希望她沒事！

布魯斯：她沒事。不過，我很失望！

❺ **sweep** [swip] *vt.* 掃；掃蕩（三態為：sweep, swept [swɛpt], swept）	• After coming home from school, I often help Mom **sweep** the floor. 放學回家後，我常幫老媽**掃**地。 • The janitor **swept** the leaves into a pile. 工友把落葉**掃**成一堆。 
❻ **be swept away by...** 被……沖走	• The houses **were swept away by** the landslide. 這幾棟房子**被**山崩**摧毀**了。
❼ **sweep sb off his / her feet** 使某人對自己一見傾心	• The first time he met Emma, Lucas **was** completely **swept off his feet**. 盧卡斯初次見到艾瑪就完全**被**她**迷倒**了。
❽ **come what may, ...** = no matter what may come, ... = no matter what happens, ... = whatever happens, ... 無論發生什麼事，……	• **Come what may,** / **No matter what may come,** / **No matter what happens,** / **Whatever happens,** I promise to support you. **不管發生什麼事**，我承諾一定會支持你。 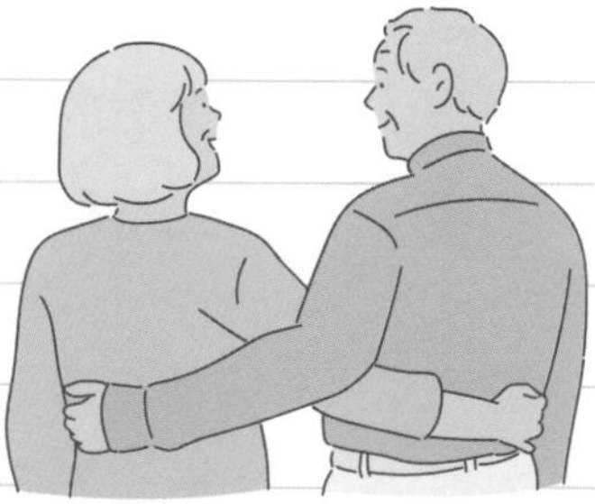

⑨ **triumph** [ˋtraɪəmf] *n.* & *vi.* 勝利，凱旋	• The soldiers came back from the front line in **triumph**. 戰士們從前線**凱旋**而歸。
triumph over... = **defeat...** 戰勝……	• I believe that sooner or later, good will **triumph over** evil. 我相信邪不**勝**正是遲早的事。
⑩ **precarious** [prɪˋkɛrɪəs] *a.* 不穩的，不確定的；搖搖欲墜的	• Jack earns a **precarious** living as an artist. 傑克當畫家謀生過著**朝不保夕的**生活。 • The ladder looks **precarious**. Don't use it. 這梯子看起來很**不穩**。別使用它。

Words in Use

Jerry: Have you heard about the terrible weather in the south?

Elaine: Yes, it's awful. Some homes have **been swept away by** the floods.

Jerry: The situation there looks **precarious**.

Elaine: The president has been on TV to say that, **come what may**, the government will find new homes for all the people affected.

傑瑞：妳有耳聞南部那糟糕的天氣嗎？

伊蓮：有，糟透了。有些民宅**被**洪水**沖走**了。

傑瑞：那裡的情況看起來**岌岌可危**。

伊蓮：總統在電視上表示，**無論發生什麼事**，政府會為所有受到影響的民眾尋找新的住處。

⑪ add insult to (sb's) injury
在 (某人的) 傷口上灑鹽

add fuel to the fire / flames
火上加油

rub salt in / into sb's wound
在某人的傷口上灑鹽

- Paul **added insult to** Mia's **injury** by breaking up with her after she got laid off.
  保羅在蜜雅被資遣後又跟她分手，簡直就是**在**她**的傷口上灑鹽**。
- The joke Sally told didn't end our argument at all. Instead, it **added fuel to the fire.**
  莎莉的笑話根本沒解決我們的爭執，反而是**火上加油**。
- Susan is already sad about her mistake, so stop **rubbing salt into her wound** by blaming her.
  蘇珊對於自己犯的錯已經很難過了，因此不要再怪罪她，以免**在**她**的傷口上灑鹽**。

⑫ bleak [blik] *a.*
不樂觀的；黯淡的

- With the pandemic still severe, the outlook for the economy in every country is **bleak.**
  疫情仍然嚴峻，各國的經濟前景**不甚樂觀**。

⑬ outlook
[ˋaut͵luk] *n.*
前景，展望；景色

- The **outlook** for the company is very bright.
  該公司的**前景**大好。

	• The villa has a pleasant **outlook** over the valley. 這棟別墅俯瞰山谷，**景色**宜人。
⑭ **glue** [glu] *vt.* (用膠水) 黏貼 & *n.* 膠水 **be glued to...** **= be fixed on...** 固定在……	• Tom's eyes are **glued to** / **fixed on** the TV all day long. He has become a couch potato. 湯姆整天**目不轉睛盯著**電視看，已成了電視迷。 

Unit 20

Words in Use

Alma: How was your trip to the south of France?

Mike: It was amazing! We stayed in a villa in the hills above Nice. The **outlook** over the city was stunning.

Alma: Did you visit many places?

Mike: To tell you the truth, I **was glued to** the view from the balcony, so we spent most of the time there.

歐瑪： 你去法國南部的行程好玩嗎？

麥克： 棒透了！我們住在一棟別墅，而這棟別墅位在尼斯上方的山丘上。望向城市的**景色**非常迷人。

歐瑪： 你有參訪許多地方嗎？

麥克： 老實告訴妳，我**像被膠水黏著似地不想離開**陽臺望出的風景，所以我們大部分的時間都待在那裡。

⑮ **It never rains but it pours.** = Whenever it rains, it pours. 不雨則已，一雨傾盆。/ 壞事不發生則已，一發生就接二連三來。 Misfortunes never come singly. 禍不單行。 Bad things come in threes. 禍不單行。/ 壞事成三。 	• First, Terry's car was towed away. Then, he realized his phone was in the car. **It never rains but it pours.** 先是泰瑞的車被拖吊了。接著他發現他把手機留在車上。正可謂「**禍不單行**」。 • Lucy's house flooded after a pipe broke in the kitchen. However, **misfortunes never come singly**. She slipped on the wet floor and broke her arm. 露西廚房裡的一根水管破掉使家中淹水。然而，真是**禍不單行**。她在溼答答的地板上滑倒還摔斷了手臂。 • After his marriage proposal failed, Larry found out his girlfriend stole money from him and is in love with another man, which really proves that **bad things come in threes.** 繼求婚失敗後，賴瑞發現他女友偷他的錢又移情別戀，這真是印證了**禍不單行**啊。
⑯ **trait** [tret] *n.* 特質，特點	• A sense of humor is one of Derek's notable **traits.** 幽默感是戴瑞克顯著的**特質**之一。 * notable [ˋnotəbḷ] *a.* 顯著的，顯要的

⑰ **somber**
[ˋsɑmbɚ] *a.*
= **melancholy**
[ˋmɛlən͵kɑlɪ]
= **pensive**
[ˋpɛnsɪv]
沮喪的，鬱悶的，憂傷的

- Why are you feeling so somber / melancholy / pensive? Is there anything wrong?
  你為何一副憂傷的樣子？發生什麼事了嗎？
- After her husband passed away, Daisy became withdrawn and somber, hardly speaking to anyone.
  丈夫過世後，黛西變得孤僻憂鬱，幾乎不跟任何人說話。

Unit 20

Words in Use

Margaret: What's up, Jack? You look somber.
Jack: My car got a flat tire today.
Margaret: Be careful: Misfortunes never come singly.
Jack: I lost my wallet, too.
Margaret: Oh, no! It never rains but it pours.
Jack: And my goldfish died, as well.
Margaret: You can relax now: Bad luck comes in threes.

瑪格麗特：傑克，怎麼了？你看起來很鬱悶。
傑克：今天我的車爆胎了。
瑪格麗特：小心：禍不單行啊。
傑克：我也弄丟了我的皮夾。
瑪格麗特：喔，不！不雨則已，一雨傾盆。
傑克：而且，我的金魚也死掉了。
瑪格麗特：那你現在可以放鬆了：壞事只會成三。

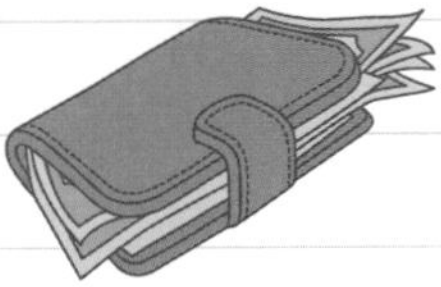

⑱ play possum 裝死 (= play dead)；裝睡	• I don't think Jim is really asleep. He is just | **playing possum.** / pretending to be sleeping. 我認為吉姆並不是真的睡著了。他只是在**裝睡**。

TIPS

possum [ˋpɑsəm] 指澳洲及北美洲的「負鼠」，這種小動物見到危險情況會立刻裝死，故有 play possum 此片語。

⑲ be like no other 獨一無二	• This car is | **like no other.** / one of a kind. / very special. 這輛車**獨樹一格**。

⑳ get out of control 失控 比較 **be under control** 在掌控中	• None of us want to see the situation get **out of control.** 我們都不願見到情況**失控**。 • Don't worry. Everything is well under **control.** 別擔心。一切都**在掌控中**。

㉑ **be out of date** 過時的 比較 be up to date 最新的；趕上潮流的	• These instruments are mostly **out of date.** 這些儀器大部分都**過時**了。 • We work hard to keep our database **up to date.** 我們努力將我們的資料庫**更新**。
㉒ **be out of luck** = be unlucky 倒楣	• I was **out of luck** / **unlucky** when my computer crashed and wouldn't restart. 我**真倒楣**，我的電腦當機又無法重新開機。

Words in Use

Son: Where's Dad? I need help with my English grammar homework.

Mom: You're **out of luck**. He's already asleep.

Son: Are you sure he's not just **playing possum**?

Mom: The snoring would suggest otherwise. Anyway, your dad's knowledge of grammar **is out of date**. I can help you with it.

Son: Thanks, Mom!

兒子：爸爸去哪了？我需要幫忙做英文文法作業。

媽媽：你**真倒楣**。他已經睡著了。

兒子：妳確定他不是在**裝睡**嗎？

媽媽：有打鼾聲表示他不是在裝睡。總之，你爸爸對文法的認知已經**過時**了。我可以幫你。

兒子：謝謝了，媽媽！

㉓ be out of work
= be out of a job
= be jobless
失業

• Phil has to live from hand to mouth now that he **is out of work**.
菲爾既然**失業**了，他只得勉強餬口來度日。

㉔ be / feel out of place
覺得格格不入

• At first, the transfer student **felt out of place**. In the end, he felt at ease in our class.
起先，這位轉學生**覺得格格不入**。最後，他在我們班上感到很自在。

㉕ be out of danger
脫離險境

• Following the operation, the patient **is** now **out of danger**.
手術後，病人現在**脫離險境**了。

比較
be in danger
有危險

• The taxi driver drove so fast that I really felt my life **was in danger**.
計程車司機開得很快，讓我感到我的生命**有危險**。

be in danger of + N/V-ing
有……的危險

• If you carry on like this, you will **be in danger of** losing your job.
=If you go on like this, you will be very likely to lose your job.
你若繼續這樣下去，**很可能會**丟掉飯碗。

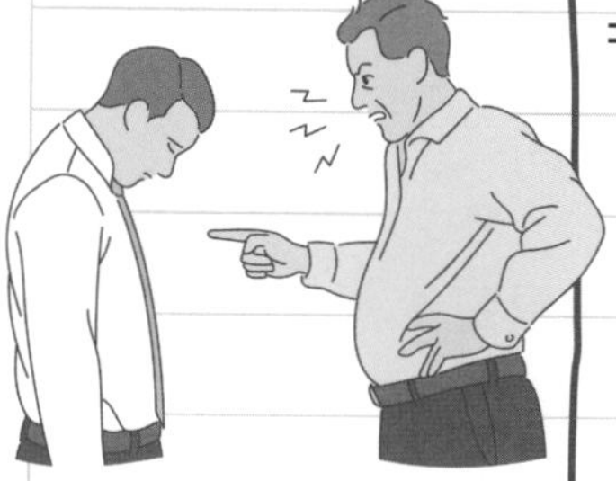

㉖ **sing out of tune** 唱歌走音	• Everyone in the audience was surprised when the world-class singer **sang out of tune.** 這位世界級的歌手**唱歌走音**時，每位聽眾都很吃驚。
㉗ **stay tuned** 保持同廣播頻率 / 頻道，請勿轉臺	• **Stay tuned**. We will be back after the commercial. **請勿轉臺**。我們廣告後即將回來。 • **Stay tuned** with us after these commercials. 廣告後請**繼續收聽**本節目。

Words in Use

Stan: How was the karaoke night?

Stella: Awful. I **felt so out of place**! Every song I sang was completely **out of tune**.

Stan: I don't know why you put yourself through these events.

Stella: Everyone in the company is expected to go. I feel like I'll **be in danger of** losing my job if I don't go.

史丹：卡拉 OK 之夜好玩嗎？

史黛拉：糟透了。我覺得很**格格不入**！我唱的每一首歌都大**走音**。

史丹：我不懂妳為什麼要勉強自己參加這些活動。

史黛拉：公司全體員工都預期要參加。讓我覺得如果不去的話，**很可能會**丟掉工作。

㉘ try one's best to + V
= do one's (level) best to + V
= do one's utmost to + V
盡全力……

• The lawyer is **trying** **his best** / **all he can** / **whatever he can** to prove that his client is innocent.

= The lawyer is **doing his (level) best to** prove his client's innocence.

= The lawyer is **doing his utmost to** prove his client's innocence.

那名律師正**盡其所能**證明他的委託人是清白的。

法庭相關人物

㉙ make every effort to + V
= spare no effort to + V
= leave no stone unturned to + V
竭盡所能……

• Mr. Chen **made every effort to** give his family a good life.

陳先生**竭盡所能**讓全家人過個好日子。

• Ms. Brown **spares no effort to** educate her students.

布朗女士教育學生**不遺餘力**。

• The police vowed to **leave no stone unturned to** find the missing boy.

警方發誓要**竭盡所能**尋找那位失蹤的男孩。

㉚ go all out to + V

= go out of one's way to + V

= go to great lengths to + V

盡力……

- Everyone can see that Ted is **going all out to** please his boss because he wants to get promoted.
  大家都看得出來，泰德正**盡心**取悅他的上司，因為他想獲得升遷。
- Carol **went out of her way to** help us when we moved.
  凱蘿在我們搬家時**盡力**幫助我們。
- The CEO's assistant always **goes to great lengths to** complete the work she has been given.
  執行長的助理總是**盡力**完成她被交付的工作。

Words in Use

Mr. Ford: Are you ready for the big meeting this afternoon, Dana? This could be a very important client for us. I need you to **do your utmost to** get him to sign with us.

Dana: Of course, Mr. Ford. I will **go all out to** win him over.

Mr. Ford: Thank you.

福特先生：戴娜，妳已經準備好參加今天下午的那場重要會議嗎？這對本公司而言可能會是非常重要的客戶。我需要妳**全力以赴**促使他與我們簽約。

戴娜：當然，福特先生。我會**盡全力**說服他的。

福特先生：謝謝妳。

Unit 20

Exercises
練習題

看圖連連看

❶

❷

❸

somber　　triumph　　glue

選出正解

❶ George made every ______________ to please his girlfriend.

(A) best　　(B) effort

(C) utmost　　(D) lengths

❷ Your criticism only added fuel to the ______________.

(A) injuries　　(B) wounds

(C) insults　　(D) flames

句子填空

tuned | swept | possum | precarious | tune

❶ Frank's financial situation is ____________, and he has to get a loan.

❷ Joe played ____________ to avoid doing chores.

❸ A special guest will be with us after the break, so stay ____________!

❹ It was funny when the comedian sang out of ____________ on purpose.

❺ My slippers were ____________ away by the large waves.

句子重組

❶ divorce / marriage / in / The couple's / ended

____

____.

❷ in / out of place / Vicky / a new environment / felt

____

____.

❸ This / no other / piece of art / like / is

____

____.

Notes

Unit 21

- [x] ❶ keep a balance between A and B
- [ ] ❷ On balance, ...
- [ ] ❸ get a kick out of...
- [ ] ❹ stimulate
- [ ] ❺ hermit
- [ ] ❻ bucket
- [ ] ❼ sb's bucket list
- [ ] ❽ kick the bucket
- [ ] ❾ device
- [ ] ❿ various
- [ ] ⓫ varied
- [ ] ⓬ variable
- [ ] ⓭ vary
- [ ] ⓮ sth of sb's dreams
- [ ] ⓯ dredge
- [ ] ⓰ impair
- [ ] ⓱ cast
- [ ] ⓲ spell
- [ ] ⓳ spell
- [ ] ⓴ spell out + why / how / what 等疑問詞引導的名詞子句
- [ ] ㉑ somewhat
- [ ] ㉒ somehow
- [ ] ㉓ countdown
- [ ] ㉔ lockdown
- [ ] ㉕ crackdown
- [ ] ㉖ breakdown
- [ ] ㉗ shutdown
- [ ] ㉘ given
- [ ] ㉙ Simply put, ...
- [ ] ㉚ Broadly defined, ...

Unit 21

❶ **keep a balance between A and B** 將 A 與 B 保持平衡 **strike a balance between A and B** 在 A 與 B 之間維持平衡 **lose one's balance** 失去平衡	• You should **keep a balance between** your family **and** career. 你應**將**家庭**和**事業**保持平衡**。 • You should **strike a balance between** work **and** play. In either case, don't go to extremes. 你應**在**工作**和**遊戲**之間找出平衡點**。不管從事哪一項，千萬不要做過頭。 • As I biked around the corner, I **lost my balance** and fell off. 我騎腳踏車過彎時，**失去平衡**而跌倒了。 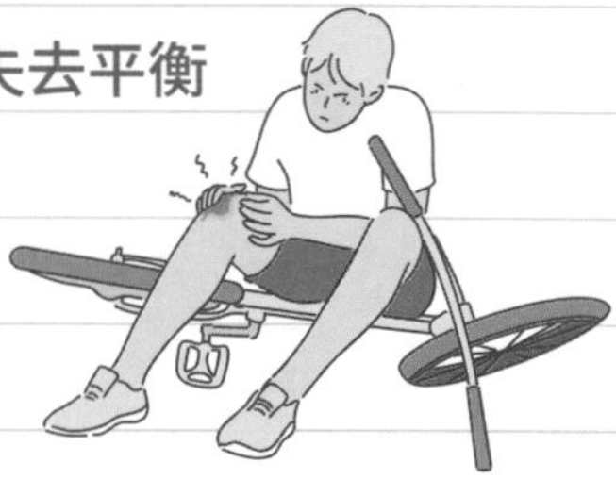
❷ **On balance, ...** = All in all, ... 總的來說，……	• **On balance,** we've had quite a successful year in terms of business. **總的來說**，就生意而言，我們這一年挺成功的。
❸ **get a kick out of...** 從……中得到樂趣	• To tell the truth, I never feel tired of teaching. Instead, I **get a kick out of** it. 老實說，我從未對教書感到厭倦。我反而從**中得到樂趣**。

❹ stimulate
[ˋstɪmjə͵let] *vt.*
激發；促進；激勵

- These courses can **stimulate** a passion for learning.
  這些課程會**激發**對學習的熱愛。
- The government should take immediate action to **stimulate** economic growth.
  政府應立即採取行動**刺激**經濟成長。

❺ hermit
[ˋhɝmɪt] *n.*
隱士；隱修者

- A **hermit** leads / lives a secluded life.
  隱士過著與世隔絕的生活。
  ⋆ secluded [sɪˋkludɪd] *a.* 與世隔絕的

Words in Use

Rosalie: Vinnie! I've not seen you at a party like this in ages. Have you been living as a **hermit** or something?

Vinnie: I guess I have. I just needed a break from the outside world.

Rosalie: And are you having a good time now?

Vinnie: I am **getting a kick out** of being back around people, actually.

羅瑟琳：維尼！我好久沒有見到你出席這種派對。你是過著**隱士**的生活還是怎樣？

維尼：算是吧。我只是需要暫時遠離外面的世界。

羅瑟琳：那你現在玩得開心嗎？

維尼：其實，我還蠻**樂於**重新與大家互動相處。

❻ bucket
[ˋbʌkɪt] *n.* 水桶

in buckets
= in great amounts
大量地

a drop in the bucket
杯水車薪

weep / cry buckets
淚如雨下

- The rain came down **in buckets** last night.
  昨晚大雨**如注**。
- The generous donation by the kind man was still just **a drop in the bucket** for the orphanage.
  那位善心男子的慷慨捐獻對孤兒院來說仍是**杯水車薪**。
- Alice **wept buckets** over the sorrowful story.
  那個悲傷的故事讓愛麗絲**淚如雨下**。

❼ sb's bucket list
某人的一生願望清單

- Benjamin completed an item on his **bucket list** when he published his first novel.
  班傑明出版了他第一本小說時便完成了他一**生願望清單**的其中一項。

❽ kick the bucket
翹辮子，死(俚語)

- Roy wants to travel around the world before he **kicks the bucket.**
  羅伊想在**死**前環遊世界。

喪禮相關物品

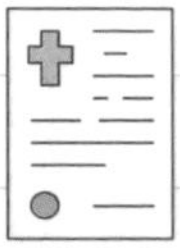
a death certificate 死亡證明書

hearse 靈車

wreath 花圈

urn 骨灰罈

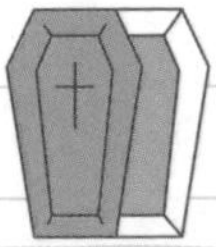
coffin 棺材

❾ **device**

[dɪ`vaɪs] *n.*

裝置，器具

比較

devise

[dɪ`vaɪz] *vt.*

設計；發明

• Rescuers used a special **device** to find survivors trapped in collapsed buildings.

救援者運用特殊**器具**搜尋被困在倒塌大樓中的生還者。

• The cartoon character Mickey Mouse was **devised** by Walt Disney.

卡通角色米老鼠是由華特．迪士尼所**創**的。

Unit 21

Words in Use

Carlos: What's that you're writing?

Miranda: It's my **bucket list**.

Carlos: Oh, no. You're not sick, are you?

Miranda: Don't worry. I'm not **kicking the bucket** anytime soon. I just like to **devise** ways to make every day on this earth count.

Carlos: (*reading*) "Try all flavors of Ben & Jerry's ice cream." Now that's my kind of **bucket list**!

卡洛斯：妳在寫什麼？

米蘭達：這是我的**一生願望清單**。

卡洛斯：喔，不。妳該不會生病了吧？

米蘭達：別擔心。我近期不會**翹辮子**。我只是喜歡**想**個方法讓我在這地球上度過的每一天都值得。

卡洛斯：(閱讀)「嚐嚐看 Ben & Jerry's 冰淇淋的每個口味。」這份**一生願望清單**真合我胃口！

⑩ various
[ˋvɛrɪəs] *a.*
各式各樣的

- The club is composed of | various / a variety of | people.
  本社團是由形形色色的人組成的。

⑪ varied
[ˋvɛrɪd] *a.*
有變化的，非一成不變的

- A varied diet will do you a lot of good.
  有變化的飲食對你會有很大的益處。

⑫ variable
[ˋvɛrɪəbl̩] *a.*
變化無常的，多變的

- The weather in the mountains is variable.
  山上的天氣變化無常。

⑬ vary
[ˋvɛrɪ] *vi.*
變化，不同（常與介詞 with 或 from 並用）
（三態為：vary, varied, varied）

- The menu at this restaurant varies with the season.
  這家餐廳的菜單隨季節變化。

餐廳重要人物

chef 廚師；主廚

sous chef 副主廚

maître d'
餐廳經理；服務生領班

waiter （男）服務生

waitress 女服務生

⑭ **sth of sb's dreams** 某人夢寐以求的東西	• I hope someday I can buy the home **of my dreams**. 我希望有一天我可以買下我**夢想的**房子。

⑮ **dredge** [drɛdʒ] *vt.* 疏浚，清淤	• Those workers are **dredging** the harbor so that larger ships can use it. 這些工人正在替海港**清淤**以供大型船隻使用。

Words in Use

Andrea: I met the man **of my dreams** last night. He's called Bradley.

Jared: And what does Bradley do for a living?

Andrea: He's got **various** jobs, actually. He's a model by day and an actor and singer by night.

Jared: I hate him already.

安德里亞：我昨晚見到了我的**夢中**情人。他叫布萊德利。

傑瑞：那布萊德利是做什麼維生的？

安德里亞：他其實從事**各式各樣的**工作。他白天當模特兒，晚上則是演員和歌手。

傑瑞：我已經討厭他了。

⑯ **impair** [ɪmˋpɛr] *vt.* 損害	• Staring at smartphone screens too long will certainly **impair** your eyesight. 盯著智慧型手機螢幕時間過久一定會**損害**視力。
⑰ **cast** [kæst] *vt.* 投射（三態同形） **cast a shadow on / over...** 使……蒙上陰影 **cast doubt on...** 使對……產生懷疑 **cast an eye over / on...** 匆匆地瀏覽……/ 看一眼…… **cast a spell on...** 對……施咒；把……迷住	• Look! The setting sun is **casting** an orange glow over the mountains. 瞧！夕陽**投射**一道光輝把這些山頭映成橘紅色。 • My grandfather's illness **cast a shadow on** the family reunion. 我爺爺的病情**讓**家族聚會**蒙上一層陰影**。 • The prosecutor **cast doubt on** the woman's alibi. 檢察官**對**該女子的不在場證明**表示懷疑**。 * prosecutor [ˋprɑsɪˏkjutɚ] *n.* 檢察官 alibi [ˋæləˏbaɪ] *n.* 不在場證明 • The editor **cast an eye over** the article and passed it to her colleague. 該編輯把那篇文章**匆匆瀏覽一遍**便傳給她同事。 • The magician **cast a spell on** the rabbit, and it vanished before our eyes. 魔術師**對**兔子**施咒**，牠就在我們眼前消失了。

⑱ spell

[spɛl] *n.*

魔咒；一段時間，一陣子

fall under sb's spell

被某人迷住；被某人下咒

- The moment I met Helena, I completely **fell under her spell.**

  我一見到海蓮娜就完全**拜倒在**她的**石榴裙下**。

- We'll have | **a spell of** / a short period of | warm weather before a cold front arrives.

  我們會有**一陣子**暖和的天氣接著會有一道冷鋒到來。

Words in Use

Meg: When I count to ten and say "abracadabra," you'll fall asleep and wake up as a frog.

Billy: Are you feeling OK, Meg?

Meg: I'm trying to **cast a spell on** you, Billy!

Billy: I don't want to **cast doubt on** your magical abilities, but I don't think it's working.

梅格： 我數到十並說出咒語時，你就會睡著，醒來後將變成一隻青蛙。

比利： 梅格，妳還好嗎？

梅格： 我正試著要**對**你**下咒語**啊，比利！

比利： 我並不想要**懷疑**妳的魔力，但是我不認為這有起作用。

⑲ **spell** [spɛl] *vt.* 拼寫，拼 (字) (三態為：spell, spelled / spelt [spɛlt], spelled / spelt)	• How to spell that word? (×，本問句無主詞，不成句) →How do you **spell** that word? (○) 要怎麼**拼**那個單字呢？ • You've **spelled / spelt** my surname wrong. 你把我的姓**拼**錯了。
⑳ **spell out + why / how / what 等疑問詞引導的名詞子句** 清楚說明為什麼 / 如何 / 什麼…… spell out sth 清楚說明某事	• Be assertive and **spell out how** you feel. 果敢地**說明**你心中的感受。 * assertive [əˋsɝtɪv] *a.* 果敢的 • The government has so far refused to | **spell out** / clarify | its plans. 政府目前仍拒絕**清楚說明**它的計畫。
㉑ **somewhat** [ˋsʌmˏ(h)wɑt] *adv.* 有點，稍微 (置形容詞或副詞前；若修飾動詞，則該置動詞後)	• It's | **somewhat** / a bit | cold today, so you should dress warm. 今天**有點**冷，因此你衣服要穿暖一點。  • Peter has changed | **somewhat** / a bit | since we last met. 自我們上次見面之後，彼得**有些**改變了。

22 somehow

[ˋsʌm͵haʊ] *adv.*
不知怎地；設法
(置句首或句尾)

- Jane is good-looking. **Somehow**, though, there is no chemistry between us.
  阿珍長得不錯。不過，**不知怎地**，我倆並不來電。
- I just got laid off because of the bad economy. However, I'm the breadwinner, so I must find a new job **somehow**.
  我因為景氣差而遭到資遣。不過我是家裡的支柱，因此我得**設法**找到新工作。
  ⋆ breadwinner [ˋbrɛd͵wɪnɚ] *n.* 負擔家中生計的人

Words in Use

Ryan: How do you **spell** "perseverance"?
Clara: Look it up in the dictionary.
Ryan: Can't you just tell me? I know you know. **Spell out** to me why I need to waste time consulting a dictionary when you could just tell me.
Clara: I won't always be around. You need to learn to cope without me **somehow**.

萊恩： 英文單字 perseverance 要怎麼拼？
克萊拉： 去查字典。
萊恩： 妳就不能告訴我嗎？我知道妳會拼。**解釋**一下既然妳可以直接告訴我，那我為什麼需要浪費時間查字典。
克萊拉： 我不會一直都在你身旁。你需要**設法**學習沒有我的時候要如何解決。

㉓ countdown
[ˋkaʊnt͵daʊn]
n. 倒數計時

- Tons of people flocked to Times Square for the New Year's Eve **countdown** party.
  人潮湧入時代廣場來參加新年前夕的**跨年**晚會。

count down (...)
倒數 (……)

- The host started to **count down** the top ten songs this week.
  節目主持人開始**倒數**播放本週前十首熱門歌曲。

㉔ lockdown
[ˋlɑk͵daʊn] *n.*
封鎖

be put / placed on / in lockdown
被封鎖

- The city was soon put / placed on **lockdown** when the pandemic broke out.
  疫情爆發後，很快就**封**城了。

㉕ crackdown
[ˋkræk͵daʊn]
n. 取締，掃蕩
(與介詞 on 並用)

- After the police launched a **crackdown** on drugs, the traffickers went underground.
  警方開始**掃蕩**毒品後，毒販便轉入地下。

crack down on...
嚴厲取締……

- Police are **cracking down on** gangs on a large scale.
  警方展開大規模**掃**黑。

㉖ breakdown
[ˋbrek,daʊn] *n.*
(機器 / 車輛) 故障；(人) 崩潰

break down
(機器 / 車輛) 故障

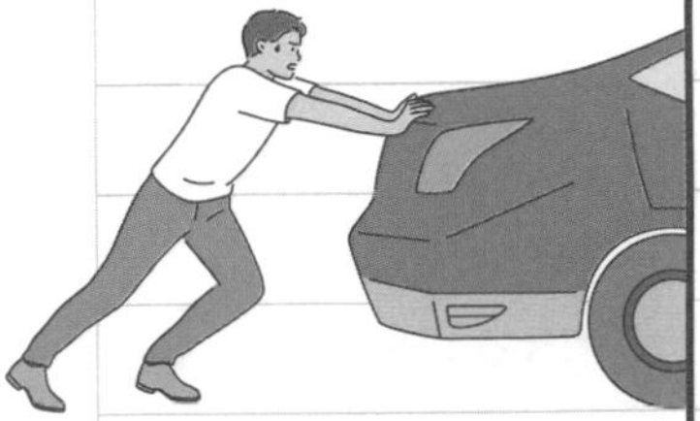

- The **breakdown** of this car was due to a mechanical failure.
  這輛車**拋錨**是機械故障造成的。
- Sarah was on the verge of a nervous **breakdown** after she heard the terrible news.
  莎拉聽到噩耗後幾近**崩潰**。
- My car **broke down** in the middle of nowhere.
  我的車子在渺無人煙之處**拋錨**了。

Unit 21

Words in Use

Charlotte: I can't wait for **lockdown** to be over!
Brendan: Me, neither. I'm **counting down** the days.
Charlotte: Sadly, it looks like it might continue for a bit longer. Too many people are wearing their masks under their nose, gathering in groups, and ignoring the rules.
Brendan: The police need to **crack down on** the rule-breakers!

夏綠蒂： 我等不及**封城**快點結束！
布萊登： 我也是。我正在**倒數**還剩幾天。
夏綠蒂： 令人難過的是，看樣子封城或許會再持續一陣子。太多人口罩都戴在鼻子下面，或是群聚並忽視規定。
布萊登： 警察應該**嚴厲取締**這些違反規定的人！

㉗ shutdown
[ˋʃʌtˏdaʊn] *n.*
停工，歇業

shut down...
將……歇業
(shut 三態同形)

- The **shutdown** of the factory was caused by the recent economic crisis.
  這家工廠**關門**是最近的經濟危機造成的。
- It's a pity that the time-honored restaurant **was** eventually **shut down** because of the pandemic.
  那家歷史悠久的餐廳因疫情爆發而**停止營業**，真令人遺憾。

  * time-honored [ˋtaɪmˏɑnɚd] *a.* 歷史悠久的

㉘ given
[ˋgɪvən] *prep.*
= **considering**
[kənˋsɪdərɪŋ]
= **in view of...**
考慮到 / 有鑑於……

given + that 子句
考慮到 / 有鑑於……

- **Given** his age, Mr. Smith is a remarkably fast runner.
  有鑑於史密斯先生這把年紀，他是跑得非常快的人了。
- I was surprised that the mayor was re-elected, **given that** he had raised taxes by so much.
  考慮到市長把稅收提高這麼多卻還是獲選連任，真是令我訝異。

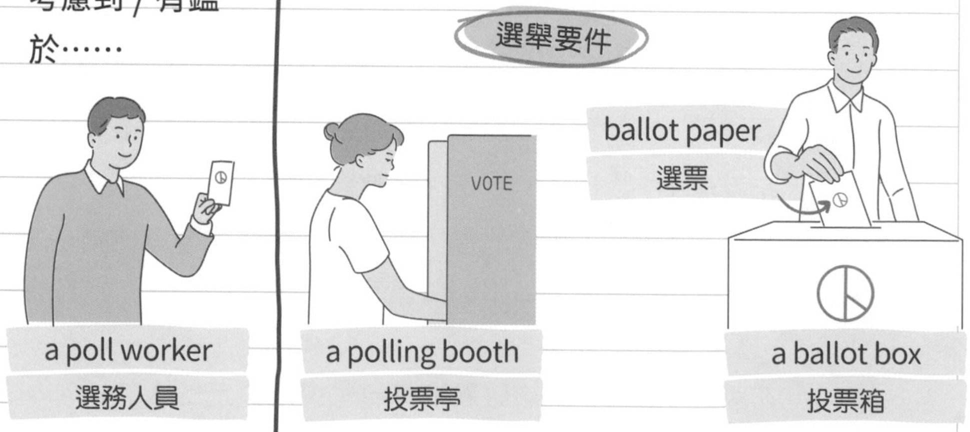

29 Simply put, ... = Put simply, ... 簡言之，……	• **Simply put,** Dean is not cut out for the job. 簡言之，迪恩並不適任這份工作。 • **Put simply,** Paul is not cut out to be a policeman. 簡言之，保羅並不適任當警察。
30 Broadly defined, ... 廣義上來說，……	• **Broadly defined,** a musical instrument is any device created for the purpose of producing musical sounds. 廣義而言，樂器是為了產生音樂而製造的任何器具。

Unit 21

Words in Use

Abby: What's wrong, Jed? You look angry.

Jed: Tony's made another mistake that's cost us a lot of money! If he carries on like this, the whole company will need to **shut down**!

Abby: Don't exaggerate. **Given** his age, I think he's very good at his job.

Jed: I disagree. **Put simply,** he's got to go.

艾比：傑德，怎麼了？你看起來很生氣。

傑德：東尼又犯錯了，讓我們損失大筆金額！如果他繼續這樣，全公司都將需要**歇業**！

艾比：別誇大。**考慮到**他的年紀，我認為他很擅於他的工作。

傑德：我不同意。**簡單來說**，他得走人。

Unit 21

Exercises
練習題

看圖選單字

❶

☐ countdown
☐ breakdown
☐ shutdown

❷

☐ devise
☐ impair
☐ dredge

❸

☐ weep buckets
☐ kick the bucket
☐ cast a spell

選出正解

❶ The police are determined to (crack / lock) down on gun violence.

❷ (Simply / Simple) put, Vince is not in the mood for visitors.

❸ There are (various / varied) solutions to solve the problem.

❹ Henry gets a (jump / kick) out of bungee jumping.

❺ It's a challenging job, but we have to finish it (somehow / somewhat).

句子填空

hermit | defined | Given | device | stimulated

❶ ____________ the circumstances, you've done quite well.

❷ The discovery of oil ____________ economic growth in the area.

❸ Kyle was tired of socializing and decided to live as a ____________.

❹ Broadly ____________, an artist is anyone who draws, paints, or sculpts.

❺ This special ____________ is used to trigger the alarm.

句子重組

❶ work and play / Tim / to strike a balance / finds it hard / between

____

____.

❷ his dreams / Ben / the woman / finally found / of

____

____.

❸ The report / the side effects / spelled out / of / the medication

____

____.

Unit 21

Notes

Unit 22

- [x] ❶ literacy
- [ ] ❷ literate
- [ ] ❸ sow
- [ ] ❹ sow doubt
- [ ] ❺ reap
- [ ] ❻ bear
- [ ] ❼ be born
- [ ] ❽ born
- [ ] ❾ be born by sb
- [ ] ❿ erosion
- [ ] ⓫ erode
- [ ] ⓬ tuck
- [ ] ⓭ reward
- [ ] ⓮ reward
- [ ] ⓯ rewarding
- [ ] ⓰ compensate
- [ ] ⓱ overwhelming
- [ ] ⓲ overwhelmingly
- [ ] ⓳ by contrast (to...)
- [ ] ⓴ stretch
- [ ] ㉑ characteristic
- [ ] ㉒ speed
- [ ] ㉓ speeding
- [ ] ㉔ speedy
- [ ] ㉕ awful
- [ ] ㉖ an awful lot of...
- [ ] ㉗ awesome
- [ ] ㉘ awe
- [ ] ㉙ considerable
- [ ] ㉚ In other words, ...

Unit 22

❶ literacy
[ˋlɪtərəsɪ] *n.* 識字
the literacy rate 識字率

• The country's **literacy rate** has steadily improved over the past few years.
該國的**識字率**在過去幾年有穩定提升。

❷ literate
[ˋlɪtərɪt] *n.* 識字的人 & *a.* 識字的
illiterate
[ɪˋlɪtərɪt] *n.* 文盲，不識字的人 & *a.* 文盲的，不識字的

• Johnson's parents, both **illiterates**, raised him by doing odd jobs.
強森的父母皆**不識字**，兩人打零工把他拉拔長大。

• According to the census last year, 30 percent of the country's population over the age of 70 are **illiterate**.
根據去年的普查，該國七十歲以上的人口有百分之三十**不識字**。

❸ sow
[so] *vt.* & *vi.* 播 (種子)
(三態為：sow, sowed, sowed / sown [son])

• **Sow** the seeds and water them well shortly after.
播種後要立刻澆足夠的水。

• As you **sow**, so shall you reap.
=You reap what you **sow**.
=You get back what you put in.
一分**耕耘**，一分收獲。(諺語)

❹ **sow doubt / confusion / fear**

製造疑慮 / 混亂 / 恐懼

• I feel betrayed now that you've sown doubt in my mind.

你現在使我**心存疑慮**，讓我覺得遭受背叛。

❺ **reap**

[rip] *vt.* & *vi.*

收穫

• Hank has worked hard for years, and he is now **reaping** the rewards of his diligence.

漢克努力多年，現在他正在**收割**他努力的成果。

⋆ diligence [ˋdɪlədʒəns]

n. 勤勉

Unit 22

Words in Use

Dean: Did you pay the bill before we left the café?

Betsy: Of course I did. I mean, I think I did. Hmm... You've **sown doubt** in my mind now. The waitress would've mentioned it if we hadn't paid, right?

Dean: Well, they were very busy. You could be a criminal now, Betsy!

迪恩： 我們離開咖啡廳的時候妳有結帳嗎？

貝琪： 我當然有啊。我的意思是，我想我有吧。嗯⋯⋯。你現在讓我**心存懷疑**了。我們沒有付錢的話服務員當時應該會提到，對吧？

迪恩： 嗯，他們當時非常忙碌。貝琪，妳可能是犯罪了！

❻ bear

[bɛr] *vt.*

攜帶；負荷；具有，帶有；忍受；承擔；生(孩子)；結(果實)(三態為：bear, bore [bɔr], borne / born [bɔrn])

bear a resemblance to sb/sth

與某人 / 某物相似

- The man was arrested for **bearing** arms.
  那名男子因**攜帶**武器而被逮捕。
- This bookshelf can **bear** a load of 50 kilograms.
  這個書架可以**荷重**五十公斤。
- The twins **bear a** striking **resemblance to** each other.
  這對雙胞胎**長得極為相似**。
- The name tag on Dora's uniform also **bears** her job title.
  朵拉制服上的名牌也**標示著**她的職稱。
- I can't **bear** / tolerate / put up with the idea of having to wait two hours.
  想到必須等上兩個鐘頭我就無法**忍受**。
- Whatever happens, I will **bear** the responsibility.
  不管發生什麼事，責任都由我**承擔**。
- The tree is starting to **bear** fruit now.
  這棵樹現在開始**結**果實了。

❼ be born

出生

TIPS

born 置 be 動詞之後，作主詞補語，有形容詞的意味。

• Where were you born?

你在哪裡出生的？

• The brothers were born in 1990 and 1998 respectively.

那對兄弟分別是 1990 年及 1998 年出生的。

• Gary was born by poor parents. (×)

→Gary was born into a poor family. (○)

蓋瑞是寒門出生。

Words in Use

Ian: What are you looking at?

Gwen: Your face, Ian. You bear a striking resemblance to a guy in my office. When were you born?

Ian: March 31st, 1975.

Gwen: He was born in 1975, too. Are you sure you don't have a twin brother?

Ian: I hope not! I couldn't bear the thought of having a brother I've never met!

伊恩： 妳在看什麼？

葛溫： 你的臉啊，伊恩。你長得跟我公司裡的某個人很像。你是什麼時候出生的？

伊恩： 1975 年三月三十一日。

葛溫： 他也是 1975 年出生的。你確定你沒有雙胞胎兄弟嗎？

伊恩： 我希望沒有！我無法承受有個從未謀面的兄弟！

Unit 22

❽ born

[bɔrn] *a.*

天生的

- Patrick is a born musician.

=Patrick was born to be a musician.

派翠克**天生**就是個音樂家。

❾ be borne by sb

某人生下的

have borne sb

生下某人

- Rumor has it that Jacob **was borne by** a poor woman. (少用)

=Rumor has it that Jacob's biological mother was a poor woman. (較常用)

謠傳雅各是一位貧窮的婦女**生**的。/ 謠傳雅各的親生母親是位貧窮的婦女。

- Mary **has borne** five children in all. (少用)

=Mary has given birth to five children in all. (較常用)

瑪麗一共**生**了五個孩子。

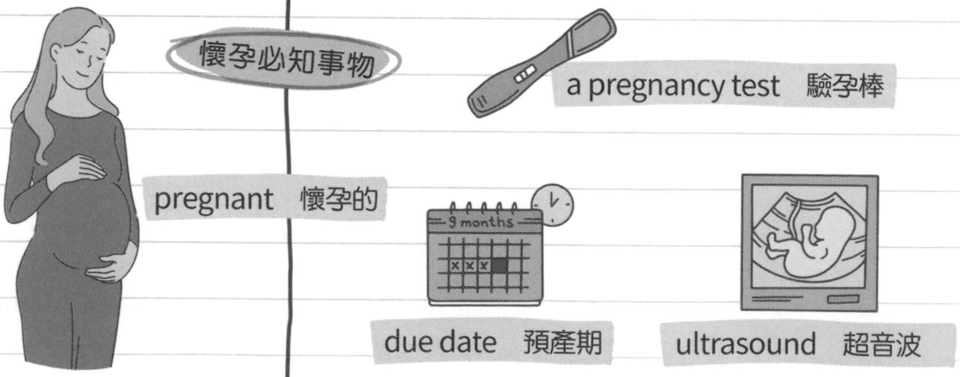

⑩ **erosion**
[ɪˋroʒən] *n.*
侵蝕；損害，削弱

- The problem of soil **erosion** in this area is getting increasingly serious.
  該地區的土壤**侵蝕**問題日趨嚴重。

⑪ **erode**
[ɪˋrod] *vt.* & *vi.*
逐漸侵蝕；損害，削弱

- The cliffs on the coast have been **eroded**.
  海岸上的這些峭壁已被**侵蝕**。
- Repeated failures have slowly **eroded** the young man's confidence.
  一再的失敗**削弱**了這位年輕人的信心。

Words in Use

Rupert: How are you, Georgia? I hope your pregnancy is going well.

Georgia: Quite smoothly, thanks, Rupert. My husband is a **born** worrier, though.

Rupert: That's natural, I think.

Georgia: His worries are starting to **erode** my confidence, though.

Rupert: Oh, well. Only a few months of worry left to go!

魯伯特：喬治亞，妳還好嗎？希望妳的孕期還順利。

喬治亞：還蠻順利的，謝謝你，魯伯特。不過，我先生**天生**就愛擔心。

魯伯特：我想這是很自然的事。

喬治亞：但是他的憂慮也開始**削弱**我的信心了。

魯伯特：喔，沒事，只需要再擔心幾個月就好了！

⑫ tuck

[tʌk] *vt.*

把(衣服、紙張等的邊緣)塞進或捲起

be tucked away in...

隱藏在……之中；位於／坐落於(僻靜的地方)

tuck sb in / up

把某人的被子蓋好

- Shawn **tucked** his shirt in.
  尚恩把他的襯衫**塞進去**。
- The girl **tucked** her skirt up and waded into the river.
  這位女孩把裙子**捲起**然後涉入河中。
  * wade [wed] *vi.* 涉水
- The letter is **tucked** under a pile of books.
  這封信被**塞**在一堆書下面。
- Some of the wildest natural scenery in the United States is **tucked away** / hidden in the state of Maine.
  美國一些最原始的天然景觀就**隱身在**緬因州內。
- The mother **tucked** her children **in** and said good night.
  媽媽**把**孩子們**的被子蓋好**並道晚安。

⑬ reward

[rɪˋwɔrd] *n.*

報酬，獎賞

as a reward for...

作為……的回報／獎賞

- The **rewards** of teaching compensate for the poor salary.
  教書所得的**回報**彌補了微薄的薪資。
- The CEO gave Tim $2,000 **as a reward for** his contribution to our company.
  執行長贈給提姆兩千美元**以酬報**他對本公司的貢獻。

⑭ reward

[rɪˋwɔrd] *vt.*

報答；獎賞

be rewarded with...

得到……作為報酬

reward sb for N/V-ing

某人因……而受到犒賞

- Billy did his chores efficiently and **was rewarded with** an ice cream cone.
  比利做家事很有效率，而得到一支冰淇淋甜筒**作為獎賞**。
- Our boss **rewarded** us handsomely / generously for completing the project successfully.
  我們成功完成該企劃案，**受到**老闆大大的**犒賞**。

Words in Use

Father: How was school today, honey?

Daughter: Very good, Dad. I got **rewarded for** doing well on the history test.

Father: Well done! What was your **reward**?

Daughter: I got a "star of the day" badge.

Father: What about your brother?

Daughter: He got told off for not **tucking** his shirt in.

爸爸：今天在學校過得如何，親愛的？

女兒：非常好，爸爸。我**因為**歷史考試成績優異**而得到獎勵**。

爸爸：做得好！妳的**獎勵**是什麼？

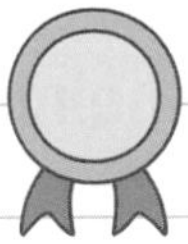

女兒：我得到「本日之星」的徽章。

爸爸：那妳的弟弟呢？

女兒：他因為沒有**將**衣服**紮進**褲子裡而受到責罵。

⑮ rewarding
[rɪˋwɔrdɪŋ] *a.*
值得的；待遇很好的；有意義的

• Teaching is by no means a financially **rewarding** job.
= By no means is teaching a financially **rewarding** job.
教書絕不是個**酬勞很高的**工作。

⑯ compensate
[ˋkɑmpən͵set]
vi. & *vt.*
補償，彌補

compensate for...
= make up for...
彌補……

• Ryan's diligence **compensates** / **makes up** for his deficiency.
萊恩的勤勞努力**補足**了他的不足之處。

⑰ overwhelming
[͵ovəˋwɛlmɪŋ]
a. 壓倒性的；難以抗拒的

• The ruling party won **overwhelming** support in the election.
這次選舉中，執政黨贏得**壓倒性的**支持。

• When Richard's ex-girlfriend saw him, she had an **overwhelming** desire to hit him.
理查的前女友見到他時，她有一股**難以抗拒的**念頭想揍他。

⑱ overwhelmingly
[͵ovəˋwɛlmɪŋlɪ]
adv.
壓倒性地；極為

• The opposition party voted **overwhelmingly** against the proposal.
反對黨以**壓倒性的**多數票反對這項提案。

⑲ **by contrast (to...)** = in contrast (to...) (與……)相較之下	• Life in the city is pretty busy. **By contrast**, living in the country is quite relaxing. 都市生活非常繁忙。**相較之下**，住在鄉間則十分輕鬆。

Words in Use

Lizzie: Do you find your job as an accountant **rewarding**, Xander?

Xander: Not particularly, to be honest. It's boring. I just do it to pay the bills.

Lizzie: There must be something to **compensate** for the boring parts.

Xander: No, not really. It's **overwhelmingly** dull.

Lizzie: I'm sorry. **In contrast to** you, I love my job as a painter!

Xander: Good for you.

麗茲：桑德，你認為你的會計師工作是份**有意義的**工作嗎？

桑德：老實說，不完全是。這份工作很無聊。我工作只是為了要付帳單而已。

麗茲：一定有一些事情可以**彌補**無聊的部分吧。

桑德：不，其實沒有。這份工作**極為**無聊。

麗茲：真可惜。**跟**你**相較之下**，我很喜歡我的畫家工作！

桑德：太棒了。

Unit 22

⑳ **stretch**

[strɛtʃ] *vt.* & *vi.*
拉長，撐大；伸展 & *vt.* 省著（用錢）；延長

stretch one's legs
伸伸腿活動

- My new shoes feel too tight. I need to find something to **stretch** them.
  我的新鞋子太緊了。我需要找個東西把它們**撐大**。
- Be sure to **stretch** before you run.
  跑步前務必要做**伸展**運動。
- I'm going to **stretch** this 100-dollar bill until payday.
  我準備**省著用**這百元美鈔直到發薪日。
- I had planned to stay here for only a few days, but I **stretched** my stay to a week to see more of this amazing city.
  我原本只打算在這裡待上幾天，但後來又將行程**延長**至一週，以便能多看看這座令人驚歎的城市。
- After such a long ride, I need to **stretch my legs**.
  坐了這麼久的車，我需要下車**伸伸腿活動**一下。

常見運動器材

dumbbell 啞鈴

kettlebell 壺鈴

resistance band 阻力帶

yoga mat 瑜珈墊

㉑ **characteristic** [ˌkærəktəˋrɪstɪk] *n.* 特色 & *a.* 典型的；特有的	• Arrogance and laziness are two of Larry's worst characteristics. / traits. 傲慢與懶惰是賴瑞最糟糕的**人格特質**其中兩項。
be characteristic of... = be typical of... 是……的特色	• The white stone houses are characteristic / typical of the island. 白色石屋**是**該島**的特色**。

Words in Use

Ella: Are you coming for a drink with us tonight, Sanjeev?

Sanjeev: I'd love to, but I've hardly got any money. I've got to stretch twenty dollars until the end of the month.

Ella: That's very characteristic of you, Sanjeev.

Sanjeev: I know. I'd like to say I'll learn my lesson, but I know I'll be in exactly the same position next month!

艾拉：桑吉夫，你今晚要和我們一起喝酒嗎？

桑吉夫：我很想，但是我沒有什麼錢。我得**省著**用二十美金直到月底。

艾拉：桑吉夫，你**總是如此**。

桑吉夫：我知道。我很想說我會記取教訓，但是我知道下個月我又會在一樣的處境下！

㉒ **speed** [spid] *vi.* & *vt.* (使) 加速；(使) 快速前進 (三態為：speed, speeded / sped [spɛd], speeded / sped) & *n.* 速度 **speed away** 快速離開	• The car suddenly **sped up** and ran a red light. 那輛車子突然**加速**並闖了紅燈。 • The ambulance | **sped** / rushed | the patient to the hospital. 救護車**把**病人**火速**送到醫院。 • After putting on a coat, Jack **sped away** on his bike. 穿上外套後，傑克就騎著腳踏車**快速離去**了。
㉓ **speeding** [ˋspidɪŋ] *n.* 開車超速	• Helen was fined $200 for **speeding**. 海倫**開車超速**，被罰了兩百美元。
㉔ **speedy** [ˋspidɪ] *a.* 快速的，迅速的	• We wish you a **speedy** recovery from your illness. 我們祝你**早日**從病中康復。 • Best wishes for a **speedy** recovery. Hope you get back on the horse soon. 祝你**早日**康復。也希望你很快重新振作起來。

㉕ **awful** [ˋɔfḷ] *a.* 差勁的；糟糕的	• We've had such **awful** weather over the past month. 過去一個月來，我們這兒的天氣一直都**很糟**。 • I feel **awful** about forgetting my wife's birthday. 我忘了老婆的生日，讓我**很過意不去**。
㉖ **an awful lot of...** 許多的……	• The landlord has **an awful lot of** money. 這位房東錢**多得不得了**。 

Words in Use

Blake: You look **awful**, Angie.

Angie: I was nearly knocked over when I was crossing the road by a driver who was **speeding**.

Blake: Oh, my God! Are you OK?

Angie: Yeah, I'm just a bit shaken.

Blake: There's **an awful lot of speeding** drivers in this area. The police need to erect more **speed** cameras.

布雷克：安琪，妳看起來**很糟**。

安琪：我過馬路的時候差點被一輛**超速的**車子撞倒。

布雷克：喔，我的老天！妳還好嗎？

安琪：還好，我只是有點受到驚嚇。

布雷克：這個區域有**許多**人會**超速**駕駛。警察必須架設更多測**速**照相機。

㉗ awesome [ˋɔsəm] *a.* 令人驚歎的 (= amazing [əˋmezɪŋ])；特棒的；令人生畏的 (= daunting [ˋdɔntɪŋ])

- The **awesome** scenery of the valley is unforgettable.
  這座山谷**令人驚歎的**風景讓人難忘。
- You look **awesome** in that white suit.
  你穿上那套白色西裝看起來**特棒的**。
- Hopefully, no one will ever experience the **awesome** power of a nuclear bomb again.
  希望再也不會有人經歷核彈的**可怕**威力。

㉘ awe [ɔ] *vt.* 使敬畏 & *n.* 敬畏；驚歎 (不可數)

- The visitors were **awed** by the splendor of the cathedral.
  這些觀光客被這座教堂的壯麗給**震攝**了。
- Evan speaks of his grandfather with **awe**.
  艾凡談到他爺爺時都會**肅然起敬**。

㉙ considerable [kənˋsɪdərəbḷ] *a.* 大量的；可觀的

- The fire caused **considerable** damage to the factory.
  這起火災對該工廠造成**很大的**損失。
- It will cost a **considerable** amount of money to rebuild the factory.
  工廠重建將會耗費一筆**很大的**經費。

30 In other words, ...
= To put it another way, ...
= To put it differently, ...
= Put differently, ...
換言之，……

- We all make mistakes. **In other words,** no one is perfect.
  我們都會犯錯。**換言之**，沒有人是完美的。

Words in Use

Dale: I hear you went to see the Taj Mahal when you were in India. It must have been **awesome**!

Florrie: I was **awed** by the beauty of it, Dale. The symmetry and the craftsmanship of it are so impressive. It really must be seen to be believed. **In other words,** you should go see it!

Dale: It's on my bucket list!

戴爾：我聽說妳在印度時有參觀泰姬瑪哈陵。那一定**很棒**！

弗蘿莉：戴爾，我被它的美給**震懾**了。建築的對稱性與工藝令人印象非常深刻。真的要親眼見到才能體會。**換言之**，你應該要去參觀看看！

戴爾：它列在我的一生願望清單上了！

Unit 22

Exercises
練習題

看圖連連看

❶ 

❷ 

❸ 

reward | stretch | speeding

選出正解

❶ The village suffered ______________ damage as a result of the typhoon.

(A) considerable (B) consider

(C) considerate (D) considered

❷ Sally can't ______________ the thought of losing her job.

(A) bore (B) bear

(C) born (D) borne

句子填空

sown | eroded | overwhelming | words | literacy

❶ Jane turned down Sam's proposal. In other ______________, she rejected him.

❷ The ______________ rate is especially low in that region.

❸ The news report has ______________ confusion among the public.

❹ Whenever Kelly hears a gossip, she has a(n) ______________ desire to tell others.

❺ Wind and rain have ______________ the rock into small pebbles.

句子重組

❶ some money / in the closet / Grandma / tucked away / has

____

____.

❷ his lack of experience / compensates / Jim's / for / hard work

____

____.

❸ These patterns / of / the local architecture / characteristic / are

____

____.

Unit 22

Notes

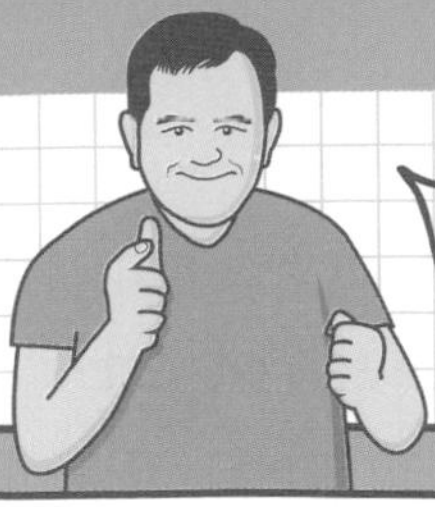

Unit 23

- [x] 1 To this end, ...
- [ ] 2 in the end
- [ ] 3 at the end of...
- [ ] 4 In the beginning, ...
- [ ] 5 at the beginning of...
- [ ] 6 prime
- [ ] 7 prime
- [ ] 8 prime
- [ ] 9 prioritize
- [ ] 10 disperse
- [ ] 11 dispel
- [ ] 12 soothe
- [ ] 13 soothing
- [ ] 14 cringe
- [ ] 15 lifespan
- [ ] 16 a multitude of + 複數名詞
- [ ] 17 apples and oranges
- [ ] 18 in the same breath
- [ ] 19 bark up the wrong tree
- [ ] 20 The apple doesn't fall far from the tree.
- [ ] 21 a chip off the old block
- [ ] 22 gigantic
- [ ] 23 vast
- [ ] 24 tremendous
- [ ] 25 massive
- [ ] 26 immense
- [ ] 27 obsequious
- [ ] 28 have a fondness for...
- [ ] 29 acclaim
- [ ] 30 acclaim

Unit 23

❶ To this end, ...
為了這個目的……，為此……

- We want to save money for a car. **To this end**, we are eating out less often.
  我們想存錢買車。**為了這個目的**，我們正減少外出用餐的次數。

❷ in the end
最後

- Originally. We wanted to take a trip to Europe. **In the end**, however, we chose to stay home to save money.
  我們原先想去歐洲玩。不過，**最後**我們為了省錢，選擇待在家裡。
- The couple got divorced **in the end**.
  這對夫婦**最後**離婚了。

TIPS
in the end 多置句首或句尾。置句首時，之後置逗點，再接主要子句；置句尾時，之前不置逗點。

❸ at the end of...
在……結束時

- Only two people remained **at the end of** the candidate's boring speech.
  該候選人枯燥乏味的演講**結束時**只剩兩個人留下來。

❹ In the beginning, ...
起先，……

- **In the beginning**, I found the book boring. By the end, though, it was quite fun to read.
  起先，我覺得這本書很枯燥。不過，到了結尾，這本書讀起來挺有趣的。

❺ at the beginning of... 在……開頭時	• At the beginning of his speech, Dr. Smith told us a joke. At the end of his speech, he told us another joke. 史密斯博士**在**他演講**開頭**講了一則笑話。演講結束時，他又講了一則笑話。

Words in Use

Olivia: Hey! How was the movie?

Marco: **In the beginning,** I thought it was pretty exciting. There were loads of car chases and action sequences.

Olivia: Sounds right up your street.

Marco: **In the end,** though, it turned into a romance movie. The hero and the main girl got married.

Olivia: Sounds right up my street!

奧莉薇亞： 嘿！那部電影如何？

馬可： **起初**，我想說電影挺刺激的。有許多飛車追逐與動作鏡頭。

奧莉薇亞： 聽起來很對你胃口。

馬可： 不過，**到了結尾**就變成浪漫愛情片了。英雄與女主角最後結婚了。

奧莉薇亞： 聽起來很合我的胃口耶！

❻ **prime** [praɪm] *n.* 盛年；鼎盛時期	• Josh is forty now, but he's still in his **prime**. 喬許年已四十，不過他仍是**英姿煥發**。 • These flowers have long passed their **prime**. 那些花早已過了**盛開時期**。 • The actor | was tragically cut off / died tragically | in his **prime**. 那位演員**英年**早逝。

電影工作人員

❼ **prime** [praɪm] *vt.* 事先指點 (某人)；使 (某人) 做好準備 **prime / prepare sb to V / with sth** 使某人準備好做……/ 某物	• The high-ranking general has **primed** his subordinates **to** give the reporters as little information as possible. 這位高階將領已**事先提點**他的部屬向記者透露愈少資訊愈好。 • The subordinates have been **primed with** good advice. 這些部屬已**得到**好建議**而胸有成竹**了。

❽ prime
[praɪm] *a.*
主要的，首要的；優質的

• Our **prime** concern is to finish the project by the end of this month.
我們的**首要**要務是在這個月底前完成這項企劃案。

• The picky gourmet eats **prime** beef only.
這位挑剔的美食家只吃**上等**牛肉。

❾ prioritize
[praɪˋɔrəˏtaɪz]
vt. & *vi.* 將……按重要性排列；按優先順序處理

• I always make a list of all the jobs I need to do and then **prioritize** them.
我一向都會將我所要做的工作列表，然後再**按重要性一一將**它們**排列**。

Unit 23

Words in Use

Nadia: Did you speak to Mike about the new project?
Gunther: Yes. I **primed** him **with** all the relevant information. And I told him to **prioritize** the most important tasks first.
Nadia: Do you really think he can cope?
Gunther: Absolutely. I promised I'd take him out for some **prime** steak if he succeeds!

娜迪亞：你有與麥克討論新的企劃嗎？
岡瑟：有的。我**向**他**說明**所有相關資訊，也告知他要**優先處理**最重要的事項。
娜迪亞：你真的認為他可以勝任？
岡瑟：當然。如果他成功的話，我答應要請他吃**頂級**牛排！

⑩ disperse [dɪˋspɝs] *vt.* 驅散（人群）& *vi.* 散開	• Police **dispersed** the demonstrators with tear gas. 警方用催淚瓦斯**驅散**了抗議者。
⑪ dispel [dɪˋspɛl] *vt.* 消除（感覺或信念）（三態為：dispel, dispelled, dispelled）	• The mother's soothing words **dispelled** any fears the child had about transferring to another school. 那位母親的安慰話語讓這孩子對轉入他校念書的恐懼**煙消雲散**。
⑫ soothe [suð] *vt.* 安慰，安撫；緩解	• The mother is trying hard to **soothe** her crying baby. 那位母親正努力**安撫**哭泣的小嬰兒。 
⑬ soothing [ˋsuðɪŋ] *a.* 安慰的，使人平靜的	• Listening to **soothing** music helps relieve your stress. 聆聽**讓人放鬆的**音樂可緩解緊張的情緒。

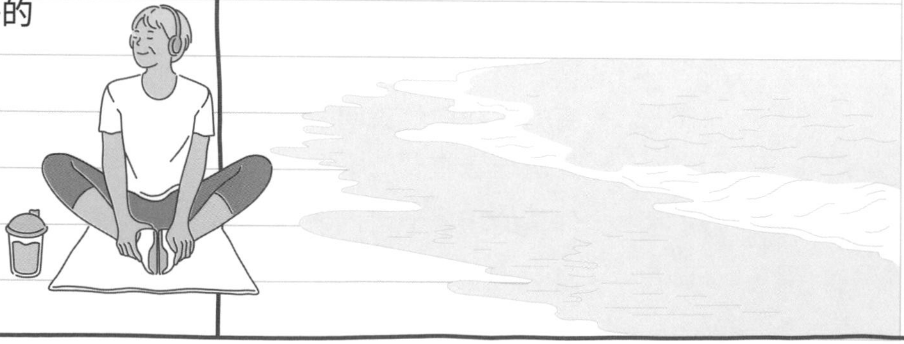

⑭ cringe

[krɪndʒ] *vi.*

退縮，畏縮；感到難為情，感到難堪

- Most people **cringe** at the thought of eating insects.
  許多人想到吃昆蟲就**畏畏縮縮**。
- I | **cringed** / felt embarrassed | at the sight of Mom and Dad kissing.
  我看到老爸與老媽親吻時**感到蠻難為情的**。

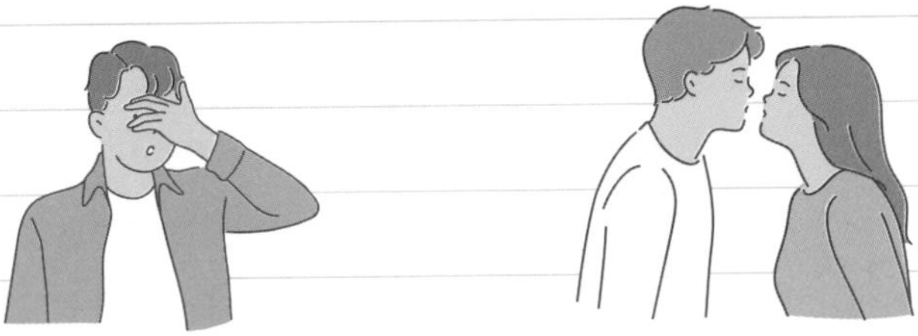

Words in Use

Lena: Why do you never kiss me in public?

Ralph: I **cringe** at the thought of public displays of affection. I'd rather wait until everyone has **dispersed**.

Lena: Well, you need to **dispel** those worries if we're going to have a future as a couple. A girl needs to see evidence that she's loved, you know!

莉娜： 為什麼你都不曾在公開場合親我？

雷夫： 我一想到公開親熱就**覺得難為情**。我寧願等到所有人都**離去**。

莉娜： 喔，如果你未來還想要跟我在一起，你就得**消除**這些擔憂。女生需要看到證據證明她是被愛的，你懂嗎？

⑮ **lifespan** [ˋlaɪf͵spæn] *n.* = life expectancy 預期壽命	• The average **lifespan** of people living in the mountains is 90 years. 居住在山裡的人們平均**壽命**是九十歲。
⑯ **a multitude of + 複數名詞** 許多……	• New York City has **a multitude of** problems, ranging from homelessness to drugs and murder. 紐約市有**許多**問題，從遊民問題到毒品及謀殺都包括在內。 • Harry is generous with his money, which is why he has **a multitude of** friends. 哈利用錢很大方，這也是他有**許多**朋友的原因。

⑰ **apples and oranges** 兩個毫不相干的事	• Japanese curry and Indian curry are as different as **apples and oranges**. 日本咖哩和印度咖哩是**截然不同的**。 • You can't compare these two companies; they're **apples and oranges**. 你不能拿這兩家公司相比；它們**完全是兩回事**。

⑱ in the same breath 同時（說出兩件相牴觸的事） 	• You say Paul treats you badly, but **in the same breath**, you tell me how much you love him! 妳說保羅對妳不好，但**同時**妳又告訴我妳有多愛他！ • You criticized the movie, but then predicted **in the same breath** it would be a great success. 你批評這部電影，但卻**又**預言它會很賣座。

Words in Use

Anita: What's that you're reading?

Raheem: It's an article about **life expectancy**. Did you know that the average lifespan in the US decreased by almost two years between 2018 and 2020?

Anita: Really? Why?

Raheem: **A multitude of** reasons, from access to healthy food to access to affordable healthcare. But mainly it was because of the COVID-19 pandemic.

安妮塔： 你在讀什麼？

拉希姆： 這是一篇關於**預期壽命**的文章。妳知道嗎，2018 年至 2020 年期間，美國的平均壽命降了將近兩年。

安妮塔： 真的嗎？為什麼？

拉希姆： 有**很多**原因，從能不能獲得健康食物到平價的健保都是。但是主要歸咎於新冠肺炎疫情。

Unit 23

⑲ **bark up the wrong tree** 錯怪某人；用錯方法（多用進行式） **bark** [bark] *vi.* 吠；叫	• I didn't take your drink. You're **barking up the wrong tree.** 我沒拿你的飲料。你**錯怪**我了。 • Franklin's proposal was rejected because he was **barking up the wrong tree.** 法蘭克林的提議被拒絕了，這是因為他**用錯方法**了。
⑳ **The apple doesn't fall far from the tree.** 有其父必有其子／有其女必有其母。	• A: Mark's father has been in and out of jail for years. And Mark, like his father, is always causing trouble. B: After all, **the apple doesn't fall far from the tree.** A：馬克的父親多年來常常進出監獄。馬克和他父親一樣，一天到晚都在惹麻煩。 B：畢竟，**有其父必有其子**。 
㉑ **a chip off the old block** 從老木塊脫落的一片碎屑（指性格、行為、長相很像父母親） **chip** [tʃɪp] *n.* 碎片	• Karen is as skilled in painting as her mother. She is **a chip off the old block.** = Karen is as skilled in painting as her mother. Indeed, like mother, like daughter. 凱倫跟她母親一樣擅長繪畫。**有其母必有其女**。

㉒ gigantic

[dʒaɪˋgæntɪk] *a.*

= enormous

[ɪˋnɔrməs]

巨大的，龐大的

- Mandy was frightened by the **gigantic** spider on the wall.

  曼蒂被牆上那隻**大**蜘蛛嚇壞了。

- Ann has a **gigantic** closet for all her clothes.

  安有個**超大的**衣櫃，可容納她所有的衣物。

Words in Use

Shop Owner: Let me see your bag. Did you pay for these comic books?

Boy: Of course.

Shop Owner: I know your father's in prison for stealing, and **the apple doesn't fall far from the tree.**

Boy: You're **barking up the wrong tree.** I'm not a criminal. My mom says she won't let me be **a chip off the old block.**

老闆：讓我看看你的袋子。你有付錢買這些漫畫書嗎？

男孩：當然有。

老闆：我知道你爸爸因為偷竊而入獄，**有其父必有其子**。

男孩：你**錯怪**我了。我不是罪犯。我媽媽說她不會讓我變得**像我爸一樣**。

㉓ vast
[væst] *a.*
巨大的；廣大的

• Google's servers are capable of holding **vast** amounts of information.
谷歌的伺服器能夠乘載**大量的**資訊。

電腦相關用詞

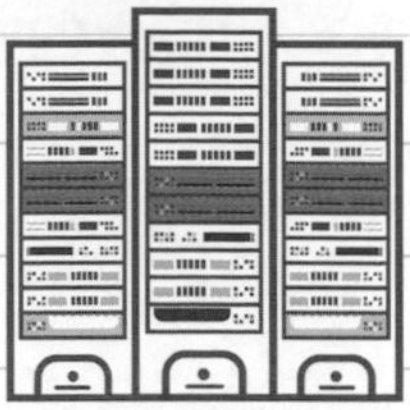

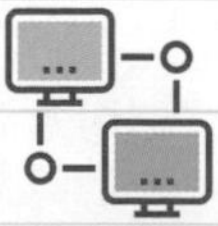

㉔ tremendous
[trɪˋmɛndəs] *a.*
巨大的；極好的

• All of a sudden / Suddenly, the passengers heard a **tremendous** explosion.
乘客突然聽到一陣**巨**響。

• The singer was praised for her **tremendous** voice.
那位歌手因她的**絕美**歌聲而受到讚賞。

㉕ massive
[ˋmæsɪv] *a.*
巨大的；大規模的

• The government troops launched a **massive** / large-scale attack on the rebels.
政府軍對叛軍發動**大規模的**攻擊。

㉖ immense
[ɪˋmɛns] *a.*
巨大的；大量的

• The **immense** structure was completed after three years of construction.
這座**巨大的**建築物在施工三年後落成。

immense wealth 大量的財富 immense value 極高的價值	• Lydia's hard work has been of immense value to our company. 莉迪亞勤奮工作對本公司來說具有極高的價值。 
27 obsequious [əbˋsikwɪəs] *a.* 諂媚的，奉承的	• The salesman's obsequious attitude was starting to irritate me. 該業務員**巴結奉承的**態度開始令我厭煩。

Words in Use

Mother: How was study group? Did you learn a lot?

Son: We had a tremendous time. I think it was of immense value. There were vast numbers of people there. It will have a massive, positive effect on our test scores.

Mother: Did you swallow a thesaurus while you were there?

Son: I just like to practice my vocabulary. I hope you don't think I'm being obsequious.

媽媽：在讀書會還好嗎？你有學到很多嗎？

兒子：我們過得**很**開心。我認為讀書會**非常有意義**。那裡有**非常**多人。它對我們的考試成績會有**很大的**正面影響。

媽媽：你在那邊吞了一本同義詞字典嗎？

兒子：我只是喜歡練一練我的單字量。希望妳不會認為我是在**巴結奉承**。

㉘ have a fondness for...

= have a liking for...
= have a passion for...
= be into...
= be fond of...
= enjoy...
喜歡……

cryptocurrency 加密貨幣

- I have a fondness for hiking in the mountains.
  我**很喜歡**在山中健行。
- It is well known that the millionaire has a fondness for donating to charity.
  眾所皆知那位百萬富翁**喜歡**向慈善機構施善。

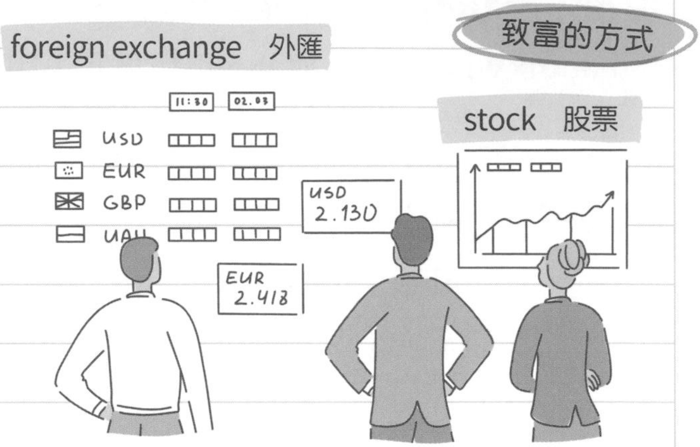

㉙ acclaim
[ə`klem] *vt.*
公開稱譽，讚揚

be acclaimed as...
被譽為……

acclaimed
[ə`klemd] *a.*
受到讚揚的

- The singer's latest album was acclaimed as a masterpiece.
  這位歌手的新專輯**被譽為**傑作。
- The artist's works were highly acclaimed by the press.
  該畫家的作品受到報章雜誌的**稱頌**。
  * the press 新聞界；平面媒體
- My good friend, Dr. Davidson, is a widely | acclaimed / praised | scholar.
  我的好友戴維森博士是個廣**受讚譽的**學者。

30 acclaim

[ə`klem] *n.*

讚揚（不可數）

• The writer's latest novel won popular
| acclaim.
| praise.

這位作家的最新小說贏得一片**讚譽**。

Words in Use

Gwen: Is that the new album by Lady Gaga?

Howard: It certainly is.

Gwen: Ooh, could I borrow it? I have a **fondness for** her music.

Howard: Sure. It has won great **acclaim**. In fact, it's **been acclaimed as** her best work yet.

Gwen: Do you agree?

Howard: Well, I'm **fond of** her early hits, such as "Bad Romance" and "Born This Way."

葛溫：那是女神卡卡的新專輯嗎？

霍華德：沒錯。

葛溫：喔，我可以跟你借嗎？我**很喜歡**她的音樂。

霍華德：可以啊。這張專輯得到很高的**讚賞**。事實上，它**被譽為**女神卡卡至今最佳的作品。

葛溫：你認同嗎？

霍華德：嗯，我**喜歡**她早期的熱門歌曲，像是《羅曼死》與《天生完美》。

Unit 23

Exercises
練習題

看圖選單字

❶

- ☐ acclaim
- ☐ prime
- ☐ prioritize

❷

- ☐ disperse
- ☐ dispel
- ☐ soothe

❸

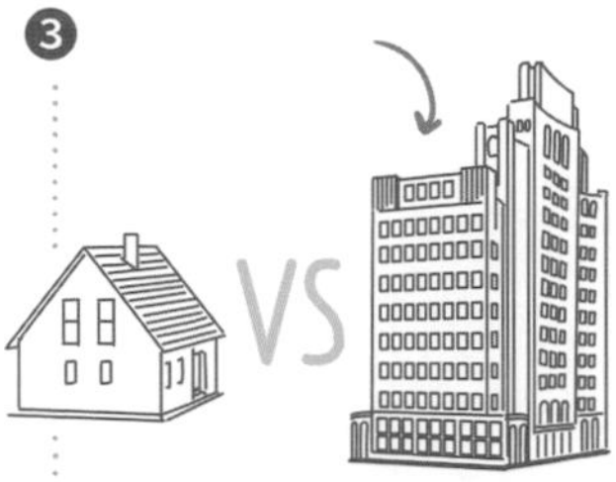

- ☐ obsequious
- ☐ tremendous
- ☐ soothing

選出正解

❶ Vicky said she's going broke, but in the same (breathe / breath), said she wants to buy a new dress.

❷ You should (prioritize / prime) your tasks to be more efficient.

❸ Like her mother, the child has a talent for singing. It proves that the (orange / apple) doesn't fall far from the tree.

❹ George has a (fondness / fond) for collecting coins.

❺ You're (climbing / barking) up the wrong tree if you think I'm the tattletale.

句子填空

dispersed | prime | cringed | end | vast

❶ Sam ______________ at the sound of his own voice on the radio.

❷ A(n) ______________ number of students signed up for the seminar.

❸ The old man was a successful businessman in his ______________.

❹ The crowd ______________ as soon as the police arrived.

❺ At the ______________ of the show, the singer bowed to her fans.

句子重組

Unit 23

❶ primed / his client / to say nothing / The lawyer / in court

____

____.

❷ a multitude / raised / The test result / questions / of

____

____.

❸ introduced / at the beginning of / himself / The speaker / his speech

____

____.

Notes

Unit 24

- [x] 1 come with...
- [ ] 2 have come a long way
- [ ] 3 Come again?
- [ ] 4 come as a shock to sb
- [ ] 5 fit in with...
- [ ] 6 shame
- [ ] 7 shame
- [ ] 8 sth of choice
- [ ] 9 put sb/sth to shame
- [ ] 10 ashamed
- [ ] 11 shameful
- [ ] 12 in the aftermath of...
- [ ] 13 soar
- [ ] 14 leave out sth
- [ ] 15 be / feel left out
- [ ] 16 catch on
- [ ] 17 catch on to...
- [ ] 18 put... under threat
- [ ] 19 itchy
- [ ] 20 be itching to + V
- [ ] 21 be itching for + N
- [ ] 22 intense
- [ ] 23 intensive
- [ ] 24 against all odds
- [ ] 25 despite...
- [ ] 26 despite oneself
- [ ] 27 season
- [ ] 28 season
- [ ] 29 seasoning
- [ ] 30 seasoned

Unit 24

❶ **come with...** (東西) 配備 有……；附有……	• The album **comes with** all the lyrics of the songs. 這張專輯**配有**所有歌曲的歌詞。 * lyrics [ˋlɪrɪks] *n.* 歌詞 (恆用複數)
❷ **have come a long way** = have made a lot of progress 大有進步	• Paul **has come a long way** from his days as an unknown singer. Now, he is a world renowned superstar. 保羅從早期還是個默默無名的歌手到現在已**大有進步**。他現在是世界知名的巨星。

❸ **Come again?** = (May) I beg your pardon? = Pardon (me)? 請再說一遍。	• A: Nice to meet you. I'm Marian. B: **Come again?** A: My name is Marian. A：很榮幸認識你。我叫瑪麗安。 B：**請再說一遍**。 A：我的名字是瑪麗安。

❹ **come as a shock to sb** (事情 / 事件) 令某人震驚	• The sudden death of the young singer came as a terrible shock to her fans. 這位年輕歌手的驟逝消息**令**她的粉絲大為**震驚**。
❺ **fit in with...** 跟……打成一片；融入……	• The transfer student quickly fit in with his classmates. 這位轉學生很快就**與**班上的同學**打成一片**。

Words in Use

Son: Mom! Mom! I won the "Boy of the Year" award!

Mom: Come again?

Son: The boy of the year in our school—it's me! I can tell that's come as a shock to you!

Mom: Well... It's just... Congratulations, son! I always knew you could do it! You've certainly come a long way since those days when you were always in trouble.

兒子：媽，媽！我贏得「年度男模範生」的獎項！

媽媽：什麼？**再說一遍**。

兒子：校內本年度男模範生 —— 就是我！看得出來這消息讓妳**很震驚**！

媽媽：嗯……只是……。恭喜你，兒子！我一直都知道你可以的！你從總是鬧事的那段日子到現在真的**大有進步**。

❻ shame

[ʃem] *n.*

遺憾（常用單數）；可恥，羞愧（不可數）

It is a shame + that 子句

真可惜／遺憾……

- A: I'm afraid I can't attend your wedding.
  B: What a **shame**! / pity!
  A：我恐怕沒辦法參加你的婚禮了。
  B：真**可惜**！
- The little boy hung his head in **shame** when his father scolded him.
  父親斥責小男孩時，小男孩**羞愧**得低下頭來。
- **Shame on you!**
  你真**丟臉**！
- **It's a shame** / pity that you missed the party last night. We all had a great time.
  = It's too bad that you missed the party last night. We all had a great time.
  真遺憾你錯過了昨晚的派對。我們大家都玩得很開心。

常見派對類型

costume party　變裝派對

slumber party / sleepover　睡衣派對

beach party　沙灘派對

❼ shame [ʃem] *vt.* 使羞愧 / 慚愧；使蒙受恥辱；使黯然失色	• It shamed me to learn that I failed the test. 我獲知考試沒及格時，我**羞愧**極了。 • Tom's great performance shamed / disgraced all the other competitors. 湯姆的優秀表現**令**其他競爭對手**黯然失色**。
❽ sth of choice 首選的事物	• Jazz is my genre **of choice** to listen to on long bus rides. 爵士樂是我坐長途巴士途中**首選的**曲類。

Words in Use

Todd: Would you like to come see Taylor Swift with me on Saturday night? I've got a ticket going spare.

Steff: Oh, I'm going to a wedding on Saturday.

Todd: That's a **shame**! I know you would love to see her.

Steff: Yeah, she's definitely my performer **of choice**. Maybe next time.

Todd: Sure thing!

陶德：妳這週六晚上要不要跟我去看泰勒絲的演唱會？我有多的門票。

史黛夫：喔，我週六要去參加婚禮。

陶德：真**可惜**！我知道妳會想去看她的。

史黛夫：對啊，她絕對是我**首選的**藝人。可能下次吧。

陶德：沒問題！

❾ put sb/sth to shame
使某人 / 某事蒙羞

- The new co-worker's excellent performance **puts us to shame**.
這位新進同仁優秀的表現**令**我們**汗顏**。
- I thought I was a great singer, but you **put me to shame**.
我還以為我歌唱得不錯，可是你比我技高一籌 / **讓我顏面無光**。
- Mary's cooking **puts** mine **to shame**.
瑪麗的廚藝**使**我（的廚藝）**相形見絀**。

❿ ashamed
[əˋʃemd] *a.*
感到羞愧 / 可恥的

- David was **ashamed** to admit (to) his mistakes.
大衛**很羞愧**不敢承認他的錯誤。

be ashamed of...
對……感到羞愧

- I **was ashamed of** having cheated on my wife.
= I was **ashamed** that I had cheated on my wife.
我對太太不忠實，**感到很羞愧**。

⓫ shameful
[ˋʃemfəl] *a.*
令人羞愧 / 可恥的（修飾行為或事情）

- I can't believe my parents kept that **shameful** secret for years.
我父母多年來一直隱瞞這**醜聞**，真是令人不敢置信。

⑫ **in the aftermath of...** 在(災難、意外、戰爭等事件)之後	• Food prices rapidly soared **in the aftermath of** the flood. 水災**過後**食物價格迅速上漲。
⑬ **soar** [sɔr] *vi.* 急升，猛漲；(鳥) 翱翔	• I spotted an eagle **soaring** high in the sky. 我看到一隻老鷹在天空中**翱翔**。

Words in Use

Javier: So, what do you think of the meal?

Penelope: It's very nice.

Javier: You don't have to say that just to make me feel better. I know your cooking **puts** mine **to shame**. That lasagna you made last week was superb!

Penelope: Actually, I'm **ashamed** to admit this, but... I didn't make it. I ordered it from a restaurant.

Javier: Penelope!

哈維爾：妳覺得那頓飯如何？

潘妮洛普：很好啊。

哈維爾：妳不用為了讓我心情好一點而那樣說。我知道妳的廚藝**使**我**相形見絀**。妳上週做的那道千層麵棒極了！

潘妮洛普：其實，我很**羞愧**不敢承認，但是……那不是我做的。我是從餐廳訂的。

哈維爾：潘妮洛普！

Unit 24

⑭ leave out sth
= leave sth out
遺漏某事物；省略某事物

- Tim **left out** some important details in his report.
  提姆在他的報告中**漏掉了**一些重要的細節。
- If you are on a diet, you should **leave** the butter **out** when baking the cake.
  你若在節食，製作蛋糕時就應**省略**奶油。

⑮ be / feel left out
遭到 / 感覺被孤立

- The little boy **felt** | **left out** / isolated | because no one wanted to be friends with him.
  小男孩**覺得遭受孤立**，因為誰都不想跟他做朋友。

⑯ catch on
流行

- I believe miniskirts will | **catch on** / come into vogue / come into fashion / be in fashion / be popular | again in the foreseeable future.
  我相信在可預見的未來迷你裙會再度**流行**。

⑰ catch on to...
= understand...
了解⋯⋯

- I'm sorry, but I still haven't **caught on to** what you said.
  很抱歉，我仍不**了解**你剛才說的話。

⑱ **put... under threat** = pose a threat to... 使……受到威脅	• Human activities have **put** the existence of many wild animals **under threat**. = Human activities are **posing a threat to** the existence of many wild animals. 人類的活動已／正**威脅**許多野生動物的生存。

Words in Use

Father: What's the matter, Sophie? You look sad.

Daughter: My friends didn't include me in their plans. I **feel left out**.

Father: Why did they do that?

Daughter: They laugh at me because I like knitting. They say it's an old-fashioned hobby.

Father: I'm sorry, honey. You'll be the one laughing when your hobby **catches on** and you find better friends.

爸爸： 怎麼了，蘇菲？妳看起來很難過。

女兒： 我的朋友們都不讓我參與他們的計畫。我**覺得被孤立**了。

爸爸： 他們為什麼要這樣？

女兒： 他們因為我喜歡編織而嘲笑我。他們說這是過時的嗜好。

爸爸： 親愛的，我真抱歉。妳的嗜好開始**流行**而且妳找到更好的朋友後，反過來笑的人會是妳。

⑲ itchy
[ˋɪtʃɪ] *a.*
發癢的

• Tamara's nose gets **itchy** from the dust and pollen in the air.
空氣中的灰塵及花粉讓塔瑪拉的鼻子**發癢**。

常見過敏原

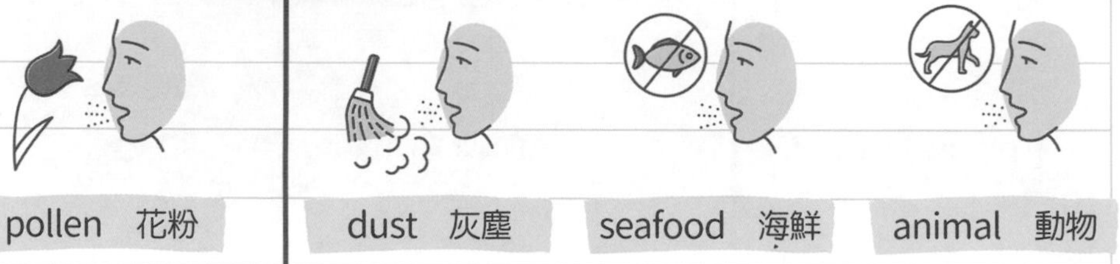

⑳ be
itching
yearning
dying
eager
to + V
渴望要……；急切想要……

• To tell you the truth, I'm **itching to** find a new job. I'm sick and tired of doing the same old job every day.
老實跟你說，我**巴不得**找份新工作。我受夠每天做一成不變的工作了。

㉑ be
itching
yearning
dying
eager
for + N
渴望……

• The audience **was itching for** the boring speech to end.
聽眾**巴不得**這場枯燥的演講馬上結束。

㉒ intense
[ɪnˋtɛns] *a.*
強烈的

• The **intense** heat of summer in southern Taiwan can be unbearable.
南臺灣夏天的**酷**熱可能會讓人受不了。

㉓ intensive
[ɪnˋtɛnsɪv] *a.*
密集的；加強的

• Ron | enrolled in / signed up for / registered for | a six-month **intensive** Korean language course.
榮恩報名參加為期半年的韓語**加強**課程。

Words in Use

Sasha: Will you stop pacing up and down the room!

Jay: I'm so bored stuck in this apartment. I'm **itching to** go outside.

Sasha: You know you're allergic to pollen. This is the worst time of the year for people with hay fever. You'd be **itchy** and sneezing in no time!

Jay: I know, I know. The pollen levels are pretty **intense**.

莎夏： 你可以不要在房間裡反覆走動嗎？

傑： 我被困在這公寓裡真是無聊死了。我**巴不得**趕快出去外面。

莎夏： 你知道你對花粉過敏。對有花粉熱的人來說，現在是一年當中最糟糕的時節。你會馬上**發癢**又打噴嚏！

傑： 我知道，我知道。花粉指數挺**高**的。

㉔ against all odds

儘管成功機率不大

TIPS

此處 odds 是名詞，恆用複數，表示「機率」、「可能性」。

• **Against all odds**, we defeated all the other teams and won the championship.

儘管勝算不大，我們還是擊敗了其他球隊並贏得冠軍。

• **Against all odds**, the patient made a full recovery.

儘管機率不大，這位病人仍完全康復了。

㉕ despite...

= in spite of...

儘管……

• **Despite** the power failure, the hospital continued to function properly.

儘管停電，醫院還是繼續正常運作。

• Poppy did well in the singing competition **despite** being sick.

= Poppy did well in the singing competition **in spite of** the fact that she was sick.

儘管生病，波比仍然在歌唱比賽表現優異。

TIPS

ⓐ despite 與 in spite of 同義，均視作介詞，表示「儘管」，之後可接名詞、代名詞、動名詞作受詞。

ⓑ 不可直接用 that 引導的名詞子句作 despite 或 in spite of 的受詞。應在 that 子句前先置名詞 the fact 作受詞，再接 that 子句，使該子句成為 the fact 的同位語。

㉖ despite oneself
不由自主地，忍不住地

• When I heard the funny joke, I laughed **despite myself**.
= I couldn't | help / resist | laughing when I heard the funny joke.
= I couldn't help but laugh when I heard the funny joke.
我聽到這則笑話時**忍不住**笑了。

Words in Use

Nick: Did you hear that, **against all odds**, England won the World Cup?

Jessica: I've got no interest in soccer.

Nick: But it was an amazing performance! They won **despite** all the injuries and the problems they experienced.

Jessica: I'm still not interested.

Nick: Just watch a soccer match with me. You might enjoy it **despite yourself**!

尼克：妳有聽說**即使勝算不大**，英格蘭仍贏了世界盃足球賽嗎？

潔西卡：我對足球毫無興趣。

尼克：可是那場表現很令人驚豔！**儘管**遭遇受傷與許多問題，他們仍贏了。

潔西卡：我還是沒興趣。

尼克：跟我一起看一場足球賽。妳或許會**忍不住**喜歡足球比賽！

㉗ season
[ˋsizn̩] *n.* 季節

in season
正值盛產季；在旺季

out of season
非盛產季；在淡季

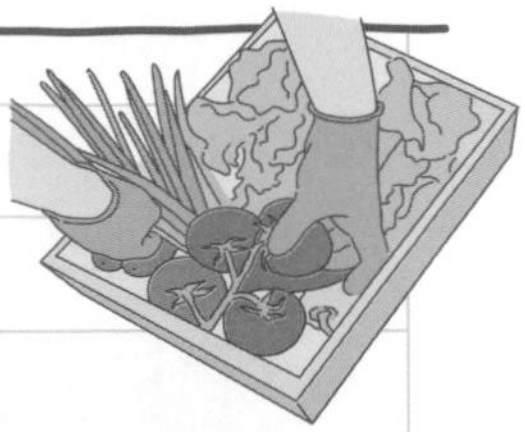

• Tomatoes won't be **in season** until late summer.
番茄要到夏末才是**盛產旺季**。

• Wax apples are **out of season** at this time of the year. They are usually in season from May to July.
每年這個時候蓮霧是**淡季**。它們通常要到五月至七月間才會盛產。

㉘ season
[ˋsizn̩] *vt.*
加調味料；(木頭) 風乾

• **Season** the pork with a bit of sugar and see how it tastes.
把豬肉加點糖**調味**，看看滋味如何。

• All wood has to be **seasoned** before being used.
所有木頭必須經過**風乾**後才能使用。

常見調味料

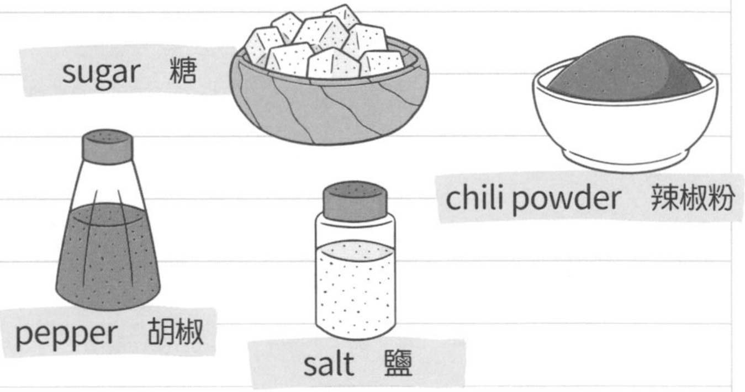

㉙ seasoning
[ˋsizn̩ɪŋ] *n.*
調味料，佐料

• Add **seasoning** to the fish and steam it for ten minutes before serving.
先把魚加上**佐料**再蒸十分鐘就可上桌了。

30 seasoned
[ˋsiznd] *a.*
經驗豐富的，老到的；(食物) 調好味的

- Dean has traveled around the world three times. He may well be called a **seasoned** traveler.
  迪恩已環遊世界三次了。他堪稱旅遊**老手**。
- This soup is highly **seasoned**.
  這道湯的**調味**很濃。

Words in Use

Irene: I hear you're going on vacation next week, Alf. Anywhere nice?

Alf: That's right, Irene. I'm going to Spain.

Irene: Why did you choose to go **out of season**? Won't it be cold?

Alf: No, it'll still be warm. And there'll be fewer people, so it'll be easier to get into museums and restaurants. Don't worry—I'm a **seasoned** traveler!

艾琳：艾爾夫，我聽說你下週要去度假。要去哪個好地方呢？

艾爾夫：沒錯，艾琳。我要去西班牙。

艾琳：為什麼你選擇**在淡季**去啊？不會冷嗎？

艾爾夫：不，那裡還會很暖和。而且那裡的人會比較少，所以比較容易進入博物館與餐廳。別擔心 —— 我是個旅遊**老手**！

Unit 24

Exercises
練習題

看圖連連看

❶ 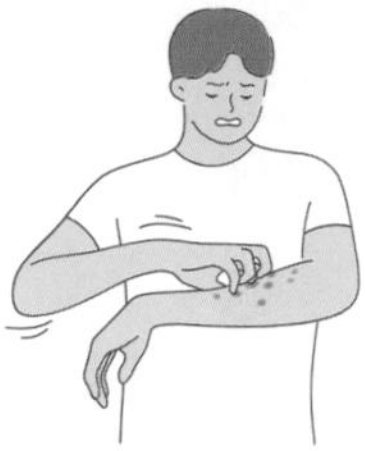

❷ 

❸ 

season　　itchy　　soar

選出正解

❶ Sarah is ____________ to try on her new dress.

(A) died　　(B) yearned

(C) itchy　　(D) itching

❷ George has been hiding his ____________ past from his friends.

(A) shameful　　(B) shame

(C) ashamed　　(D) shamed

句子填空

Against | despite | shock | intense | aftermath

❶ Arthur felt sorry for the poor child ______________ himself.

❷ The news of Margery's resignation came as a(n) ______________ to us all.

❸ In the ______________ of the war, many people were living in poor conditions.

❹ ______________ all odds, Phil's start-up became a worldwide business.

❺ Donald suddenly felt a(n) ______________ pain in his back.

句子重組

❶ his colleagues / William / fit in / finds it hard to / with

____

____.

❷ Lillian / changed / sugar / by leaving out / the recipe

____

____.

❸ couldn't / the lesson / to / The new student / catch on

____

____.

Notes

Answers
解答

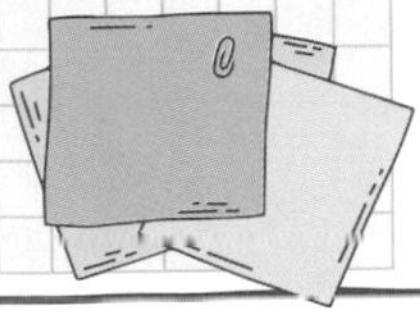

Unit 1

看圖選單字

❶ exhausted ❷ scorching hot ❸ cough

選出正解

❶ off ❷ shoulders ❸ fortune ❹ on ❺ bite

句子填空

❶ out ❷ temper ❸ buried ❹ favor ❺ sold

句子重組

❶ The bad man cheated Cindy out of her money
❷ It takes luck to win the lottery
❸ Our company has come a long way in the past 30 years

Unit 2

看圖連連看

❶ grab a bite to eat ❷ look into the mirror ❸ It's ten exactly.

選出正解

❶ C ❷ B

句子填空

❶ feet ❷ knowledge ❸ relate ❹ dark ❺ talent

句子重組

❶ Ethan doesn't want to let his father down
❷ Ben chowed down on his food because he was starving
❸ When it comes to sports, Matt has no equal

Answers
解答

Unit 3

看圖選單字

❶ smash into pieces ❷ pull over ❸ go sightseeing

選出正解

❶ well-known ❷ afford ❸ by ❹ dye ❺ word

句子填空

❶ boast ❷ sight ❸ wordy ❹ plate ❺ appreciate

句子重組

❶ I recommend Henry without reservation

❷ Word has it that Sam is having an affair

❸ Claire is not in the mood for games

Unit 4

看圖連連看

❶ bumper to bumper ❷ toss a coin ❸ litter

選出正解

❶ A ❷ D

句子填空

❶ liking ❷ chipped ❸ ends ❹ cautious ❺ show

句子重組

❶ Frank looks sharp in that outfit

❷ We have no option but to start over

❸ The old man is dead set against moving to a new house

Unit 5

看圖選單字

❶ slip ❷ weight ❸ with care

選出正解

❶ spot ❷ anything ❸ mind ❹ up ❺ off

句子填空

❶ mind ❷ end ❸ short ❹ well ❺ miss

句子重組

❶ Sally is striving to maintain a healthy lifestyle

❷ Mason knows the ins and outs of the project

❸ Ben is weighed down by the responsibilities

Unit 6

看圖連連看

❶ heartbreaking ❷ take sb on a ride ❸ stubborn

選出正解

❶ C ❷ B

句子填空

❶ nothing ❷ slim ❸ home ❹ point ❺ Though

句子重組

❶ It's a one-hour drive from my house to the beach

❷ Irene jumped at the chance to meet her idol

❸ It came as no surprise that Gary proposed to Helen

Answers
解答

Unit 7

看圖選單字

❶ dance to the music ❷ a bolt of lightning ❸ cheeky

選出正解

❶ blue ❷ fullest ❸ date ❹ With ❺ eye

句子填空

❶ wonders ❷ reference ❸ pastime ❹ dates ❺ handy

句子重組

❶ I can't believe Henry asked me out on a date
❷ In Sam's eyes, Tess is the prettiest girl in school
❸ This meal is low in calories

Unit 8

看圖連連看

❶ a spare tire ❷ go bad ❸ flood

選出正解

❶ D ❷ A

句子填空

❶ associated ❷ go ❸ leave ❹ duty ❺ to

句子重組

❶ The last thing my boyfriend would ever do is betray me
❷ I'm happy to call this house my own
❸ Karen is the last person who would steal things from me

Unit 9

看圖選單字

❶ see red ❷ keep in shape ❸ yellow

選出正解

❶ borrowed ❷ on ❸ Upon ❹ thumb ❺ white

句子填空

❶ smiled ❷ immune ❸ impulse ❹ black ❺ root

句子重組

❶ Oil prices will remain high for a long time to come

❷ Let's paint the town red to celebrate your birthday

❸ Roger is in the pink after a good rest

Unit 10

看圖連連看

❶ signature ❷ eat like a horse ❸ needy

選出正解

❶ B ❷ C

句子填空

❶ budget ❷ short ❸ genuine ❹ top ❺ drawbacks

句子重組

❶ Your well-being is above everything else

❷ This jacket comes in various sizes

❸ The chairman laid stress on protecting the environment

Answers
解答

Unit 11

看圖選單字

❶ shut-eye ❷ fulfilled ❸ ditch sb

選出正解

❶ word ❷ chord ❸ broke ❹ fear ❺ aside

句子填空

❶ dares ❷ suit ❸ trace ❹ burn ❺ best

句子重組

❶ Samuel was awakened to the dangers of smoking
❷ Charlie and I enjoy each other's company
❸ Betty is married to her childhood friend

Unit 12

看圖連連看

❶ bony ❷ feel at ease ❸ map

選出正解

❶ C ❷ A

句子填空

❶ penciled ❷ treats ❸ halt ❹ amount ❺ threatened

句子重組

❶ Sam made the most of the beautiful day and went hiking
❷ Ben was replaced because he wasn't cut out for the job
❸ The customer made no bones about his dissatisfaction

Unit 13

看圖選單字

❶ break down ❷ hit the sack ❸ set the table

選出正解

❶ out ❷ realized ❸ horizons ❹ into ❺ effect

句子填空

❶ record ❷ example ❸ heyday ❹ nervous ❺ seclusion

句子重組

❶ Fiona was set up by her colleague

❷ Phil is all set for the trip to Paris

❸ Dylan was reduced to living on the streets

Unit 14

看圖連連看

❶ bush ❷ caregiver ❸ slimy

選出正解

❶ B ❷ C

句子填空

❶ discount ❷ quitting ❸ cheap ❹ discreet ❺ hype

句子重組

❶ New job opportunities are just around the corner

❷ The number of new students has reached a record low

❸ It's beyond me why anyone would hate chocolate

Answers
解答

Unit 15

看圖選單字

❶ launch a rocket ❷ answer the phone ❸ heaven

選出正解

❶ elbow ❷ habitable ❸ independent ❹ perceives ❺ alert

句子填空

❶ pace ❷ fought ❸ conceive ❹ odds ❺ unfazed

句子重組

❶ Gary came close to winning the match
❷ The car accident left five people injured
❸ Let's put your ideas into practice

Unit 16

看圖連連看

❶ sniff ❷ takeaway ❸ maze

選出正解

❶ D ❷ A

句子填空

❶ cracked ❷ handle ❸ credited ❹ air ❺ dispose

句子重組

❶ The pop star has a huge following around the world
❷ Keith tends to weigh people up quickly
❸ The actress took the world by storm with her performance

Unit 17

看圖選單字

❶ be soaking wet ❷ sprain ❸ grin

選出正解

❶ day ❷ pride ❸ broke ❹ disagree ❺ before

句子填空

❶ numbered ❷ far ❸ mistake ❹ effect ❺ drudgery

句子重組

❶ Sally holds her mentor in high esteem
❷ There is no point in arguing about the issue
❸ Calvin studied English all day long

Unit 18

看圖連連看

❶ double ❷ lose one's sight ❸ perspiration

選出正解

❶ C ❷ D

句子填空

❶ bargain ❷ exasperated ❸ sight ❹ lone ❺ scrambled

句子重組

❶ Harry resigned as the CEO of the company
❷ The manager cashed in on the singer's fame
❸ Joe is quick to point out other people's mistakes

Answers
解答

Unit 19

看圖選單字

❶ ship ❷ take notes of... ❸ prey

選出正解

❶ lead ❷ note ❸ disappointment ❹ rather ❺ forces

句子填空

❶ terms ❷ faulty ❸ mindset ❹ eye ❺ addicted

句子重組

❶ It's unhealthy to bottle up your emotions
❷ The clerk had trouble handling the customer
❸ The rabbit disappeared in the blink of an eye

Unit 20

看圖連連看

❶ triumph ❷ glue ❸ somber

選出正解

❶ B ❷ D

句子填空

❶ precarious ❷ possum ❸ tuned ❹ tune ❺ swept

句子重組

❶ The couple's marriage ended in divorce
❷ Vicky felt out of place in a new environment
❸ This piece of art is like no other

Unit 21

看圖選單字

❶ shutdown ❷ devise ❸ weep buckets

選出正解

❶ crack ❷ Simply ❸ various ❹ kick ❺ somehow

句子填空

❶ Given ❷ stimulated ❸ hermit ❹ defined ❺ device

句子重組

❶ Tim finds it hard to strike a balance between work and play

❷ Ben finally found the woman of his dreams

❸ The report spelled out the side effects of the medication

Unit 22

看圖連連看

❶ stretch ❷ reward ❸ speeding

選出正解

❶ A ❷ B

句子填空

❶ words ❷ literacy ❸ sown ❹ overwhelming ❺ eroded

句子重組

❶ Grandma has tucked away some money in the closet

❷ Jim's hard work compensates for his lack of experience

❸ These patterns are characteristic of the local architecture

Answers
解答

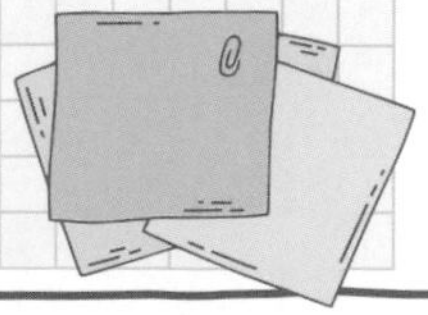

Unit 23

看圖選單字

❶ acclaim ❷ soothe ❸ tremendous

選出正解

❶ breath ❷ prioritize ❸ apple ❹ fondness ❺ barking

句子填空

❶ cringed ❷ vast ❸ prime ❹ dispersed ❺ end

句子重組

❶ The lawyer primed his client to say nothing in court

❷ The test result raised a multitude of questions

❸ The speaker introduced himself at the beginning of his speech

Unit 24

看圖連連看

❶ itchy ❷ soar ❸ season

選出正解

❶ D ❷ A

句子填空

❶ despite ❷ shock ❸ aftermath ❹ Against ❺ intense

句子重組

❶ William finds it hard to fit in with his colleagues

❷ Lillian changed the recipe by leaving out sugar

❸ The new student couldn't catch on to the lesson

Notes

Notes

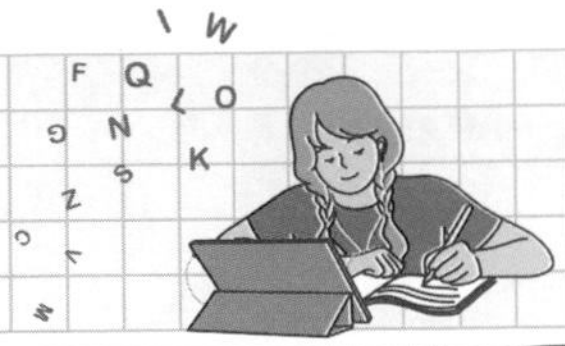

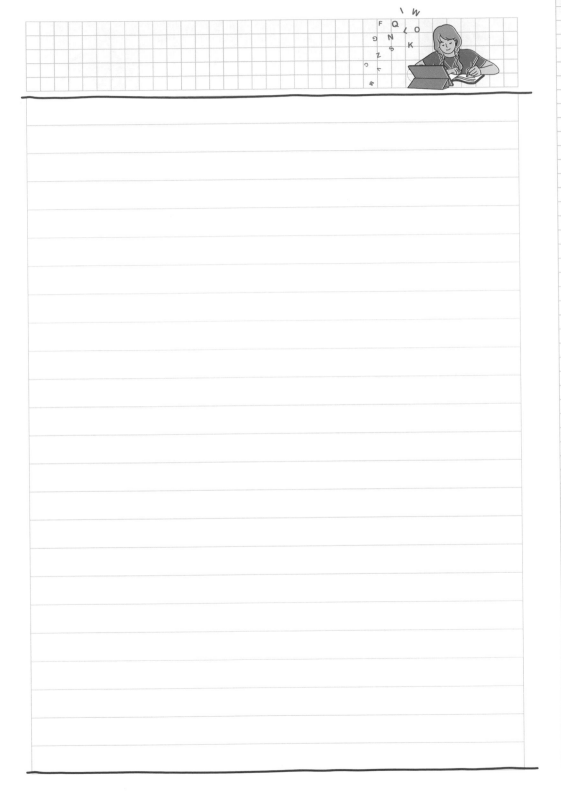

Notes

國家圖書館出版品預行編目（CIP）資料

用賴世雄筆記法學英文：每天 10 分鐘，單字片語一本通／賴世雄作. -- 初版. -- 臺北市：常春藤有聲出版股份有限公司, 2022.06　面；　公分.
--（常春藤生活必讀系列；BA20）
ISBN 978-626-96046-5-4（平裝）
1. CST：英語　2. CST：詞彙
805.12　　111007148

常春藤生活必讀系列【BA20】

用賴世雄筆記法學英文：每天 10 分鐘，單字片語一本通

編　　著　賴世雄
終　　審　李　端
執行編輯　許嘉華
編輯小組　鄭筠潔・Nick Roden・Brian Foden
設計組長　王玥琦
封面設計　王玥琦
排版設計　王玥琦・王穎緁・林桂旭
錄　　音　李鳳君・劉書吟
播音老師　內文朗讀：Jacob Roth・Terri Pebsworth・Tom Brink・Leah Zimmermann
內容講解：賴世雄
法律顧問　北辰著作權事務所蕭雄淋律師
出 版 者　常春藤數位出版股份有限公司
地　　址　臺北市忠孝西路一段 33 號 5 樓
電　　話　(02) 2331-7600
傳　　真　(02) 2381-0918
網　　址　www.ivy.com.tw
電子信箱　service@ivy.com.tw
郵政劃撥　50463568
戶　　名　常春藤數位出版股份有限公司
定　　價　460 元

郵票黏貼處

100009 臺北市忠孝西路一段 33 號 5 樓

常春藤有聲出版股份有限公司　行政組　啟

常春藤 英語集團

讀者問卷【BA20】

用賴世雄筆記法學英文：每天 10 分鐘，單字片語一本通

感謝您購買本書！為使我們對讀者的服務能夠更加完善，請您詳細填寫本問卷各欄後，寄回本公司或傳真至（02）2381-0918，或掃描 QR Code 填寫線上問卷，我們將於收到後七個工作天內贈送「常春藤網路書城熊贈點 50 點（一點 = 一元，使用期限 90 天）」給您（每書每人限贈一次），也懇請您繼續支持。若有任何疑問，請儘速與客服人員聯絡，客服電話：（02）2331-7600 分機 11～13，謝謝您！

線上填寫
免郵寄最環保

姓　　名：＿＿＿＿＿＿ 性別：＿＿＿ 生日：＿＿年＿＿月＿＿日

聯絡電話：＿＿＿＿＿＿ E-mail：＿＿＿＿＿＿

聯絡地址：□□□□□□

教育程度：□國小　□國中　□高中　□大專／大學　□研究所含以上

職　　業：1 □學生

2 社會人士：□工　□商　□服務業　□軍警公職　□教職　□其他＿＿＿

1 您從何處得知本書：□書店　□常春藤網路書城　□FB／IG／Line@ 社群平臺推薦　□學校購買　□親友推薦　□常春藤雜誌　□其他＿＿＿

2 您購得本書的管道：□書店　□常春藤網路書城　□博客來　□其他＿＿＿

3 最滿意本書的特點依序是(限定三項)：□APP　□試題演練　□字詞解析　□內容　□印刷　□編排方式　□音檔朗讀　□音檔講解　□封面　□售價　□信任品牌　□其他＿＿＿

4 您對本書建議改進的三點依序是：□無（都很滿意）□APP　□試題演練　□字詞解析　□內容　□編排方式　□印刷　□音檔朗讀　□音檔講解　□封面　□售價　□其他＿＿＿

原因：＿＿＿

對本書的其他建議：＿＿＿

5 希望我們出版哪些主題的書籍：＿＿＿

6 若您發現本書誤植的部分，請告知在：書籍第＿＿＿頁，第＿＿＿行

有錯誤的部分是：＿＿＿

7 對我們的其他建議：＿＿＿

感謝您寶貴的意見，您的支持是我們的動力！　常春藤網路書城 www.ivy.com.tw